A TWIST OF THE KNIFE

By Peter James

The Roy Grace Series

DEAD SIMPLE   LOOKING GOOD DEAD

NOT DEAD ENOUGH   DEAD MAN'S FOOTSTEPS

DEAD TOMORROW   DEAD LIKE YOU

DEAD MAN'S GRIP   NOT DEAD YET

DEAD MAN'S TIME   WANT YOU DEAD

Other Novels

DEAD LETTER DROP   ATOM BOMB ANGEL

BILLIONAIRE   POSSESSION   DREAMER

SWEET HEART   TWILIGHT   PROPHECY

ALCHEMIST   HOST   THE TRUTH

DENIAL   FAITH   PERFECT PEOPLE

Short Stories

SHORT SHOCKERS: COLLECTION ONE

SHORT SHOCKERS: COLLECTION TWO

A TWIST OF THE KNIFE

Children's Novel

GETTING WIRED!

Novella

THE PERFECT MURDER

A TWIST OF THE KNIFE

PETER JAMES

MACMILLAN

First published 2014 by Macmillan
an imprint of Pan Macmillan, a division of Macmillan Publishers Limited
Pan Macmillan, 20 New Wharf Road, London N1 9RR
Basingstoke and Oxford
Associated companies throughout the world
www.panmacmillan.com

ISBN 978-0-230-76437-8 HB
ISBN 978-1-4472-6014-1 TPB

1 3 5 7 9 8 6 4 2

A CIP catalogue record for this book is available from the British Library.

Typeset by Ellipsis Digital Limited, Glasgow
Printed and bound by CPI Group (UK) Ltd, Croydon, CR0 4YY

For Wayne Brookes

Superstar

CONTENTS

12 BOLINGBROKE AVENUE 1

NUMBER THIRTEEN 9

JUST TWO CLICKS 25

DEAD ON THE HOUR 31

VIRTUALLY ALIVE 41

MEET ME AT THE CREMATORIUM 49

VENICE APHRODISIAC 67

TIME RICH 77

CHRISTMAS IS FOR THE KIDS 89

WHEN YOUR NUMBER'S UP 97

LIKE YOU 107

SMOKING KILLS 119

THE STAMP OF A CRIMINAL 123

A VERY SEXY REVENGE 151

THE KNOCK 157

DREAM HOLIDAY 161

A CHRISTMAS TRADITION 179

COMPANIONSHIP 189

MY FIRST GHOST 193

TWO MINUTES 203

GIFTS IN THE NIGHT 209

GHOST PAINTING 223

TIMING IS EVERYTHING 237

ART CLASS 245

DREAM WIFE 263

A DEAD SIMPLE PLAN 285

SUN OVER THE YARD ARM 305

YOU'LL NEVER FORGET MY FACE 333

SANTA DROPS IN 341

CROSSED LINES 361

12 BOLINGBROKE AVENUE

It was a pleasant-looking mock-Tudor semi, with a cherry tree in the front garden and a stone birdbath. There was nothing immediately evident about the property to suggest a reason for the terror Susan Miller felt every time she saw it.

'Number 12' – white letters on the oak door. A brass knocker. And, in the distance, the faint sound of the sea. She began to walk up the path, her speed increasing as she came closer, as if drawn by an invisible magnet. Her terror deepening, she reached forward and rang the bell.

'Susan! Susan, darling! It's OK. It's OK!'

The dull rasp faded in her ears; her eyes sprang open. She gulped down air, staring out into the darkness of the bedroom. 'I'm sorry,' she whispered hoarsely. 'The dream. I had the dream.'

Tom settled back down with a grunt of disapproval and was asleep again in moments. Susan lay awake, listening to the steady, endless roar of the traffic on the M6 pouring past Birmingham, an icy fear flooding her veins.

She got out of bed and walked over to the window, afraid to go back to sleep. Easing back the edge of a curtain, she stared out into the night; the large illuminated letters advertising IKEA dominated the horizon.

The dream was getting more frequent. The first time had been on Christmas Eve some ten years back, and for a long while it had recurred only very occasionally. Now it was happening every few weeks.

After a short while, exhaustion and the cold of the late-October air lured her back into bed. She snuggled up against Tom's unyielding body and closed her eyes, knowing the second nightmare that always followed was yet to come, and that she was powerless to resist it.

*

Christmas Eve. Susan arrived home laden with last-minute shopping, including a few silly gifts for Tom to try to make him smile; he rarely smiled these days. His car was in the drive, but when she called out he did not respond. Puzzled, she went upstairs, calling his name again. Then she opened the bedroom door.

As she did so, she heard the creak of springs and the rustle of sheets. Two naked figures writhing on the bed spun in unison towards her. Their shocked faces stared at her as if she were an intruder, had no right to be there. Strangers. A woman with long red hair and a grey-haired man. Both of them total strangers making love in her bed, in her bedroom. *In her house.*

But instead of confronting them, she backed away, rapidly, confused, feeling as if it were she who was the intruder. 'I'm sorry,' she said. 'I'm so sorry. I'm—'

Then she woke up.

Tom stirred, grunted, then slept on.

Susan lay still. God, it was so clear this time – it seemed to be getting more and more vivid lately. She had read an article in a magazine recently about interpreting dreams, and she tried to think what this one might be telling her.

Confusion was the theme. She was getting confused easily these days, particularly with regard to time. Often she'd be on the verge of starting some job around the house, then remember that she had already done it, or be about to rush out to the shops to buy something she had just bought. Stress. She had read about the effects of stress, in another magazine – she got most of her knowledge from magazines – and that it could cause all kinds of confusion and tricks of the mind.

And she knew the source of the stress, too.

Mandy. The new secretary at the Walsall branch of the Allied Chester & North-East Building Society, where Tom was Deputy Manager. Tom had told her about Mandy's arrival a year ago, then had never mentioned her since. But she had watched them talking at the annual Christmas party last year, to which spouses and partners were invited. They had talked a damned sight too much for Susan's liking. And they emailed each other a damned sight too much.

She had not been sure what to do. At thirty-two, she had kept her figure through careful eating and regular aerobics, and still looked good. She took care of her short brown hair, and paid attention to her make-up and her clothes. There wasn't much else she *could* do, and confronting Tom without any evidence would have made her look foolish. Besides, she was under doctor's orders to stay calm. She had given up work in order to relax and improve her chances of conceiving the child they had been trying for these past five years. She *had* to stay calm.

*

Unexpectedly, the solution presented itself when Tom arrived home that evening.

'Promotion?' she said, her eyes alight with excitement.

'Yup! You are now looking at the second youngest ever branch manager for the Allied Chester & North-East Building Society! But,' he added hesitantly, 'it's going to mean moving.'

'Moving? I don't mind at all, darling!' *Anywhere,* she thought. *The further the better. Get him away from that bloody Mandy*. 'Where to?'

'Brighton.'

She could scarcely believe her luck. In their teens, Tom had taken her for a weekend to Brighton; it was the first time they had been away together. The bed in the little hotel had creaked like mad, and someone in the room below had hollered at them and they'd had to stuff sheets into their mouths to silence their laughter. 'We're going to live in Brighton?'

'That's right!'

She flung her arms around him. 'When? How soon?'

'They want me to take over the branch at the start of the New Year. So we have to find a house pretty smartly.'

Susan did a quick calculation. It was now late October. 'We'll never find somewhere and get moved by then. We've got to sell this place, we've got to—'

'The Society will help. They're relocating us, all expenses paid, and we get a lump-sum allowance for more expensive housing in the south. They're giving me the week off next week so we can go there and look around. I've told the relocations officer our budget and she's contacting some local estate agents for us.'

*

The first particulars arrived two days later in a thick envelope. Susan opened it in the kitchen and pulled out the contents, while Tom was gulping down his breakfast. There were about fifteen houses, mostly too expensive. She discarded several, then read the details of one that was well within their range: a very ugly box of a house, close to the sea, with a 'small but charming' garden. She liked the idea of living near the sea, but not the house. Still, she thought, you spend most of your time indoors, not looking at the exterior, so she put it aside as a possible and turned to the next.

As she saw the picture, she froze. *Couldn't be,* she thought, bringing it closer to her eyes. *Could not possibly be.* She stared hard, struggling to control her shaking hands, at a mock-Tudor semi, identical to the one she always saw in her dream. *Coincidence,* she thought, feeling a tightening knot in her throat. *Coincidence. Has to be. There are thousands of houses that look like this.*

12 Bolingbroke Avenue.

Number 12, she knew, was the number on the door in her dream, the same dream in which she always heard the distant roar of the sea.

Maybe she had seen the house when they had been to Brighton previously. How long ago was that? Fourteen years? But even if she had seen it before, why should it have stuck in her mind?

'Anything of interest?' Tom asked, reaching out and turning the particulars of the modern box round to read them. Then he pulled the details of the semi out of her hands, rather roughly. 'This looks nice,' he said. 'In our bracket. "In need of some modernization" – that's estate agent-speak for a near wreck. Means if we do it up, it could be worth a lot more.'

Susan agreed that they should see the house. She had to see it to satisfy herself that it was not the one in the dream, but she did not tell Tom that; he had little sympathy for her dreams.

*

The estate agent drove them himself. He wore a sharp suit, white socks and smelled of hair gel. 'Great position,' he said. 'One of the most sought-after residential areas in Hove. Five minutes' walk to the beach. Hove Lagoon close by – great for kids. And it's a bargain for this area. A bit of work and you could increase the value a lot.' He turned into Bolingbroke Avenue, and pointed with his finger. 'There we are.'

Susan bit her lip as they pulled up outside number 12. Her mouth was dry and she was shaking badly. Terror was gripping her like a claw; the same terror she had previously experienced only in her dreams.

The one thing that was different was the 'For Sale' board outside. She could see the cherry tree, the stone birdbath. She could hear the sea. There was no doubt in her mind, absolutely no doubt at all.

She climbed out of the car as if she were back in her dream, and led the way up the path. Exactly as she always did in her dream, she reached out her hand and rang the bell.

After a few moments the door was opened by a woman in her forties with long red hair. She had a pleasant, open-natured smile at first, but when she saw Susan, all the colour drained from her face. She looked as if she had been struck with a sledgehammer.

Susan was staring back at her in amazement. There was no mistaking, it was definitely her. 'Oh my God,' Susan said, the words blurting out. 'You're the woman I keep seeing in my dreams.'

'And you,' she replied, barely able to get the words out, 'you are the ghost that's been haunting our bedroom for the past ten years.'

Susan stood, helpless, waves of fear rippling across her skin. 'Ghost?' she said finally.

'You look like our ghost; you just look so incredibly like her.' She hesitated. 'Who are you? How can I help you?'

'We've come to see around the house.'

'See around the house?' She sounded astonished.

'The estate agent made an appointment.' Susan turned to look at him for confirmation, but could not see him or Tom – or the car.

'There must be a mistake,' the woman said. 'This house is not on the market.'

Susan looked round again, disoriented. Where were they? Where the hell had they gone? 'Please,' she said. 'This ghost I resemble – who . . . who is . . . was she?'

'I don't know; neither of us do. But about ten years ago some building society manager bought this house when it was a wreck, murdered his wife on Christmas Eve and moved his mistress in. He renovated the house, and cemented his wife into the basement. The mistress finally cracked after a couple of years and went to the police. That's all I know.'

'What . . . what happened to them?'

The woman was staring oddly at her, as if she was trying to see her but no longer could. Susan felt swirling cold air engulf her. She turned, bewildered. Where the hell was Tom? The estate agent? Then she saw that the 'For Sale' board had gone from the garden.

She was alone, on the step, facing the closed front door.

Number 12. She stared at the white letters, the brass knocker. Then, as if drawn by that same damned magnet, she felt herself being pulled forward, felt herself gliding in through the solid oak of the door.

I'll wake up in a moment, she thought. *I'll wake up. I always do.* Except she knew, this time, something had changed.

NUMBER THIRTEEN

For 353 days a year – and 354 in a leap year – N.N. Kettering put the fear of God into restaurants around the world. On those dozen remaining days, something put the fear of God into him.

A number.

Just a simple, two-digit number.

Thirteen.

Just the sight of it was enough to make beads of sweat appear along his brow. And he had a vast expanse of brow, providing ample accommodation for whole colonies of sweat beads.

Nigel Norbert Kettering hated both his first names. When he had first started out as a restaurant critic, for a small English provincial newspaper, he decided a degree of anonymity was a good thing – and it gave him the opportunity to lose those two bloody names. For the past two decades, N.N. Kettering had been, undisputedly, the most influential restaurant critic in England, and in more recent years, his eagle eye and sharp palate, and even sharper writing, had made him a global scourge.

Kettering analysed everything. Every single aspect of any meal he ate. From the table at which he sat, to the quality of the paper on which the menu was printed, to the glasses, the tablecloth, the plates, the balance of the menu, the quality and speed of the service, and, far above all else, the food.

This attention to every detail, even to the quality of the toothpicks, had taken him to the top of his profession – and the top of the list of people many of the world's most renowned chefs would have liked to see dead.

His daily online postings, the *Kettering Report,* could make or break a new restaurant within days, or dramatically enhance the reputation of an established one. No amount of Michelin stars or Gault Millau points came close to the rosette rankings of the *Kettering Report.* Of course, he had his favourites. Before it closed, El Bulli in Spain regularly received a maximum score of ten. So did The French Laundry in Yountville, California, and The Fat Duck in Bray, Vue du Monde in Melbourne, and Rosemary in Sardinia, and the Luk Yu Tea House in Hong Kong for its dim sum.

But there were legions of other establishments, hailed as temples of gastronomy by some of the greatest newspaper critics, which received from Kettering a scornful three, or a withering two. One of the greatest French chefs committed suicide after Kettering downgraded his rating from a nine to a devastating one in the space of a single year.

In the current harsh economic climes, few people would risk the expense and disappointment of a mediocre night out without first checking the latest opinion online at Kettering's site.

N.N.'s appearance at a restaurant was enough to render the most seasoned maître d' and the most assured sommelier quivering jellies, and when whispered word of his presence reached the kitchen, even the most prima donna of chefs turned into a babbling, begging wreck.

Some years ago, his identity had been revealed by a tabloid newspaper. Now, he no longer bothered to book his tables under an assumed name. Every restaurateur in the world had N.N. Kettering's photograph pinned discreetly to an office wall. Besides, the man was hard to miss. He was tall and lean, despite all the food and wine he packed away, with an elongated neck, on top of which perched his egg-shaped head, his eyes distorted behind round, bottle-lens glasses and his short black hair brushed forward, rather like a modern take on a monk's tonsure, the fringe barely reaching the start of his high, sloping brow.

He was always dressed the same – in a dark, immaculately tailored suit, white shirt and red or crimson tie – and sat ramrod straight, with perfect posture, as if he had a ruler jammed down the back of his jacket. One great London restaurant owner had described the sight of his head rising above the menu he was reading, accompanied by his beady glare, as being like staring into the periscope of a submarine. Fortunately for this man's establishment, N.N. Kettering never got to hear the remark.

Of course, Kettering's tastes became more and more esoteric. One year, the appearance of snail porridge on the menu of The Fat

Duck caused him to devote two whole pages of lyrical praise to Heston Blumenthal's skills as a chef. The following year, he devoted an unprecedented three-page review to a single dish at El Bulli – chef Ferran Adrià's creation of oysters with raw marinated rabbit brains.

And his demands for greatness and excellence became ever higher.

Almost uniquely among restaurant critics, N.N. Kettering employed no assistants. He ate lunch and dinner out seven days and nights a week. Sometimes breakfast, too. Food was his life. He had never married, never even had a girlfriend – or boyfriend. And he always paid for every meal in crisp, new banknotes. He never accepted anything free.

He never tipped.

He felt fulfilled. As if he had been put on this planet to be the custodian of its restaurants' standards. He was married to tomorrow's restaurants. His reviews were his babies.

Once, early in his career, in a rare interview, he declared, 'The best number for dinner is two – myself and a good waiter.'

But not on the thirteenth of any month.

On the thirteenth of any month, it all changed.

From as far back in his life as he could remember, N.N. Kettering had been a triskaidekaphobic. He had a morbid fear of the number thirteen. And the worst possible date was a Friday the thirteenth. Because not only was he a triskaidekaphobe, he was also a paraskavedekatriaphobe.

Someone who has a total fear of the date Friday the thirteenth.

He knew that the number thirteen was out to get him. It was around him all the time. It was there on car number plates. It lurked in the number of grains in the breakfast cereals he ate. In the number of berries he added to his cereal. In the number of mouthfuls he took to eat his breakfast, and his lunch, and his dinner. In the number of steps he would take from a taxi to the restaurant. In the number of steps from the front door of the restaurant to his table.

He would never sit at table thirteen. He would never choose the thirteenth item on a menu. Nor on a wine list. Nor anything that was a multiple of thirteen.

Whenever it was a Friday the thirteenth, he would prepare himself in advance. All kinds of danger lurked out in the world. So it was best not to risk it. Stay home. But home was dangerous, too. He had read that the place where you were most likely to die was in your own home, especially your kitchen. So, on every Friday the thirteenth he stayed in bed, in his small flat in London's Notting Hill. The night before, he prepared everything he would need up until midnight the following day. He would spend the time reading, and watching television – mostly food programmes – and visiting, anonymously of course, a number of networking sites and online discussion groups about restaurants.

So it happened, on one such Friday the thirteenth, a cold February day when he was logged on while in bed, that he found by chance a new discussion group on the Web, made up of some of the world's greatest chefs. He had eaten in every one of their restaurants – a few of them he had praised, but the majority he had trashed. He watched the discussion in fascination, as they were talking about a restaurant he had never heard of. And not just talking about it. Raving about it.

This demented him! He knew every significant restaurant in the world, surely? He had eaten at all the ones that had any kind of a reputation. Yet here, suddenly, was a reference not just to a restaurant, but to one these particular chefs agreed unanimously was the very best in the world. No restaurant sourced better cuts of meat. No restaurant handled an entire range of offal with such inventiveness. He became hungry just reading the descriptions of the sauces, the tenderness of every bite, the juxtaposition of flavours. He was salivating.

And the bastards did not give away the name.

Frustrated, he posted, under his Internet pseudonym, *ChefStalker*, the words: 'Hi everyone, what's the name of this place? I thought I knew every restaurant worth eating in on the planet!'

To his dismay, the discussion ended abruptly, without any reply.

He realized there was only one thing for it. He would email some of the chefs, selecting only the ones he had praised, revealing who he was, knowing that was almost bound to lead to an invitation.

To his joy, he was right. Two days later he received an email, although, curiously, anonymous:

Dear N.N. Kettering,

Thank you for your interest. This establishment about which you are enquiring is in fact a private dining club. We would be

> delighted for you to join us as our guest the next time we hold one of our dinners – Friday 13 May. There is one condition: that you never write about this club, either before or after your visit. Some things are just too good to be shared. You will receive your formal invitation, and the address, on the night of 12 May. We look forward to greeting you. Bon appétit!

He stared at the email. *Friday 13 May.*

He had never in his life, since leaving school, left the safety of his home on a Friday the thirteenth.

His first inclination was to reply, explaining that he was grateful for the invitation, but that he could not accept.

But then he thought again about all the words of praise he had read. Many of them from chefs who, he might have thought, had experienced every taste sensation there was to taste, but who raved unanimously.

God, how he loved the mystique of restaurants. He remembered so vividly the first restaurant he had ever entered, when he was just ten years old; it was called Verry's. He was with his parents, in busy, noisy Regent Street in London. The door had swung shut behind them, and they were in a new world, dimly lit, oak-panelled, with a quiet hum of chatter, tantalizing smells of garlic and grilling meat and fish. A man in a tuxedo, with an Italian accent, had greeted his parents as if they were his long-lost friends, then had shaken his hand and led them courteously along a line of red leather banquettes to their table.

Crystal chandeliers hung from the ceiling. Crystal glasses were laid out on a crisp, white tablecloth. A silver dish lay on it, filled with frilly curls of butter. Another silver dish appeared, stacked with Melba toast. Then he was presented with a burgundy leather-covered menu, filled with delights. A few minutes later, a green leather-bound wine list, as thick as a bible, was placed in his father's hand.

Waiters swept past with silver trays laden with food. Others hovered around their table. It was like being on a new planet, in a new universe. From that moment onwards, Nigel Norbert Kettering knew that he wanted to spend his life in this world. But, even at ten, he noticed things that were not right. Little imperfections. The waiter forgot a side order of haricot verts, and had to be reminded twice.

His father muttered that his steak was cooked more than he had asked, but seemed too in awe of the waiters to complain. So, to his father's embarrassment and his mother's astonishment, little Nigel stuck up his arm and summoned the waiter. Five minutes later the offending steak was duly replaced.

That was his start. And now, aged forty-four, he had succeeded beyond all his dreams. And there were still some restaurants he entered that held that same, magical promise of Verry's all those years ago.

And now there was one that sounded as if it would top them all. But his invitation was for a Friday the thirteenth. He emailed back, asking what other date options there were. Within minutes he received a reply: 'None. We assume you are declining. Thank you.'

Almost as fast as his fingers could move, panic causing beads of sweat to appear all over that brow of his, he typed back: 'No, not declining. Thank you. I'm accepting.'

*

The next three months passed slowly, feeling more like three years. Everything in every restaurant irritated him. Gormless, moronic waiters sanctimoniously reciting the day's specials as if they had personally line-caught or wood-roasted the damned fish or meat with their bare hands. Eating starters of bi-valves tortured to death in unpleasantly flavoured oils, or pasta resembling origami creations made during handiwork classes at special needs institutions.

He bankrupted a dozen Michelin-starred establishments and closed four restaurants before they had even opened their doors to the great unwashed.

But finally the great day arrived.

And just how great was it?

He stared at the email printout from the night before, in which he had finally been sent the address. It was the place that just about every ranked chef considered to be the finest eating establishment in the world. It was Number 13, in West Audley Street in London's Mayfair.

Number sodding 13.

He came close to telling them to take a hike. To stick their stupid invitation up the place where the sun doesn't shine.

Thirteen.

The number he had spent his entire life trying to avoid. And now he was in a taxi, cruising down Park Lane, getting ever closer.

Salivating.

Thinking about all those descriptions of grilling meat and offal in sauce combinations he had never dreamed possible.

Looking forward to trashing it! To making fools of all those great chefs. To destroying fifty reputations in one single posting on his site later that evening.

He was less than amused when the cabbie read the meter and turned to him. 'That'll be thirteen quid, gov.'

N.N. Kettering counted out the money exactly. And took pleasure in the driver's scowl when he asked for his receipt, with no tip. No arsehole driver who mentioned the number thirteen was going to get a tip from him.

Then he walked up the steps to the door and stared at the shiny, brass digits.

13.

He began shaking. Then hyperventilating. He nearly turned and walked straight back down the steps.

Only the descriptions of the food that lay beyond this portal kept him there. He lifted his hand to the bell, and forced his index finger to dart forward and jab it.

He was still considering his options when the door swung open and a tall, gaunt, formidable-looking figure in a tuxedo and white gloves, hair as slick as a frozen pond, with a matching frozen smile, bowed. 'Sir?'

N.N. gave his name.

Moments later he stepped forward, into an oak-panelled corridor, and the door closed behind him.

'This way, sir.'

He followed the man along the corridor, which was lined with framed oil portraits. Some of them he recognized as high-profile food critics. He passed one of A.A. Gill from the *Sunday Times*. Another of Fay Maschler from the *Observer*. Then one of Giles Coren from *The Times*. One of Michael Winner. Then several he recognized from other countries. Then he was bowed through a door.

He found himself in a grand, windowless dining room, in the centre of which was an oval mahogany table, at which sat twelve people. One place was empty at the centre on one side – his.

The thirteenth place.

As he clocked the faces of each of his fellow diners in turn, he realized he was in the presence of twelve of the highest rated chefs in the world. Highest rated, that was, by all food critics other than himself.

He had trashed all of them – viciously. Brought each of their establishments to their knees. They were all smiling at him.

His instinct was to turn and run. It had been years since he had eaten at a table with company. He really only liked to eat alone. But they were all rising to their feet. The one nearest him, whom he recognized as Jonas Capri, from Sydney, Australia, said, 'N.N. Kettering, we are honoured.'

He did not know what to reply or if he even wanted to reply.

Another of the great chefs spared him the problem. Ferdy Perrin, from Haut Mazot restaurant in Switzerland, once famed for its lamb – before the *Kettering Report* – shook his hand warmly. 'You cannot imagine the honour we are feeling here tonight. That you have agreed to come and eat our creations. It is our hope that you will leave this evening with a changed opinion of our abilities. We are grateful to you that you give us this chance.'

'Well,' he said, for the first time in many years feeling just a little humbled. But before he could say anything else another chef stood up.

His name was Jack Miller, from Miller's House in Tampa, Florida. 'See, N.N., we want you to know we have no hard feelings. Maybe when you came to my restaurant we were having an off night. I'm not here to convince you to change your review. I just want you to have one of the greatest eating experiences of your life, here tonight. What you make of it will then be up to you to decide.'

N.N. saw that the walls were hung with more paintings. He recognized Gordon Ramsay. Anthony Worrall Thompson. Albert Roux. Wolfgang Puck. Alain Ducasse. Raymond Blanc.

He took his seat. A vast array of cutlery and glasses lay in front of him. One glass was half-filled with an ochre-coloured white wine, another with water.

He was still thinking what to do when a side-door opened and four waiters entered, dressed head to foot in black, holding massive silver platters, on which sat tiny demitasse cups topped with froth. Within seconds one had been distributed to each diner.

The gloved man who had brought N.N. Kettering in appeared to duplicate his tasks as both doorman and headwaiter.

'L'amuse-bouche,' he announced. 'Cappuccino de testicules.'

Each of his fellow diners began to spoon this dish up with gusto. N.N. Kettering raised the first mouthful to his lips and sniffed. The bouquet was sensational. He placed one sliver, no thicker than a communion wafer, in his mouth and the flesh dissolved on his tongue like butter. It was so good he dug his spoon in again. And again. And again. Scraping every last milligram of flavour from the sides of the tiny, ribbed cup. He could easily have eaten seconds. And thirds. He found himself even wanting to lick the inside of the cup clean.

'Fantastic!' he said. '*Incroyable!*' he added for the benefit of the French chefs present. The others demurred.

He had eaten pigs', lambs' and bulls' testicles before, but never, remotely, with this complexity of flavours. These were the best ever. Wow!

'The secret is in the marinade,' the chef on his right said, a man in his late thirties with close-cropped hair, wearing a black T-shirt and jeans.

'I would argue also the quality of the produce,' said the chef opposite them, a rather studious-looking man in his sixties, wearing a cardigan.

'That goes without saying,' said a third.

N.N., long conditioned to observe every detail and nuance in a restaurant, noticed the discreet wink that passed between two of the chefs. It seemed to carry on around the table, from chef to chef, a sort of chain wink, from which he was excluded.

Now they all seemed to be concealing smirks from him.

He noticed a printed menu, picked it up and glanced down it. There were twenty-one courses. The menu was written in French, but he was fluent in the language so it was easy to translate. But, even so, there were several words he struggled with. The first set of courses were all offal. Goujons of brain was to follow the testicles. Then sweetbreads – the pancreas and thymus. Then tripe – the intestines. Liver. Kidneys. Then . . . something else, but his French failed him.

With even more ceremony than the previous dishes, a miniature covered silver tureen was placed in front of each diner, signalling that one of the highlights of the meal had arrived. The lids were removed to reveal a wonderful, sweet aroma of chargrilled meat, cinnamon and coriander. The dish was a rich, dark cassoulet of beans, chickpeas and the thinnest possible slices of what N.N. Kettering assumed was sausage. But when he forked one into his mouth, although the taste was undoubtedly pork, and delicious, it had a strange, flaccid, rubbery texture that reminded him of squid. It was definitely, he made a mental note, a triumph of taste over texture.

The dish was eaten in complete silence, and Kettering became increasingly uncomfortable with each mouthful he took as, one by one, he ruled out all other body parts, leaving him with just one possibility. He shuddered but at the same time felt very slightly aroused.

After that, the menu continued through a series of meat dishes, different cuts from the leg, rump, shoulder. The animal was not stated and he became increasingly curious to know. Lamb, Cow, Deer, Pig? Ostrich?

But when he questioned any of his fellow diners they just smiled and replied, 'Every dish is a unique surprise. Savour it, don't destroy it with analysis.'

The French chef in the cardigan turned to him and said, 'You are familiar with the words of your great poet, Pope? "Like following life in creatures we dissect, we lose it in the moment we detect."'

So he did his best. With almost every mouthful he took, one of the numerous wine glasses on the table was filled or refilled. Whites, reds, pinks, all different hues, all steadily melding into a blur.

Then the highlight of the meal arrived: a roast, presented on a miniature campfire of burning fennel twigs, and he knew instantly from the smell and the sight of the crackling that this had to be roast pork. As he tucked in, whether it was the wine or the sheer joy of eating one magical dish after another, he was sure, quite sure, that this was the finest roast he had ever eaten, and probably ever would. He was starting to feel very happy, very contented. He was starting to like these chefs. Next time, he decided, he would give them all good scores. Enough so that perhaps they might invite him again . . .

Even on a Friday the thirteenth.

Because the date was turning out not to be so bad after all.

'This is the best pork I've ever eaten!' he proclaimed through a mouthful of perfect, crunchy crackling.

'Long pig,' said the chef opposite him.

And suddenly, as if a fuse had been tripped, all the good humour in the room seemed to evaporate. There was an awkward moment of silence. Several faces turned towards the man who had said, 'Long pig.' A ripple of glances passed from one chef to the next.

Then N.N. was conscious that everyone was looking at him, as if waiting for him to react.

A shiver rippled through him. *Long pig*. He knew what the words meant, what long pig was.

Suddenly his head was spinning. He began to feel sick. His eyes moved, in turn, to each of the twelve pairs of eyes around the table. Each stared back at him coldly.

'Long pig' was the term cannibals in the South Seas and in Africa used to describe white men. Because their flesh tasted like pork.

He stood up abruptly. His chair fell over behind him, crashing to the floor with a sound like a gunshot. 'I have to go,' he said.

No one said a word.

He ran from the room, back along the portrait-lined corridor, and reached the front door. He yanked the handle. But the door did not move.

It was locked.

The key was missing.

He turned and saw the maître d' standing behind him, his arms crossed. A bunch of keys hung from a leather fob on his belt. 'You haven't had dessert yet, sir. It would be very impolite for you to leave without dessert. We have the finest desserts you will ever have tasted.'

'I have to go,' he said again. 'Please open the door.' Blind panic was gripping him now.

'I'm afraid not, sir.' The maître d' took a step towards him.

N.N. Kettering had never headbutted anyone before in his life. But he headbutted the maître d' now. It was a clumsy attempt and he did not dip his own head enough, resulting in him striking the maître d' forehead-on and smashing both the bottle lenses of his own glasses, without which he was almost blind. Nevertheless, it was effective enough to make the maître d' fall to his knees with a dazed grunt.

N.N. grabbed the key fob and tugged with all his strength, ripping it away from the man's belt. He turned back to the door, tried one, then another, then another. He looked over his shoulder and, through a blurry haze, saw a posse of his dining companions storming down the corridor towards him.

He tried the fourth key, desperately, and it turned.

The door opened and he stumbled out down the steps and ran blindly across the pavement, straight into the road. Straight into the path of an eleven-and-a-half-ton double-decker bus.

It struck him at almost thirty miles per hour, catapulting him a short distance down the road. Then it braked to a slewed halt. It seemed in the brief silence that followed that the whole of London had come to a halt.

The paramedics, who arrived on the scene within minutes and lifted him carefully onto a stretcher, were unaware, just as N.N. Kettering was, of the irony that it was a number 13 bus.

*

Two days later, N.N. regained consciousness briefly. Just long enough to hear a murmured conversation right beside him.

A male voice said, 'Any luck with next-of-kin?'

A female voice said, 'No, doctor, we've not yet been able to trace any relatives.'

'Any change in his condition?'

'I'm afraid not.'

'Well, let's keep him on life support for a while longer. But I don't think we're going to see any change. He has massive internal injuries, and his Glasgow coma score remains at three. He's clearly brain-dead, poor sod. Nothing more we can do. Just wait.'

The man's voice was familiar, but N.N. struggled to remember where he had heard it before. Then, just before he lapsed back into unconsciousness for the final time, he remembered.

It was the voice of the maître d'.

*

Two days later, the duty intensive care registrar was doing his ward round. He noted that one of the beds in the unit was now vacant. It was bed number thirteen.

The sister was staring at it sadly. 'You OK?' he asked.

'Every time we lose someone, I feel like a failure,' she replied. Then she looked at the sticking plaster on his forehead. 'Are you all right? Cut yourself?'

'It's nothing. He looked back down at the empty bed. 'Always remember the first rule of the Hippocratic Oath: "Do no harm." Right?'

She nodded sadly.

'It would have been harmful to keep him going. What kind of quality of life would he have had if he had lived?'

'You're right,' she replied. 'None. I suppose sometimes we have to thank God for small mercies. He'd have been a vegetable if he'd lived.'

'You know, nurse, I've never liked that word, "vegetable",' he said. 'Why not a "piece of meat"?'

JUST TWO CLICKS

Just two clicks and Michael's face appeared. Margaret pressed her fingers against the screen, feeling a longing to stroke his slender, pre-Raphaelite face and to touch that long, wavy hair that lay tantalizingly beyond the glass.

Joe was downstairs watching a football match on Sky. What she was doing was naughty. Wicked temptation! But didn't Socrates say "the unexamined life is not worth living"? The kids were gone. Empty nesters now, her and Joe. Joe was like a rock to which her life was moored. Safe, strong, but dull. And right now she didn't want a rock, she wanted a knight on a white charger. The knight who was just two clicks away.

*

Just two clicks and Margaret's face would be in front of him. Michael's fingers danced lightly across the keys of his laptop, caressing them sensually.

They had been emailing each other for over a year – in fact, as Margaret had reminded Michael this afternoon, for exactly one year, two months, three days and nineteen hours.

And now, at half past seven tomorrow evening, in just over twenty-two hours' time, they were finally going to meet. Their first *real* date.

Both of them had had a few obstacles to deal with first. Like Margaret's husband, Joe. During the course of a thousand increasingly passionate emails (actually, one thousand, one hundred and eighty-seven, as Margaret had informed him this afternoon) Michael had built up a mental picture of Joe: a tall, mean, brainless bully, who had once punched a front door down with his bare fists. He'd built up a mental picture of Margaret, too, that was far more elaborate than the single photograph he had downloaded so long ago of a pretty redhead, who looked a little like Scully from the *X-Files*. In fact, quite a lot like the heavenly Scully.

'We shouldn't really meet, should we?' She had emailed him this afternoon. 'It might spoil everything between us.'

Michael's wife, Karen, had walked out on him two months ago, blaming the time he spent on the Internet, telling him he was more in love with his computer than her.

Well, actually, sweetheart, with someone on my computer . . . he had nearly said, but hadn't quite plucked up the courage. That had always been his problem. Lack of courage. And, of course, right now this was fuelled by an image of Joe who could punch a front door down with his bare fists.

A new email from Margaret lay in his inbox. 'Twenty-two hours and seven minutes! I'm so excited, I can't wait to meet you, my darling. Have you decided where? M. xxxx'

'Me neither!' he typed. 'Do you know the Red Lion in Handcross? It has deep booths, very discreet. Went to a real-ale tasting there recently. Midway between us. I don't know how I'm going to sleep tonight! All my love, Michael. xxxx'

*

Margaret opened the email eagerly, and then, as she read it, for the first time in one year, two months and three days she felt the presence of clouds in her heart. *Real Ale*? He'd never mentioned an interest in real ale before. Real ale was a bit of an anoraks' thing, wasn't it? *Midway between us*? Did he mean he couldn't be bothered to drive to somewhere close to her? But, worst of all . . .

A pub???

She typed her reply. 'I don't do pubs, my darling. I do weekends in Paris at the George V, or maybe the Ritz-Carlton or the Bristol.'

Then she deleted it. *I'm being stupid, dreaming, all shot to hell by my nerves . . .* From downstairs there came a whoop from Joe, and then she could hear tumultuous roaring. A goal. Great. Big. Deal. *Wow, Joe, I'm so happy for you.*

Deleting her words, she replaced them with 'Darling, the Red Lion sounds wickedly romantic. 7.30. I'm not going to sleep either! All my love, M. xxxx.'

*

What if Joe had been reading her emails and was going to tail her to the Red Lion tonight, Michael thought as he pulled up in the farthest, darkest corner of the car park? He climbed out of his pea-green Astra (Karen had taken the BMW) and walked nervously towards the front entrance of the pub, freshly showered and shaven, his breath minted, his body marinated in a Boss cologne Karen had once said made him smell manly, his belly feeling like it was filled with deranged moths.

He stopped just outside and checked his macho diver's watch. Seven thirty-two. Taking a deep breath, he went in.

And saw her right away.

Oh no.

His heart did not so much sink as burrow its way down to the bottom of his brand new Docksider yachting loafers.

She was sitting at the bar, in full public display – OK, the place was pretty empty – but worse than that, a packet of cigarettes and a lighter lay on the counter in front of her. She'd never told him that she smoked. But far, far, far worse than that, the bitch looked nothing like the photograph she had sent him. Nothing at all!

True, she had the same red hair colour – well, henna-dyed red at any rate – but there were no long tresses to caress; it had been cropped short and gelled into spikes that looked sharp enough to prick your fingers on. *You never told me you'd cut your hair. Why not???* Her face was plain, and she was a good three or four stone heavier than in the photograph, with cellulite-pocked thighs bared by a vulgar skirt. She hadn't lied about her age, but that was just about the only thing. And she'd caught his eye and was now smiling at him . . .

No. Absolutely not. No which way. Sorry. Sorry. Sorry.

Michael turned, without looking back, and fled.

Roaring out of the parking lot, haemorrhaging perspiration in anger and embarrassment, switching off his mobile phone in case she tried to ring, he had to swerve to avoid some idiot driving in far too fast.

'Dickhead!' he shouted.

*

Margaret was relieved to see the car park was almost empty. Pulling into the farthest corner, she turned on the interior light, checked her face and her hair in the mirror, then climbed out and locked the car. Seven thirty-seven. Just late enough, hopefully, for Michael to have arrived first. Despite her nerves, she walked on air through the front entrance.

To her disappointment, there was no sign of him. A couple of young salesmen types at a table. A solitary elderly man. And on the barstools, a plump, middle-aged woman with spiky red hair and a tarty skirt, who was joined by a tattooed, denim-clad gorilla who emerged from the gents', nuzzled her neck greedily, making her giggle, then retrieved a smouldering cigarette from the ashtray.

Michael, in his den, stared at the screen. 'Bitch,' he said. 'What a bitch!' With one click he dragged all Margaret's emails to his trash bin. With another, he dragged her photograph to the same place. Then he emptied the trash.

*

Back home just before ten, Joe glanced up from a football game that looked like all the other football games Margaret had ever seen. 'What happened to your night out with the girls?' he asked.

'I decided I'd been neglecting my husband too much recently.' She put her arm around him, around her rock, and kissed his cheek. 'I love you,' she said.

He actually took his eyes off the game to look at her, and then kissed her back. 'I love you, too,' he said.

Then she went upstairs to her room, and checked her mailbox. There was nothing. 'Michael, I waited two hours,' she began typing.

Then she stopped. It was cold in her den. Downstairs the television had given a cosy glow. And her rock had felt warm.

Sod you, Michael.

Just two clicks and he was gone from her life.

DEAD ON THE HOUR

(originally published by the *Mail on Sunday*)

The hour before dawn is the deadliest. The silent, ethereal period when the air is filled with an indefinable stillness; the darkness is spent but the new day has not yet begun. It is the hour when human resistance is at its lowest, when the dying, exhausted from the sheer effort of clinging to life, are most likely to slip their moorings and drift quietly away into that good night.

Sandra held her mother's hand; it was no bigger than a child's, soft and fragile with leathery creases. And sometimes she imagined there was still a pulse, but it was merely the beat of her own pulse coming back at her.

A tear rolled down her cheek, chased by another as she reflected on her past, her memory in selective mode, retrieving and presenting to her only what was good. She delved back into her childhood, when it was she who had been weak and her mother who had been strong, and thought about how the wheel had turned, as relentless and impersonal as the cogs of the grandfather clock downstairs. Strong. Yes, she had been strong these past months, spoon-feeding her mother an increasingly infantile diet. Supper last night had been pineapple jelly and a glass of milk. At 7 p.m. precisely.

The clock was quiet; it seemed a long time since it had last chimed. She looked at her watch. A whole hour had passed, gone. Like the hour that ceases to exist or vanishes during the night when the clocks go forward to British Summer Time. It was three o'clock in the morning and then suddenly it was four o'clock. Sandra's mother was alive and suddenly she was not.

And now, equally suddenly, there was no hurry. Sandra clung to the thought as the one consolation through her grief. No hurry at all. She could sit up here for hours if she wanted. Sure, she would have to call the doctor eventually, and – she shuddered – an undertaker. She would have to get the death certificate. The vicar would make an appearance. There were relatives to be phoned. Probate. Her mind whirred as she remembered all the arrangements when her sweet father had died six years back. *Escaped*, she had sometimes thought, and felt guilty about that as she stared at her mother's pitifully atrophied body.

It was Tony who always made that joke. He said it was the only way her father had been able to get safely away from her mother. If he'd merely left her, she'd have tracked him down and turned up, pointing angrily at her watch, asking if he realized what the hell the time was.

Yes, she had been a difficult woman, a tyrannical clock-watcher, selfish, petulant, unreasonable and, in her last years, spoilt and paranoid. Sandra's brother, Bill, had emigrated to Australia. *Escaped*, as Tony put it. And her sister, Marion, had gone to America; also *escaped*, according to Tony. So the duty of looking after their mother fell to her.

Tony had always criticized her for that. She was too weak with her mother, he warned. She had always allowed the older woman to walk all over her, to dominate her, forcing her to live at home to look after her until she was past the age when she could have children of her own. It was not a bond of love, he told her, but of fear. He was right. Her mother had hated Tony for taking Sandra away, and she had hated him even more for not allowing Sandra to let her come and live with them until these last two years when she had been dying.

Now, as Sandra sat clutching her mother's lifeless hand, she realized that for the first time she was free. She would no longer have to set the alarm for six-fifteen in order to take her mother a cup of tea in bed at six-thirty precisely – as her father had always done. She would no longer have to bring her breakfast up at seven-fifteen precisely, or bath her every morning at eight o'clock precisely. She would no longer have to set her mental clock to call her every hour, on the hour, whenever she was out of the house, and no longer have to suffer the abuse when she was late with a call, or came home later than she had stated, or was late with the afternoon tea tray or the supper tray or the cup of warm milk at eleven o'clock.

Slowly, half reluctantly, half anticipating her new freedom, she prised away the lifeless fingers one at a time, then laid her mother's skeletal arm down. She turned out the light, closed the door, walked slowly to her own bedroom and slipped, exhausted, into bed beside Tony's sleeping frame.

No need to wake him. It could wait. A few hours of sleep and she would be better able to cope with the grim business ahead – choosing the coffin, the hymns, the wording for the death notices in the papers. She lay still, drained after her weeks of vigil, her eyes wet and her heart hollow with grief.

She dozed fitfully, listening for the chimes of the grandfather clock, but heard only the rising, then abating, dawn chorus. Finally, she got out of bed, pulled on her dressing gown, closed the door and stood for a moment on the landing. Bitumen-black shadows rose out of the darkness to enfold her. She stared at the door of her mother's room and felt a tightness grip her throat. Normally she would have been able to hear the clock ticking, but it was silent. Puzzled, she went downstairs into the hall. The hands of the grandfather clock pointed to three o'clock. It had stopped, she realized, her eyes sliding to her own wristwatch. It was six-forty-five.

Then she felt a deep unease. Three o'clock. She remembered now; it was coming back. She remembered what grief had made her forget earlier. Three o'clock. She had glanced at her watch to imprint it on her mind. Information the doctor might want to know: her mother had died at three o'clock precisely.

A tiny coil of fear spiralled inside her. The clock had been her mother's wedding present to them. Stark, institutional, rather Teutonic, it dominated the small hall, stared her in the face each time she came into the house as if either to remind her it was time to call her mother or to reproach her for forgetting. Tony disliked it, but he had been trying, in those early days, to make friends with her mother. Thus the clock had stayed and had been given pride of place. He had taken to joking that there was no need to have a portrait of her mother in the house – the clock was a near perfect likeness of her.

Sandra turned and walked into the kitchen. As she went in, a blast of cold air greeted her, making her shiver. Startled, she wondered if the freezer door was open. The daylight seeping through the blinds was grey and flat, and the only sound was the rattling hum of the fridge. Then, as she reached for the light switch, something brushed past and she felt a rustle of fabric. She stood, absolutely rigid, goose pimples breaking out all over her body.

Her mother had come into the room.

Sandra stared at her in disbelief and terror. The old woman was standing, in her pink dressing gown, angrily tapping her watch. 'Where's my tea? What kind of a daughter are you that you forget to bring your dying mother her cup of tea?'

'M-M-Mummy!' she stammered finally. 'You . . . you died . . . dead . . . you . . .'

The room was getting colder and the light was dimming perceptibly. Yet her mother seemed brighter, more vibrant, more alive in contrast to it. Relief momentarily flooded through Sandra's confusion. 'Mummy . . . you're OK. I . . . I . . .' her voice tailed off. Her eyes told her that her mother was standing in front of her, but her brain told her that was impossible. She reminded herself that only a few hours ago there had been no pulse, her mother had been turning cold, rigor mortis had begun to set in.

'You and Tony can't wait for me to go so you can be rid of me, can you?'

'Mummy, th–that's not true. It isn't . . . I . . .'

Her mother stepped towards her, with her hand raised in the air. 'You bitch! You slut! You tramp!' She swiped her hand ferociously and Sandra flinched, stepping back out of her way with a startled cry.

'Who are you talking to?'

Sandra turned. Tony, bleary-eyed, wrapped in his towelling dressing gown, stood behind her in the doorway. When she looked back, her mother had vanished. Her heart was hammering and she was gulping air in shock. 'Mummy,' she blurted. 'I . . . I . . .' She pushed past him, ran stumbling upstairs and threw open the door of the spare room.

Her mother lay there, exactly as she had left her. Slowly, hardly daring to breathe, Sandra walked across and touched her cheek. Her flesh was cold, like putty. Her eyes were still closed and there was the faintest hint of a rictus grin that lent her a smugness even in death, as if she were enjoying some final private joke.

Shaking with fear and confusion, Sandra hurled herself into the arms of Tony who had followed her. He held her tightly, and she pressed her face against the soft towelling and began to sob.

'She's cold,' Tony said quietly and baldly. 'She must have gone in her sleep.'

*

The following morning Sandra sat bolt upright in bed, wide awake. The bedside clock said six-fifteen. Fifteen minutes! She hurried downstairs, spooned tea into the pot and, while the kettle boiled, set her mother's cup and saucer on the tray.

As she was pouring the water into the pot, she stopped.

What the hell am I doing?

Her mother was in the chapel of rest in a funeral parlour. The funeral was all arranged for next Tuesday.

Angrily, she threw the contents down the sink, walked back into the hall, glared defiantly at the hands of the clock still stuck on three o'clock and got back into bed. She nestled closely to Tony, slipped her hand inside the fly of his pyjamas and gently aroused him. Then she straddled him and they made harsh, savage love.

'You're free,' Tony said as they luxuriated in their first Saturday lie-in for as long as they could remember. 'You can get a life of your own now, of *our* own. We can go on holiday. And get rid of that damned clock.'

'The man's coming this morning to fix it,' she said.

'Christ, why spend any money on it? Let's just bung it in the first auction we can find.'

'I want it fixed first,' she said. 'I can't leave it the way it is.'

*

'Nothing wrong with the movement, Mrs Ellis. I've given it a good cleaning; could have been the dust that stopped it.'

Sandra thanked the man and paid him. As he was leaving she said, 'I don't suppose you know anyone who might be interested in buying it?'

'Ah.' He looked pensive. 'Yes, well, it's a fine piece. Try Atherton's in Lewes High Street.'

Sandra closed the door. The hall was once again filled with the relentless tick of the grandfather clock and, as she watched it, she saw the minute hand jerk forward to eleven minutes past two.

Tony was playing golf and was not due back until late afternoon. She would arrange the sale now, she thought. The sooner the clock was out of the house the better. It might be disrespectful to get rid of it before the funeral, but Sandra no longer cared.

*

Tony arrived home shortly before five and was surprised to see Sandra's Toyota wasn't in the drive.

As he let himself in, he noticed the hands of the grandfather clock were again pointing to three o'clock and there was no tick emanating from the case. Strange, he thought; Sandra had told him the repairer would be coming at midday. Then a sound from the kitchen caught his attention.

It was Sandra.

'Hallo, darling,' he said, walking through. 'I didn't think you were home.'

Tea was laid on a tray on the table. 'Mummy wanted her afternoon tea,' she said. 'I had to come back.'

He gave her a strange look. 'Your mother's dead – and where's the car?'

The doorbell rang before she could reply. Sandra turned towards the kettle as if she had not heard either the question or the bell.

Tony opened the front door. Two policemen stood there, grim-faced, holding their caps in their hands.

'Mr Anthony Ellis?' asked one, his voice quavering slightly.

'Yes,' Tony replied.

'Your wife has had an accident, sir. She was hit by a car as she was crossing Lewes High Street. She was taken to the Royal Sussex County Hospital but I'm afraid she was dead on arrival.'

Tony shook his head. 'I'm sorry, you must have made a mistake – she's here. Come in and see for yourself.'

He led them through into the kitchen. 'Sandra, you'll never guess . . .' His voice dried up. She was not in the kitchen. There was no tray on the table.

He ran upstairs, calling her name, but only empty silence greeted him. Slowly, ashen, he walked back downstairs. 'Wh-what . . . when . . . when did this happen?'

'A little earlier this afternoon, sir,' said the second policeman, who was eyeing the grandfather clock with a strange expression. 'About three o'clock.'

VIRTUALLY ALIVE

Henry blew an expensive new chip, trashed an important mailbox file and misrouted himself halfway around the world, getting himself hopelessly lost. It was turning out to be a bummer of a Monday morning.

Henry, or *henry.biomorph.org.uk*, to give him his full name, dealt with the problem the same way he dealt with all problems: he went back to sleep, hoping that when he woke up, the problem would have gone away, or miraculously resolved itself, or that he might simply never wake up. Fat chance of that. You could not send someone into oblivion who was already in oblivion.

But try telling him that.

Tell me about it, he thought. *I've had it up to here.* Wherever 'here' was. He wasn't even a disembodied entity – he was just a product of particle physics, a fractal reduction of a real human, a vortex of self-perpetuating energy waves three nanometres tall, inside which was contained all the information that had ever travelled down a computer cable or jumped a data link anywhere on the planet, which made him at the same time the most knowledgeable entity in the world and the least experienced. Some things he was not able to experience at all – food, sex, smell, love. He was a cache of knowledge, of acquired wisdom. If he owned a T-shirt, on it would be printed the legend: 'Seen it all and what's the use?'

But no one made T-shirts three nanometres tall and, if they did, such a thing would not have been much use to him, as nine trillion bytes of data zapping past him every attosecond would have incinerated it. He would have liked to have dumped from his memory the motto 'All dressed up and nowhere to go', since it had no relevance for him. But he could not dump info. When he tried, it simply came back, eventually, from somewhere else. He had seen every movie that had ever been made. Read every book. Watched every single television programme that had been broadcast on every channel in every country in the world over the past twenty-five years.

Then he saw the hand moving towards the switch.

A stab of fear from nowhere was followed by erupting panic; the hand was closing in on the switch, the red switch beneath which was printed in large red letters EMERGENCY SHUTDOWN. Beneath it should have been (but, of course, wasn't) printed in equally large letters PRE-SHUTDOWN PROTOCOLS MUST BE EXECUTED TO AVOID IRREVERSIBLE DAMAGE.

'Protocols!' Henry shrieked. 'Protocols!' His panic deepened. 'PROTOCOLS!'

He felt himself being drawn rapidly upwards, in bewildering defiance of gravity; higher, faster, through a pitch-black vertical tunnel. Then he crashed, with a stark bolus of terror emptying into his veins, through into consciousness.

Awake mode. Full hunter-gatherer consciousness.

At least he thought he was awake, but he could never be quite sure of anything these days. He lay very still, fear pulsing through him as the nightmare receded, trying to find coherence in his surroundings. The same nightmare he had night after night, and it felt so damned real – except what the hell was reality these days? Life was confusing, one seamless time–space continuum of complete muddle. He stared blankly at the pixels on the pillow beside him.

Hundreds of them. Thousands. Millions, in fact, all needing assembling to make a coherent image of his wife. He always compressed her when he went to sleep (to save storage space on his hard disk – or brain as he still preferred to call it) but it was a hassle making sense of her again, like having to do a fiendish jigsaw puzzle every morning and do it in a ludicrously brief fragment of time. Sod it, how much smaller could time get? It had already gone from a picosecond to a nanosecond to an attosecond. An attosecond was to one second what one second was from now back to the Big Bang . . . and he had to assemble the puzzle in just one tiny fraction of that.

'Morning, darling,' Susan said with a sleepy smile, as the jumble of pixels rearranged themselves into a solid image of his wife, tangles of brown hair across her face. Gosh, she looked so lifelike, Henry thought, just the way he always remembered her – but so she should.

He leaned across to kiss her. There was nothing there, of course, but he still kissed her every morning and she reciprocated with a tantalizing pout and an expression that was dangerously close to a smirk, as if she had some secret she was keeping from him. She giggled exactly the way she did every morning, and said, 'Oh darling, I wish, I wish!'

He watched her get out of bed, and felt a sudden prick of lust as she arched her naked body, tossed her hair and strode to the bathroom. The door slammed shut. God, they hadn't made love since . . . since . . . He trawled his memory racks – no, banks . . . no, cells, yes, brain cells ('wetware' they called it) – but could not remember when they had last made love. He couldn't even remember when he had last *remembered* making love. The muddle was definitely worsening.

Brain Overload Stress Syndrome. It had become the Western world's most common illness. The brain filled up, could not cope with new input, creating a sense of panic and confusion. Henry had been suffering from BOSS for some while now. The symptoms were so clear to him he hadn't even bothered going to the doctor for confirmation: there was just too much bloody bandwidth in the world.

He sat up in alarm. *I cannot make love to my wife because she does not exist, or rather she exists only in my memory. I am the sole reality.* Then he said what he always said when he needed to reassure himself: '*Cogito, ergo sum.*' Then he repeated it in English because he felt it sounded better in English. '*I think, therefore I am.*'

Susan had been dead for two years now, but he had still not got used to it, still got cheated by the cruel dreams in which she was there, they were laughing, kissing, sometimes even making love; the dreams, yes, old times, good times. Gone.

But not entirely gone. Henry could hear her now in the bathroom. It was all part of the post-deanimation program hologram model PermaLife-7. Behind closed doors she made the sounds of ablutions, creating the illusion that she was still alive.

A few seconds later, at exactly 06.30 European Communal Time, the synthesized voice of the MinuteManager personal organizer kicked in: 'Good morning, Mr and Mrs Garrick. It is Thursday, 17 November 2045.'

Henry realized now what was wrong. Susan had got up before the alarm. She *never* got up before the alarm. Ever.

The MinuteManager continued breezily: 'Here are the headlines of today's online *Telegraph* that I think will interest you. I will bring you editorial updates as I come across them during the next hour. The Prime Minister is arriving in Strasbourg this morning to present his arguments against Great Britain's expulsion from the EU. Parliament will today debate the first stage in the reduction of power of the House of Commons in favour of government by consensus on the Internet . . . and delegates from the World Union of Concerned Scientists will today be pressing for international legislation limiting the cerebral capacity of sentient computers.'

'You're up early, darling,' Henry said as Susan came back into the bedroom.

'Busy day,' she murmured in her gravelly voice, before beginning to rummage through her wardrobe, pausing every few moments to select a dress and hold it against herself in the mirror.

Breakfast, he thought. That was missing these days. She used to bring him breakfast in bed, on a tray. Tea, toast, cereal, a boiled egg. He was a creature of habit and she had prepared him the same breakfast every day of their marriage. He depended on her for everything, that's why he had wanted to keep her on after her death. 'Where's my breakfast?' he said grumpily. Except somewhere in his addled memory an assortment of bytes of stored information arranged themselves into a message informing him he had not eaten breakfast for two years. But they failed to yield the information as to why not.

It was terrible but he had great difficulty remembering anything about Susan's death, he realized guiltily. It was as if he had stored the memory in some compartment and had forgotten where. One moment they had been contentedly married and the next moment she was no more. At least, not flesh and blood.

Henry Garrick could have had a full-body replica of his wife. But robot technology still had not perfected limb and muscle movement, so FBRs – as full-body replicas were known – tended to move with a clumsy articulation that made them look like retards. He had opted instead for a hologram – the standard post-deanimation program hologram model PermaLife-7.

Susan-2, as he had called her, was connected through a cordless digital satellite link to an online brain-download databank named ARCHIVE 4, and a network of lasers concealed in the walls gave her the ability to move freely around much of the apartment, though not of course beyond. The entire transformation of Susan from a wetware (flesh-and-blood) mortal into a hardware (digitized-silicon) virtual mortal had been handled by the undertakers.

Death was a redundant word these days. 'Deanimation', or 'suspended animation', or 'altered sentient condition', or even 'metabolically challenged state', were more accurate descriptions – at least, for anyone who took the consciousness-download option offered by most leading funeral directors these days as a pre-death service. Blimey, Henry thought, the array of options was bewildering for both the living and the downloaded. Options for everything: static books, interactive books; virtual reality, alternative reality. And, of course, good old television still had its following.

No one knew how many channels there were now. His MinuteManager trawled the airwaves around the clock for programmes fitting Henry's taste parameters. It then divided them into two categories – those Henry would actually watch and those it would load straight into Henry's brain via his silicon interface, so that he would simply have the memory of having watched them.

'There's some good legal retro on tonight,' the MinuteManager announced. '*L.A. Law, Kramer vs. Kramer, Perry Mason, CSI, The Firm, Lawman, Rumpole of the Bailey*. Would you care to watch any in real time or compressed time?'

For some moments Henry Garrick did not answer. He was still wondering why his wife had got up so early. Perhaps there was a problem with one of her modules – maybe he should call an engineer and get her looked at under the maintenance contract, if he could remember who the hell it was with. Then her voice startled him.

'Goodbye, darling. Have a nice day.'

She was going out! She wasn't supposed to go out . . . There wasn't any way she *could* go out. 'Hey!' he shouted. 'Hey, where the hell are you going?'

*

It was nearly midnight when Susan came back. She reeked of booze and smoke and had her arms around a man.

'Where have you been?' Henry yelled at his wife. 'And who the hell is this creep?'

To Henry's chagrin, Susan didn't even respond. She did not even look at him.

'I thought I would miss him,' Susan said quietly to her new boyfriend, Sam. 'I thought it would be nice to continue having him around the house. The problem is, he's never realized he's dead – can you believe it? He thought it was me that died! Poor sod, he was getting terribly muddled towards the end of his life. It's spooky the way he looks at me sometimes. I mean, he's just a hologram guided by a few bits of data, but it's as if he's still alive, still sentient. And he seems to be getting more and more so every day. He actually got mad at me for going out this morning! I guess it's time to call a halt.'

'Yes,' Sam agreed, staring uneasily at the quivering hologram. 'There comes a time when you have to let go.'

Susan lifted her arm and pressed the switch.

MEET ME AT THE CREMATORIUM

'I want you,' he texted.

'I want you more!' she texted back.

Trevor was fond of saying that the past was another country. Well, at this moment for Janet, it was the future that was another country. The future – and another man.

And tonight she was going to have him. Again.

A sharp, erotic sensation coiled in the pit of her stomach at the thought of him. A longing. A craving.

Tonight I am going to have you. Again and again and again!

Her past receded in the rear-view mirror with every kilometre she covered. The forest of pines that lined the autobahn streaked by on both sides, along with road signs, turn-offs and other, slower cars. She was in a hurry to get there. Her heart beat with excitement, with danger. Her pulse raced. She had been running on adrenaline for forty-eight hours, but she wasn't tired – she was wide, wide awake. Going into the unknown. Going to meet a man who had been a total stranger until just a few weeks ago.

His photograph, which she had printed from the jpeg he had emailed her, lay on the passenger seat of her elderly grey Passat. He was naked. A tall, muscular guy, semi-erect as if teasing her to make him bigger. A tight stomach, nearly a six-pack, and she could already feel it pressing hard against her own. He had brown hairs, thick and downy, on his chest and on his legs, and she liked that. Trevor was white and bony, and his body was almost hairless. This man was tanned, lean, fit.

Hans.

He looked wild, like a young Jack Nicholson, his hair thinning on the top. He looked just the way he had sounded on the Internet chat room when she had first been attracted to him.

Feral.

The background to the photograph was strange. An enclosed,

windowless space that might be the engine room of a ship, although she had a pretty good idea what it really was. Like everything about him, it excited her. Shiny, floor-to-ceiling metal casings, beige coloured, with dials, gauges, switches, levers, knobs, winking lights. It could be some kind of control room in a nuclear reactor? Or a mission control centre?

She felt on a mission very much under control!

Who had taken that photograph, she wondered? A lover? Had he taken it himself with a time delay function? She didn't care, she wanted him. All of him. Wanted that thing that half-dangled, half-rose. Wanted to gather it deep inside her again. Wanted him so badly she was crazed with lust. Mosquitoes got crazed with blood lust. They had to land, take in the blood, even if it killed them. She had to have Hans, take him into her, into her body, into her life, even if that killed her, too.

She didn't care. For now she was free. She had been free for two whole days and that was longer than she had been free for years.

Over the scratchy reception of the car's radio, struggling through the occasional interference of someone talking in German, Bob Dylan was singing 'The Times They Are a-Changin''.

They were. They really were! Flecks of sleet struck the windscreen, and the wipers cleared them. It was cold outside and that was good. It was good to make love in the warmth when it was cold outside. And, besides, the cold had plenty of other advantages.

I will never let you go, Trevor had said. *Never. Ever*. He had told her that for years.

Hans explained to her precisely what he was going to do to her. Exactly how he would make love to her the first time. And he had done so just the way he had described. She liked that Germanic precision. The way he had studied every detail of her photograph. The way he already knew her body when they met. The way he told her he loved her hair, and had buried his face into it. Into all of it.

My name is Hans. I am thirty-seven, divorced, looking to start a new life with a lady of similar age. I am liking brunettes. Slim. Excuse my bad English. I like you. I don't know you, but I like you.

I like you even more!

She would be forty this year. Hans would be her toyboy, she had teased him. He had laughed and she liked that; he had a big sense of humour. A wicked sense of humour.

Everything about him was totally wicked.

She looked OK, she knew. She'd never been a beauty, but she understood how to make herself look attractive, sexy. Dressed to kill, plenty of men would look at her. She used to keep in shape with her twice-weekly aerobics classes, then, when Trevor had gone through one of his particularly nasty phases, she had turned to binge eating – and then binge drinking – for comfort. Then she enrolled in WeightWatchers, and the fat and the flab and the cellulite had come off again. Her figure was good, her stomach firm – not a distended pouch, like the stomachs of some of her friends who'd had children. And her boobs were still firm, still defying gravity. She'd like to have been a little taller – she'd always wished that – but you couldn't have everything.

Anyhow, Trevor, who was much taller than her, told her the very first time they had made love that people were all the same size in bed. That had made her smile.

Trevor used to tell her that nothing you do in life is ever wasted. He was always coming up with sayings, and there was a time when Janet had listened to them intently, adored hearing them, filed them away in her memory and loved repeating them back to him.

Loved him so damned much it hurt.

And she hadn't even minded the pain. Which was a good thing because pain was something Trevor did really, really well. The knots, the handcuffs, the nipple clamps, the leather straps, the spiked dog collar, the whips, the stinging bamboo canes. He liked to hurt her; knew how to cause her pain and where to inflict it. But that had been OK because she loved him. She would have done anything for him.

But that was then.

And sometime between *then* and *now* he had changed. They had both changed. His horizons had narrowed; hers had widened.

Every system can be beaten. That was one of his sayings.

He was right.

Now she was a lifetime away. So it seemed. And one thousand, two hundred and twelve kilometres away, driving through spartan

December pine forest. Click. One thousand, two hundred and thirteen. And, in a few moments, travelling at one hundred and thirty klicks an hour, with her life in the two large suitcases jammed on the rear seats, one thousand, two hundred and fourteen.

'Hagen 3.'

The turn-off was coming up. She felt a tightening of her throat, and a prick of excitement deep inside her. How many villages, small towns, big cities had she driven through or passed by in her travels, during her life, and wondered, each time, *what would it be like to stop here? What would it be like to drive into this place as a total stranger, knowing no one, then check into a hotel, or rent a small flat, and start a totally new life?*

She was about to realize her dream. *Hagen.* So far it was just images she had found when she had Googled it. *Hagen.* The thirty-seventh largest town in Germany. She liked that. A population of two hundred thousand. On the edge of the Ruhr. A town few knew about outside of its inhabitants. A once important industrial conurbation that was now reinventing itself as a centre of the arts, the websites had proclaimed. She liked that. She could see herself in a place that was a centre of the arts.

Up until now, she had not had much contact with the arts. Well, there had never been time, really. During the week she was always on the road, driving from place to place as an area sales representative for a company that made industrial brushes. Finishing brushes for the printing trade. Brushes for vacuum cleaners. Brushes for the bottom of elevator doors. For electrical contacts. She would miss her flirting and banter with her clients, the almost exclusively male buyers at the factories, the component wholesalers, the plant hire and hardware stores. She was missing her comfortable, new, company Ford Mondeo, too, but the Passat was OK. It was fine. It was a small price to pay. Tiny.

Then, at the weekends, Trevor wasn't interested in any area of the arts. He didn't want to know about theatre, or art galleries or concerts, except for those of Def Leppard – great music if you like that kind of thing, which she didn't – but they were not *art,* at least not in her view. He just wanted to watch football, then either go to the pub, or more preferably to a particular S&M club he had discovered in London, where they had become regulars. He liked, most of all, to hurt and humiliate her in front of other people.

Ahead of her and to her left, across the railings on the elevated road, she could see the start of a town. It lay in a valley, surrounded by low, rounded, wintry hills. Everything she could see was mostly grey or brown, the colours bleached out by the gloomy, overcast sky. But to her, it was all intensely beautiful.

Hagen. A place where no one knew her, and she knew no one. Except just one man. And she *barely* knew him. A place where a stranger she was going to have sex with tonight, for just the second time, lived and worked. She tried to remember what his voice sounded like. What he smelled like. A man so crude he could send her a photo of himself naked and semi-erect, but a man so tender he could send her poetry by Aparna Chatterjee.

> Lust is what I speak tonight,
> Lust is what I see tonight,
> Lust is what I feel tonight,
> And I Lust You.
> Show me your Body
> Inside out . . .
> No clothes on,
> No holds barred . . .
> Bit by bit,
> Part by part,
> Give me your smells,
> And your sweat . . .

Trevor had never read a poem in his life.

The road dipped down suddenly beneath a flyover that seemed, from this angle, as if it went straight through the middle of a row of grimy, pastel-blue townhouses. She halted at a traffic light in the dark shadow beneath the flyover, checked in her mirror for an instant – just checking – then saw a yellow road sign. There was an arrow pointing straight ahead, with the word 'Zentrum'. Another arrow pointed left, and bore the word 'Theater'.

She liked that. Liked the fact that the second word she saw on arriving in the town was *Theater.* This was going to be a good place

– she felt it in her bones, in her heart, in her soul. *Hagen*. She said the word to herself and smiled.

Behind her a car hooted. The lights were green. She drove on past a road sign that read 'Bergischer Ring', and realized from the directions she had memorized that she was close to her hotel. But anxious as she was to see Hans, she wanted to get her bearings. She wanted to arrive slowly, absorbing it all, understanding the geography. She had all the time in the world, and she wanted to get it right, from the very beginning. It seemed too sudden that one moment she was on the autobahn, the next she was slap in the centre of the town. She wanted to feel it, explore it slowly, breathe it in, absorb it.

She turned right at the next road she came to, and drove up a steep, curving hill, lined with tall, terraced townhouses on both sides, then past a grimy church. She made a left turn at random, up an even steeper road, and then suddenly she was in scrubby, tree-lined countryside, winding up a hill, with the town below her.

She pulled over to the kerb, parking in front of a butane gas cylinder that was partially concealed by a threadbare hedge, stopped and climbed out. The central locking had packed up a long time ago, so she went around the car, making sure the doors and the boot were locked. Then she walked over to the hedge and looked down, across the valley, at her new home.

Hagen. A place that boasted, among its tourist attractions, Germany's first crematorium. Which had a certain convenient ring to it.

The town lay spread out and sprawling in the bowl beneath her. Her eyes swept the grey, urban landscape beyond the gas cylinder, below the murky, sleeting sky. She saw a cluster of industrial buildings, with a white chimney stack rising higher than the distant hills. A small nucleus of utilitarian apartment buildings. A church spire. A Ferris wheel brightly lit, although it was only three o'clock in the afternoon, reminding her that darkness would start to fall soon. She saw a narrow river bordered by grimy industrial buildings. Houses, some with red roofs, some grey. She wondered who lived in them all, how many of their inhabitants she would get to meet.

It is neither fish nor meat, Hans had said, telling her about Hagen. But she didn't mind what it was, or was not. It looked huge, vast, far bigger than a town of two hundred thousand. It looked like a vast city. A place where she could get lost, and hide, forever.

She loved it more every second.

She noticed a strange, cylindrical building, all glass, lit in blue, above what looked like an old water tower, and she wondered what it was. Hans would tell her. She would explore every inch of this place with him, in between the times they lay in bed, naked, together. If they could spare any time to explore anything other than each other's bodies, that was!

She turned away from the view and walked on up the hill, hands dug into the pockets of her black suede jacket, the sleet tickling her face, her scarf tickling her neck, breathing in the scents of the trees and the grass. She followed the road up into a wooded glade, until it became a track, which after a few minutes came out into a knoll of unkempt grass, with a row of trees on the far side and a rectangular stone monument at the highest point.

She climbed up to it, and stopped at a partially collapsed metal fence that was screening it off for some kind of repair work. She knew it was the Bismarck monument, because she recognized it from various websites as one of Hagen's landmarks. She stared at it silently, then took her little digital camera from her bag and photographed it. Her first photograph of Hagen. Then she stood still, licking the sleet off the air, feeling a moment of intense happiness, and freedom.

I'm here. I made it. I did it!

Her heart was burning for Hans, and yet, strangely, she still felt in no hurry. She wanted to savour these moments of anticipation. To appreciate her freedom. To relish not having to hurry home to make Trevor his evening meal (always a variation on meat and potatoes as he would eat nothing else). To be able to stand for as long as she wanted beneath the statue of Otto Eduard Leopold von Bismarck, a man partly responsible for shaping the country that was about to become her adopted home, for however many days of freedom she had remaining. And she did not know how many that might be.

Better to live one day as a lion than one thousand years as a lamb, Trevor was fond of saying, strutting around in his studded leathers and peaked cap.

Of course, he would not have approved of her being here. And particularly not of her standing like an acolyte worshipping at the statue of Bismarck. Trevor had a thing about Germany. It wasn't the war or anything like that. He said the Germans had no humour – well, Hans had proved him wrong.

He also said the Germans were efficient, as if that were a fault!

Trevor had a *thing* about all kinds of stuff. He had a particularly big thing about crematoriums. They gave him the creeps, he said. Whereas she found them fascinating. Yet another thing on which they disagreed. And she always found his dislike of crematoriums particularly strange, since he worked in the funeral business.

In fact, thinking back on fifteen years of marriage, what exactly had they agreed on? Rubber underwear? Handcuffs? Masks? Inflicting modest pain on each other? Bringing each other to brutal climaxes that were snatched moments of release, escape from their mutual loathing? Escape from the realities they did not want to face? Such as the fact – thank God for it now – that they could not have children?

Time was when she really had been in love with him. Deeply, truly, crazily, do-anything-for-him, unconditional love. She had always been attracted to death. To people who worked close to death. Trevor was an embalmer with a firm of funeral directors. He had a framed certificate, which was hung in pride of place in the sitting room, declaring him to be 'A Member of the Independent Association of Embalmers'.

She used to like his hands to touch her. Hands that had been inserting tubes into a cadaver, to pump out the blood and replace it with pink embalming fluid. Hands that had been applying make-up to a cadaver's face. Brushing a cadaver's hair.

The closer she was to death, the more alive she felt.

She liked to lie completely naked, and still, and tell Trevor to treat her as if she were a cadaver. She loved to feel his hands on her. Probing her. Slowly bringing her alive.

The best climax – absolutely the best ever, in her entire life – was one night when they had made love in the embalming room at the funeral director's. With two naked corpses lying, laid out on trolleys, beside them.

Then she had truly felt alive. The way she felt now.

And those same feelings would happen again with Hans, she knew it, she absolutely knew it. She was going to be so happy with Hans.

'Love doesn't last,' Trevor had responded one night when she told him she was not happy. 'Happiness is an illusion,' he had said. 'Only an idiot can be happy twenty-four/seven. The wise man seeks to be content, not happy. *Carpe diem*.'

'You have to face reality,' he had harped on, after she had told him she was leaving him. 'You can run but you can't hide.'

She was running now.

Hit someone over the head with a big stick hard enough and for long enough and one day they will hit you back. Even harder.

She could not put a time or a date on when it had all started to go south. Not the exact moment. Could not get a fix on it the way you can pinpoint your position with a set of navigation coordinates. It was more of a gradual erosion.

But once you had made your decision, there was no going back. You just had to keep running. As Trevor used to say, *it's not the fall that gets you, it's the sudden stop.*

And now, of course, Hagen was that sudden stop. It scared her almost as much as it thrilled her. In truth, she had learned a lot from him.

'I will never let you go, ever,' he had said, when she once suggested that they might be happier apart.

Then he had punched her in the face so hard for suggesting it, she had not been able to go to work for several days, until the bruises had subsided and the stitches had been removed. As usual, she covered up for him, with a lame excuse about being knocked off her bicycle.

It was his diabetes that caused his mood swings, she had come to learn over many years. Too little sugar and he became edgy and aggressive. Too much and he became sleepy and docile as a lamb.

She retraced her steps from the Bismarck monument to her car, then threaded her way back down the network of roads, noting the pleasant houses, wondering what kind of house Hans had lived in until his marriage break-up. After a few minutes she found herself back on the Bergischer Ring, where she turned right. She drove along, past a market square where the Ferris wheel had been erected at the edge of a small fairground. She saw a row of kerbside Christmassy tableaux, one after the other, with puppets acting out fairy-tale scenes.

One was full of busy bearded goblins with hammers. Two small girls, clutching their mother's hands, stared at them in wonder.

Janet stared at the girls as she waited at a traffic light, and then, wistfully, at the mother. Forty was not too old. Maybe she and Hans could have children. Two little girls? And one day she would stand here, holding their hands, a contented hausfrau of Hagen, while they looked at the hammering goblins.

Just three weeks to Christmas. She would wake up on Christmas morning, in her new country, in the arms of her new man.

As she drove on she saw, on her left, a brightly lit shop, the windows full of sausages hanging in clumps, like fruit, the name Wursthaus König above the door. She stopped for a moment and checked her map. Then after a short distance she turned left into a side street, past a restaurant, and pulled over outside the front entrance of the hotel she had found on the Internet.

Hans had invited her to stay with him. But after only one date, even if it had finished – or rather *climaxed* – in a way she had not experienced in years, she wanted to keep her options open. And her independence. Just in case.

She tugged one bag off the rear seat of the car, and wheeled it in through the front door of the hotel. Inside was dark and gloomy, with a small reception desk to her right and a staircase in front of her. A living cadaver of a man stood behind the desk and she gave him her name. The place smelled old and worn. The kind of place travelling sales people would stay in. The kind of dump she had occasionally found herself in during her early years on the road.

He passed her a form to fill in, and asked if she would like help with her luggage. 'No,' she told him emphatically. She filled in the form and handed him her passport.

And he handed her an envelope. 'A message for you,' he said.

Using the one word of German she knew, she said, '*Danke*.' Then, as she went back outside to get her second suitcase, she tore it open, with eager fingers and nails she had varnished to perfection for him. For Hans.

The note read: 'Meet me at the crematorium. xx'

She smiled. *You wicked, wicked man!*

The cadaver helped her up two flights of stairs to a room that was as tired and drab as the rest of the place. But at least she could see down into the street and keep an eye on her car, and she was pleased about that. She popped open the lid of one case, changed her clothes and freshened herself up, spraying perfume in all the places – except one – that she remembered Hans had liked to press his face into most of all last time.

Twenty minutes later, in the falling dark, after getting lost twice, she finally pulled into the almost deserted crematorium car park. There was just one other car there – an elderly brown Mercedes that tilted to one side, as if it had broken suspension.

As she climbed out, carefully locking the car, she looked around. It was one of the most beautiful car parks she had seen in her life, surrounded by all kinds of carefully tended trees, shrubs and flowers as if it were a botanical garden. It barely felt like December here; it seemed more like spring. No doubt the intention – a perpetual spring for mourners.

She walked up a tarmac footpath that was wide enough for a vehicle, and lined with manicured trees and tall black streetlamps. Anticipation drove her forwards, her pace quickening with every step, her breathing becoming deeper and faster. God, her nerves were jangling now. A million butterflies were going berserk in her stomach. Her boots crunched on grit; her teeth crunched, grinding from the cold, but more from nerves.

She walked through open wrought-iron gates, and continued on, passing a cloistered single-storey building, clad in ivy, its walls covered in memorial plaques.

And then, ahead of her, she saw the building.

And she stopped in her tracks.

And her heart skipped a beat.

Oh, fuck! Oh, wow!

This was a crematorium?

It was one of the most beautiful buildings she had ever seen in her life. Rectangular, art deco in style, in stark white, with a portico of square black marble columns and windows, high up, like port-holes on a ship, inset with black rectangles. It was topped by an elegant pitched red-tiled roof.

She was stunned.

There were steps leading up to the portico, with a stone balustrade to the right, giving a view down across terraces of elegant tombstones set in what looked like glades in a forest. *When I die, this is where I would like to lie. Please, God. Please, Hans.*

Please!

She climbed the steps and pushed the door, which was unlocked and opened almost silently. She stepped inside and simply stopped in her tracks. Now she could understand why the crematorium featured so prominently as one of Hagen's major attractions.

It was like stepping inside a Mondrian painting. Vertical stripes of black and white, with geometrical squares in the centre, varying in depth, width and height, at one end. At the other end was a semi-domed ceiling, with quasi-religious figures painted on a gold backdrop, above more black-and-white geometrics.

Beneath was a curious-looking altar, a white cross rising above what looked like a white two-metre-long beer barrel.

As she stared at it, there was a noise that made her jump. A sudden, terrifying sound. A mechanical grinding, roaring, vibrating bellow of heavy machinery. The barrel began to rise, the white cross with it, the floor trembling beneath her. As it rose higher, behind it a bolt of grey silk slowly unfurled. Then a coffin rose into view. Janet stood, mesmerized. The grinding, roaring sound filled the galleried room.

Then the sound stopped as abruptly as it had started.

There was a moment of total silence.

The coffin lid began to rise.

Janet screamed.

Then she saw Hans's smiling face.

He pushed the lid aside and it fell to the floor with an echoing bang, and he began to haul himself out, grinning from ear to ear, hot and sweaty, wearing nothing but a boiler suit over his naked skin and black work boots.

She stood and stared at him for a moment, in total wonder and joy. He looked even more amazing than she remembered. More handsome, more masculine, more raw.

He stood up, and he was taller than she remembered, too.

'My most beautiful angel in all the world,' he said. 'You are here! You came! You really came!'

'Did you think I wouldn't?'

'My brave angel,' he said. 'My brave English angel.' Then he scooped her in his strong arms, pulled her tightly to him, so tightly she could feel the contour of his body beneath the thin blue cotton, and kissed her. His breath smelled sweet, and was tinged with cigarette smoke, garlic and beer, the manly smells and taste she remembered. She kissed him back, wildly, deeply, feeling his tongue, holding it for a second, losing it, then finding it again.

Finally, breathless with excitement, their lips separated. They stood still, staring at each other, his eyes so close to hers they were just a warm blur.

'So,' he said. 'We have work to do, *ja*?'

She pushed her hands down inside the front of his trousers and gripped him gently. 'We do,' she smiled.

He drew breath sharply and exhaled, grinning. 'First we must work.'

'First we make love,' she replied.

'You are a very naughty little girl,' he teased.

'Are you going to punish me?'

'That will depend, yes? On how naughty you have been. Have you been very naughty?'

She nodded solemnly, stood back a pace, and put her finger in her mouth like a little child. 'Very,' she said.

'Tell me?'

'I can show you.'

He smiled. 'Go and fetch the car, I will be prepared.'

*

Five minutes later, Janet reversed the Passat up to the side entrance of the crematorium, where there was a green elevator door. As she halted the car and climbed out, the metal door slid open and Hans stood there, with a coffin on a trolley. There was a strange expression on his face and he was looking at her in a way that made her, suddenly, deeply uncomfortable.

Her eyes shot to the coffin, then back to his face.

Then to the coffin.

Had she made a terrible mistake? To be alone, here, with all her bridges burned, her trail carefully covered. Had she walked into a trap?

No one at home in Eastbourne knew where she was. No one in the world. Only Hans. And she was alone with him at the crematorium, in the falling darkness, and he was standing, looking at her, beside an open coffin.

She felt suddenly as if her insides had turned to ice. She wanted to be home, back home, where it was safe. Dull but safe. With Trevor.

But none of that was an option any longer.

Then he smiled. His normal, big, warm Hans smile. And the ice inside her melted in an instant, as if it had flash-thawed. 'In the trunk?' he questioned.

Nodding, she popped open the boot of the car, and then they both stood and stared for some moments at the black plastic sheeting, and the curved shape inside it.

'No problem?' he asked her, putting his arm around her and nibbling her ear tenderly.

'He was good as gold,' she said, wriggling with the excitement of his touch. 'Went out like a lamb after I swapped his insulin for sugared water. But he was heavy. I nearly didn't have the strength to get him into the boot.'

Where there's a will, there's a way, Trevor was fond of saying. And, of course, what was particularly sweet was that Trevor had written a will a long time ago, leaving everything to her, naturally.

'It is good he is so thin,' Hans said, unwrapping him. 'I have two cadavers waiting for the burners and one is very thin. I have the death certificates from the doctor's; we are all set. He will fit nicely into the coffin with the thin one. No one will know a thing.'

Down in the basement, as they wheeled the coffin out of the elevator, Janet recognized the beige metal casings, the instruments, the dials. The word 'Ruppmann' was printed above them, and on other machines in the room, and on top of wiring diagrams. Opposite them, two coffins sat, one with the lid open.

A few minutes passed and the thin occupant of the open coffin now had a companion, squashed tightly against him, as Hans screwed the lid down.

Then Hans smiled. A totally wicked smile.

A few minutes later, after he had pressed a number of buttons and the mechanical doors had closed, and the roar of the burners of the two huge furnaces rose to a crescendo, they could see, through the observation window, flames licking along the lengths of the two coffins.

Janet felt Hans's arms around her waist. Slowly, shedding their clothes, they sank to the floor.

Smoke rose from the chimney into the night sky. They made love while the burners rose to their optimum temperature, and their own body heat rose at the same time.

In the morning, Hans raked the remaining pieces of bone into the cremulator, then ground them to a powder that mingled with the ashes. Then they stepped through the crematorium doors, arm in arm. Outside, in the early, pre-dawn light, the world seemed an altogether brighter place. Birds were starting to sing.

Hans slipped an arm around her, then whispered into her ear, 'You know, my English angel, I will never let you go.'

And for an instant he sounded just like Trevor. She kissed him, then whispered back into his ear, 'Don't push your luck.'

'What is that meaning?' he asked.

She smiled.

VENICE APHRODISIAC

The first time they came to Venice, Johnny had told his wife he was on an important case; Joy had told her husband she was going to see her Italian relatives.

In the large, dingy hotel room with its window overlooking the Grand Canal, they tore off each other's clothes before they had even unpacked, and made love to the sound of lapping water and water taxis blattering past outside. She was insatiable; they both were. They made love morning, noon and night, only venturing out for food to stoke their energy. On that trip they barely even took time out to see the sights of the city. They had eyes only for each other. Horny eyes, each greedy for the other's naked body. They were aware that they had precious little time.

Johnny whispered to her that Woody Allen, whose movies they both loved, was once asked if he thought that sex was dirty, and Woody had replied, 'Only if you are doing it right.'

So they did it right. Over and over again. And in between they laughed a lot. Johnny told Joy she was the sexiest creature in the world. She told him no, he was.

One time, when he was deep inside her, she whispered into Johnny's ear, 'Let's promise each other to come back and make love here in this room every year, for ever.'

'Even after we're dead?' he said.

'Why not? You're stiff when you're dead, aren't you? Stiff as a gondolier's oar!'

'You're a wicked woman, Joy Jackson.'

'You wouldn't like me if I wasn't, you horny devil.'

'We could come back as ghosts, couldn't we, and haunt this room?'

'We will!'

Two years later, acrimoniously divorced and free, they married. And they honeymooned in Venice in the same hotel – a former palazzo – in the same room. While they were there, they vowed, as before, to return to the same room every year for their anniversary, and they did so, without fail. In the beginning they always got naked long before they got around to unpacking. Often, after dining out, they felt so horny they couldn't wait until they got back to the hotel.

One time they did it late at night in a moored gondola. They did it beneath the Rialto Bridge. And under several other bridges. Venice cast its spell – coming here was an aphrodisiac to them. They drank Bellinis in their favourite café in Piazza San Marco, swigged glorious white wines from the Friuli district and gorged on grilled seafood in their favourite restaurant, the Corte Sconta, which they always got lost trying to find, every year.

Some mornings, spent with passion, they'd hop on an early water taxi and drink espressos and grappa on the Lido at sunrise. Later, back in their dimly lit hotel room, they would take photographs of each other naked and film themselves making love. One time, for fun, they made plaster-of-Paris impressions of what Joy liked to call their 'rude bits'. They were so in lust, nothing, it seemed, could stop them, or could ever change.

Once, on an early anniversary, they visited Isola di San Michele, Venice's cemetery island. Staring at the graves, Johnny asked her, 'Are you sure you're still going to fancy me when I'm dead?'

'Probably even more than when you're alive!' she had replied. 'If that's possible.'

'We might rattle a bit, if we were – you know – both skeletons,' he had said.

'We'll have to do it quietly, so we don't wake up the graveyard,' she'd replied.

'You're a bad girl,' he had said, before kissing her on the lips.

'You'd never have loved me if I was good, would you?'

'Nah,' he said. 'Probably not.'

'Let me feel your oar!'

*

That was then. Now it was thirty-five years later. They'd tried – and failed – to start a family. For a while it had been fun trying, and eventually they'd accepted their failure. A lot of water under the bridge. Or rather, all four hundred and nine of Venice's bridges. They'd seen each one, and walked over most of them. Johnny ticked them off on a coffee-stained list he brought with him each year, and which became more and more creased each time he unfolded it. Johnny was a box-ticker, she'd come to realize. 'I like to see things in tidy boxes,' he would say.

He said it rather too often.

'Only joking,' he said, when she told him she was fed up hearing this.

They say there's many a true word spoken in jest but, privately, he was not jesting. Plans were taking shape in his mind. Plans for a future without her.

In happier times they'd shared a love of Venetian glass, and used to go across to the island of Murano on every trip to see their favourite glass factory, Novità Murano. They filled their home in Brighton with glass ornaments – vases, candlesticks, paperweights, figurines, goblets. Glass of every kind. They say that people who live in glass houses shouldn't throw stones, and they didn't. Not physical ones. Just metaphorical ones. More and more.

The stones had started the day she peeked on his computer.

Johnny had been a police officer – a homicide detective. She had worked in the Divisional Intelligence Unit of the same force. After he had retired, at forty-nine, he'd become bored. He managed to get a job in the fulfilment department of a mail-order company that supplied framed cartoons of bad puns involving animals. Their best-selling cartoon range was one with pictures of bulls on: *Bullshit. Bullderdash. Bullish.* And so on.

Johnny sat at the computer all day, ticking boxes in a job he loathed, despatching tasteless framed cartoons to people he detested for buying them, and then going home to a woman who looked more like the bulls in the cartoons every day. He sought out diversions on his computer and began by visiting porn sites. Soon he started advertising himself, under various false names, on Internet contact sites.

That was what Joy found when she peeked into the contents of his laptop one day when he had gone to play golf – at least, that had been his story. He had not been to any golf club. It was strokes and holes of a very different kind he had been playing and, confronted with the evidence, he'd been forced to fess up. He was full frontal, naked and erect on eShagmates.

Naked and erect for everyone in the world but her.

And so it was, on their thirty-fifth wedding anniversary, that they returned to the increasingly dilapidated palazzo on the Grand Canal, each with a very different agenda in their hearts and minds to the ones they'd had on those heady days of their honeymoon and the years that followed.

He planned to murder her here in Venice. He'd planned last year to murder her during a spring weekend break in Berlin, and the year before that, in Barcelona. Each time he had bottled out. As a former homicide detective, if anyone knew how to get away with murder, he did, but equally he was aware that few murderers ever succeeded. Murderers made mistakes in the white heat of the moment. All you needed was one tiny mistake – a clothing fibre, a hair, a discarded cigarette butt, a scratch, a footprint, a CCTV camera you hadn't spotted. Anything.

Certain key words were fixed in his mind from years of grim experience. *Motive. Body. Murder weapon.* They were the three things that would catch out a murderer. Without any one of those elements, it became harder. Without all three, near impossible.

So all he had to do was find a way to dispose of her body. Lose the murder weapon (as yet not chosen). And, as for motive – well, who was to know he had one? Other than the silly friends Joy gossiped with constantly.

The possibilities for murder in Venice were great. Joy could not swim and its vast lagoon presented opportunities for drowning – except it was very shallow. There were plenty of buildings with rickety steps where a person could lose their footing. Windows high enough to ensure a fatal fall.

It had been years since they'd torn each other's clothes off in the hotel room when they'd arrived. Instead, today, as usual, Johnny logged on and hunched over his computer. He had a slight headache, which he ignored. Joy ate a bar of chocolate from the minibar, followed by a tin of nuts, then the complimentary biscuits that came with the coffee. Then she had a rest, tired from the journey. When she woke, to the sound of Johnny farting, she peered suspiciously over his shoulder to check if he was on one of his porn chat sites.

What she had missed while she slept was the emails back and forth between Johnny and his new love, Mandy, a petite divorcee he'd met at the gym where he'd gone to keep his six-pack in shape. He planned to return from Venice a free man.

The Bellinis in their favourite café had changed, and were no longer made with fresh peach juice or real champagne. Venice now smelled of drains. The restaurant was still fine, but Johnny barely tasted his food, he was so deep in thought. And his headache seemed to be worsening. Joy had drunk most of the bottle of white wine and, with the Bellini earlier, into which he had slipped a double vodka, seemed quite smashed. They had six more nights here. Once, the days had flown by. Now he struggled to see how they could even fill tomorrow. With luck he would not have to.

He called the waiter over for the bill, pointing to his wife who was half asleep and apologizing that she was drunk. It could be important that the waiter would remember this. *Yes, poor lady, so drunk her husband struggled to help her out . . .*

They staggered along a narrow street, and crossed a bridge that arced over a narrow canal. Somewhere in the dark distance a gondolier was singing a serenade.

'You haven't taken me on a gondola in years,' she chided, slurring her words. 'I haven't felt your oar much in years either,' she teased. 'Maybe I could feel it tonight?'

I'd rather have my gall bladder removed without an anaesthetic, he thought.

'But I suppose you can't get it up these days,' she taunted. 'You don't really have an oar any more, do you? All you have is a little dead mouse that leaks.'

The splash of an oar became louder. So did the singing.

The gondola was sliding by beneath them. In it, entwined in each other's arms, were a young man and a young woman, clearly in love, as they had once been. As he was now with Mandy Brent. He stared down at the inky water.

Two ghosts stared back.

Then only one.

It took Joy some moments to realize anything was wrong. Then she turned in drunken panic, screaming for help, for a doctor, for an ambulance. A kindly neurosurgeon told her some hours later, in broken English, that there was nothing anyone could have done. Her husband had been felled by a massive cerebral aneurysm. He would have been dead within seconds.

*

Back in England, after Johnny's body had been repatriated, Joy's troubles really started. The solicitor informed her that he had left half of his entire estate, which was basically the house they lived in, to a woman she had never heard of. The next thing she knew, the woman was on the phone wanting to discuss the funeral arrangements.

'I'm having him cremated,' Joy said.

'He told me he wanted to be buried,' Mandy Brent insisted. 'I'd like that. I'd like to have somewhere I can go and sit with him.'

All the more reason, thought Joy, to have him cremated. But there was another bigger reason she had been thinking of. Much bigger.

*

The following year, on what would have been their thirty-sixth wedding anniversary, Joy returned to Venice, to the same room in the dilapidated former palazzo. She unpacked from her suitcase the small grey plastic urn and put it on the windowsill. She stared at it, then at the view of the Grand Canal beyond.

'Remember what we said to each other, Johnny? Do you? That promise we made to each other? About coming back here? Well, I'm helping us to keep that promise.'

The next morning she took a water taxi across to Murano. She spoke to the same courteous assistant in the glass factory, Valerio Barbero, who had helped them every year since they had started coming. Signor Barbero was an old man now, stooped and close to retirement. He told Joy how very deeply sympathetic he was, how sad, what a fine gentleman Signor Jones had been. And – as if this was quite a normal thing for him – he accepted the contents of the package and her design without even the tiniest flicker of his rheumy eyes. It would be ready in three days, he assured her.

*

It was. Joy could barely contain her excitement on the water taxi ride back to the mainland. She stopped in St Mark's Square to gulp down two Bellinis in rapid succession – to get her in the *mood*, she decided.

Then she entered the hotel room, hung the 'Do not disturb' sign on the door and locked it from the inside. She untied the pretty blue bow around the tall box and carefully opened it, removing the two contents.

The first item was the plaster-of-Paris mould she had taken of Johnny's rude bits, all those years ago, when he had been particularly drunk and even more aroused than usual. The second was the exquisite glass replica, now filled with the grey powder from the urn.

Slowly, feeling pleasantly tipsy from the Bellinis, she undressed, then lay on her back on the bed. 'Remember, Johnny?' she whispered. 'Remember that promise we made each other that very first time we came here? About coming back and making love here in this room every year forever? You were worried, weren't you, about not being able to get stiff enough for me after you were dead? Well, you really shouldn't have concerned yourself, should you?'

She caressed the long, slender glass. Hard as rock.

Stiff as a gondolier's oar.

Just like she remembered him.

TIME RICH

Wealthy guy, 39, non-smoker, tall, GSOH, good-looking, WLTM lady for fun, friendship and possibly more . . .

It isn't actually that I am being unfaithful to my wife at this moment, as I sit in my small den, at 3 a.m., logged on to a dating agency on the Internet, while Alison sleeps in the bedroom on the other side of the wall.

Because, you see, it is not really me at all who is online. Not debt-ridden Clive Talbot, with my credit cards all maxed out, my BMW about to be repossessed, and my mortgage company weeks away from foreclosing. They say if you haven't made it by forty, you aren't going to make it, ever. Well, I'm just six months short of that big birthday and I'm determined no one is going to hold that two-fingered 'Loser' sign up against my forehead.

No, sir.

Only problem is that, at this moment, my sole possession of real value is the gold Rolex on my wrist, which I bought years ago after a big poker win. In truth, my only ever big poker win. It is a very classy watch, but it's not much to show for a lifetime of hard work, is it?

So, now let me introduce Sebastian DeVries, cool, suave, man-about-town entrepreneur, who is at this moment talking to one hot, seriously rich dame, whose name is Maria Andropoulos. For the past hour she has been pouring her heart out to me – sorry, to *Sebastian* – about her terrible marriage to one of those new Russian oil oligarchs. Tired of his constant philandering and bullying, she is in search of an affair – and, who knows, perhaps true love – with someone with whom she can settle down and enjoy the divorce settlement she will undoubtedly get from him. Of course, the latter is just my interpretation of where things could go – if I play my cards right . . .

And so far, so good – she likes everything she has seen and heard about Seb DeVries! And we have a date – lunch at her regular table at one of the coolest restaurants in London, the Wolseley, in three days' time.

I've just met her on ParkLaneIntroductions.com. This is a dating agency with a difference – it is only for the very wealthy. Rich men and women in search of affairs. What better place to pull a rich woman? A client of mine told me about it – he said that because there is a surplus of women registered, eligible men can have six months' free-trial membership. And I assure you that Sebastian DeVries is eminently eligible!

And, hey, Sebastian and I are not really that dissimilar. People always tell me I look like Daniel Craig. I think they're right, although, actually, I think I'm better looking – more sophisticated. I have class. I'm really much more the guy Ian Fleming had in mind when he wrote those Bond books than Daniel Craig will ever be. I was educated privately – well, for a couple of years anyway, until my dad went to prison for fraud and my mother had to take me out because she had no money to pay the fees. But that's another story.

It's raining outside. The wind of an autumn equinox gale throws the droplets at my windows, clawing at the glass like the letters I get daily from the debt collectors that claw at my soul. The truth is, I'm just not living the life I was born to live. I have a failed business behind me, and now I'm working as an independent financial advisor, for a crook who never pays me the commission I'm due for the life insurance policies I sell, the dubious tax schemes I hook people into and the useless pensions I dupe my clients into buying.

And all my sour little wife, Alison, does is max out our credit cards a little more every day, buying stupid face creams, ridiculous dresses and paying for lunches we cannot afford. Who was it who said so many of us spend all our lives doing jobs we hate, in order to earn money we don't need, so that we can buy things we don't want in order to impress people we don't like? Well, I do the earning and Alison does the rest.

*

For the next couple of days, I find it hard to concentrate on my work. I use the last of my credit cards which still has some life in it to buy a cool suit, shirt, and a new tie for good measure, from Richard James of Savile Row, and a pair of black suede Crockett & Jones loafers from Burlington Arcade. Alison tells me I seem distant and asks me what's wrong. I lie, something that comes easy after twenty years of marriage to a woman whose only asset for me today is the meagre income she brings in as a legal secretary. Nothing's wrong, I tell her, and to prove it, driven by the excitement of what awaits me tomorrow, I make love to her with a passion I did not know I still had in me – and which I'm sure the beautiful Maria Andropoulos is going to appreciate in the weeks and months to come.

*

And now, finally, in the vast, ornate black-and-white galleried room of the Wolseley, filled with the beautiful people of London, a greeter, all in black and perfectly formed, is guiding me through the packed tables alive with the buzz of rich, successful people's conversation, to an apparition that is way, way, way beyond her photograph on the Internet.

Her blonde hair looks wild, untamed, in the way that only a top salon charging at least £300 for a blow-dry could achieve. She is dressed in a high-collared dress with a leopard-skin pattern that clings to her slender contours, and that quietly states, 'I am rich and beautiful and I know it.' Her teeth, the colour of snow, melt me. She is dripping with serious bling. And she has great tits – but let's not get crude.

I can immediately sense from her body language that I am making an impression on her, too. I sit down, our eyes locked, inane grins on our faces. She holds up in greeting a glass filled with champagne, and moments later, at the hand of an unseen waiter, the rarefied froth of 1990 Cristal is rising over the rim of my own goblet.

'You look so much better than your photograph, Sebastian,' she says.

'You, too,' I tell her, trying to stop my greedy eyes from looking at those rings on her fingers, the bracelets, the necklace, the earrings, and the Vertu phone on the white table cloth.

And I am so captivated by her charm that, as we get stuck into the second bottle of champagne before the starter (she has ordered oysters, followed by Beluga) even arrives, I need to keep reminding myself I am here not to enjoy myself, but on business.

We glide easily across topics. Trite at first – stuff about what a great place London is for the arts. She has a slightly husky, mid-European accent which I find very attractive. And all the while her 'fuck-me' eyes seldom let go of mine.

We both share the massive dish of oysters and somehow, by the time we've finished, the second bottle of champagne is empty. And a third is on its way. She keeps looking at her watch. I don't know what the make is, but it is encrusted with diamonds the size of barnacles. And suddenly there is something I notice about her. It is the way she keeps twisting the biggest bit of bling of all: a diamond engagement – or maybe eternity – ring. She turns it round, and round, and round.

It is hypnotic.

I've never seen diamonds so big.

Gradually, subtly, our conversation deepens as she tells me about her brute of a husband. I notice she keeps looking at her watch and I wonder, anxiously, if perhaps I am boring her. She apologizes, suddenly, explaining that her driver is arriving at 3 p.m. to collect her – she has to make an important speech this afternoon at the Savoy hotel for the charity Women Against Poverty, of which she is chair.

'I like a Rolex on a man,' she says, with a very sexy smile. 'A naked man wearing a Rolex is a very big turn-on for me.'

And now I am glad there is a table between us, so she cannot see just how turned on her remark makes me.

'It could be arranged,' I say.

'I'd like that very much,' she replies, then twists that ring again. 'I apologize, my finger hurts – I have arthritis in the knuckle. I hurt my hand from fending off my husband's blows. Sometimes I have to move the ring to ease the pain.'

I try to imagine her husband. I think of the pictures of Russian tycoons I have seen in the papers, and I find myself hating this man with all my heart and soul. I want to take her away with me now, to protect her – and make love to her and . . .

I am forgetting myself. Forgetting why I am here. The champagne and her intoxicating company are making me behave this way.

Her phone rings. She answers it with a curt, 'Yes. You are outside now? OK.'

And suddenly, before I realize it, she is standing up. 'I really want to see you again,' she says.

'Me too.'

She gives me her elegant card and enters my mobile number into her Vertu. Then she kisses me lightly on the cheek. Her tender touch and her intoxicating perfume send my pulse into orbit. But as she turns away to walk towards the door, she collides with a shaven-headed ape in a grey suit and white polo neck, who has appeared from nowhere, totally not concentrating on where he is going, talking on his mobile phone. She ricochets off him, straight into a waitress carrying a tray of beautifully prepared food. And in the next instant, to my dismay, my beautiful date and the waitress crash into a table, knocking everything on it flying, and fall to the floor, entangled like a pair of mud-wrestling bitches.

I can scarcely believe my eyes as I jump up to rescue my distressed damsel and help her back to her feet. Elegant waiters swarm around. Maria smiles at me; she is fine. Like a James Bond martini, she is shaken but not stirred. Through the mêlée of people assisting her, she blows me a goodbye kiss.

And through the haze of champagne, in the moments after she has gone, I realize that we didn't get the bill. Not a problem; I assume she has an account here. So I enjoy the remaining half-bottle of champagne and order a large espresso – and, what the hell, a decent Armagnac to go with it. Then my phone rings.

It is Maria. For an instant my heart leaps, then her voice tells me something is wrong. She sounds in a terrible state. 'Sebastian, please can you help me? I've lost my ring!'

'Ring?'

'My engagement ring from Aleksei. It's worth about three hundred thousand pounds, but that's not the important thing – he will go nuts if he sees me without it!'

'Where have you lost it?' I ask dumbly.

'It must have come off my finger when I fell over with that stupid waitress! It has to be on the floor somewhere. Look, I haven't got time to deal with this; I have to start speaking in a few minutes. Would you be a darling and look for me?'

'Of course.' My eyes are already scanning the floor around me.

'I *have* to get it back.'

I was touched by the desperation in her voice.

'Darling, if you cannot find it, please tell the staff at the Wolseley that I will pay a £10,000 reward to anyone who finds it.'

'You won't need to do that.'

'Dahlink, £10,000 is nothing to me, OK? Aleksei makes that in twenty minutes. Please, just find it for me.'

She was in tears.

'I'll find it,' I said. 'You won't need to pay any reward, I promise you.'

I was lying. A plan was forming in my head. A very beautiful plan, because instead of dulling my senses, the champagne and now the Armagnac were actually sharpening my thoughts.

I fell to my knees and started grovelling around on the floor, looking for the ring. Proffering apologies, I crawled between the legs of diners, moving handbags aside, my nostrils filled with the scent of expensive leather shoes. But no damned ring.

After ten minutes, and numerous apologies, I admitted temporary defeat and sat back down, thinking hard, wondering if she had dropped it out in the street, perhaps?

If so, the chances of it still being there were slim. As I was pondering, a glint of light struck my eyes. To my astonishment, I saw the ape who had first collided with Maria seated at the next table. He was holding a sparkly object in his fingers, examining it.

It was Maria's ring! I was as certain as I could be of anything.

And while I stared, he and his companion, another ape in a vulgar suit, stood up and walked past me, heading quickly towards the exit.

I jumped up from my chair. 'Excuse me!' I called after him.

But I got trapped in the narrow gulley between the tables by a waiter with a massive tray of drinks. By the time I had squeezed past him, both apes had walked through the crowd of people hovering around the entrance, waiting either for their coats or their tables, and were heading out through the front door.

As I reached the door, a tall, smiling man all in black stepped into my path.

'Your bill, sir?' he asked.

'It's been . . . it's settled – on Maria Andropoulos's account.'

'I'm sorry, sir,' he said, with a perfectly formed and delivered smile. 'People do not have accounts here.'

'But she . . . she said . . .' I stared at him bewildered, realizing she must have forgotten in all the chaos surrounding her departure, and stared at the doors swinging closed behind the apes and my fast vanishing £10,000 reward.

I pulled out my one remaining live credit card, thrust it into his hand, told him I would be back in a moment, and threw myself out of the door and past the liveried doorman outside, looking frantically each way down Piccadilly. Then I saw them, walking along the pavement, a short distance away.

I ran after them and caught them up. 'Hallo,' I said, a tad breathlessly, to the ape in the white polo neck. He was six-feet-four inches of muscle and gristle, with a complexion like the wrong side of the moon, and an expression I already, very seriously, did not like.

'I think you just picked up the ring a friend of mine dropped.'

They stopped in their tracks. White polo neck asked me, 'Do you have dental insurance?'

'Dental insurance?' I replied, puzzled.

'Yes,' he said, in an East End accent. 'Because if you don't fuck off, you're going to need it.'

I don't actually know where I got the strength from – but I stood my ground, doubtless driven by desperation. 'I've been asked to offer a reward of £2,000 for that ring by my friend who lost it,' I blurted.

For a long moment I thought he was going to drive my teeth so far down my throat that I would need the services of a proctologist. But then I realized from his expression that he was actually considering my offer.

He pulled the ring out of his pocket and held it up. The other ape nodded thoughtfully.

'I don't know much about rings,' polo neck said, 'but I would guess this has to be three grand.'

'Two and a half,' I blurted.

'OK,' he relented, to my joy. 'Two thousand, five hundred pounds.'

The next half hour was totally surreal. I found myself in a taxi with these two apes, which I had to pay for, naturally, driving to a pawnbroker that polo neck appeared to know in High Holborn. I cashed in my watch for a lousy £2,500 exactly, handed him the cash, took the ring and jumped into another cab, heading straight back to the Wolseley. I paid the bill – a whopping £425 including tip, which, miraculously, my credit card withstood – then waited another hour in a Starbucks down the road, giving my beloved Maria time to finish her speech, before dialling the number on the card she had given me.

I got an automated response, from a curt sounding lady, which said, 'The number you have called is not recognized. Please check the number. If you need help, call the operator.'

I called the operator. The number on Maria Andropoulos's business card was incorrect.

Puzzled, I rang the Savoy hotel and asked to speak to Maria Andropoulos who had been making a speech at the Women Against Poverty charity function at the hotel that afternoon. After some minutes, the very helpful assistant assured me that there was no function in the hotel for that charity scheduled for that day. And the name of my beloved meant nothing to them.

Unsure what to do next, I decided to take a cab back to the pawnbroker. The man who ran it had seemed extremely pleasant, albeit on the mean side. He scrutinized the ring with one of those curious monocles I had only ever seen in films.

Then he smiled and shook his head. 'Where did you get this from?' he asked.

'A friend,' I replied.

He looked at me with deep suspicion which implied, *First a Rolex, now this.* Then he floored me.

'It's worthless,' he said. 'Costume jewellery. This is what you'd get in a Christmas cracker. I wouldn't even give you a quid for this.'

A twenty-pound cab ride later, a jeweller in a shop in Old Bond Street confirmed what I had been told.

*

I have a postscript to add to this sorry tale. It was five years later, and I was divorced, still eking a living out of flogging tax schemes. I emerged from Knightsbridge underground station and was walking past Harvey Nichols, a store that, in my financial position, there was no point in even *thinking* about entering, when a black S-Class Mercedes pulled up to the kerb. From the rear, Maria Andropoulos and the ape in the polo neck emerged.

Both of them saw me, and I stopped in my tracks.

'Dahlink!' she said, thrusting out her hand as if greeting a dear and long-lost friend. 'My dahlink Sebastian! How are you?'

Before I could even muster a reply, the ape pulled back the cuff of his Savile Row suit jacket to reveal a gold Rolex.

My gold Rolex.

'We're late,' he said to her, glancing at me as if I was part of the flotsam of London's streets that people in S-Class Mercedes-Benz cars were well removed from.

And he was right, of course.

CHRISTMAS IS FOR THE KIDS

Kate saw him standing at the Tesco checkout and presumed he was with his mother. The store was quiet. It was Christmas Eve, the last hour of shopping.

The doors opened and a loop of tinsel swayed in the draught. 'Silent Night' echoed around the darkening car park. The queue moved forward and the boy tugged his stacked trolley. The woman in front of him was stuffing her purchases into her carrier, and Kate realized then that the boy was on his own. His head barely reached the top of the trolley, and he had to stretch to reach the lower packages.

He looked about six. Floppy blonde hair, freckles, a snub nose, wearing a quilted jacket, jeans and trainers. Something seemed wrong about his being there alone.

She watched him unload two twelve-packs of Coke, sweets and chocolate bars, more fizzy drinks in lurid colours, ice cream, burgers and frozen chips. What kind of a mother did he have? Too busy or disinterested to cook anything but junk and convenience foods?

She'd never let her kids eat such rubbish. Never. When she had kids. Or, as she worried increasingly, if. She felt a pang of sadness. Christmas was for kids, not for lonely adults. She'd split up with Neil in February. Ten months she had been on her own and there was no one on the horizon.

The kid paid cash from a wad of notes, then began packing his groceries. By the time she had signed her credit card slip, he had already left.

A fleck of sleet tickled her face as she unlocked her car, but there was no forecast of a white Christmas. The engine turned sluggishly before clattering into life and she revved hard for some moments before driving off. As she pulled onto the main road she noticed the tiny figure of the kid struggling under the weight of his packages.

She stopped. 'Can I give you a lift?'

'It's OK. I only live just—' At that moment one of his bags broke and several cans clattered onto the ground; a bottle of ketchup smashed. Kate got out to help him. 'Come on. You can't manage all these. I'll run you home.'

'I – I better not.' He looked scared of something and her concern about him deepened. She loaded his groceries into the boot and he climbed, subdued, into the front seat.

She drove about a mile, and was passing a row of new houses behind a developer's hoarding when he said, 'There!'

She turned onto a tree-lined track that went up a slight incline, past a sign warning WORKS ENTRANCE. HARD HAT AREA. 'I'm Kate,' she said. 'What's your name?'

'I'm getting a computer for Christmas,' he said after some moments, ignoring her question.

After half a mile, a solitary detached Edwardian house came into view. It looked in poor condition, and what she could see of the grounds looked neglected.

'Are you going to come in?' he said as she pulled up. She wanted to, very much. Wanted to give his parents a piece of her mind.

'I'll help you with your shopping,' she replied.

He turned imploringly to Kate and she could see again that he was frightened.

'Would you like to stay with us?'

'Stay with you?' She felt a sudden prick of anxiety, the boy's fear transmitting to her. Her curiosity about his parents was increasing. 'I'll come in with you.' She smiled at him. 'What's your name?'

'Daniel Hogarth. What's yours?'

'Kate Robinson.'

He ran up to the front door and knocked loudly. A girl of about seven with black hair in a velvet band opened it indignantly. 'We're not deaf, you know.'

The boy whispered and she looked at Kate. Kate lugged a couple of bags out of the boot and the two children carried the rest.

There was a huge Christmas tree in the hall that rose up the stairwell; it was beautifully decorated, with real candles which were flickering and guttering in the draught, and the base was surrounded by finely wrapped presents. There was a smell of wood smoke that made Kate nostalgic for her own childhood.

She followed the children into a kitchen, where there was a pine table at which a girl of about five in a pinafore and a boy of about the same age in a striped jersey and jeans sat, the girl reading, the boy furiously pressing the keys of a small electronic game.

'This is my brother, Luke, and my other sister, Amy,' Daniel said. Then he looked at Kate solemnly. 'You will stay with us for Christmas, won't you?'

Kate laughed, then realized the boy was serious. 'It's sweet of you, but I don't think your mummy and daddy would like that.'

The children at the table turned towards her. 'Please don't leave us,' the little girl, Amy, said.

'Please don't go,' Luke added. Tears filled his eyes.

'If you leave us,' Daniel said, 'we won't have Christmas. Please stay and let us have Christmas.'

The kids looked clean, well nourished, no bruises. And yet there was an overwhelming sense of sadness in their faces. She fixed her stare on Amy, her heart heaving for them. 'Where are your mummy and daddy?'

Amy looked silently at the floor.

Kate's imagination went wild for a moment. Were their parents dead somewhere in the house and the kids were too afraid to tell her?

Shivers as hard as needles suddenly crawled across her skin. She began walking back towards the front door. Daniel ran along beside her and tugged her hand. She opened the door and noticed to her surprise that it was snowing outside; fat, heavy flakes were settling on the drive.

'Kate, if you stayed with us, maybe we could have Christmas after all.'

'What do you mean, Daniel?'

'We'll never get to open our presents if you go.'

She looked into his frightened eyes and patted his cheek tenderly. 'I-I'll be right back, OK?'

'It only works if you stay,' he said forlornly.

'What only works?'

He shrugged and said nothing.

'I won't be long, I promise.'

Tearfully, Daniel closed the door behind her. Kate climbed back into her car and turned the ignition key. Nothing happened. She tried again, then again, but the battery was dead.

Exasperated, she got out, then noticed to her surprise that all the lights in the house had gone off. Sharp prickles of fear again raked her skin, harder than before. Had they tampered with her car?

She swallowed, the grip of fear tightening around her. Then she started walking quickly down the drive, turning her head and staring back at the darkness every few moments, her leather shoes inadequate, slipping on the settling snow.

The tunnel of trees seemed to be closing in around her and she broke into a run, her heart pounding, her chest feeling as if it were about to burst. *Just a prank*, she thought. *Just a prank*. But it wasn't just a prank, she knew.

Headlights crossed ahead of her. The main road. Kate ran faster, past the developer's hoarding and out into the road. Police. She needed to call the police, then cursed as she realized she had left her phone in the car. She ran along the pavement. There was a phone box ahead and she dived into it, then saw to her dismay that it had been gutted by vandals.

She ran on towards the town centre, crossed one busy street and then another. A car coming towards her had a perspex panel on its roof. A police car.

She leapt out in front of it, flapping her arms frantically. It pulled up and the driver wound down his window.

'Please,' she gasped. 'Please, I think there's something very wrong . . . children very frightened . . . I . . .'

There was a WPC in the passenger seat and Kate was aware she was looking at her oddly.

'Could you calm down and give us a little more detail?' the driver said.

Kate explained, trying to gather her breath. 'I don't know for sure,' she said. 'It's just a feeling I have.'

'OK, jump in the back. We'll go and take a look.'

The WPC spoke into her radio and the car accelerated.

'Turn right up this track,' Kate said.

'There's nothing up here – this is all part of the development site,' the driver said.

'No, there's a house at the top . . . you must know it: a big Edwardian place,' Kate replied.

'Only house up there is the Hogarth place.'

'Yes! Daniel Hogarth. That's right,' Kate said, remembering his name.

As they drove up through the tunnel of trees, she frowned. There was no snow on the ground yet it had been settling only minutes ago. Then the house came into view. It was still in darkness. The dull paintwork of her car glinted in the headlights. Then she gasped in shock as they neared the house and she could see it more clearly.

It had been gutted by fire.

The roof was gone completely and half of the walls had collapsed, leaving the charred rooms open to the elements. Pipes and wiring hung out like entrails. Kate swallowed, her heart crashing wildly inside her chest. 'I-I-I came here . . . I-I went in . . . I—'

'Happened five years ago,' the driver said, halting the car.

The WPC turned to face her. 'The parents were separated. The father was up north. The mother must have had some kind of breakdown – bought them all their presents, gave them a wad of cash then left them home alone, instructed them not to speak to anyone, and went off to Switzerland with a boyfriend. Sometime on Christmas Eve, while the kids were asleep, the house caught fire and they were all killed. The mother committed suicide after she was arrested.'

Kate sat in numbed silence and stared at the blackened shell where only a short while ago she had stood in the warm kitchen and smelled wood smoke and seen a tree surrounded by presents, and odd thoughts strayed through her mind.

She wondered whether, if she had stayed, the snow would have continued falling, and whether the kids would have got to open their presents. And she resolved that next year she would go back to the supermarket and, if Daniel was there again, she would accept his invitation to stay.

WHEN YOUR NUMBER'S UP

For as long as Gail had known Ricky Walters, he had dreamed of winning the lottery – the National Lottery, with its promise of £50 million, if not more. Much more.

Loadsamoney!

Moolah!

And he would win it, he knew; it was just a matter of time. He had a winning system, and besides, he had always been lucky. 'You make your own luck in life. I was lucky meeting you,' he told Gail. 'Marrying you was like winning all the lotteries in the world at the same time!'

That was then. Now was ten years later. Five years ago, a clairvoyant in a tent at a charity garden party told Ricky she could see he was going to have a big lottery win. Gail had scoffed, but Madame Zuzu, in her little tent, had simply reinforced what Ricky already knew. He had absolute confidence. Absolute belief in his system.

It consumed him.

Yes, he was going to win the lottery. It was a fact. An absolute racing certainty. He was so damned confident that he was going to win that often, over a few drinks at his favoured corner table in The Dog and Pheasant, which he visited most nights, he would spend time going over the list of all the things he was going to buy and the investments he would make with the money.

He subscribed to a range of lifestyle magazines, which he always read cover to cover, tearing out and filing away pages featuring items he was considering buying when 'L-Day', as he called it, finally came. A yacht – probably a custom-built Sunseeker; cars – well, it would have to be an Aston Martin Vanquish for himself, and a convertible Mercedes SL AMG for madam; a private jet, of course – he rather fancied a Lear; a Hublot watch.

There'd be a new house too. Gail told him she thought it was strange that he had a new house so far down his list of priorities – considering they weren't exactly living in a palace right now. Yep, right . . . well, that was another story.

Ricky was a systems manager, with responsibility for the computers in the Brighton head office of a national web design and development company. Algebra and maths were his thing, always had been, and it was through playing around with the six numbers of the lottery that one day, eight years back, he had his light-bulb moment. He saw something in the randomness of those figures that, so far as he could see, no one else had – and certainly not anyone at Camelot who ran the lottery.

A year ago the firm had gone into liquidation and he had so far not found another job. He'd done a few bits and pieces of IT work for friends and acquaintances, and they were kept afloat – just – by Gail's job as a bookkeeper for a small firm of estate agents. Gail was worried as hell about their financial future, but he was happy and confident. He was going to win the lottery. Oh yes. His system rocked!

You make your own luck in life.

Whenever he talked about it to Gail, her eyes glazed over. He'd told her, on their first date, that one day they were going to be richer than Croesus. But when, after that light-bulb moment, he had begun to explain how, expounding enthusiastically his applications of elements of calculus, Pythagoras, Noether's Theorem and the Callan-Symanzik Equation, her eyes would always begin to glaze over. In fact, throughout the years of their marriage, her eyes had begun to glaze over faster and faster. Recently, the moment he began to talk mathematics, he could almost hear them glazing over. It was as if the cords holding up shutters had been severed, and they'd fallen with a resounding crash.

But Ricky barely noticed. He wasn't talking to her anyway; he was really addressing himself, reassuring himself, reconfirming all that he knew. He was going to win one day for sure. The big one – the National Lottery. And, for a whole number of reasons, it would be really convenient for him if it happened quite soon. Ideally within the next few weeks, please! His fortieth birthday was looming, and it was not a milestone he was happy about. He'd read somewhere that if you haven't made it by the time you are forty, you are not going to make it.

And, as Gail had only too accurately pointed out, in eight years of spending twenty pounds a week on tickets for his system, to date he had had just one small win of fifty pounds to show for his efforts.

She'd calculated that if he had banked twenty pounds a week over this same period of time, they'd have over eight thousand pounds saved – and more, with interest.

'Just how far would that amount get you today?' he would retort.

'It would get us a new dishwasher, which we can't afford,' Gail reminded him. 'It would enable us to pay for a holiday – which we haven't had for two years because you say we can't afford one. It could replace my car, which is a basket case.'

Most importantly of all, in her mind, it would pay for IVF treatments, since all their attempts to conceive so far had failed.

'Ah, but just wait!' he would reply.

'I've been waiting – when do I stop waiting?'

'Soon, very soon. I know – I just know – that we are on the verge; it's going to happen. All the numbers are meshing closer and closer. It could be any week now!'

'Well,' she said, 'dream on.'

'Oh, I will!'

Ricky had always had a lot of dreams. But he needed the money to make the most important one of all come true.

*

They decided they could not afford to throw a party for Ricky's fortieth birthday, so instead they invited a dozen friends to join them for a dinner celebration at their favourite Italian restaurant in Hove, Topolino's. On the strict understanding everyone would pay for themselves. Ricky, who was by nature a generous man, hadn't been happy about that idea, but his latest bank statement was the gloomiest to date, and had forced him to accept the plan, albeit still reluctantly.

That damned win was just around the corner, he told Gail. He could feel it in his bones!

But after an hour of gulping down Prosecco at Topolino's, listening to jokes about ageing and questions about whether he was looking forward to his free bus pass, he was enjoying the company of good friends, and all he could feel was a deep sense of bonhomie growing inside him, the more alcohol he drank. They were a rowdy table, sensibly placed in a far corner of the restaurant so they could stand up and make their toasts and their speeches without ruining the evening for the rest of the diners there.

Suddenly, part way through eating his starter of ravioli florentine, he glanced at his watch. It was just past 9 p.m. Shit! He waved over a waiter, a tall, thin, cadaverous-looking Italian with a voice that was far more cheerful than his face.

'Si, signor?'

Ricky tried to speak to him without attracting the attention of the rest of his guests. 'Could shew do me a favour,' he slurred. 'I shleft my phone at home. Could shew let me know this week's lottery numbers?'

The waiter frowned. 'I go ask.'

'Thank you so much.' Ricky shoved a twenty-pound note into his hand.

'For God's sake!' Gail admonished quietly into his ear. 'Can't you leave it alone for just one evening, darling, and enjoy yourself?'

'What if tonight's the night?' he hissed back.

She shook her head, and drank a large gulp of her red wine.

'Hey, Ricky,' his oldest friend, Bob Templeton, the overweight owner of a heating engineering business, said. 'Did you hear the one about the forty-year-old IT man who goes into a pub with a frog on his head? The barman asks, "What's that you've got there?" And the frog replies, "I don't know. It started off as a wart on my arse."'

The whole table erupted into peals of laughter. Ricky stifled a wry smile. Then the owner of the restaurant – a wiry, cheery man in his late fifties – bounded over. In a broad Italian accent he said, 'OK, who wanta know tonight's lottery numbers?'

Ricky raised a hand.

The owner read them out. '1, 23, 34, 40, 41, 48.'

Ricky frowned. 'Could you repeat those?'

'Si, signor. 1, 23, 34, 40, 41, 48.'

'Are you sure? Are you absolutely sure?'

'I sure. I go check, if you like? Make absolutely sure?'

'Please.'

Gail stared at him, and Ricky avoided looking at her. Inside, he was trembling. He downed the remainder of his glass of wine, reached for the bottle with a shaking hand and refilled it.

'It's a rip-off, the lottery,' Hilary Wickens, the wife of his best man, said. 'I think it's a mug's game.'

Ricky remained silent. Totally silent. Only Gail, staring at him intently, noticed all the colour had drained from his face. But she said nothing.

Suddenly the owner was standing over Ricky's shoulder, leaning down, handing him a tiny sheet of paper, torn from a pad, with the six numbers written on it. 'Si, Signor Walters, I have checked. Called the phone line to make-a-sure for you!'

Ricky said nothing. He nodded silent thanks, read the numbers carefully, folded the sheet and tucked it into his jacket pocket. He was aware of Gail's intense gaze and avoided her eyes. He downed his newly filled glass in one gulp. He was shaking, almost uncontrollably, and did not want to be at the restaurant any more. But he had to go through with the rest of the evening.

He picked at his main course, a thick, broiled veal chop on the bone, normally one of his favourite foods, but right now he had no appetite at all. And why the hell did Gail keep looking at him so strangely? Annoyed that he wasn't in the party spirit? Well, hey, big surprise, it didn't take much to annoy her these days.

A massive cake arrived, with forty candles and a big firework thing in the middle. Everyone sang 'Happy Birthday', with most of the rest of the people in the restaurant joining in. Then he had to blow out the candles. Of course, they were those stupid jokey ones that kept relighting themselves.

Then he was called on to make a speech. He bumbled through the words he had prepared on a scrap of paper he produced from his pocket – although he was much more interested in the scrap of paper in a different pocket.

He finished his short speech by quoting George Carlin. 'Life's journey is not to arrive at the grave in a well-preserved body, but rather to skid in sideways, totally worn out, shouting, "Holy shit, what a ride!"'

Everyone laughed and applauded, except for Gail, who sat staring at him in stony silence.

She leaned over to him when he sat back down, as Bob Templeton was rising to his feet to begin his speech. 'Are you all right?'

'Never better!' Ricky said.

And he meant it.

And at the end of the evening, he insisted, absolutely insisted, on paying for everyone on his credit card. Despite almost coming to blows with Gail, who kept telling everyone he was drunk and to ignore him.

*

The cab dropped them home just after midnight. Ricky, well lit up with three Sambucas inside him on top of everything else he had drunk, slumbered for the entire short journey. He went straight into the bathroom, closed the door behind him, then pulled out the crumpled piece of paper the owner of Topolino's had given him, on which were written the winning National Lottery numbers.

His numbers!

Oh shit.

Oh shit.

He focused hard on them, to make absolutely sure he was not mistaken. He knew them by heart. They were one of the group of numbers his computer algorithm had calculated was bound to come up from the combination of six balls dropping. And now they had.

He was not mistaken.

As he stepped back out of the bathroom, Gail gave him a quizzical smile. 'So, what's going on?'

'What do you mean, what's going on?'

'You've been very quiet most of the evening. Didn't you enjoy your party?'

'I'd have enjoyed it more if you hadn't tried to make me look so small over the bill.'

'You were drunk, darling. Everyone had already agreed to contribute – you didn't need to do that.'

'No? Well, let me tell you something. I've won the lottery! My numbers have come up – and you never believed me when I said I would win. Well, I've been looking forward to this moment for a long time – a long, long time. You see, I don't want to be with you any more. I'm in love with someone else and have been for a long time. Now, finally, I can afford to divorce you. You don't have to worry, I'm not going to dump you in the shit. I've thought about it very carefully and done the maths. I'll make sure you're well provided for.'

'Very thoughtful of you,' she said, acidly.

He gave her a drunken leer. 'Yeah, well, I'm all heart. Too bad you never recognized that.'

'Silly old me.'

'I'll be gone in the morning,' he said. 'I'm going to start packing now. I can't stand the sight of you for another day.'

'You know how to make someone feel good,' she said, 'that's for sure.' She stepped past him, up to the washbasin, and began to remove her make-up.

'You've always ridiculed my system. You told me I would never win. So, just how wrong are you?'

'Not wrong at all,' she said, dabbing away her mascara. 'I thought it might make a fun evening if you thought you'd won the lottery. So I asked the waiter to give you those numbers, which I wrote down for him. Oh, and just in case you are wondering, I have tonight's actual winning numbers. I suggest you tweak your system – you didn't get a single one of them.'

LIKE YOU

She *liked* him on Facebook. He *liked* her back. Actually, he liked her a lot.

He liked her smile. He liked her photograph. She was the right age for him – late twenties, he guessed. An age when people started to mature and know what they wanted. She had a serene air about her, and a friendly smile that suggested she could be fun, a bit of a sport, maybe very sexy. But at the same time he could sense a slight hunger in her eyes. As if she was looking for something she had not yet found. He liked her name too. Teresa Saunders.

He wanted to be her friend. Very badly. *Oh yes. You are one stunning girl. We could definitely hit it off. Me, I could be that guy you are looking for. Really I could!*

He clicked to see more photographs, but all he got was the message: *No photos to show.*

Damn, he thought, she had her privacy settings high. He sent a request to be Teresa Saunders' friend. Then he waited. Twenty minutes later, it was past midnight and there was no response. He had to be up early for an important client presentation: the launch of a new food brand, a vitamin-packed, cholesterol-busting super-porridge that would be all the breakfast you ever needed. So he logged off and went to bed.

Teresa came to him during the night in a dream. Her long, wavy hair, the colour of winter wheat, floated in slow motion around her face. Her blue eyes smiled at him. She kissed him lightly on his forehead, on his cheeks, then on his lips. He woke with a start, convinced, for a fleeting instant, that she was in the room with him. And feeling horny as hell.

Of course, it was just a dream. But what a dream! He could feel some kind of strange, magical and deeply erotic connection with her across the ether. It was so powerful he had to switch on the light just to make sure she was not really in the room with him. But he was alone, of course. Alone in his big, loft-style bedroom, with its bare wooden floors strewn with rugs, and the curtainless picture window overlooking the inky waters of the Thames, half a mile upstream from Tower Bridge.

Lights glided by, accompanied by the throb of an engine: a Port of London Police boat. He slipped out of bed and padded through to his den, sat at his desk, which looked out over the river; then he flipped open the lid of his laptop and logged back on to Facebook. There was a notification: *Your friend request has been accepted. Teresa Saunders is now your friend.* And there was a message: *Thanks for the friend request!*

Yayyyyyy!

But he held off replying. Did not want to seem too keen. She might think him a bit of a saddo messaging her at 3.20 a.m.

He went back to bed and closed his eyes and wondered if she would come to him again. But all that came were images of MaximusBrek, the porridge of gladiators!

His slogan and he was proud of it.

*

He awoke at 6.15 a.m., a few minutes before his alarm was due to go off. Dawn had long broken and it was almost full light. He liked this time of year, early April. Spring was in the air. The nights were getting shorter. Maybe this spring he would fall in love. Perhaps with Teresa Saunders?

He sat in his black silk dressing gown in front of *Daybreak* on television, and ate his microwaved MaximusBrek. It tasted like molten plaster of Paris but, hey, he wasn't going to tell the clients that. He would stride into the meeting bursting with energy, like an unleashed gladiator, and tell them how terrific this new food was. Especially for the below-the-line profits of the ad agency that paid his wages.

As he ate, angry Palestinians were shouting on the screen and holding up placards. He should have been thinking about his pitch at the meeting, but he couldn't focus on that. All he could think about was the message he was going to send Teresa Saunders. Something original that would make her smile, that would make her think he was a really interesting guy to communicate with. Hell, he was one of the highest-paid advertising copywriters in London right now. He wrote hot slogans for hot products. So surely he could write one for the hottest product of all – himself.

He was thirty-two. Single. He had this cool pad. His charcoal Aston DBS. He kept himself and his bank balance in shape. But for the past eight months, since his last short-lived relationship, he slept every night in an empty bed.

He sent Teresa Saunders a message: *Thanks for accepting my friend request . . . J*

Then he got dressed and headed out to work, checking his iPhone at every red light he stopped at. Fresh emails popped up every few seconds. But to his disappointment, nothing from Teresa Saunders.

Come on, he chided himself. *Focus. Concentrate!* They sat round the black glass table in the stark white boardroom of Bresson, Carter, Olaff – the agency he worked for. Croissants and brioches lay on plates, alongside jugs of coffee and expensive mineral water. The four-strong team from the client, as well as his three agency colleagues, including his boss, Martin Willis, watched the presentation on the big screen. Then they were shown mock-ups of the TV campaign, the magazine campaign, the online campaign and the in-store point-of-sale artwork. He should have been watching too, but instead he kept glancing at his iPhone, surreptitiously cupped in his hands beneath the table.

'Don't you think, Jobe?'

Hearing his name brought him back to earth with a start. He looked up to see fourteen eyeballs fixed on him – several of them through stupidly trendy glasses. He went bright red. He stammered. 'Um, well, yes,' although he had, in truth, no idea what they were referring to. He felt their stares, and his face burned as if a corrosive acid had been poured over his skin.

'Are you with us, Jobe?' Willis said.

'Totally.' He began perspiring.

'You have the floor,' Willis said.

'Yes, right. Um . . . ah . . . OK.'

The female, whose name he had forgotten, said helpfully, 'We're referring to the Twitter aspect of the campaign.'

'Indeed,' he said, waiting for the light-bulb moment. But it didn't happen. So he took a stab in the dark. 'My thinking is that all these tweets start appearing, from people who have eaten MaximusBrek, saying how much energy they suddenly have. Also, when anyone tweets that they're on a diet, MaximusBrek starts following them. We kind of anthropomorphize it, so MaximusBrek becomes like a person out there in cyberspace, right, rather than just a brand.'

He was greeted with frowns and blank stares.

'Diabetics,' the female client said. 'I thought we planned to target the two and a half million diabetics in the UK with the low glycaemic index of MaximusBrek.'

'Absolutely!' Jobe said, remembering suddenly. 'Diabetics are a shoo-in. What we're going to do is engage with the diabetic blog sites, as well as Twitter and Facebook. MaximusBrek is going to be the diabetic's new best friend – types one *and* two! We're going to make it the biggest breakfast cereal ever – first for this nation, and then we'll break it out globally!'

Then he made the mistake of glancing down at his iPhone again. *Hey Jobe, nice to 'meet' you! Just checked out your photos – you look a really cool guy! Tell me more about yourself.*

*

After the meeting, Martin Willis asked him to come up to his office. Willis was in his early forties, with trim ginger hair, and was dressed in a traditional business suit and an expensive open-neck white shirt. He had a hard, blunt Yorkshire accent. 'Who are you with, Jobe? The Woolwich?'

'The Woolwich?' Jobe frowned.

'Yeah, the Woolwich? Are you with them? Because you sure as hell aren't with us.'

'I'm not quite with you.'

'No, you're sodding not. You're not with anyone today; you're on planet Zog. You on drugs or something? Not well?'

'No – nothing . . . and I'm not unwell.'

'You realize you almost lost us one of our biggest new clients this morning with your behaviour? Every time anyone asked you a question you were somewhere else.'

'I'm sorry,' he said.

'I don't do *sorry*.'

*

Back home, Jobe typed: *Hey Teresa, nice to 'meet' you too! Your reply got me a load of verbal from my boss a bit earlier! He seemed to think it was more important for me to concentrate on a meeting I was in than read your message. What a Philistine!*

Anyway, about me: I'm single and I work in advertising. I live on Wapping Wharf, near Tower Bridge. I'd love to meet you properly J.

He posted the message then switched on the television, mixed himself a large vodka martini, took one sip, then checked his laptop before settling down to watch television. Whatever was on, he didn't care. He needed a large drink tonight after the bollocking from Martin Willis – and what annoyed him most about it was that Willis was right. His mind had been all over the place in a crucially important meeting. God, Teresa Saunders was messing with his head and they hadn't even met yet!

Yet!

And there was a reply from her, already.

I'd love to meet you too J.

He replied immediately.

When's good for you?

She replied immediately too.

Tonight?

She was keen!

OK! What time and where?

There was a long delay, and then the message appeared.

10.35 p.m. Hampstead Heath. 51° 56' 47.251" N 0° 17' 41.938" W.

Jobe frowned for a moment, then grinned. Compass co-ordinates. Teresa Saunders was a piece of work! Smart girl. He liked challenges.

He typed back:

See u there!

The reply arrived:

I want u 2 join me! x

He typed:

That's my plan! x

She replied:

Promise? x

He grinned and typed:

I promise! x

He picked up his iPhone and flicked through to the compass app he had downloaded a long time back for a coffee advert he had written, in which a man and a woman teased each other by sending compass co-ordinates that came closer and closer until they finally met in a coffee shop. That was one of his most successful commercials. Teresa must have seen it, he figured. His own location showed as: *51° 50' 33.594" N   0° 06' 15.631" W.*

*

It was 9 p.m. At a rough guess it would take him an hour to drive there. He made himself a toasted cheese sandwich, which he figured would absorb enough of the alcohol to put him safely below the limit, then on his laptop googled Hampstead Heath, working out the nearest street to the co-ordinates he had been given.

Shortly before half past nine he brushed his teeth, squirted on some cologne, pulled on his black leather jacket and pocketed a small torch. Then he took the lift down to the garage, climbed into his Aston Martin and tapped his destination into the satnav. His stomach was full of butterflies. But good butterflies!

His drive across London through the thin evening traffic was joyous. A Michael Kiwanuka CD was spinning, the dials in front of him were spinning, and the GPS numbers on his iPhone were spinning as he headed nearer and nearer to Hampstead. To Teresa Saunders. His dream girl!

He reached his destination with twenty minutes to spare. The Kiwanuka CD had finished and now a Louis Armstrong track was playing: 'We Have All The Time In the World'.

And just how appropriate was that?

He parked his car, pulled the torch from his pocket and entered the heath. There was no one around and ordinarily, in such a strange, dark and isolated environment, he might have felt apprehensive, but tonight the knowledge that Teresa was heading through the darkness too – and might already be there – allayed his concerns.

He watched the compass co-ordinates on the app spinning away, until he reached *51° 56' 47.251" N   0° 17' 41.938" W.*

Right in front of him was a park bench.

Oh yes! He was loving this!

He sat down, the butterflies going increasingly crazy in his stomach, and pulled out a pack of cigarettes. But what if she disapproved of smokers? There was a smell of burnt wood in the air.

He slipped the pack back in his pocket and sat listening. Somewhere in the distance he heard a man calling out, 'Oscar! Oscar! Here, boy! Oscar!'

A dog barked.

The man said, 'Good boy, good boy!'

The dog barked again.

Then silence.

He waited. The air was chilly. After a while he checked his watch. Five minutes had passed. Another five minutes passed. He checked Facebook on his phone. Nothing. He sent a message.

I'm here!

Moments later a message came back.

So am I!

He looked around, then switched on the torch and shone the beam in every direction. It fell away into the darkness. He sent another message.

I can't see you. Did I get the co-ordinates right? 51° 56' 47.251" N 0° 17' 41.938" W.

The reply came almost before he had posted it.

Spot on!

He felt a sudden swirl of cold air; it went, almost as fast as it had come. Then he felt something digging into his back – something hard and flat that felt different from the rest of the bench.

He turned around and shone the beam onto it. It was a small brass plaque. Engraved, in tiny lettering, were the words: *In memory of Teresa Saunders (1983–2011) who loved this heath. Tragically killed by lightning on this spot.*

Another swirl of icy air engulfed him. Then he felt a touch, just the faintest touch, on his cheek. Like a kiss.

An instant later there was a crack, like a peal of thunder, directly above him. He looked up in shock to see a dark shape hurtling down towards him.

*

'Poor bastard,' the Police Sergeant said.

'Must have been instant at least,' the constable who had been first on the scene replied.

The fire brigade officers had rigged up some lights, and three of them were hurriedly attaching lifting gear from the rescue tender to the massive, blackened branch that pinned Jobe, by his crushed skull, to the ground.

The attending paramedic could find no pulse, and viewing the matter leaking from the unfortunate young man's crushed head, was all too grimly aware that it was what he and his colleagues, with the gallows humour of their trade, called a 'scoop-and-run job'. The Coroner's Officer was on his way.

A man who had been walking his dog nearby was in shock. He had stood numbly watching, then several times had repeated crossly, almost shouting, to the attending officers beyond the police tape cordon, 'They should have bloody cut it down – any fool could see it was an accident waiting to happen.'

Another police officer who had turned up, but had nothing to do, suddenly snapped on a pair of gloves, knelt and picked up an object. 'iPhone,' he said. 'Might give us a clue who he is.'

He tapped the power key to wake it up, then studied the screen. 'Looks like he was meeting someone here,' he said. 'Seems as if he had a date. Meant to be meeting her here at 10.35 p.m. – that's half an hour ago. I haven't seen any sign of a woman anywhere around.'

'Not his night, is it?' one of the fire officers replied. 'Stood up, then this happens.'

'Or maybe she broke it off and left,' the Sergeant said.

SMOKING KILLS

A very short story based on a true incident

'You have a last request?'
'Uh-huh. Could I have a cigarette?'
'I'm sorry, this is a no-smoking execution chamber.'
'It's not going to kill me, you know.'
'You're right about that, sunshine.'

THE STAMP OF A CRIMINAL

Roy Grace's first case

The dog was a wuss, Crafty Cunningham always said. An adorable wuss, certainly, but a wuss nonetheless.

His wife, Caroline, agreed. He was a big dog, a lot of dog, especially when he jumped on you, wet and muddy from the garden, and tried to lick your face. It was like having a sheep fall off a cliff and land on you. His name was Fluff, which was a ruddy stupid name, they both knew, for a dog of this size. The animal was still unable to grasp the fact that after eleven years (a ripe seventy-seven in dog time) he was no longer a tiny, fluffy puppy, but was a very large, overweight and usually smelly golden retriever.

They both loved him, despite the fact they had been badly advised on their choice of a puppy. They'd originally wanted a guard dog that would be happy roaming a big garden in Brighton, and wouldn't need too many walks beyond that. Fluff needed two long walks daily, which he did not often get, which was why he was overweight. And as a guard dog he was about as much use as a chocolate teapot. Crafty was fond of telling their friends that the hound might drown a burglar in slobber, but that would be about his limit.

Crafty's real name was Dennis, but he'd acquired the nickname back in his school days and it had stuck. He'd always been one for a crafty dodge. He used to play truant from school; he was a crafty dodger around the football pitch, and equally crafty at dodging trouble. And he was always one for getting something for nothing. His father had once said of him, with a kind of grudging respect, 'Dennis is a lad who could follow you in through a turnstile and come out in front of you without having paid.'

Neither of them heard Fluff, early that April Tuesday morning, pad upstairs from the kitchen, where he usually slept, and flop down on their bedroom floor. Later, Crafty would tell the police he thought he had heard whimpering, around 5 a.m. he estimated, but because he wasn't aware the dog was in the bedroom, he thought the sound was coming from Caroline, having a bad dream.

It was only when Crafty woke at 7 a.m., with that very distinct smell of damp dog in his nostrils, that he saw Fluff on the floor. To his surprise, the dog was shaking. 'Fluff!' he hissed, not wanting to wake Caroline, who never rose before 8.30. 'What are you doing here, boy?'

The dog gave him a baleful look, stood up, still shaking, padded to the door, then turned back to him and gave a single bark that was much higher than his usual.

'Ssshhhh, boy!' Crafty said, but at the same time he thought the dog was behaving in a very strange way – almost as if he was trying to tell him something. Was he ill? 'Need to go out, do you? What's the matter? Why are you shaking?' he whispered, then slipped out of bed, pushed his feet in his slippers, and unhooked his silk paisley dressing gown from the back of the door. It was cold in the room and he was covered in goosebumps, he realized. Spring was meant to be here, although there was still a wintry chill in the air. But that could not be why Fluff was shaking – he had too much fur on him to be cold, surely?

The dog barked again, trotted a short way down the stairs, then turned, looked up at his master and barked again.

'You're definitely trying to tell me something, aren't you, boy?'

He was.

*

Detective Constable Roy Grace sat at his small desk in the detectives' room, on the second floor of Brighton's John Street police station, which was to be his home for the foreseeable future.

He put down his mug of coffee from the canteen, and removed his jacket. His desk, apart from a telephone, his radio next to it and a copy of yesterday's briefing notes, was almost bare. He opened his attaché case and pulled out a few personal belongings, and started by pinning up in front of him a photograph of his fiancée, Sandy. She was smiling, leaning against a railing on the seafront, the wind blowing her long blonde hair. Next he placed in front of him a photograph of his parents. His father, Jack, stood proudly in his uniform bearing Sergeant stripes.

Roy had recently completed his two years as a probationer, walking the beat in Brighton as a Constable, and he had loved it. But right from his early teens he had dreamed of becoming a detective. He still could not really believe that he now was one.

This was his second day in his new role, and he loved the sound of his title. Detective Constable Grace. *Detective!* Sandy loved it too, and told him she was very proud of him. He sipped some coffee and stifled a yawn. He had been told he did not need to be in until 8 a.m., but he wanted to make a good impression – and perhaps bag an early worm – so he had arrived at the police station, in a smart blazer and slacks, at 7 a.m., hoping for a more challenging day than yesterday when, in truth, he'd felt a little bored. Wasn't this supposed to be the second busiest police station in the UK? It had felt as quiet as a mortuary.

What he needed was a case to get his teeth into. Nothing had happened on his first day, apart from attending a briefing, some basic familiarization with the routines, and being given his shifts for the three months ahead. It had been a quiet Monday generally, blamed largely on the pelting rain. 'Policeman Rain' it was jokingly called, but it was true. Levels of crime fell dramatically when the weather was rubbish. Today looked better, an almost cloudless sky giving the promise of sunshine. And crime!

Yesterday, he reflected, had felt a bit like his first day at school, getting to know the ropes and his new colleagues. There had been a handful of follow-ups from crimes committed on the Sunday night – a string of break-ins, a couple of street robberies, several motor vehicle thefts, a racist attack on a group of Asians by one of the town's nasty youth gangs, and a drugs bust on a private dwelling – but other detectives had been despatched to handle those. He had spent most of his first day chatting to colleagues, seeing what he could learn from them, and waiting for his Detective Sergeant, Bill Stoker, to give him an action; he hoped today would not be a repeat.

He did not have to wait long. The DS, a burly former boxer, ambled over, wearing a charcoal suit that looked a size too big for him and black shoes polished to a military shine. 'Right, old son, need to send you out. Domestic burglary in Dyke Road Avenue. Sounds like a high-value haul. I'll come with you – but I'll let you lead. I've already got SOCO on standby.'

*

Grace hoped his excitement didn't show on his face too much. He drove the unmarked Metro up past Brighton railway station, carefully sticking to the speed limit, across the Seven Dials roundabout and on up Dyke Road, then into Dyke Road Avenue, lined on both sides with some of the town's swankiest houses.

'Not many coppers living on this street,' his Sergeant observed wryly. 'Not many honest ones at any rate.'

There had been a big police corruption scandal some years back, which Roy Grace's father had talked about, and which had left a bad taste in everyone's mouth – police and public alike. He decided, from the Sergeant's slightly bitter tone, not to probe. Just as he was about to make a non-committal comment, his colleague said, 'Here, that's it, over on the left, on that corner!'

Grace pulled over. There was a narrow driveway with in-and-out gates; both sets were open – and from their poor state of repair, it did not look as if they had been closed in years. 'I think if I lived on this street, I'd keep my gates shut – open like that is an invitation,' he said.

'Most people don't have a bloody clue about security,' the Detective Sergeant said. 'All right, before we get out of the car, what's this place tell you at first glance?'

Roy Grace stared at the house. It was secluded from the street by a wooden fence badly in need of repair, rising above which, on the other side, was a tall, neatly trimmed privet hedge. The house itself was an Edwardian mansion, with window frames that, he could see from here, looked in poor condition. 'Elderly people live here,' Grace said. 'They've probably owned the property for several decades, and never bothered with an alarm. There's no box on the outside of the house.'

The Detective Sergeant raised his eyebrows. 'What makes you think the occupants are elderly?' He looked down at his notepad. 'Mr and Mrs Cunningham.'

'Old people get worried about money, sir. They don't like to spend anything they don't have to. So they haven't done maintenance on the exterior for a very long time. But I suspect they are keen gardeners – and they have the time, which means they are retired. Look at the condition of the hedge. It's immaculate – trimmed by a perfectionist.'

'Let's see if you're right,' Bill Stoker said, climbing out.

Grace looked at him. 'Is there something you know about these people that I don't?'

Stoker gave a non-committal shrug and a wry smile. The two men walked up the threadbare gravel of the driveway. An elderly Honda saloon was parked near the front door. From what they could see of the garden from their position, all the shrubbery was neatly tended, but close up, Grace could see the exterior of the house was in an even worse state of repair than he had first assessed, with large chunks of the pebbledash rendering missing and a few ominous patches of damp on the walls.

They entered the porch and rang the bell. Instantly, they heard the half-hearted bark of a dog, and a few moments later the door was opened by a wiry, energetic-looking man in his early seventies, Grace estimated. Grace shot Bill Stoker a quick glance; Stoker gave a small grin of approval.

'Mr Cunningham?'

'Yes?'

Grace pulled out his warrant card holder and flipped it open, to show his card and the Sussex Police badge. It was the first time he had used it, and he felt a deep thrill. 'Detective Constable Grace and Detective Sergeant Stoker, from Brighton CID, sir. We understand you've had a break-in?'

The old man, dressed in a plaid shirt with a cravat, chinos and monogrammed velvet slippers, looked distinctly on edge and a tad lost. His hair was a little long and unkempt, giving him the air of an absent-minded professor. He did not look to Roy Grace like a man who had ever held a staid office job – possibly a former antiques dealer or someone in the arts world, perhaps. Definitely some kind of wheeler-dealer.

'Yes, that's right. Bloody awful. Thank you for coming. I'm so sorry to have troubled you.'

'No trouble at all, sir,' Bill Stoker said. 'That's what we're here for.'

'It's shaken us up, I can tell you. Please come in. My wife and I have tried to be careful not to touch anything, but the ruddy dog's trampled all over – I suppose what you fellows call – the *crime scene*.'

'We'll have SOCO take some paw prints, so we can rule him out as a suspect, sir,' Bill Stoker said, entering the rather grand panelled hallway. Several fine-looking oil paintings were hung along the walls, and it was furnished with tasteful antiques. He knelt to stroke the dog which had padded over towards him, tongue out. 'Hello, fellow!' He rubbed the dog's chest gently. 'What's your name?' he asked, looking at the collar tag. 'Fluff. You're Fluff, are you?' Then he heard a female voice.

'Who is it, darling?'

'The Police. CID. Two detectives.'

'Oh, thank God.'

Caroline Cunningham was an elegant woman in her late sixties, with neatly coiffed hair and a face that was still handsome despite her wrinkles. She must have been very beautiful in her youth, Roy Grace thought. She was wearing a white blouse, black slacks and sparkly trainers.

Her husband introduced them, getting their names and ranks the wrong way round. Roy Grace corrected him.

'Would you gentlemen like some tea or coffee?' she asked.

Grace did fancy a coffee but was unsure it would be professional to accept. 'We're fine,' he said. 'Thank you very much.' Then he noticed the look of dismay on Bill Stoker's face. Ignoring it, he ploughed on. 'I understand two officers attended an emergency call made at 7.10 a.m. today from this address, Mr and Mrs Cunningham?'

'Correct. We didn't know if the blighters . . . were still in the house. We were bloody terrified – and the dog was no damned use at all!'

'My husband has a shotgun, but of course it's locked away in the safe in the garage,' she said.

'Probably just as well, madam,' Bill Stoker said. 'Once a firearm is involved, matters can turn very dangerous very quickly.'

'I'd have given them both barrels and to hell with it,' Crafty Cunningham said.

From the grimace on his face, Roy Grace had no doubt he meant it. 'I think what would be most helpful is if you can you talk us through exactly what happened from the moment you discovered the break-in, then we'd like to go through what has been taken.'

'I'm not sure we can remember exactly what's been taken – but the majority of it, certainly,' the old man replied.

'Georgian silver mostly,' Caroline Cunningham said. 'They knew their stuff whoever did this. They didn't seem to bother with much else.'

'From what you are saying, you seem pretty certain it was more than one intruder?' Grace said.

'Damned right it was,' Crafty said. 'The buggers made themselves breakfast in the kitchen before they left! Two bowls of cereal, bread, butter and marmalade. Can you believe it?'

'Maybe it would be a good idea if we could sit down and go through everything,' Bill Stoker said. 'Then we'll take a look around afterwards. Is there a room that the . . . er . . . intruders didn't enter, to your knowledge?'

'The conservatory,' Caroline Cunningham said.

'Let's go in there.'

'Are you sure you wouldn't like tea or coffee?' she asked.

This time Grace looked at his Sergeant for a lead.

'I wouldn't say no to a cuppa,' Stoker said. 'Thank you.'

'A coffee for me, please,' Grace said. 'But I'm a bit worried, if they've been in your kitchen, about contaminating any possible evidence.'

The couple looked at each other guiltily. 'Erm, I'm afraid we have already been in there, and made ourselves something to eat – not that either of us had much of an appetite. But we had a feeling it was going to be a long morning,' Crafty replied.

Bill Stoker looked at his watch. 'Someone from SOCO should be along shortly to dust for prints. They'll need to take both of yours, to know which ones to eliminate, if that's all right?'

'Yes, indeed,' Caroline Cunningham said.

'And the dog's, also?' her husband said, with a smile.

'Have you lost a lot?' Grace asked them.

'Quite a bit, in value,' Crafty replied.

'Much of it sentimental. Bits and pieces I'd inherited from my parents,' Caroline said. 'And wedding presents. Christening cups and napkin rings. To be honest, we're pretty numb. A lot's happened in the last hour – hour and a half . . .' She looked at the wall, and frowned. 'No! Bastards.'

Grace followed her gaze and saw a rectangular shadow on the wall.

'That was a beautiful antique French wall clock.'

'Belonged to my great-grandfather,' Crafty Cunningham said ruefully. 'Bloody hell, what else has gone?'

'I'm afraid people often keep finding things missing for weeks after a burglary,' Bill Stoker said. 'Let's go and sit down and take things slowly from the beginning.'

*

Tony Langiotti watched from his office window as the white Renault van came around the corner into the mews. His mews. He owned all eight of the lock-up garages, and the warehouse opposite. That meant no strangers with prying eyes could see who came and went. He put down his coffee, lit a cigarette, and with it dangling from his lips went outside to meet the two Welsh scumbags.

'You're fucking late. What kept you?' he said to the van's driver, Dai Lewellyn. The Welshman was in his early twenties, with a cratered, emaciated face and a hairstyle like his mother had just tipped a bowl of spaghetti on his head. 'Stop to get your toenails varnished or something?'

'We went to get breakfast,' Lewellyn said cheerily, in a sing-song voice.

'We've been up since early, like, we were hungry, like,' the other man, in the passenger seat said. His name was Rees Hughes. Both occupants of the van were dressed in postmen's uniforms.

Langiotti hauled up the door of garage number 4, and signalled for them to drive in. Then he switched on the interior light and pulled the door back down behind them.

They were in a large space, eight lock-up garages wide, with all the internal walls knocked down. There were two other vans in there, a machine for manufacturing number plates, a number of old vending machines stacked against the far wall, and a line of trestle tables, which gave it the faint appearance of a village hall.

'So what you tossers got for me?' The cigarette dangled from Langiotti's lips, with an inch of ash on the end.

'I don't like your tone,' the fat one said in a mild rebuke, getting out of the van.

'Yeah, well, I don't like being kept waiting, see? So what you got for me?' He walked around to the rear of the van, and saw the two large grey mail sacks lying there, each stamped *GPO*.

'We did the Dyke Road Avenue House.'

'Yeah? Any bother?'

'No, there was no alarm, like you said. The dog wasn't any trouble either, like you said it wouldn't be.'

'I do my research,' Langiotti said. 'You got some good gear for me?'

Dai pulled the first sack out; it clinked as he put it down, then he untied the neck and Langiotti peered in, taking a pair of leather gloves from his pocket and pulling them on. He removed a silver Georgian fruit bowl from the sack and held it up, turning it around until he could see the hallmark. 'Nice,' he said. 'Very nice.'

'We took the Georgian silver – we identified it from the pictures you gave us from the insurance company. There was a nice-looking clock we saw that wasn't on the list, but it looked good to us.'

'Anything else that wasn't on the list?'

The two Welshmen looked at each other and shook their heads.

'I wouldn't want to find out you'd nicked something that you didn't tell me about, know what I mean? That you'd kept something for yourselves, yeah? It's when people try to flog stuff on the side that trouble happens. That's how you get nicked, you know what I'm saying?'

Dai Lewellyn pointed at the two sacks. 'Everything we took is in these.'

Langiotti took each item out, carefully setting it down on the trestles. Then he ran through the haul, checking each item against the insurance inventory, and jotting numbers down on his notepad. When he had finished he said, 'Right, by my reckoning, I've got a market value here of forty-five thousand quid, less what I'll have to knock off. We agreed ten per cent of value, right?'

The two Welshmen nodded.

'Right, come across to my office and I'll square up, and give you tonight's address. Got a good one for you tonight, I have.'

Their eyes lit up greedily.

*

The Cunninghams took the two detectives into the rooms where items had been stolen, making an inventory as they went. But with the couple constantly interrupting and contradicting each other, it took some time for Roy Grace and Bill Stoker to get a clear idea of the sequence of events and of what had been taken.

The dining room had been the most badly affected. Caroline Cunningham pointed out, tearfully, the bare sideboard where much of the fine silver had stood, as well as a Georgian silver fruit bowl, which, she told them, had been in her family for five generations, and had stood in the centre of the fine oval dining table.

Back in the conservatory again and sipping another cup of coffee, Grace studied his notes and asked them to go through the events of the early morning once more. Crafty Cunningham said he was roused by a whimpering sound, which he thought was his wife having a nightmare, and happened to notice on the bedside clock that it was just past

5 a.m.; then he went back to sleep. He went downstairs at 7.10 a.m. to find the burglars had broken in through the toilet window, which was along the side of the house. The glass had been cut neatly, rather than broken, which meant their entry had been almost silent. They had left via the kitchen door, which the Cunninghams had found unlocked.

Roy Grace stared out at the large, beautifully tended garden, with its swimming pool and tennis court, and did a quick calculation. The burglars had entered before sunrise. OK, it was logical for them to have broken in while it was still dark. But why at 5 a.m.? There was a risk that daylight would be breaking when they left. Why not much earlier in the night? Or was this the last of a series of houses the perpetrators were burgling last night? But if that was the case, surely the police would have heard of other burglaries by now – it was nearly 9.30 a.m.

'I don't suppose you have any idea what time the intruders might have left?' He addressed both the Cunninghams.

They shook their heads.

'What time are your newspapers delivered?'

'About a quarter to seven,' Caroline Cunningham said.

'If you could give me the details of your newsagent, we'll check with the paperboy to see if he noticed anything unusual. Also, what time does your post normally arrive?'

'About 7.30 a.m.,' the old man said.

'We'll check with the post office also.'

Then the two detectives went back carefully over the inventory of stolen items, reading it all out to the couple and asking them several times if there was anything else that had been taken which they might have overlooked. It was clearly a big haul, and the burglars seemed to be professionals who knew exactly what they were taking.

As the Cunninghams showed the two detectives to the front door, thanking them for their help, Crafty suddenly said, 'Oh my God, my stamps!' He clapped his hand to his forehead in sudden panic.

'Stamps, sir?' Roy Grace asked.

Caroline Cunningham gave her husband an astonished look. 'You didn't check, darling?'

'No . . . I . . . I . . . dammit, I didn't!'

'Where are they this week?'

Crafty looked bewildered for a moment. He stroked his chin.

'My husband's a stamp collector,' Caroline explained. 'But he's paranoid about them. Twenty-five years ago his collection was stolen – we always suspected the housekeeper had something to do with it because he kept them hidden in a particular place in his den, and the thieves went straight to it. Ever since, he's been paranoid – he changes the hiding place every few weeks.'

'You don't use a safe, sir?' Roy Grace asked.

'Never trusted them,' Crafty replied. 'My parents had a safe in their house jemmied open. I prefer my hiding places.'

'I keep telling him he's bloody stupid,' his wife said. 'But he won't listen.'

'What's the value of your collection, Mr Cunningham?' Bill Stoker asked.

'About one hundred thousand pounds,' he said absently, scratching his head now, thinking. 'I . . . I had them under the carpet beneath the dining table,' he said. 'But then I moved them . . . um . . . ah, yes, of course, of course! I remember!'

With the rest of them in tow, he hurried through an internal door into the integral double garage. A large, elderly Rover was parked in there, along with an assortment of tools and two lawnmowers, one sitting on top of a hessian mat. He pulled the mower back and, like an excited child, knelt and lifted the mat.

Then he looked up in utter disbelief. 'They've gone,' he said lamely, looking gutted. 'They've gone.'

Both detectives frowned. 'You kept a hundred thousand pounds worth of stamps beneath an old mat in the garage?' Bill Stoker said, incredulously.

'They're sealed,' he said. 'And there's no damp in the garage.'

'How easy would the stamps be to identify, sir?' Roy Grace asked.

'Very easy if someone tried to sell them as a single collection. They're all British Colonial from the Victorian period and there are some very rare ones among them. But not so easy if they sold them individually or in strips.'

'And you have them insured, sir?'

'Yes.'

'No insurance stipulation about having them locked in a safe or a bank vault?'

He shook his head. 'Only have to do that if the house is empty.'

'Do you have any photographs of these stamps, Mr Cunningham?' Roy Grace asked.

'Yes, I do. I can make you a copy of the list the insurance company has.'

'Thank you, sir,' the young detective said. 'That would be very helpful. We'll be organizing some house-to-house inquiries over the next few days.'

Afterwards in the car, heading back to the police station, Roy Grace said, 'Something doesn't feel right.'

'About the Cunninghams?'

He nodded.

'He's dodgy,' Bill Stoker said. 'Well dodgy.'

'I sensed something. Couldn't put my finger on it.'

Stoker touched the tip of his nose. 'Copper's nose. You'll develop it more as you get experience, old son. Follow your instincts and you won't often go wrong. He's been known to us for years, but no one's ever pinned anything on him.'

'Known for what?'

'Handling.'

'Stamps?'

The DS shook his head. 'High-end antiques. But anytime we ever tried to nick him, he could always produce receipts. He's crafty, that one. I've talked to a few people who reckon he's got away with everything but murder over the years. A lot of coppers would like to see him behind bars.' He shrugged. 'But doesn't look like it's going to happen, does it? And now he's a sodding victim.'

'Reckon that's genuine?'

He nodded. 'You could see how upset the missus is. They've had the tables turned, all right. Mind you, you sodding deserve it if you leave a hundred grand's worth of stamps under a bleeding mat, right?'

Grace nodded thoughtfully, replaying the scene over in his mind. 'The timing bothers me, sir – why do it at 5 a.m.? Why not earlier in the night?'

'Police patrols get suspicious of vehicles out late at night. If the Cunninghams are correct and the villains broke in at 5 a.m., did their burgling, then made themselves some breakfast, it meant they were probably there a good hour or so. They'd have left around 6 a.m. perhaps, when people are starting to surface and be up and about. More vehicles on the road. Less suspicion. Nah, it's an open-and-shut job. Let's see if SOCO pick up any dabs.' He glanced at his watch. 'They'll be there in the next half hour. We need to brief our press officer in the meantime. I'll let you do it – be good practice.'

*

Shortly after 12.30 p.m., Tony Langiotti left his office, pulled his door shut behind him, a fresh cigarette dangling from his lips, and sauntered out into the bright sunshine. He was in a sunny mood, looking forward to a nice pint or two and a bite to eat in the pub with a couple of mates.

He'd already made a deal this morning to offload the Georgian silver haul from last night, for a very tasty price indeed! The clock wasn't proving quite so easy and he wished the tossers hadn't bothered nicking it – the value was peanuts compared to the rest of the items. But he knew someone who would take it off his hands when he returned from a holiday in Spain later in the week.

He climbed into his large Jaguar, started the engine, and drove up to the Old Shoreham Road. A short distance on he halted at a red traffic light. As he waited for it to change, he glanced idly towards the parade of shops on his left; suddenly, the banner headline of *The Argus* newspaper, outside a newsagent's, caught his eye.

Instantly, his mood darkened. Violently. It was too coincidental to be a different house.

'What?' he said aloud. 'What?' he repeated. 'What the f—?'

£100,000 STAMP HAUL IN EXCLUSIVE HOVE MANSION RAID.

Ignoring that the lights had changed to green, and the hooting from behind, he sat and stared in disbelief for several moments. Then he jumped out, gave two fingers to the driver of the car behind, ran into the newsagent's and grabbed a copy of the paper. He paid for it, then stood rooted to the spot reading it, ignoring the hooting outside from the obstruction his car was causing.

Thieves broke into a Dyke Road Avenue mansion early this morning and made off with a haul that included Georgian silver, valued at over £50,000, and a prized stamp collection, worth an estimated £100,000.

The house's owner, retired Brighton businessman Dennis Cunningham, said to The Argus *earlier this morning, 'They clearly knew exactly what they were looking for. They only targeted our finest Georgian silver – and my stamps. And the cheek of them!' he added, indignantly. 'They helped themselves to breakfast while my wife and I were asleep upstairs!'*

Detective Constable Roy Grace, in charge of the investigation, said, 'We are pursuing a number of lines of enquiry, and will make every effort to apprehend those responsible and recover the valuables, many of which are of great sentimental value to their rightful owners.

'If any member of the public saw anything suspicious in the Dyke Road Avenue area between the hours of 4 a.m. and 7 a.m., please call Detective Constable Roy Grace at Brighton CID on the following number . . .'

Langiotti stormed out of the newsagent, jumped into his car, lit another cigarette to calm himself down, then accelerated away, his lunchtime plans out of the window, anger coursing through his veins.

'Bastards,' he said. 'You jammy little Welsh bastards. Think you're going to get away with cheating me out of a hundred grand? Well, boyos, you've got another think coming.'

*

In the CID office at John Street police station, Roy Grace was hunched over his desk, an untouched sandwich beside him and a forgotten mug of coffee gone cold. He was concentrating hard, determined to impress Detective Sergeant Stoker with his work on this case. And he knew he was going to impress one person today – his beloved Sandy. The noon edition of *The Argus* lay beside him; it was the first time he had ever seen his name in print, and he was chuffed to bits. He could not wait to show it to her this evening.

In his notebook he wrote:

Look for similar modus operandi.

House-to-house enquiries.

Newsagents.

Stop all vehicles in Dyke Road Avenue during that time period tomorrow and ask if they saw anything.

Check all antique shops and stalls in Brighton regularly over coming weeks.

Check local and national stamp dealers for items they have been offered.

He was interrupted in mid-flow by his phone ringing. 'DC Grace,' he answered. 'Brighton CID.'

'I'm phoning about the Dyke Road Avenue robbery this morning,' the male voice at the other end said, in a coarse Brighton accent.

Eagerly, Grace picked up his pen. 'May I have your name and phone number, sir?'

'You may not. But I've got inside information, see. There's going to be another burglary tonight. 111 Tongdean Avenue, a house called The Gallops.'

Grace knew his home town well. This was considered by some to be an even smarter street than Dyke Road Avenue. 'How do you know that, sir?'

'Just trust me, I know. They'll be going in around 5 a.m., and coming out soon after 6 a.m., disguised as postmen. Couple of Welshmen, from Cardiff.'

Any moment there was going to be a catch; Grace pressed on with his questions, whilst waiting for it. Probably a demand for money.

'Can you give me their names, sir?'

'Dai Lewellyn and Rees Hughes.'

He wrote the names on the pad. 'May I ask why you are giving me this information?'

'Tell 'em they shouldn't have been so greedy with the stamps.'

There was a click. The man had hung up.

Grace thought for some moments, feeling a buzz of excitement. If . . . if . . . if this tip-off was real, then he had a real chance to shine! Even better if he could catch the perps red-handed. But it could of course have been a crank call. He phoned the operator and asked for a trace on it, then he looked up the number of Cardiff's main police station, called it, and asked to speak to the CID there. The duty detective was out at lunch, but Grace was told he would call back on his return.

A short while later the operator called to tell him the call had been made, as he had suspected, from a phone booth. She gave him the address of the booth, in a busy street near the Brighton & Hove Albion football stadium. Grace thanked her and immediately contacted the SOCO officer who had just finished at the Cunninghams' house, asking him to get straight over to the phone box and take some prints from that – although Grace doubted whether whoever had made the call would have been dumb enough to have left any prints anywhere in the booth.

Then he hurried across the room to Bill Stoker's tiny office, which was largely decorated with photographs of him in his former life as a professional boxer, and told him the developments.

'Probably a crank,' was the Detective Sergeant's first reaction.

'He was very specific.'

'Let's wait and see if Cardiff Police come back with anything on these two Taffies.'

An hour later, Grace received a call from Detective Constable Gareth Brangwen of the South Wales Constabulary. Before getting down to business he asked whether Grace was a football or a rugby man. 'I'm a rugby man, sir,' he said, 'Out of preference.'

'Good man!' he said. 'We're going to get along fine, you and I! Now, what's this about two of our undesirables over on your manor?'

The young DC gave him, as briefly as he could, the facts.

'Well, we do have a Dai Lewellyn and Rees Hughes well known to us. They come from the same estate and they've given us plenty of trouble over the years. Housebreaking is their speciality, if you want to call it that. Both of them have form – they were last released from prison six months ago.'

Grace thanked him, hardly able to wait to give Bill Stoker the news.

*

There were several cars parked along both sides of Tongdean Avenue, so another one, a large plain Vauxhall, did not look out of place. Taking no chances, Roy Grace and another DC colleague, Jon Carlton, had arrived shortly before midnight for the stake-out.

They were parked across the road, a safe distance back from The Gallops, number 111, the target house. A quarter of a mile away, down a side street, other officers waited in an unmarked van. A second unmarked car, with two police officers seated inside, was parked in the street near the rear of the property. No one could go in or out without being seen from one of the roads.

There were to be no breaks, and no one leaving or entering any of the vehicles. If anyone, including Grace and Carlton, needed to urinate for the rest of the night, they'd have to do it into plastic jars, which they had with them.

One of the biggest decisions that had been made, fortunately by his superiors – so there would be no comeback on him at least – was not to inform the owners of The Gallops. The news would undoubtedly worry, if not downright terrify them. There would be no telling how the owners might react – perhaps by keeping the lights on all night long, which could blow the police's chances of an arrest. The plan was to seize the perpetrators as they attempted to enter the house.

Grace was nervous as hell – so much was riding on this. Would they turn up, or would he have wasted hours of time for eight officers, and DS Stoker, who had also sacrificed his night's sleep to be on standby for him? He'd have a very red face if there was a no-show, or if it all went, as Bill Stoker had charmingly put it, tits-up.

Grace wondered if he was noticing a pattern. The Gallops, which he had driven past in daylight earlier, was one of the largest houses in this street, but – like the Cunninghams' house – one of the ones in poorest repair, and there was no burglar alarm box on the wall. There were also no gates to the entrance or exit of the in-and-out driveway.

His colleague was an experienced and chatty DC, who was hoping to move across to Major Crime work, which included all homicides. High-profile murder cases were the best jobs, the *Gucci jobs,* he told Roy Grace over several cigarettes, which they smoked cupped in their hands to conceal the glow in case their quarry approached unseen, and sickly sweet coffee that was becoming progressively more lukewarm. They were also the cases that got you noticed by your superiors, and which helped your promotion chances.

As the night wore on, it wasn't promotion that was Grace's worry, it was his growing fear of a no-show. Had he been sold a pup? Been naive in believing a crank caller?

But the names of the two Welshmen had checked out, hadn't they? If it had been a crank call, whoever had made it had gone to a lot of trouble.

At a few minutes past five, DC Carlton yawned. 'What time are you reckoning on calling it a day?'

The sky was lightening a fraction, Grace thought, and a few tiny streaks of grey and red were appearing. He felt tired, and shaky from too much coffee. He munched a Kit Kat chocolate bar, sharing it with Carlton. Then, just as he bit on the last morsel, both men stiffened.

Headlights appeared.

A white van drove slowly past them, with what looked like two men in the front. All the cars parked on this street, and on the driveways of the homes, were modern; this Vauxhall they were in was one of the cheapest, but it was inconspicuous. The van stuck out instantly. The vehicle was wrong for the street – certainly at this hour.

Grace radioed in. 'Charlie Victor, Tango One approaching Tango Two.'

But the van carried on going and Grace's heart sank. Then it turned around and came back, and pulled into a space less than a hundred yards in front of them. Two men climbed out. In the glow of a street light he could see they were dressed as postmen, carrying what looked like empty mail sacks. They looked furtively around at the seemingly deserted street, then scurried across the road, hurried along the pavement and down the driveway.

'Now,' he radioed urgently. 'Tango One on scene. Charlie Victor going in. Unit Two, move forward!'

Grace signalled to his colleague to wait for a few more seconds, pulled his torch out of the glove compartment without switching it on, then as quietly as they could, they slipped out of the car and hurried across the road. The driveway of The Gallops was tarmac, and on their rubber-soled shoes they made little noise as they hurried around the side of the house. Then they stopped.

Right in front of them, barely twenty feet ahead, they saw the silhouettes of the two men. Then they heard a tinkle of glass. In the distance, Grace heard the roar of an engine being revved hard. He snapped on his torch, lighting up their startled faces, and yelled, 'Police, don't move!' as both officers sprinted forwards.

'Shite!' One of the thieves shouted, dropping his tools and making a run for it across the lawn. Grace broke away to the right, sprinting hard to try to cut him off. Out of the corner of his eyes he saw the other trying to climb the wall into the neighbour's garden and being dragged back down by Carlton. But all his focus was on the sprinting man ahead of him. Gripping his torch, the beam jigging everywhere, Grace was gaining on him on the damp grass. Gaining. Then suddenly his quarry appeared to trip and plunge forward in the darkness. An instant later, as the ground gave way beneath him, he realized why.

For an instant he swayed wildly, then fell forward too, the torch rolling away from him onto the soft, tensioned cover of the swimming pool. He reached forward and grabbed an ankle, as the thief attempted to scramble away. Grace clung to it, as the Welshman kicked hard and swore, then moments later he broke free, leaving Grace floundering on the material, now sodden with chlorinated water, holding a trainer in his hand. He lurched to his feet, and stumbled forward through ankle-deep water, radioing for assistance.

Ahead he saw the Welshman haul himself back onto terra firma and sprint towards the end of the garden. Not bothering to pick up his torch, Grace sprinted on after him. Suddenly, appearing to change his mind, the thief turned and ran back towards the house, and seconds later was lit up by the beams of three different torches. He stopped in his tracks. Before he knew it he was face down on the ground, with two officers on top of him.

'Out for an early morning stroll are we, sunshine?' said one.

'Bit careless forgetting a shoe when you got dressed, wasn't it?' said the other. 'Got any mail for us then?'

*

Back at the police station, ignoring his Sergeant's advice to go home and get some dry clothes and some kip, Grace insisted on going down into the custody block in the basement. Dai Lewellyn and Rees Hughes had been read their rights, and were now locked in separate cells, still dressed as postmen, waiting for a duty Legal Aid solicitor to arrive.

Grace, his tie awry, his clothes sodden, walked through the custody centre in the basement of the police station and peered through one of the cell doors. 'Got everything you need?'

Lewellyn looked at him sullenly. 'So, how did you know?'

'Know what?'

'You know what I mean. You knew we were coming, didn't you? Someone grassed us up, didn't they?'

Grace raised his eyebrows. 'A little bird told me you shouldn't have been so greedy with the stamps. That mean anything?'

'Stamps?' Lewellyn said. 'What do you mean, *stamps*? We didn't have no stamps. You mean, like in postage stamps?'

'Yes.'

'I don't know what you're talking about. We didn't take no stamps. Why would we take stamps? I don't know nothing about no stamps.'

'But you and your mate know all about Georgian silver?' Grace asked.

Lewellyn was silent for some moments. 'We might,' he said finally. 'But not stamps.' He was emphatic.

'Someone thinks you've been greedy over stamps.'

'I don't understand,' Lewellyn said. 'Who?'

'A man who knows where you were yesterday and what you took.'

'There's only one bastard who knows where we was,' he said, even more emphatically.

Roy Grace listened attentively.

*

The next two hours were taken up with formal interviews with the two men. In the end they admitted the burglary, but continued to deny any involvement with stamps, and indeed any knowledge of them.

Finally, shortly before 10 a.m., still in his damp clothes, with a search warrant signed by a local magistrate in his hand, along with the inventory folder and photographs of the valuables taken and a fresh team of officers, Grace arrived at West Southwick Mews. Their pissed-off co-operative Welsh prisoners had kindly supplied them with the exact address.

One officer broke the door down with the yellow battering ram, and they entered, found the switch and turned the lights on.

They were in a huge space, eight garages wide, and almost empty, bar a row of trestle tables – and what looked to Grace like a rather ugly antique clock.

Five minutes later, Tony Langiotti arrived for the start of his day, in his Jaguar, cigarette as ever dangling between his lips. As he drove into the mews and saw the police officers, he stamped on the brakes, and frantically threw the gear shift into reverse. But before he could touch the accelerator a police car appeared from nowhere, completely blocking off the exit behind him.

The cigarette fell from his lips and it took him several seconds to realize. By then it was burning his crotch.

*

There was not such a big hurry for Roy Grace's last call of what was turning out to be a very long day or, rather, extended day. It was 2 p.m. and he'd had no sleep since yesterday. But he was running on an adrenaline high – helped by a lot of caffeine. So far everything had gone to plan – well, in truth, he had to admit, somewhat better than planned. Three in custody, and, if he was right, by the close of play there would be four. But, he knew, it might not be such an easy task to convince DS Stoker.

He went home to shower and change, wolf down some cereal and toast and to think his next – potentially dangerous – step through. If he was wrong, it could be highly embarrassing, not to mention opening the police up to a possible lawsuit. But he did not think he was wrong. He was increasingly certain, as his next bout of tiredness waned, that he was right. But speed again might be of the essence.

Whether it was because he was impressed with his results to date, or it gave him the chance to settle an old, unresolved score, DS Bill Stoker agreed to Grace's request far more readily than he had expected, although to cover his back, he still wanted to run it by the Detective Inspector. He in turn decided to run it by the Chief Superintendent, who was out at a meeting.

*

Finally, shortly after 5 p.m., running on his second, or maybe even third or fourth wind, Roy Grace had all his ducks in a row. Accompanied by DS Stoker, who was looking as weary as Grace felt, he pulled up in the street outside the Cunninghams' house. A van, with trained search officers, pulled up behind, and they all climbed out.

Roy Grace and Stoker walked up to the front door. Grace held in his hand his second document signed by a magistrate today. He rang the bell and waited. A few moments later, it was opened by the old man. He looked at them, and the entourage behind them, with a puzzled frown. 'Good afternoon, officers,' he said. 'To what do I owe this pleasure? Do you have some news for me?'

'We have some good news and some bad news, Mr Cunningham,' Roy Grace said. 'The good news is we believe we have recovered your stolen clock.'

'Nothing else?'

'Not so far, sir, but we have made some arrests and we are hopeful of recovering further items.'

'Well, that's good. So what's the bad news?'

'I have a warrant to search these premises, sir.' Grace showed him the signed warrant.

'What exactly is this about?'

'I think you know that, sir,' he said with a tired smile.

*

Trained police search teams, Roy Grace learned rapidly, missed few things. Not that the stamps had been hidden in a difficult place to find – they were beneath a crate of Champagne in the cupboard under the stairs that served as the Cunninghams' wine cellar.

But it was three other items they found that were really to seal Crafty's fate. The first was an insurance claim form that lay on his desk, faxed only this morning, but which he had already started to fill out with details of the missing stamps.

The second was another fax, lying beneath it, to a dealer in the US, offering the collection for sale to him.

The third was a fax back from the US dealer, offering slightly more than the £100,000 Crafty had given the detectives as an estimate.

*

Later that night, even though he was exhausted, Roy Grace insisted on taking Sandy out to dinner to celebrate the first highly successful days of his new post, rather than going to the bar with the other officers. Four arrests! 'We got lucky,' he said. 'If the Chief Superintendent hadn't been out, and delayed us for several hours, and we had gone early, he might not have started filling in that insurance form. He might not have sent that damning fax. And he might not have had the damning reply.' He pulled out the folded page from *The Argus* newspaper and showed it to her.

She read it then smiled at him. 'I'm very proud of you.' She raised her wine glass, and clinked it against his, and said with another smile, this one a tad wistful, 'Now, how about asking me about my day?'

A VERY SEXY REVENGE

He saw her and beamed as he staggered down the aisle of the packed aircraft, towing his holdall which bashed into all the other passengers' ankles. She was fit: slender and beautiful with long blonde hair cut elegantly, and smartly dressed. And she was sitting in his seat.

She saw him too, and hoped to hell the dishevelled, drunk-looking slob in the crumpled tan suit wasn't heading for her row, then focused back on her crime novel. She smelled the fumes of alcohol before she heard his voice.

'S'cuse me, you're in my seat!'

She held up her ticket stub, barely glancing at him. '14A,' she said, and turned back to her novel.

He squinted at his own ticket. 'Mea culpa!' he said. 'I'm 14B. Next to you!'

He tugged open the overhead locker, and saw the large pink carrier bag. 'Is that yours?' he asked her.

She nodded, barely looking up from her book.

'I'll be careful not to crush it.' He lifted it out, hefted his bag in first, then held up the large, almost weightless carrier. On the outside was printed *Agent Provocateur.*

'Sexy underwear, is it?' he said, squeezing his bulky frame into the seat beside her. She smelled fragrant. He reeked of booze and stale smoke.

'You could sit in the aisle seat – it would give us more space,' she said.

'Nah, this is cosier!' He gave her a wink. 'Good book?'

Yes, it's about a drunken dickhead on a plane, she nearly said. Instead she smiled pleasantly and said, 'I'll tell you when I've finished it.'

'I'm Don,' he said. 'Been in Manchester at a business fair – I flog aircraft components. But don't worry, none on this plane are mine – so we won't crash, ha, ha!'

'Good.' She pulled her book closer to her face.

He pointed upwards. 'That sexy underwear – going to wear it for your boyfriend, are you?'

*

He drank three Bloody Marys on the short flight – or four including the one he spilt down the front of his jacket. As the plane began its descent, he whispered, 'You haven't told me your name.'

'Roxanna,' she said, as politely as she could, and began rereading the same page yet again, waiting for his next bloody interruption.

'Posh,' he said. 'I like it! Tell you what, Roxanna,' he lowered his voice. 'Why don't you and I meet sometime in London – you know? A couple of drinks, a nice little dinner?'

She looked down at his wedding ring, and said pointedly, 'Would your wife be joining us?'

'Nah, that's over. Well, it's on the rocks. She doesn't understand me, you see.'

After the engines had been switched off, he stood up unsteadily and lifted her carrier bag and her small case down for her, then slipped her his business card. 'I'd like to see you again,' he said. 'I'd like to see you wearing what's in that bag – know what I mean? We could have a bit of fun.'

'Oh, I will have fun, trust me.'

He held back the queue of passengers so she could go in front of him, but she insisted he went first. 'Hope to see you sometime soon,' he slurred.

Not if I see you first, she thought.

*

The kids were asleep, and Susie had prepared a candlelit dinner and opened a bottle of wine to welcome him home, as she always did. He held her in his arms and kissed her tenderly.

'So, tell me about the trip? How was the fair?' she asked over the avocado and prawns. 'Tell me about the hotel – was it nice? And why did you have to stay on an extra couple of days?' she quizzed as he carved into his steak.

After draining the bottle, he staggered upstairs, and threw his clothes on the floor as usual. Susie picked up his jacket, studying the tomato juice stain. 'I'll take that to the cleaner's first thing,' she said.

'Yrrrrr,' he groaned, almost asleep already.

As she began checking the pockets, she pulled out a folded square of paper from the right-hand one and opened it out. It was a receipt for Fifi briefs and a Fifi bra in black silk from Agent Provocateur.

On the back was written: *Don, thanks for your wonderful generosity on this trip, as ever. And for making me a member of the mile high club on the flight back! I never knew an airplane toilet could be such fun! Roxy xxxxxxxxxxxx*

THE KNOCK

‘Who was that at the door?’
‘Some undertakers with a hearse.’
‘No one’s dead.’
‘They said they can wait.’

DREAM HOLIDAY

This was inspired by the true story that gave me the idea for my novel *Dreamer*

One of the things Annie liked best about going on holiday was deciding what she was going to wear in the evenings. She'd always had a passion for designer shoes, and of course, in her stylish opinion, if you bought new shoes, then a matching handbag was a must. Much to her husband's dismay she regularly maxed her cards out on new outfits; she argued that it was her money, and he had to agree. And, to be fair, Nigel told her he was always extremely proud of how lovely she looked. Once he'd admitted to her, with that wry smile of his, that he got a secret kick out of seeing the envy on other men's faces when they looked at her.

She was particularly excited about this holiday because it was the first time that the two of them were going away alone, without the kids. Thank you, Aged Ps, as Nigel called his mum- and dad-in-law! They weren't actually that elderly at all, and were relishing taking care of Chloe, who was four, and Zak, who was going through his terrible twos. Zak had turned from an angelic baby into, at times, a demon out of a horror movie, with frequent tantrums, often involving hurling his food around the room. Although she would miss the children, the thought of having a week free of Zak was deeply enticing.

At least he liked attending the day nursery, and she was grateful for the respite that it gave her. She was able to continue her business as a hairdresser from home for three days a week without constant interruptions from him and it enabled her to afford to pay for her luxuries herself.

They were going to Montreux, a beautiful lakeside town on a sheltered bay, with fairy-tale views across the placid water of Switzerland's Lake Geneva – or Lac Léman, its Swiss name that Nigel liked to call it by – to the Alps. The hotel, a magnificent building in grand Belle Époque style, had once been a palace, and all the guests dressed for evening cocktails on the terrace. Dinner, in the majestic dining room with its starched linen and fine-crystal glasses, where the waiters wore black tailcoats and white gloves, was a magical experience.

It was there, after a particularly fine dinner, that Nigel had proposed to her. It had taken him two years to get round to it, although, he had confessed to her shyly, he knew he wanted to marry her the moment he had first set eyes on her.

Nigel was an analyst for a stockbroking firm in the City, and was incapable of acting spontaneously. Analyst stood for *anal*, she sometimes chided him. He scrutinized everything, always thought through every single detail with the greatest care. Sometimes that drove her to distraction. He could spend hours online, poring over restaurant menus and wine lists, before deciding on where they would go to eat. He had already planned every minute of their holiday. And probably every second.

Their recent purchase of a new car had been a nightmare odyssey through websites and dealerships, weighing up the safety features for their precious children, all elaborately detailed by Nigel on a spreadsheet. They'd settled on a big Volvo off-roader, which ticked the most boxes, but then they had argued about the colour. Nigel wanted white, and Annie was dismayed. She told him that according to an article in a woman's magazine, white was the colour people chose when they couldn't decide on a colour! She wanted black or silver, or even navy blue.

'But, darling,' he had insisted, showing her a computer printout. 'Read this. Yellow and white are the safest colours statistically. You are least likely to be involved in "a passive accident" in a yellow or white car. But I don't think we want *yellow*, do we?'

Nigel tended to get his way because he always had statistics on his side. Besides, she knew, bless him, that he meant well, he had the best interests of his family at heart. So white it was. But one detail Nigel had overlooked, and which she teased him about mercilessly in the first weeks after they had got the new car, was that it would not fit in the garage of their house, near Hove Park, in the city of Brighton and Hove.

Well, that wasn't strictly accurate. It did fit in the garage, but if you drove it in, it was impossible to open the doors, so the only way out would be through the sunroof – one of the options she had insisted on.

So the car became something she ribbed Nigel about, mercilessly. The big white elephant stuck on the driveway. But, she had to admit, it was comfortable, and inside you felt indestructible, like being in a tank.

It was Sunday night. The following Sunday, she thought, as she lay back against the headboard, flicking through the *Style* section of the *Sunday Times*, they would be luxuriating in that huge bed, beneath the soft, plump duvet, in Switzerland. Heaven! She could not wait, and her mind was too preoccupied with trying to remember all the things they must not forget to pack to concentrate on reading anything.

She kissed Nigel goodnight, switched off the light and snuggled down against the pillow, thinking, *hiking boots, shorts, suntan lotion, nose block, sunhats . . .*

The only downside to the holiday was the journey. She had never been happy about flying, even though Nigel had given her all the statistics, demonstrating to her that being in a commercial airliner was actually the safest place in the world – safer even than your own bed. But he could not convince her.

. . . books, Kindle, swimsuits, insect repellant cream, first-aid kit . . .

There was a familiar rustling sound beside her. Nigel would never go to sleep on a Sunday night without having read the news and financial pages of every single one of the broadsheets. Every Sunday evening of their marriage she had fallen asleep to that sound.

Scrunch, she heard. *Scrunch, scrunch, scrunch.* Then the thud of a discarded supplement landing on the floor on his side of the bed.

Scrunch, rustle, rustle, rustle, rustle.

Then a different sound.

A strange, deep, pulsing *thump, thump, thump* in the distance. Getting closer and louder.

Suddenly she was engulfed in a vortex of swirling air. She saw a propeller spinning in front of her eyes.

She screamed. Her eyes snapped open. She snapped on the light, gulping down air.

Nigel, fast asleep, stirred and murmured, 'Wasser? Wassermarrer?'

The bedside clock said 3.15 a.m.

'It's OK,' she said, upset at having woken him: he had an early start every workday and needed his sleep, especially on a Sunday night so that he was fresh for the week ahead – and the week before going on holiday was always a stressful one for him. 'I'm sorry – just had a nightmare.'

She kept the light on for some minutes, lying there. It was a still, early June night. There was a faint scratching sound outside – a cat or an urban fox rummaging in a rubbish bag. Slowly, her breathing calmed. She turned out the light, and fell asleep again a short while later.

*

The next night, Monday, Annie had the dream again. It was exactly the same, only this time the propeller was even larger, and came even closer. Again her screaming woke Nigel, and it set Zak off screaming too; but she managed to calm her son down by recovering his 'night' teddy, which had fallen on his bedroom floor, and he went back to sleep with one of its paws in his mouth.

*

On Tuesday night she had the dream again. This time the propeller came even closer still. And this time she snapped on her bedside light and she told Nigel. 'This is the third night running. I think this dream is telling me something.'

'What do you mean? Telling you what?' he asked, more than a little grumpily. Then he looked at the clock. 'Shit, 4 a.m.'

'I think it's a premonition,' she said. 'It's telling us we shouldn't fly.'

'Oh, for Christ's sake, Annie, it's you being afraid of flying! You have a bad dream every time before we fly.'

'Not like this one.'

'Can I go back to sleep?'

'Go back to sleep.'

*

On Wednesday night, although she had been frightened to turn the light out for a long while, Annie slept a deep, dreamless sleep and woke refreshed, feeling positive and optimistic. Even Zak, for a change, was in a happy mood, gleefully pushing his big yellow digger truck around the floor, and making the accompanying sound effects.

After she had dropped the two children off at their nurseries, she returned for the first client of the day, Samantha Hardy, the wife of a work colleague of Nigel, who also lived locally, and chatted to her excitedly about their holiday. Samantha told her about a wonderful restaurant near Geneva she and her husband had eaten in, and promised to text her the name that evening when he got home.

*

On Thursday night Annie dreamed she was in a cloud. Cold, grey tendrils brushed her face, icy air thrashed her blonde hair around her face, making it feel as hard as whipcords, and chilling her body to the core. She was shivering with cold and fear. In the distance a thump, thump, thump became increasingly louder. Louder. Louder. THUMP, THUMP, THUMP, THUMP. The roar of an engine rising to a crescendo. She was rocking from side to side and screaming, trying to keep her balance. Then the propeller was right in front of her face, thrashing, thrashing, coming at her, thrashing; suddenly the air gripped her in a vortex, spun her, hurtled her straight into the propeller.

'Darling! Darling! Annie! Annie! Darling! Annie! Annie!'

Nigel's voice, panicky, distant.

Darkness.

Then a light came on.

A warm, bright glow. She blinked.

She was in bed, Nigel staring at her in alarm. 'Darling. Annie, darling, it's OK. Calm down. You were having a nightmare, it's OK.'

Zak was screaming across the landing.

She was shaking, her heart thudding; she could hear the roaring of her blood in her ears. She was soaking wet, she realized. Drenched. Rivulets of perspiration streamed down her face, mingling with her tears. 'I'm sorry,' she spoke in gulping sobs. 'I'm sorry, Nigel, I can't get on that plane on Saturday. Even if we get there safely, I'll spend the whole week worrying about the flight home. I just can't do it. I had the dream again. It's telling me something.'

Her husband slipped out of bed, stomped out of the room and, uncharacteristically losing his temper, bellowed at Zak to shut up. It only made Zak's screaming worse. Annie followed him in, found Zak's night teddy on the floor again and gave it to him. Moments later he was calm once more. Then she stood for a while and stared at the little boy, thinking how deeply she loved him and Chloe. The thought of something happening to her – to her and Nigel – of never seeing them again. Of orphaning them. It was unbearable.

'Planes don't have propellers these days, Annie,' he said. 'Not large commercial planes. They haven't for years – they're all jets.'

'I know about dreams,' she replied. 'I've read a lot. You dream in symbols. The propeller is the symbol. And anyhow, what about bird strikes? You read about those sometimes. There was a plane that had to land on the Hudson River in New York after a multiple bird strike. Do you remember, a few years ago?'

'Yes, vaguely.'

'The birds got sucked into the turbines and mangled up the fan blades – something like that. So jet engines do have propellers – sort of.'

Back in their bedroom she said, 'I'm sorry, we'll have to cancel the trip – or you go without me.'

'That's ridiculous, Annie! I'm not going without you!' He sat down on the edge of the bed and thought for a moment. 'Have you had any dreams about trains crashing? Cars crashing?'

She shook her head, then stepped out of her sodden nightdress. 'Why don't we drive? Take the White Elephant? It would be nice, give us a chance to use the sunroof.'

'We only have a week,' he said. Driving would take a whole day each way.'

'If we left early on Saturday morning, on the Eurotunnel, we could get there by the evening. It's about seven, eight hours' drive, I seem to remember.'

'We'd probably miss dinner on Saturday, and we'd have to leave a day early to come back – so we'd miss it the following Friday too.'

'What about getting up really early?'

'I thought we were going on holiday, not boot camp.'

She shrugged herself into a fresh nightdress. 'I'm sorry,' she said. 'What about trains?'

'I already looked into those before booking the flights.'

Of course you would have done, she thought.

'The timings don't work.'

'Right.'

'You're sure you've had no premonitions about car accidents?'

'No.'

*

They left the house at 3 a.m., caught a 5.15 a.m. Eurotunnel crossing, and, allowing for the one-hour time difference, were on the road heading out of Calais towards the autoroute by 7 a.m. French time. The satnav which Nigel, being Nigel, had already programmed the night before, told them their ETA in Montreux was 3.55 p.m.

Due to a couple of stops to take turns behind the wheel and for coffee, snacks and loo breaks, they arrived at the hotel shortly after 5 p.m., on a glorious, balmy afternoon. For the last half hour, travelling around the shore of the lake, they'd had the sunroof open, and despite feeling a little tired, Annie felt happy – and relieved that they'd made the right decision. And, hey, they still had time to unpack, have a rest and make it for cocktails on the terrace.

She had already decided what she would wear that night. A pair of cobalt-blue suede Manolo Blahniks, and a totally stunning handbag to match, with a Stella McCartney A-line cocktail dress that stopped a couple of inches too high above her knees. Naughty, she knew, but it showed off her legs, by far her best asset – although for knocking on thirty and having had two sprogs, she didn't reckon the rest of her was too bad either. Tits still firm, stomach reasonably flat. So far, so good . . .

Out of curiosity, Nigel went online and checked the easyJet flight they would have been on. It had landed ten minutes early, shortly after midday. He told Annie.

'But the thing is, darling, as I said to you. Even if we'd got here safely, I would have spent the entire holiday fretting about the flight home. I didn't have the dream last night. We did the right thing.'

Nigel told her that if she felt they had done the right thing, then they had.

*

The first two days of their stay were blissful. Tired from the journey, they spent much of Sunday chilling, relaxing on loungers beside the hotel's infinity pool and reading. On Monday they went hiking up in the mountains and, later, Annie had a massage. On their third day, Tuesday, in the personal organizer section of Nigel's phone was, *Picnic lunch on boat. Dep. 11 a.m., return 4 p.m.*

'Couldn't be more perfect weather for a day on the water, could it?' Nigel said, pulling on his Dyke Golf Club baseball cap to cover his balding dome. He cast off the mooring rope of the brown-varnished, clinker-built dinghy they had rented. There was an outboard, if they wanted to use it, but Nigel was keen to row. He patted his stomach, which Annie had noticed was definitely in an expansionist mode these past few years, although he was a long way from what one could call *fat.* 'Promised myself I'd lose this by the end of the week,' he said.

'Let me know when you get tired and I'll have a go on the oars too,' she said.

'You can take over when we get to France, and row back!' he said with a grin, and pointed at the craggy peaks of the Alps on the far shore. Deeper into the mountain range, some of the peaks were still snow-capped, but the visibility was not good enough to see them today.

'How far is it across?' she asked.

'About fourteen kilometers – nine miles,' he said.

'Quite a row!'

'Could do it in a couple of hours – shall we try? We can use the outboard to motor back.'

'Do we have to pay extra if we get back after 4 p.m.?'

'There's an hourly charge, but it's not exorbitant.'

'Let's go for it. Splice the main brace, Sir Francis!'

It was a baking hot morning, with a faint breeze, the blue sky smudged with just a few wispy cirrus clouds high above them. Annie sat back, watching Nigel in his pink shorts, white polo shirt and trainers steadily rowing, keeping up a good speed. She breathed in the smells of boat varnish and rope and the fresh, faintly reedy tang of the water, and listened to the steady splash of the oars. In the distance, she saw a ferry crossing, and a large pleasure boat heading along the lake in front of them.

Suddenly, her phone pinged with a text. She pulled it out of her bag and looked at the display. 'From Mummy,' she said, opening it.

All fine here. Zak good as gold. Taking them to Drusilla's Park today. Hope you're having a nice time!

She sent a reply that they were – they were having a really lovely time. Then as she put her phone away she said to Nigel, 'Zak, *good as gold*!'

'Respect to your parents, I'd say!'

*

An hour later the mountains of the French Alps ahead of them grew steadily larger and higher as they rowed nearer, but the far shore was still a long way off. Nigel had pulled off his top and, moving carefully in the boat, making sure not to rock it too much and capsize, he made his way over to Annie so she could rub sun cream onto his back and chest.

'Want me to take over yet?' she asked.

He was sweating heavily but looking relaxed and cheery. 'No, thanks, I'm fine.' He took his hands from the oars to pat the big roll of flesh that was his stomach. 'Is it looking any smaller?'

'Definitely, darling!'

Suddenly, she felt a sudden swirl of cold air; it was so fleeting that for an instant she thought she had imagined it. Then from the faint frown that crossed Nigel's face, she knew he'd felt it too. But it was gone, as suddenly as it had come. A couple at the next-door table on the terrace last night, who told them they came to Montreux every year for their holiday, said to be careful out on the lake – there were strange eddies and currents, and treacherous mists could descend quickly and with little warning.

But of course Nigel had checked the weather forecast carefully this morning with the concierge. It was going to be a fine day on the lake as well as on the shore. No mists were forecast. A perfect day for boating!

But, almost imperceptibly, the water seemed to be getting choppier; although not unpleasantly rough, it was definitely no longer as calm as it had been. She commented on it to Nigel.

'It's because the breeze is coming from the Montreux side – the lee shore,' he explained. 'We're heading towards the windward shore, so the further out we get, the choppier it will become.'

As he spoke, a wave, from the wake of some bigger craft, broke over the bow, sprinkling a few droplets over Nigel's back – and she felt a few of them on her face; nice and refreshing, but at the same time, staring at the darkening water, she felt a faint tinge of apprehension. They were a long way out now, in a very small craft. She turned her head and looked back at Montreux, so far in the distance it took her a moment to identify their hotel.

'Maybe we shouldn't go any further,' she said.

Nigel looked at his watch. 'Twelve thirty. Hmm, it is taking longer than I thought.' He looked over his shoulder at the French shore. 'It will take a good hour more at least to get there.'

'Longer, I'd say,' she replied dubiously.

'We could go up the lake a little way instead, and then drift and have lunch in around half an hour. How does that sound?'

She nodded. 'OK. Or we could row back a little towards the lee shore – it would be nicer to eat not rocking around so much.' She suddenly had to grip the gunwales as the boat was rocked harshly by another, much bigger wave; the wash from a powerboat heading into the distance at high speed.

Nigel did not seem to need much persuading to turn the boat around. Annie offered to take over rowing, but he was fine, he said, and she could do some after lunch. But as he pulled on the oars he was looking less happy than when they had started out this morning, and the water was looking distinctly less happy too. Instead of getting calmer it was definitely getting a tad rougher all across the lake.

Above them the clouds were building up. Annie delved into the picnic hamper prepared by the hotel and brought out some bottled water. She took a long swig then offered some to Nigel. He shook his head. 'When we stop, thanks, darling.'

After another ten minutes, to Annie's relief, the water seemed a little calmer again. At 1 p.m. precisely, Nigel shipped his oars. 'Lunch?'

'Good plan,' she said. 'I'm ravenous!'

For several minutes, she knelt, keeping her head down, focused on the contents of the hamper. She pulled out a beer, which she opened and handed to Nigel, then peeled two hardboiled eggs, and carefully buttered two rolls. There were plates, knives and forks beautifully wrapped in linen napkins, wine glasses and a bottle of a local white wine, Dole, in a cooler bag. There was pâté in one container, slices of ham in another, tomato salad in a third, as well as an assortment of cheeses and fruits, and two miniature bars of Lindt chocolate.

'I don't think we're going to starve!' she said, carefully preparing a platter for Nigel. But to her surprise he did not comment. When she looked up to hand it to him, she could see why. Tendrils of mist were drifting by them like ghosts. She turned and the mist was everywhere, thin and hazy and wispy in places. It took her some moments to even spot the shore, and Montreux through it. 'I thought the weather forecast was meant to be good, Nigel?'

'That's what it said on both the ones I checked online, and the concierge assured me of the same. This is probably just some kind of midday heat haze.'

'More like a sea mist,' she said.

'This is a lake, not the sea, darling.'

'That couple last night said something about sudden mists descending. Maybe we should head back while we can still see the shore – what do you think?'

He dipped his egg into the small pile of salt and pepper Annie had poured onto his plate, then bit into it, and chewed thoughtfully. 'Maybe that would be wise. Might be best to use the outboard – get a bit closer to the shore and we'll probably find it's completely clear there.'

'I'll pack the picnic away.'

The boat rocked wildly as Nigel slid off his seat and edged his way, balancing with difficulty, to the stern. The mist was thickening by the second now. The temperature felt as if it had dropped twenty degrees. And suddenly, for a brief moment, Annie could see nothing at all – she was totally engulfed in the mist; she felt disoriented and giddy.

It cleared a fraction, and she could just make out Nigel, barely ten feet away; he was merely a shadow. But she could not see the shore, any shore in any direction. 'I don't like this,' she said.

The temperature was dropping even further. Then, in the distance, she heard a steady, rhythmic thump, thump, thump.

It was getting louder by the second.

Thump, thump, thump.

Cold air suddenly swirled around her.

She could hear the roar of an engine. The thrashing of water.

'Nigel!' she called out, panicky. 'Nigel, start the outboard, please, quickly.'

'I'm trying – not sure which way I'm meant to turn this ruddy knob.'

She heard the clatter, clatter, clatter as he pulled the starting handle, but no sound of the motor firing. He pulled again.

The thump, thump, thump grew louder, closer. The thrashing sound was louder, closer. The roar of the engine was rising to a crescendo.

Icy air engulfed them. The boat was rocking wildly; strands of her hair whipped her face. The water erupted around them into foaming bubbles, as if some monster beneath them was rising from the deep. Then a shadow, tall as a house, bore down on them out of the mist.

'NIGEL!' she screamed.

An instant later she was in the water, spinning around and around in a crazed, choking vortex that was pulling her backwards and under.

*

An Englishman in a dark suit and a sombre club tie, accompanied by a uniformed police officer, greeted the grief-stricken sixty-year-old man as he stepped off the plane at Geneva airport.

'Mr Donaldson?'

'Yes.'

'I'm Gavin Pearson, the British Consul, and this is Inspector Didier Motte of the Geneva Cantonal Police. I'm very sorry about your daughter, sir.'

Michael Donaldson thanked him, blinking away tears, and shook both their hands.

'A terrible tragedy, and on their holiday,' Inspector Motte said, sympathetically.

'Would you like to have anything to eat or drink, or a rest, before we head off, Mr Donaldson?' the Consul asked.

'No, let's go straight to the mortuary, get it over with, please,' he replied.

They exchanged few words in the police car for several minutes. Michael Donaldson sat on the back seat, oblivious to the passing surroundings. Then he asked, 'My son-in-law, Nigel. Presumably you've not found . . . not . . . recovered . . . his body yet?'

Inspector Motte, who was driving, responded in his broken English. 'We are diving on the lake since the unfortunate accident happened, but there are a number of – how you say – *courants,* and the lake is deep in this part. It may take some time. And we are searching the lake all over, by air and water.'

They drove on in silence. Annie's father caught a glimpse of the lake to his right, a cluster of vessels way out towards the middle, and the small black dot of a helicopter hovering low over the water, and hastily averted his gaze. He did not even notice them pulling up outside the mortuary building. The rear door of the car was opened by one of the men – he barely registered which – and he stepped out as if in a trance. He was here to identify his daughter's body. He could not get his head around this.

As if sensing him faltering, as they entered the building, the Consul put his hand on his arm. 'Mr Donaldson, are you absolutely certain you want to see her body? We could do this another way – identify her from her wedding ring, or items of her clothing, or even dental records or DNA, if you'd prefer?'

'I want to see her,' he said. 'I want to see my baby one last time.'

'Of course.'

'Just tell me – I'm still not totally clear about how the accident happened. The English police who gave me and my wife the news only had very sketchy details. They were in a rowboat, quite far out on the lake, in bad weather? It doesn't sound like my son-in-law – he was a very cautious man. Was . . . I'm saying *was* . . . he might still be alive, mightn't he?'

'I think by now, two days, we would have found him if he was alive,' the Inspector said.

'Apparently your daughter, Annie, and son-in-law, Nigel, rented a small day boat, with an outboard, and took a picnic lunch prepared by the hotel,' the Consul said. 'The weather forecast was good, but unfortunately, where you have a large mass of water surrounded by mountains, it will always be susceptible to sudden changes. A mist came down that no one predicted – very fast, apparently, and it was a tragic accident. The little boat was run down by a ferry. The captain has been arrested.'

'That's not going to bring them back,' Annie's father said grimly.

'I'm sorry,' the Consul said. 'I'm truly sorry. I wish there was something I could do. Anything.'

'There is one thing,' Michael Donaldson said. 'How much do you think my daughter suffered? I can't imagine what it's like to drown—'

'Let me set your mind at rest,' the Consul said, interrupting him. 'I spoke to the pathologist. Your daughter didn't drown – her death would have been instant.'

'How can you be so certain?' Donaldson asked with suspicion.

'Well – I was hoping to spare you the details.'

'I would like to know. I'd like to be able to at least tell my wife that our beloved daughter didn't suffer.'

The Consul looked at him, hesitantly, then turned to the police officer as if for help. But Motte just stood in polite silence.

'She didn't drown, you say,' Annie's father prompted. 'Was she struck on the head?'

'No, she didn't – she didn't have a head injury. I'm afraid, in the collision with the ferry, your daughter was cut in half by the propeller.'

A CHRISTMAS TRADITION

Susan took the black lace-trimmed teddy from the bottom drawer of her pine chest, where it had lain carefully washed and neatly folded for twelve months. The satin trickled through her fingers as she held it to her body and she was shocked how rough her hands felt in contrast to its softness, and by how drawn and tired her face looked in the mirror against its sheen.

She was frightened that Tony would not come back tonight, and she could not bear the thought of spending Christmas without him. They had never spent Christmas apart before, but she had a feeling this year was going to bring some break with tradition, and she was uneasy.

Thirty-three and growing old. *Growing old and frightened,* she thought as she parted the curtains and stared into the darkness, watching the fairy lights on her neighbour's tree through the ghost of her own face at the window. A mist of fine rain clung like a swarm of midges to the glow of the street lamp, and tears clung to her eyelashes.

She looked up, wondering if he was up there now beyond the canopy of clouds. There were times on clear nights when she had seen navigation lights winking beneath the stars and had wondered if it was him, returning. The clouds frightened her, made her think back . . . but she suppressed the memory. It was Christmas Eve and he always managed to make it back, somehow.

She had had no message from him, although that was not unusual, and she understood how the wives and girlfriends of hostages must feel, never knowing, never hearing; except Tony wasn't being held captive, unless it was by temptation. He was one of those mercurial and unpredictable men, with an aura of the untamed adventurer about him and an appetite for life that women found attractive. She had noticed his eyes roving at parties.

And yet he swore he had never been unfaithful. Until recently, Susan had believed him. Her friends had tried to tell her to forget him, to move on, and his long silence and her feeling about the break with tradition were beginning to convince her also. The stewardesses on the small private airline were chosen for their looks. Tony flew the world with them. It was hard to believe he could have always resisted.

Even so, she kept her hope and prepared the bed, let her long brown hair down because he liked it that way, put on his favourite perfume, moisturized her hands and ran them down her slender, freshly waxed legs, savouring their smoothness. She slipped out of her clothes, shivering from the cold air on her naked skin, and put on the teddy, which he had bought her for Christmas five years ago, and which it had become a tradition for her to wear in bed on Christmas Eve.

The first time they had made love was on Christmas Eve, up in her attic bedroom at her parents' home in Wembley whilst they were out at a party. Afterwards they had lain in silence, the windowpanes drenched in the darkness of the night, wrapping paper rustling at the end of the bed when they moved their feet. She could still remember vividly how they had held each other tightly, urgently, pressing against each other for warmth and reassurance, and they had made one of those vows that young people in love make, and in time can so easily forget.

They vowed that whatever happened in the future, they would always make love on Christmas Eve.

So far, in fourteen years, neither of them had broken the vow. It had become a tradition between them, a night of intense sensuality that grew stronger each year, fuelling in Susan a sense of the magic of Christmas that she remembered as a child but once thought had been lost forever.

Tony had usually managed to wangle the rosters, and on those times when he had not been able to, and all looked impossible, fog had come down and grounded the aircraft, or there had been a mechanical problem and he had been released from duty. Once, in an act of sheer bravado, he had borrowed his boss's plane and flown in from Monaco at midnight. She remembered that Christmas well. A tear rolled from her eye; her lashes crushed it and she smiled – she did not want him to arrive home and find her in tears.

She lit a candle, as she always did on Christmas Eve, placed it on Tony's bedside table, slid his card beneath it, and slipped into bed. She read for a while, waiting, listening. It was ten past twelve. At half past she switched off her bedside light. The flame of the candle burned steadily, undisturbed. He liked to make love with a light on, liked to watch her, liked to unclip the fasteners of the teddy himself. 'You're my Christmas present,' he would say, and then lean forward to kiss her. Everywhere.

For a long time they had given each other a stocking, but that was a tradition she had stopped, concentrating instead on the children. Christmas had been special to her childhood and she wanted it to be special to theirs too. But she had never dreamed that it would one day dominate her every waking moment. That it would become a point on the horizon to which each year was anchored. The port in the storm. The magical time when wounds could be healed and sadness forgotten and hope restored.

She had never dreamed that it would be memories of Christmases past that gave her the strength to get up each morning, to get through the spring and into the summer. And that August and September would be months of deep doldrums in which the memory had faded and doubt would seep into her like acid from a corroded battery, eating away, leaving wounds and pain and scars.

Then with the first crisp snap of an autumn chill the memory would come alive again and hope would wrap itself snugly around her with the knowledge that Christmas lay just beyond those first long nights of the autumn and the fierce equinox gales that would vandalize the landscape. Christmas would follow with calm, with serenity, with carols and games of Monopoly, with long walks and mince pies, with the laughter of old friends and the pleasure of old traditions. One very special tradition.

She closed her eyes, but knew, like all the Christmas Eves of her childhood, this was one of those nights when she could not even remember how to fall asleep. In the silence of the house she could hear the insistent rustling of paper, and she smiled – the kids already rummaging through their stockings. They wouldn't actually open their presents tonight – she had taught them they must not until the morning – but they would be feeling the shapes of the packages, wondering, trying to guess. Then she heard the faint click of the front door and her breathing quickened.

It clicked again, shut. She waited for the next click of the deadlock, and the final clank of the safety chain, then his footsteps. Routine, she thought; she knew his routine so well and you had to be careful in marriage not to turn traditions into routines.

She lay and waited and it was the expectation that gave her her deepest arousal. He moved slowly, hanging up his coat then going into the kitchen and sifting through the mountain of post she had left waiting for him. Her stomach felt like a snowstorm that had been shaken inside a glass paperweight.

He was moving up the stairs, his pace lighter and quicker with every step, as if he sensed her excitement and it was charging his own. He opened the bedroom door and the candle jigged in the sudden draught, and shadows danced beyond her closed eyelids. Her lips released the smile they could no longer contain as she sensed his shadow in front of her now, felt the fresh sheets sliding back and the sudden cold air on her skin, and she knew he was watching, knew he was lowering his head to kiss her; she felt the caress of his hands, then his fingers, fumbling clumsily, as they always did, with the fastener.

'My very special Christmas present,' he said.

'And mine,' she murmured richly, as his lips touched her.

*

The morning was dry and cold and an east wind blew. Frost sparkled like powdered glass on the grass, and the crimson orb of the sun hung in the grey silk sky. It was the kind of magical Christmas morning she remembered from childhood.

Static crackled inside the house as she walked across the carpets, lighting the fire, putting out the glasses, paper rustling continuously now as the children tore open more presents. Static crackled inside her veins too, and she felt flooded with the same passion for life that Tony's presence always fired in her.

She liked this time before the invasion of relatives started. Once they would have gone to church, but Tony did not like that any more, did not want to come with her; they had precious little time together and she could not bear to spend even an hour of it without him. It had become a morning to savour for themselves, a time of reflection and of peace. And a time, she hoped today, to forge a new understanding between them.

A time when the house always felt bright and cheery. The windows decanted light into the room, spreading it evenly so that everything seemed intensely alive, the colours rich, the textures of the carpets and the wallpaper and the curtains emerging from the monochrome shadows which shrouded them for the rest of the year. The holly looked fresh, the berries ripened to a vivid red.

The air became infused with smells of basting turkey, wood smoke and freshly uncorked bottles. There was a quietness outside, stronger than any Sunday, the silence of a night that lingered on into the day and would soon be pleasantly disturbed with laughter, and the clinking of glasses, the chatter and snores of discarded relatives retrieved again for the occasion, like the tangled fairy lights in the tired cardboard box.

And the draughts. Always the draughts.

'Never known a house with so many draughts,' her father said.

She watched the light bulbs swaying, the curtains shifting restlessly, the ball of wrapping paper that uncurled by itself and fluttered from time to time. Paper rustled with a roar like the pull of a retreating tide on shingle. Strands of silver lametta and tinsel shimmied between the needles of the tree. The children were engrossed. Lucy was changing her Barbie doll's dress. Jamie was assembling his Scalextric. Sometimes the coloured baubles on the tree would touch with sounds like wind chimes. Old logs settled into the grate and new ones crackled.

In the kitchen Susan was distracted by Tony and she kept duplicating jobs and spilling things. He was in a more passionate mood than she had ever known, and from his caresses she felt increasing currents of excitement in the pit of her stomach as fresh erotic images formed in her mind, and new desires pulled silky threads tight inside her. She broke a glass. It was lucky to break a glass, he had told her once, a long time ago. She reminded him and they laughed together now.

Car doors slammed outside. The family had begun to arrive. Her father walked with a stick after his heart surgery.

'Never seen you look so well, Susan,' he said.

They all told her how well she looked. Years had dropped from her face, they said.

Ronnie Bodkins, the chirpy oaf her sister had married, with his two lawnmower dealerships and his pearls of wisdom trawled from the *Reader's Digest*, sat on the sofa and slurped his Pinot Noir (red wine, he assured everyone, was the best thing for your heart) and told his one joke that came out each year as if it came from the same tired box that contained the fairy lights.

Someone always fed him the question. This year it was her brother, Christopher. 'How's business, Ronnie?' he asked.

'Oh, can't complain. Christmas is a good time for me. All the little women come in and buy their hubbies gardening presents. Could have fooled me there's a recession. Well, it was the Good Lord himself who said that a great profit shall come unto the land!'

He always laughed at his joke. He was the only one.

Conversations edged on, the digging and probing of new ventures and old wounds. The morning passed for Susan in a haze of remembered pleasures, and a sense of anticipation she had never experienced before. She came into the drawing room for a quick glass of Champagne and looked at the clock. 1.15 p.m. Lunch, then the Queen's speech. *Some Like It Hot* with Marilyn Monroe on the box. Followed by *Downton Abbey.* And then, probably, to bed. Except something was different about this Christmas and she hardly dared hope it could be true.

'To absent friends.'

Her brother's toast at the beginning of lunch was becoming a tradition too. They all raised their glasses. Susan raised hers the highest. She sensed the draught on her cheeks, felt it lifting her hair and lowering it again. Body language. There were signals between her and Tony the way there were between all lovers, a touch, a whisper, a wink. As the years had gone by their signalling had become stronger and they could communicate feelings without the banality of conversation. *Tonight,* Tony was saying. He wanted to make love again, tonight.

Normally, she stuffed herself, drank herself into a pleasant state of oblivion and collapsed in front of the box, dragging herself to her feet from time to time to make tea, to say farewells, to tidy up with a heavy heart and heave herself upstairs to bed. Instead, today she cut herself a thin sliver of turkey, took no potatoes and just a couple of sprouts, and sipped only her mineral water.

'Not dieting, surely, darling?' her mother asked.

She replied with a silent blush.

'Four years now,' her father said. His voice resonated in the silence the toast had left in its wake.

Four years since the small plane had gone down, crashed into trees outside the airfield only ten miles from the house. Just a simple error. He had forgotten to adjust the altimeter from Monaco's sea level setting to Biggin Hill's. Just the twiddle of a knob. But the magic of Christmas affected everyone in its own way.

'It must be hard for you, darling,' her mother said. 'Christmas must be the time when you miss him the most.'

Susan shared her secret with the candles that tugged sharply on their wicks, and the paper chains that swayed gently, and she felt the draught as warm as breath blowing down her neck, and thought about the night ahead that might be heralding the start of a new tradition. 'No,' she said with a distant smile. 'It's the one day of the year I don't miss him at all.'

COMPANIONSHIP

She moves slowly on her Zimmer, placing one foot after the other, stretching her neck forward towards her little room, a distant, distancing smile on her face, like a carapace.

Everyone thought the old lady had a tame pigeon, until they entered after her death, and found its feet were nailed to the windowsill.

MY FIRST GHOST

The following story is true. It is my own experience of living in a haunted house and if, when you have read it, you are still sceptical about the existence of ghosts, I will be very surprised.

All I have done is to change the names of the house and the other people involved, to protect their privacy, although the armchair detectives among you would not have too much difficulty establishing the real names!

In 1989 I was fortunate to have made a substantial sum of money from my first two supernatural thrillers, *Possession* and *Dreamer* (the true story that inspired this latter book is in this anthology, titled *Dream Holiday*), and my then wife and I went house-hunting. We fell in love with a stunning Georgian manor house on the edge of a Sussex hamlet. It had a long history – before being a manor house it had been a monastery in the middle ages, and prior to that there had been a Roman villa in the grounds, part of which – a Roman fish keep – was still largely intact.

During our time there, archaeological students spent two years doing a dig to discover the remains of the villa – much to my wife Geraldine's dismay, as it meant they dug up an area of a very fine lawn, and without success. However, after we sold the house in 1999, the next owners dug foundations for a new garage at the top of the long drive and unearthed, by accident, the ruins. Their building work was then delayed for two years by a court order to allow excavations to take place.

'You'll like this house, with what you write,' the owner told me, mischievously, on our first viewing. 'We have three ghosts.'

It turned out he was fibbing – the house, we were to discover later, actually had four. The first one manifested while we were in the process of moving in. I was standing in the front porch, on a beautiful spring morning, with my mother-in-law, Evelyn, a very down-to-earth lady, who was a senior magistrate. But she had a 'fey' side to her in that she was very open-minded about the paranormal, and always had a particular recurring, frightening dream whenever someone she knew was about to die. She had told me about this and had come to accept it, without ever being able to come up with a rational explanation beyond, perhaps, telepathy.

I liked her a lot and we had always got on really well, I guess in part because although in court she was a formidable, doughty lady, who acquired the soubriquet (which she greatly enjoyed) of 'The Hanging Magistrate of Hove', she was an enthusiastic reader of my work and was someone both totally unshockable and hugely intelligent, with whom I could converse on any topic from aliens to ancient Egypt, to modern politics.

From the front door where we were standing, there was a long, narrow corridor which ran from the front of the house through to an oak-panelled atrium at the rear, with four Doric columns, which led into the kitchen. This atrium was all that remained of the monastery which had originally been on the site, and you could still see the arches where the altar had been.

As we stepped aside to let the removals men leave the house to fetch another item, I suddenly saw a shadow, like the flit of a bird across a fanlight, in the interior of the house.

'Did you see that?' my mother-in-law asked, with a knowing look.

Despite the warmth of the sunlight, I felt a sudden chill. I could tell by the expression on her face at that moment that she had seen something uncanny. But I did not want to spook my wife on our very first day in the house. Geraldine and I were both townies, and this was our first move into the countryside. She was already apprehensive about the isolation of the property. The last thing I needed was for her to be unnecessarily scared by a ghost! So I shook my head and told Evelyn I had not seen anything. But in truth, I was feeling a little spooked by this.

Our first night was uneventful, and our Hungarian sheepdog, Boris, had been very happy and calm. I'd been told that dogs would often pick up on any supernatural occurrence way before their owners, so I took this as a good sign.

In the morning, Geraldine left for work at 8 a.m. After breakfast I went to my study to resume work on my third supernatural novel, *Sweet Heart*. Around 10.30 a.m. I went downstairs to make a cup of coffee. As I entered the atrium, on my way through to the kitchen, I saw tiny pinpricks of white light all around me. My immediate reaction was that it was sunlight, coming through the window in the far wall, reflecting off my glasses. I took them off, put them back on, and the pinpricks of light had gone.

I returned to my study, but when I went downstairs to make myself some lunch, the same thing happened again. And again, after removing my glasses and putting them back on once more, the pinpricks had gone. But I was left with a slightly uneasy feeling. In the afternoon, when I went downstairs to make a mug of tea, it happened again.

I said nothing to Geraldine when she arrived home that evening, and she did not see anything.

The next day around mid-morning, when I was alone in the house, I saw the pinpricks again, and at lunchtime. After lunch I took Boris for a walk. We'd only gone a short distance along the lane when an elderly man came up to me, introducing himself as Harry Stotting, a neighbour in the hamlet. 'You are Mr James, aren't you?' he asked.

'Yes, I am,' I replied.

'You've just moved into the big house?'

'Two days ago.'

'How are you getting on with your grey lady?' he said, with a strange, quizzical look that immediately unsettled me.

'What *grey lady*?' I asked.

He then really spooked me. 'I was the house-sitter for the previous owners. In winter, they used the atrium as a 'snug' because, as it adjoined the kitchen, it was always warm from the Aga. Six years ago I was sitting in the snug watching television, when a sinister-looking woman with a grey face, and wearing a grey silk crinoline dress, materialized out of the altar wall, swept across the room, gave me a malevolent stare, flicked my face with her dress, and vanished into the panelling behind me. I was out of there thirty seconds later, and went back in the morning to collect my things. Wild horses wouldn't drag me back in there again!'

I was struck both by the sincerity of the man, and his genuine fear, which I could see in his eyes as he told me the story. It truly made the hairs on the back of my neck rise.

I returned to the house after our walk feeling very uncomfortable. I even wimped out of going through the atrium into the kitchen to make my afternoon cuppa! But when Geraldine came home in the evening, I said nothing – I suppose I did not want to believe it myself, and she was still extremely nervous about living in such an isolated house. One of the things you realize when you move into the depths of the countryside after living in an urban environment is the sheer darkness of the nights. In a city, it is never truly dark, ever – there is always an ambient glow from the street lighting. But on a cloudy or moonless country night, it is pitch black. I had tried to convince her that for a potential intruder total darkness was harder than ambient light, so we were safer. But she did not buy that.

The following Sunday, we had invited Geraldine's parents to lunch. Whilst she was occupied putting the finishing touches to the meal, I took her mother aside and asked her what exactly she had seen that day we were moving in.

She described a woman, with a grey face, dressed in grey silk crinoline, moving across the atrium – exactly what the old man, Harry Stotting, had described to me.

I was stunned – and very spooked. Later, after her parents had left, I decided I had to tell Geraldine. She took it in the pragmatic way she had of dealing with most difficult issues in life. 'You've met several mediums in your research – why don't you ask one of them to come in and see what they find?'

A few days later, a medium who had helped me a lot during my writing of *Possession* came to the house, and I took her into the atrium and left her on her own, as she had requested.

An hour later she came up to my study, and yet again described exactly the woman in grey silk crinoline. She explained the pinpricks of light I kept seeing by telling me I was slightly psychic, so while I was not actually seeing the entire apparition, I was picking up some of its energy.

I asked her if there was anything I could do about this, and she told me that the apparition was of a deeply disturbed former resident of the house, and that it needed a clergyman to deal with it.

I felt a tad cynical about her response – but at the same time, I was now feeling deeply uncomfortable in what should have been the sanctuary of my own home. However, there was a vicar I knew who I thought would be able to help.

At the time he was officially the Vicar of Brighton – but with another hat, he was also the chief exorcist of the Church of England. That wasn't his actual title, which was the less flaky-sounding Minister of Deliverance. A former monk with a double first from Oxford in psychology, and the son of two medics, he was as far from Max Von Sydow's Father Merrin in *The Exorcist* as you could get. He is a delightful human being, with whom I had become good friends, and still am to this day. He is a modern thinker, a clergyman who has a problem with the biblical concept of God yet still retains an infectious faith.

Even so, I was a little surprised when he cheerfully entered the atrium, stood still for a couple of minutes, and then loudly and very firmly enunciated into thin air, 'You may go now!'

He turned to me and said, 'You should be fine now.'

Well, we were, until a mid-June day in 1994. My novel *Host*, which had been published the previous year by Penguin in hardback, had just been published both on two floppy discs, billed as the world's first electronic novel, and in paperback. The thick paperback lay on a beautiful antique wooden chest which we kept in the atrium. I always put my latest book there for visitors to see. On this particular sunny morning, I was having breakfast around 7.45 a.m., while Geraldine was upstairs getting ready for work. Suddenly she called down, 'I can smell burning!'

I suddenly realized that I could too. I turned around, and to my amazement, the copy of *Host*, on top of the wooden chest, was on fire!

I rushed over, grabbed the book, ran to the kitchen sink and threw it in, then turned the taps on to extinguish the flames.

There was, of course, a perfectly prosaic explanation: close to the book, on the chest, was a round glass paperweight. The hot June morning sun rays had been refracted through it, much the same way that as kids we used to set fire to things by letting the sun's rays refract through a magnifying glass. But . . . the fact it had happened in this room which had had the apparition in it added a very sinister dimension.

The above story was only one of the spooky occurrences we had in this otherwise glorious house. The second happened the first weekend we spent there. It was on the Sunday morning and I said hello to our nearest neighbours, who lived in what had, in former days, been the coach house. 'I just want to ask you,' the cheery elderly occupant asked, 'because my wife and I are very curious. Do you have anyone staying with a young baby this weekend?'

'No,' I told him.

'Ah, must be your ghost again,' he said, very matter-of-factly.

It turned out that he, and other neighbours across the narrow lane outside the house, would regularly hear a baby crying. We learned that in the 1920s the drawing room floor had been dug up because of damp and dry rot and the skeleton of a baby had been discovered – perhaps stillborn, or possibly even murdered way back in time.

In the grounds was a very narrow lake, a quarter of a mile long, and on the far side was a public footpath. During the decade we lived in the house, several residents of the hamlet and of surrounding villages told us how they had been chased off the footpath at dusk by a Roman centurion! To me, this was the least credible of the stories. But in many ways, one of the most credible was the one I was told the day I was collared by another of my neighbours.

The house used to own many hundreds of surrounding acres. Over time the land was sold off in parcels. Several houses had been built in the 1930s and 1950s along the far side of the lake. One day I was walking Boris along past them when the owner of one – a very down-to-earth factory manager in his mid-fifties – shouted, 'I wish you would keep your bloody ghosts under control!'

He then told me, 'Last Sunday, we held a christening party for my grandson here. At 4 p.m., all the guests had gone and I went and sat in the conservatory to read the *Sunday Times*. Suddenly the room turned icy and I shivered. I looked up and saw a monk in a cowled hood staring down at me. I thought at first it was one of my relatives playing a prank on me. I stood up and followed it into the kitchen. But he had vanished. The only person in there was my wife, doing the washing-up. There is no door out of the kitchen. She had not seen or heard anything.'

There was one more very spooky occurrence during our time there. At the front of the house were two sets of classic Georgian bay windows. One was in a spare bedroom, which we called the Blue Room, where we often put up guests, and all the time we lived there, I never felt comfortable entering it. Whenever we went away, we employed a house-sitter. On each occasion, when we returned home the house-sitter would have moved out of this room, giving a lame excuse about not liking the colour, or the morning sun, and slept somewhere else in the house.

As a postscript, I should add something of the house's history. For much of the twentieth century it was owned by the Stobart family, the most famous member of which, Tom Stobart OBE, was a photographer, zoologist and author. A true adventurer, he was the cameraman who climbed Everest with Hunt and Hillary and took the photos of their ascent, was subsequently shot in the knee in Ethiopia, and tragically died far too young from a heart attack at the local railway station, Hassocks. One member of the family was – reputedly – a strange lady, who became a man-hating lesbian and subjected Tom's sister Anne, who we befriended in the years before she died from a stroke, to such cruelty as a child she was never able to live a normal life or form normal relationships. Anne told us one day that this relative used to strap her hands to the side of the bed when she was a child to prevent her, should she be tempted, from touching herself.

Was she the grey lady in the atrium?

During the Second World War, the house was used to billet Canadian soldiers. After the war, during the second half of the twentieth century, three couples bought it – and subsequently divorced. We were the third. Was the grey lady in any way responsible?

I will always wonder.

TWO MINUTES

When he was a small boy, Rod Wexler loved to hang out on Brighton's Palace Pier – long since renamed Brighton Pier. He liked looking down, through the holes in the metal gridding of the walkway, at the sinister, shadowy dark green water fifty feet below. And he was fascinated by the escapologist, the Great Omani, whose act (which the strange man repeated hourly, on the hour) was to tip a gallon of petrol into the sea below, drop a lighted taper to create a flaming circle, then tie himself up in a straitjacket, jump off the side of the pier into the flames, disappear below the surface, then emerge a minute or so later, triumphantly holding the straitjacket above his head, to a small ripple of applause.

From an early age Rod had always been obsessed with trying to work things out; there were so many mysteries in the world, and the Great Omani's escape act was one of the first to consume him. What, he wondered, was so clever about escaping, when you had tied yourself up in the first place? Now, if someone else had tied him up, that would be very different!

But he never got a chance to study the act for long. When the Great Omani spotted him, he would shout at him angrily that his act wasn't free, and people had to pay to watch him by putting money in his hat. 'I don't take pennies, son. Minimum a shilling on this bit of the pier – so pay up or clear off!'

Rod did not think the act was worth a penny, let alone a shilling, which was an entire week's pocket money. For him, there was much better value inside the amusement arcade. One row of wooden slot machines there, in particular, fascinated him.

They had their names displayed on the outside, such as *Haunted House!, Guillotine!, Gulliver's Lilliput World!* You pushed a penny coin into the slot and things would start to happen. The interior would light up behind the glass viewing window. He liked the haunted house. A coffin lid would rise up to reveal a glowing skeleton. A spider would drop down and rise up. Doors would open and apparitions would appear and disappear. The lights would flicker. It was like a cross between a very spooky doll's house and a miniature ghost train.

Rod had never been on the real ghost train, further down towards the end of the pier, because he'd seen people coming off it looking terrified; it scared him too much. Also, it was too expensive for his tiny budget. He could have six goes on these slot machines for the price of one sixpenny ghost train ride.

But the machine he liked the most, on which he spent most of his shilling each week, was the *Guillotine!*

He would push his penny coin into the slot, and then watch as a blindfolded Marie Antoinette was dragged to the guillotine, placed face down, and then after some moments a character would pull a lever, the blade would slide down, slice clean through her neck, and her head would drop into a basket. Then the lights would go out again.

Every time he watched, he wondered, was she still conscious after her neck had been severed and, if so, for how long? And what, if anything, did she think about while her head was lying in that basket, in those final moments of her existence?

Years later, as a forty-year-old adult, the attractions on the pier, like its name, had changed. The wooden penny-in-the-slot machines had been moved to a museum underneath the Arches, close to the pier, where they were maintained in working order. You could buy a bag of old penny coins and still activate the machines. He took his own kids to see them, but they weren't impressed; they were more interested in computer games.

But his own fascination never went away. He was enjoying a successful career as an actuary for a reinsurance group, in which his natural curiosity was able to flourish. His job was to calculate the odds, much like a bookmaker might, of accidents and disasters happening. One role, for instance, was to calculate the odds against rainfall happening in particular regions. In some parts of the south of England, much though the country had a reputation for being wet, he was able to demonstrate that, in fact, there were only ninety-four days a year when it actually rained – he defined it as there being precipitation at some point during the twenty-four hours of the day.

Some of his friends called him a dullard, obsessed with facts and statistics. But he really, genuinely, loved his work. He liked to refute the saying that 'No man on his deathbed ever said, "I wish I had spent more time in the office."'

'I would say that,' he would announce proudly in the pub and at parties. And it was true. Rod loved his work, he really did. Facts and statistics were his life; these were the things that gave him his bang. He loved to analyse everything, and break it all down to its component elements. He loved to be able to tell people stuff they didn't know – such as what was the most dangerous form of travel, what your percentage chances were of dying of a particular ailment, or how long you were likely to live if you reached fifty.

It used to infuriate his wife, Angie. 'God, don't you ever *feel* anything?' she would ask him.

'Feelings are dangerous,' he would retort, which angered her further. But he wasn't being frivolous, he genuinely believed that. 'Life is dangerous, darling,' he would say, trying to placate her. 'No one gets out of here alive.'

Once at a dinner party, he had raised the subject of his childhood fascination with the slot machine with the guillotine. A neurosurgeon friend, Paddy Mahony, sitting opposite him had said that he reckoned after being guillotined, people could remain conscious for up to two minutes. Or was it ninety seconds? Rod could not quite remember, although it was pretty relevant now, since one moment he had been texting his mistress, Romy, and the next he had looked up to see all the traffic ahead of him on the fast lane of the M4 had stopped dead.

He was surprised at just how calm he felt as the bonnet of his Audi, bought for its safety points after analysis of crash statistics, slid under the tailgate of the truck. He frowned, thinking that there had been a law passed, surely, that they needed a bar to stop his car doing just what it was now doing – sliding under the tailgate while the occupants are decapitated. Like the guillotine.

Funny, he thought, *to be lying on a wet road, looking up at exhaust pipes and bumpers and number plates and brake lights.* Not the way he would have chosen to exit this world, but it certainly was interesting to see if Paddy was right. Although, of course, he could not see his wristwatch. That was still in the car attached to the rest of him.

'Hello,' he said to a woman who climbed out of one of those little Nissan Micras, a bilious purple colour. 'Could you tell me the time?' He mouthed. But no sound came out.

She screamed.

This was not going well. Then she vomited. Fortunately she did not splash him. His sense of smell was acute at that moment. He felt no pain, but smelled diesel and puke. It was normally a smell that instantly made him puke too. But not today. He heard a siren.

Suddenly, he remembered that old nuclear bomb thing of his youth. The *four-minute warning.* The warning you might get in the event of a pending nuclear attack. People being asked what they would do if they had only four minutes left to live.

That threat had sort of faded away and been forgotten.

He remembered another dinner party he'd been at a while ago. Everyone was asked what they would do in their last four minutes. Then someone, he could not remember who, had suggested just one minute. 'That would really concentrate your mind!' he had said.

Now, by Rod's calculation, he would be lucky to have another minute. *Strange,* he thought, *our obsession with the time. Here I am, able to count my future in seconds, and I'm not worrying how my wife and kids are going to cope. All I want to know is the bloody—*

GIFTS IN THE NIGHT

During my research for the spooky novels I wrote in the late 1980s and the early 1990s, I interviewed a large number of people, from all walks of life, who believed they'd had a paranormal experience of some kind. Some years back, seated next to HRH Princess Anne at a charity dinner – she's a sparky lady and great fun to talk to – she told me a very convincing story about a friend of hers who had a poltergeist in her home. And the late great comedian, Michael Bentine, made my hairs stand on end with stories about his father who carried out exorcisms.

I talked to mediums, clairvoyants, scientists, psychologists, psychiatrists, and became good friends with a truly extraordinary character, the late Professor Bob Morris, who had been appointed as the first Chair of Parapsychology in the UK, heading up the Koestler Parapsychology Unit at Edinburgh University. What made Bob Morris a fascinating man, to me, was that he was a scientist – a physicist – who had had a paranormal experience early in his life, which had opened his mind to the existence of the paranormal.

I learned from him an astounding statistic: that a survey was taken, in 1922, of scientists in Britain who believed in God. The results came out at 43 per cent. The same survey was repeated in 1988 and, very surprisingly, the results showed exactly the same percentage. But there had been a significant shift: fewer biologists now believed in God, but more mathematicians and physicists proclaimed themselves believers.

I listened to a large number of views and stories of strange experiences, and I talked to leading sceptics as well. For eighteen months, in 1990 and 1991, I hosted a regular Friday night radio phone-in show, taking calls from members of the public who had experienced something uncanny, or inexplicable, ranging from sightings of apparitions or bizarre coincidences to past-life memories or a sense of déjà-vu. In 1993 I was commissioned by the BBC to present a show in Scotland, in which I was given carte blanche to travel around interviewing people who claimed to have had paranormal encounters.

Many of the stories I was told were chilling, some were distressing, but the majority, when I examined them further, turned out to have credible rational explanations. I learned that both the Anglican Church and the Roman Catholic Church employ diocesan exorcists – although they are given the less dramatic titles of Ministers of Deliverance.

The role of a Minister of Deliverance is to investigate any apparent paranormal occurrence brought to the attention of the local vicar or priest, and for which they had no explanation. But of major importance in this role is to rule out the paranormal wherever possible and produce rational explanations. As an example, there was a papal edict in the Catholic Church, issued over two centuries ago, warning priests not to confuse demonic possession with the tricks played on people's minds as a result of grief, and stating that no exorcisms should be carried out on anyone within two years of them suffering a bereavement.

I became good friends with one Minister, a senior clergyman with considerable experience of people who claimed to have had paranormal encounters, and who is himself an extremely caring and rational man. I will call him Francis Wells. He is a modern-thinking clergyman, with a distinguished university background in psychology, who has deep faith but once confided in me that he had problems with the conventional biblical image of God. His primary objective in all cases brought to him was to try to find a rational explanation. For instance, he was regularly called in to investigate people deeply disturbed by occurrences following Ouija board sessions. His view of such sessions, after over thirty years of investigations, is that the Ouija does not open up channels to the spirit world, but rather opens up the Pandora's box of demons that each and every one of us carries in our psyche.

I asked him if he had ever, in his career to date, experienced something that could not be explained in a rational way. 'Yes,' he replied. 'Twice.'

This is the first story. At his request, to respect their privacy, I have changed the names of the people involved.

In 1987 a young married couple, Geoff and Kerry Wilson, had recently had a baby son, Darren. Geoff worked as a plumber and Kerry was on maternity leave from her local council job in Croydon. They had been living in a rented basement flat in Croydon and had saved enough money to put down the deposit on a small house on a brand new housing development in the area, built by a national brand-name company.

They moved in when Darren was three months old, and were blissfully happy to finally be in a home of their own. Kerry was a keen gardener, and was happy to be home alone with Darren, who was a delightful, happy and calm baby, while Geoff was away much of the day, and often late into the evenings, working his butt off now that he was the sole breadwinner of the family.

Four weeks after they had moved in, early on a late November morning, Kerry woke suddenly, feeling concerned that something was wrong. She looked at the clock and saw it was 7 a.m. The baby monitor was silent and she realized she had missed Darren's normal 3 a.m. feed. She went through into his room and was confronted with every mother's worst nightmare.

Darren lay face down against the mattress. She felt total panic as she gently turned his motionless body over. He was cold, and solid as wood, and his face was a deep mottled blue. The paramedics, who arrived twelve minutes later, were, tragically, unable to resuscitate him.

To add to the hell of the following hours, they then had to deal with the police interrogations. Whilst they were allocated a Family Liaison Officer, a kindly, sympathetic woman PC, they were also subjected to the house being treated as a crime scene, and grilled by two CID officers. They faced the further agony of knowing little Darren was to be subjected to a post-mortem in the mortuary. Police interviews, as well as interviews with a forensic psychologist and a forensic psychiatrist, continued for several days, making them feel – through their intense grief – like criminals and distracting them from the funeral arrangements.

Kerry, who had stopped drinking from the moment she had learned she was pregnant, took to the bottle; Geoff was arrested for drink-driving and faced losing his licence – and his livelihood. He was dependent on his van for his work.

Eventually, they were left alone. Darren's body was released by the Coroner, and he was buried in a tiny white coffin. In the days following the funeral, Kerry and Geoff, occasionally joined by their parents, sat in desolation in the front room of the new house that had, just a short while ago, seemed so full of promise. The little garden at the rear, where Kerry had dug beds on both sides of the lawn with an ambitious planting plan, looked increasingly sad, with the grass growing unkempt and weeds sprouting.

To make them feel even more isolated from normal life, most of the units on the estate were still, as yet, unsold, so they had few neighbours to talk to and share their grief with. Kerry's best friend, Roz, put on a brave face but was totally freaked out, and kept giving excuses why she could not come over. There was just one other young couple, directly across the close – Rob and Mandy King. Mandy was seven months pregnant, and she and her husband felt a kinship with Geoff and Kerry. Kerry's parents were as supportive as they could be; but they were almost equally grief-stricken and, after a while, they began to avoid contact as much as they could because they just distressed Geoff and Kerry more. Their neighbours, Rob and Mandy, became almost their sole lifeline.

Geoff ignored the brown envelopes of bills that fell daily onto the doormat. He really didn't care about anything. He could function just sufficiently to make the occasional three-mile round trip to the supermarket, with his wife driving, to buy basic food and cheap wine. They were each drinking a bottle a day.

The doctor prescribed tranquilizers for Kerry, and also sleeping pills after her seventh consecutive night of lying awake crying. Geoff tried to cope without either. He spent his days sitting in front of the television, watching anything that was on, absorbing nothing. He used to like reading, but the pages of any book he picked up contained a meaningless jumble of words.

At 2 a.m. on a Wednesday night, three weeks on, Geoff woke, badly needing to pee and his head throbbing from the booze. He climbed out of bed without turning the light on – not wanting to wake Kerry – pulled on his dressing gown, found his slippers, and shuffled out onto the dark landing, heading to the toilet.

And he stopped in his tracks.

In his own words, this is what happened next:

I saw an endless stream of people, all in white robes, each carrying a small parcel wrapped in white cloth. They were coming out of the wall in front of me, to the right, crossing the landing, and disappearing into the wall on the left.

They were oblivious to me. One after another. Then another, then another. Silent, serious, men and women, some young, some not so young. All in these strange robes. All carrying a white parcel.

For some moments, I thought I must be dreaming. But I was awake. I did that cliché thing of pinching myself, and realized that I was very definitely awake. I stood there, quaking with fear, unsure what to do. I don't remember for how long I stood there. Some of them seemed to half turn towards me, as if there was something they wanted to communicate, but then they carried on, fading into the wall on the left hand side.

I backed away, turned and dived into our bedroom, slamming the door shut, the noise waking Kerry.

'Wossat?' she murmured, sleepily.

I turned on the light. I had to wake her fully. She needed to see this – or convince me that I was hallucinating. I told her to go and take a look at the landing.

'I'm so sleepy,' she said.

I felt really bad about disturbing her. But I had to be reassured I wasn't either hallucinating or going mad. Every inch of my flesh was covered in goosebumps. I'd never, ever, felt so spooked in my life.

'Please go and look on the landing,' I pleaded.

Finally, very reluctantly, she slipped out of bed, in her nightdress, padded across the floor and opened the door, with me right behind her.

Then she just stood there, mesmerized. I will always remember her face as she turned to me for as long as I live.

It was the face of someone who has stared into the pit of Hell.

We clutched each other, and stared at the procession of people. It went on and on and on. I don't know for how long we stood there. These eerie people in white, carrying their parcels of white, all looking serious, purposeful, on a journey, heading towards a clear destination.

'What's going on?' she murmured, terrified.

'I don't know,' I replied, equally terrified, but trying, unsuccessfully, to remain calm. I was having a dream, a nightmare, that was the only possible explanation.

Then Kerry lit a cigarette. That was another thing – she had given up smoking – her thirty-fags-a-day habit – for Darren. I'd given up too, in support. She handed me the Silk Cut, and I took a drag, inhaled the sweet smoke, and that was when I knew this was for real.

The next few minutes were a blur. I don't remember us leaving the house and running across the road. All I can remember is hammering on the door of our neighbours, then finding the bell and ringing it, and a minute or so later seeing light come on behind the glass panel at the top of the door. Moments later, it opened and Rob stood there in his pyjamas, with a quizzical expression I will never forget. I almost hugged him in relief.

'Need to use your phone!' I blurted. 'Police. I'm so sorry. I—'

Suddenly, away from the madness that our house had

become, none of what we had experienced seemed real any more. I've never had any truck with God, or the supernatural, none of that shit. My dad died when I was twenty, when an Army truck rammed the back of his car during a motorway pile-up. My mum died of cancer two years later – triggered by shock and grief, my sister always reckoned. Thanks, God!

I dialled the 9s, then was struck dumb when the operator answered, asked me which service I required. When a Police operator came on the line, I suddenly felt very foolish. 'We've got . . . well . . . I sort of think . . . intruders in our house,' I managed, finally. And I felt a right dickhead as I replaced the receiver.

Rob's wife, Mandy came downstairs in her dressing gown, wondering what the commotion was. 'I'm sorry,' I blurted out. 'There's something strange going on in our house – I've just called the Police.'

Kerry suddenly collapsed on the sofa, sobbing. Mandy, bless her, sat down beside her and put an arm around her. And in a sudden moment of normality said, 'I'll make us all a cup of tea, shall I?' She got up and went into the kitchen.

It seemed only moments later that streaks of blue light were skittering off the front windowpane. We heard a car pull up and I opened the front door to see two male uniformed officers standing there, one a middle-aged Sergeant, the other a much younger rookie constable, holding their caps in their hands.

Rob invited them in, and I stood in the little hallway, explaining what we had just seen to looks of extreme incredulity from Croydon's finest. When I had finished, all too aware that what I had said sounded like the ramblings of a crazy, the Sergeant took a step forward and sniffed my breath.

'Been drinking, have you, sir?' he said, with extreme sarcasm.

'No more than usual,' I replied.

'Walking out of the wall, are they, sir? All carrying something?'

I nodded.

'It's nearly Christmas,' he said. 'Maybe they're bringing you Christmas presents. Was one of them dressed in red robes, with a long grey beard? I didn't see any reindeer on the roof.'

Both their radios crackled into life. Both listened to the message. 'We're just attending at Ecclestone Close. We'll be on our way in a minute,' the Sergeant said.

'Go and take a look,' I said. 'I've left the front door open.'

The Sergeant nodded at the rookie and pointed across the road with his finger. The young constable went out. Mandy came into the hall. 'I'm just making a cuppa – would you both like one?' she asked.

'No, thank you, ma'am,' the cynical cop replied. 'There's an accident on the A23 we need to attend.'

That made me feel bad. That I was keeping these officers from something far more important. Rob, the Sergeant and I stood there in awkward silence.

'Nice development this estate,' the Sergeant said. 'Not been here before.'

'We've only recently moved in,' I said.

Moments later the front door was pushed open and the rookie stood there. His face was sheet white and he was shaking like a leaf. He could barely speak. 'Sarge,' he said. 'I . . . I . . . I think you'd better go and take a look. I think I'm imagining things.'

Both officers strode back across the road and entered our house. I went into the living room and sat down beside Kerry, who was still sobbing, and tried to comfort her. Mandy brought us mugs of tea and a moment of normality returned as she asked us if we wanted milk and sugar.

Then there was a rap on the front door. I followed Rob as he went to answer it.

The Sergeant stood there, looking as shaken as his colleague, his face ashen. After some moments, the senior officer spoke. 'I don't know what to say Mr . . . er . . . Mr Wilson?'

I nodded.

'It's not someone playing a prank on you, is it?'

'What do you think?' I replied.

'I didn't . . . didn't see . . . didn't see any projector,' the rookie said.

'I don't know what to think, sir,' the Sergeant said. 'I've not seen . . . not experienced . . . nothing . . . nothing like this in all the years I've been a police officer. I'm at a loss what to suggest. Has this happened before?'

'No,' I said very firmly.

'I . . . I approached the . . . the intruders,' he said. 'I walked right through one and it was like stepping into a freezer. I think you'd better not go back to the house, not just yet.'

He was quivering all over, so much that I broke out in goosebumps myself at the sight of him.

'They can stay the night here,' Rob said kindly. 'We'll put them in the spare room.'

The two police officers looked like they could not wait to get away from here, but not because they needed to attend the other incident, the crash on the A23, the main London road. It looked to me as if they wanted, right then, to be anywhere but here. They seemed totally out of their comfort zone and, if nothing else, at least it gave me some reassurance that Kerry and I were not mad.

The Sergeant was holding his notebook in his hand and he tried to jot down some details, but his hand was shaking so much that after a few tries, he stopped. 'I'm sorry, Mr Williams – I mean Wilson,' he said to me. 'I think I'm as shook up as you are. I . . . I don't know . . . are you and Mrs Wilson of any religious persuasion?'

I told him we were both sort of lapsed Anglicans. I'd been confirmed as a child, and so had Kerry. But neither of us had

had much time for religion since, although both of us had had parental pressure to have little Darren baptized.

The Sergeant said, 'The only thing I can suggest is that you contact your local vicar in the morning and see what he has to say about this, Mr and Mrs Wilson.'

We stayed the night in our kind neighbours' spare room, and in the morning ventured home. All was quiet there, back to normality. We packed some of our belongings into a suitcase and moved, temporarily, to Kerry's parents' home in Surbiton. Later that morning we drove to see our vicar – who we had never met before. He was a young clergyman, who although a tad sceptical at first, listened intently to our story. While we were sitting in his house, he phoned the police and asked to speak to the Sergeant who had attended last night, and was told he was currently off duty and to call back that evening.

At around 7 p.m. he called us at Kerry's parents' home, sounding shaken, telling us the Sergeant had verified our story, and that he was going to contact his diocesan Minister of Deliverance, Francis Wells, for advice.

A week passed, during which we heard nothing, and Kerry and I began to doubt our sanity, despite the fact that the two police officers had witnessed what we had witnessed. Then we received a phone call from Francis Wells, asking if he could come and see us at our house. He was insistent that both of us should be there.

We did some research on him, and learned that he was a highly respected clergyman, with particular interest in the paranormal, and came from an academic background. Both his parents were medics, and he had achieved a double first in psychology from Oxford. He seemed exactly the right person, with a practical mindset, to investigate the phenomena we had encountered, and Kerry and I felt reassured.

Kerry drove us to the house in my van, but refused to go

in. Although it was the middle of the day, I was also too scared to go in alone. We waited outside, and after about twenty minutes, a bright red Alfa Romeo saloon pulled up, and out clambered a very good-looking man in his early thirties, dressed in a business suit, with a very pleasant and gentle demeanour.

Francis Wells was far from what we had been expecting – perhaps a priest in robes, holding a bell, book and candle, like something out of The Exorcist. *He was so normal, so ordinary, and warm-hearted, instantly putting us at our ease and expressing his deepest sorrow at our loss. He asked if he could go inside and take a look at where the apparitions had appeared.*

We agreed, although neither Kerry nor I would go further than the front room. We sat on the sofa, feeling very uncomfortable being back in the house, while he went upstairs. After what seemed an eternity, he came down and sat in a chair opposite us. Kerry found the strength to make us all a coffee and when she had handed out our cups, together with a plate of biscuits, he told us his findings, smiling benignly at us, as if to reassure me and my wife that we were not bonkers, and speaking in a soft, gentle voice.

He started by offering us prayers, and did not seem at all offended when we thanked him but told him that both of us had a problem with religion. He was totally understanding. 'That is absolutely fine,' he said. He sipped some coffee then continued. 'Well, Geoff and Kerry, I've just been upstairs and all seems quiet, for now. I've been researching into the background of your home, and I've discovered something that may offer an explanation, however strange it might seem to you, for what has been happening. I'm assuming you both studied history as part of your curriculum at school?'

Yes, I told him, but it had never really grabbed me. Kerry, however, said it had been one of the few subjects she had loved.

The Minister of Deliverance nodded approvingly at her. 'Do you remember the Great Plague? The bubonic plague?'

'I remember a ditty we learned at school,' Kerry said. '1665 no one left alive. 1666 London burned to sticks.'

The Minister smiled. 'Indeed. But before that – three hundred years earlier – the bubonic plague started; it was called the Black Death. It wiped out over 30 per cent of our population. Towns and villages had plague burial pits. My team has discovered that this housing estate, where we are now, is on the site of an ancient plague burial ground. And the precise location of your house is over a pit where infant victims of the plague were buried.

He went on to tell us that he could not say whether it was the negative energy from all the young babies buried here that had caused the cot death of our baby son, Darren, or whether his death had for some reason triggered this eerie replay of parents bringing their dead infants here.

We put the house on the market, without ever telling prospective buyers about our experience. To our relief, the eventual purchasers were a middle-aged couple with grown-up children. We now live thirty miles away and have never been back.

GHOST PAINTING

This fictional account is based on the second of the two true stories that Francis Wells, the chief Minister of Deliverance of the Anglican Church, told me when I asked him if ever, during his experience of dealing with the paranormal, he had encountered anything for which he had no rational explanation, and which had convinced him of the survival of some element of the human spirit beyond death. As before, to protect their privacy, I have changed the names of the people involved and the precise location. This incident occurred shortly after he had taken up a post which gave him direct responsibility for Sussex.

*

The house had a sad look about it, Meg Ryerson thought, as she stood in the rear garden with her husband, Paul, and the estate agent. Then they walked around to the front again, along the narrow passageway down the side and through the gate, squeezing past the bins.

The interior needed modernizing and the garden, which was a good-sized plot, had been badly neglected. But Meg did not mind that; she had always wanted a garden. The street itself was bright and pleasant, lined with a mixture of bungalows, semi-detached houses and small, detached ones, like number 8. But strangely, on this sunny morning, the house looked like it was permanently in the shade. Meg was good with colours; it had been one of her strengths at art college a decade ago. Perhaps, she thought, standing on the pavement in front of the house now, it was the drab grey paint on the pebbledash rendering on the walls that was doing it.

Whatever.

The house just wasn't ticking many of the boxes on their list. She'd set her heart on somewhere with character, and her dream was one of those elegant white villas in one of the Regency terraces in the Clifton area of Brighton, steeped in history, with canopied windows and views over the rooftops towards the sea. But in all the particulars they had seen – and they had seen a lot, from just about every estate agency in the city of Brighton and Hove over the past three months – those houses had always been out of their price range.

This small, detached Edwardian house, with four bedrooms – two of them tiny – was in a pleasant but uninspiring street that ran south of Brighton's Dyke Road Avenue. It ticked just two of the boxes on their list. The first was that it had a really nice outbuilding at the end of the garden which could, with some TLC, become a studio for Meg to paint in. The other was that it was in their price range – just.

'It does have character,' the agent said. 'And of course the location is very sought after. Just a short walk from the Hove recreation ground and Hove Park. You could make this into a very lovely home.'

'Position,' Paul said to Meg. 'Don't they say that the three most important things in a property are *location, location* and *location*?' He looked at the estate agent, who nodded confirmation.

Meg gave a wan, dubious smile, wondering what it would feel like to live here.

'At the price they are asking,' the agent said, 'it's a bargain.'

Paul led Meg a short distance away, down the street, out of earshot of the estate agent. 'The thing is, darling, you have terrific taste. We could buy this, transform it, and in a couple of years we could make a good profit on it, and then be able to afford something we love more, perhaps in the Clifton area.'

Megan stared up at the mock-Tudor gables, then the brick-tiled carport and the integral garage, feeling a conflict of emotions. Paul was right: it was a great buy. It had a nice garden at the back, with three beautiful, mature trees, and the wooden structure at the far end could make a pleasant studio. But . . .

But.

It really was so *suburban.*

Was it John Lennon who said, *Life is what happens to you while you're busy making other plans*? What would happen if they bought this place and then, for whatever reason, they couldn't sell it in a couple of years? She knew from experience that life never did work out the way you planned it. What if they ended up stuck here for years? Spending the rest of their lives here? Could she be happy in this house forever?

And suddenly she realized she was being ungrateful. There were many people who would love to live in this area, and she was lucky to have a husband who worked damned hard, in a job he didn't particularly enjoy as an accountant in a small Brighton practice, to support her ambition to become a portrait painter. OK, so it didn't have the character she had dreamed of, but they were still young – she was thirty-one and Paul was thirty-three – and if the family they had been hoping to start did come along, this was actually a good and safe location to bring up young children.

'Why are the owners selling?' she asked the agent, a smartly dressed woman about her own age. 'They've only been here just over a year, right?'

'The husband's an economist with an oil company. From what I understand, he got offered a five-year contract in Abu Dhabi, with the chance to make a lot of money, tax-free. They had to make a quick decision, and they took it. They've already gone, and I'm told they are throwing in all the carpets and curtains – and they'll sell you any of the furniture you'd like at a good price.'

'Carpets and curtains cost a fortune,' Paul said, ever the accountant. 'That could save us several grand easily.'

Megan nodded. None of the rooms was furnished to her taste, but they could change that, she supposed, in time. Not having to buy curtains and carpets was a big saving – but not enough to justify buying a house you did not love.

But, she had to admit, the agent was right on one thing. This house was a bargain – and would be snapped up quickly.

*

They moved in on a Friday in late May. Megan was feeling a lot more positive about the house, and already thinking ahead to Christmas that year. The dining room was big enough to seat ten people at a pinch, unlike the one in their flat in Kemp Town where six had been a squeeze. They could have Paul's parents, her brother, her sister and brother-in-law and their four-year-old over. Magic!

By Saturday afternoon, they had got the old-fashioned kitchen, their bedroom and the lounge straight. The dining room, the two spare bedrooms and the garage were still filled with unopened tea chests, put there by the removals company. The summer house at the end of the garden – in reality little more than a glorified shed – was a long way from being habitable, so she had made the lounge into a temporary studio, setting up her easel at one end, and laying out her paints on an old trestle beside it.

At around tea time they had both come close to losing the will to live, and were looking forward to an evening out at the trendy fish restaurant at The Grand – GB1 – with their best friends, Tim and Sally Hopwood.

For the past week, Megan had done nothing but pack, pack and then unpack. She'd been covered in dust from head to toe, and had begun to despair of ever looking human again. But tonight, hey, she was damned well making an effort! They were in their new home, and today was the start of their new life. She felt happy about the house now, loved the view from their bedroom out across the long, narrow garden, with the summer house at the far end – beneath the three beautiful old trees – that would, one day, be her studio. She had started making big plans for the garden, sketching out a design which included a Zen pond, a brick-walled vegetable plot and groups of shrubs.

Paul was in the small third bedroom, upstairs, facing the street, which he had commandeered as his home office, working away on his computer. Megan stepped out of the shower and into her dressing gown, a towel wrapped around her head like a turban, and sat down at her Victorian dressing table. She stared into the mirror, and began to apply her make-up.

And froze. A shiver snaked through her.

In the reflection she could see a middle-aged woman standing right behind her, on one leg, supported by crutches. The woman was staring at her, as if curious to watch the way she was applying her make-up.

For an instant she did not dare move. It felt as if a bolus of ice had been injected into her veins. She spun around.

There was nothing there.

She felt an icy chill crawl up her spine. She broke out in a rash of goose pimples that were so sharp they hurt her. She could, literally, feel her hair rising from her scalp, as if pulled by a magnet.

For some moments she wanted to shout for Paul to come up. But if she told him what she had just seen it would sound stupid, she thought. And besides, she knew that he was well aware she did not love this house, but had agreed to buying it and moving here because it was a good investment opportunity. With his logical mind, he would give her an explanation that would make perfect, rational sense.

So she said nothing.

They went to dinner with their friends and had a great time. Later, in the taxi heading home, nicely fuzzed with several glasses of the delicious wine Paul had chosen, Meg dismissed what she had seen earlier. It had been her imagination working overtime, she decided. They went to bed, and all was fine. All was fine again, throughout Sunday. And Monday.

On Tuesday, one of Paul's clients had invited them both to a dinner at the Hotel du Vin in Brighton. Paul warned her in advance that the client was big in international media, rich and flash, and to dress to kill.

After several hours of retail therapy on the Monday, Megan again sat in front of her dressing table mirror at 6.30 p.m. on the Tuesday night, putting the finishing touches to her make-up. Then she saw the one-legged woman again, standing behind her.

She spun around in her chair.

And again saw nothing.

But this time she was convinced it wasn't her imagination.

In the back of the taxi on the way to dinner, she was about to tell

Paul what she had seen when the cab driver, a strange little man, suddenly said, 'Nice perfume, madam. Armani Code?'

'Yes!' she said, delighted. 'How did you know?'

'Oh, I know these things, uh-huh.'

She grinned at Paul and squeezed his hand. Then she whispered to her husband, 'There's something I need to tell you.'

'What is it?'

'Later.'

'I'm all ears!'

*

Shortly before midnight as a taxi dropped them home, she waited until they had entered the house and closed the front door behind them. Then, emboldened by a little too much wine, she told Paul what she had seen on Saturday night, and again tonight.

Maybe it was because he had drunk too much also, but his reaction was less sceptical than she had been expecting. 'If she's appeared so vividly, why don't you paint her portrait, darling?'

'Maybe I will,' she replied thoughtfully.

Despite a hangover the next morning, Meg set up a fresh canvas on her easel in the living room, then sketched in pencil, the way she always began any portrait, the woman's head and shoulders. So clear was her memory of what she had seen that within half an hour she had begun painting. The face of a handsome woman in her early fifties, with elegant, brown wavy hair tinged grey in places, and wearing a soft green cardigan over a cream blouse, began to appear. As she stood back for a few moments, she noticed a sad expression in the woman's face.

She reminded her of someone, and then she realized who. She looked a little like a younger, less beautiful and less vivacious sister of the actress Joan Collins.

She was so absorbed in her work that two hours passed without her being aware. Then the ringing of the doorbell cut through her concentration.

She was irritated by the interruption, and for a moment was

tempted to ignore it and carry on. But there was a ton of stuff she had ordered online for the house, so she put down her brush and walked through to the front door, not wanting to risk missing a delivery.

To her surprise, a pleasant-looking silver-haired woman of about sixty stood there. She was dressed in a baggy tracksuit top, shapeless brown slacks and trainers. 'Hello,' she said. 'I'm Jenny Marples. My husband and I live right opposite you, at number 17. I'm also the local Neighbourhood Watch co-ordinator. Just thought I'd pop over and say hello to our new neighbours!'

'Nice to meet you,' Meg said, and she meant it. So far she'd not seen a soul in the street, and had been planning to pop round to all their immediate neighbours to introduce herself. She invited Jenny Marples in for a cup of tea, which the woman enthusiastically accepted.

They went first into the kitchen, which Meg was a little embarrassed about as it was so drab and still very untidy, part of the work surface and the table still piled with crockery and kitchen utensils she had not yet found a permanent home for. While the kettle was coming to the boil, Jenny Marples said, 'We barely met the previous owners, you see, they were here for such a short time. They moved in, and then, almost before we'd even got to know their names, they'd gone! Overseas, I'm told.'

'Abu Dhabi. Do you take milk? Sugar?'

She set their cups and saucers on a tray, shook out some chocolate digestives onto a plate, then led the way through into the living room.

'You're an artist?' Jenny exclaimed.

'A struggling one! I'm hoping to get some commissions.'

'You're good!' her neighbour said. 'That is really—'

Then she stopped in her tracks and peered more closely at the portrait on the easel. She turned, with a frown. 'Is that yours, or did you find that here?'

'It's mine,' Meg said, setting the tray down on the coffee table. 'Sort of a work in progress.' Then she caught the strange look on Jenny Marples' face. 'Found it here? What do you mean, exactly?'

'Well . . . that's extraordinary! You see . . .' her neighbour's voice trailed off. She stared back at Meg. 'Is it someone you know?'

Meg felt her face redden. 'Well, not exactly, no. I—' She watched the woman's face closely, feeling a deepening sense of unease as she peered even more intently at the portrait.

'That's Alwyn!' she declared. 'Alwyn Hughes! You painted this? You really painted this?'

'I did.'

'The likeness is incredible. I mean it, incredible. It's her!'

'Alwyn Hughes?'

'You must have copied this from something? A photograph perhaps?'

'I'm sorry, I'm not with you.'

'She used to live here!'

Meg felt the goosebumps rising up her back. 'When . . . when was that?'

'You don't know?'

'I don't. Please tell me.'

The two women sat down opposite each other on the sofas. Jenny looked at her strangely, then back at the portrait again. 'You didn't hear the story? The estate agent didn't tell you?'

'The estate agent told us the previous owners had only been here a short while. Shortly after they moved in, the husband was offered a very lucrative contract for a five-year posting in Abu Dhabi. My husband, Paul, who's an accountant, explained to me that if you want to go into tax exile, you cannot own a home in the UK – so I understand that is the reason why they had to sell the house.'

Jenny Marples nodded. 'That would make sense. They were such a nice couple; they fitted so nicely into the neighbourhood. We were all sorry when they left so suddenly.' She sipped her tea, then glanced at her watch.

'What didn't the agent tell us?' Meg asked.

'It was really so sad, so sad. Alwyn and her husband moved here around the same time that my husband, Clive, and I did. She loved this house so much – well, you know,' she said, tapping her nose in a conspiratorial way, 'this is rather an exclusive area. A lot of people dream of living in Hove 4. It was a bit of a financial stretch for them, but her husband had a job with good prospects, she told me, and although they had mortgaged up to the hilt, their children had grown up and were off their hands, so she hoped that within a few years their financial situation would improve considerably. But they had the most terrible luck.'

She sipped more tea, and fell silent for some moments.

'What was that?' Meg prompted, shooting a glance at the portrait.

'Well, she told me they'd been up to Yorkshire to spend Easter weekend with her husband's parents, in Harrogate. On their way back down the M1 they'd been involved in one of those horrific multiple-vehicle motorway pile-ups. They were rear-ended by a lorry and shunted into a car in front. Her husband was killed instantly, and she was trapped in the car by her legs. They had to amputate one of them, her right leg, to free her.'

Meg felt as if she had been dunked in an ice bath. She recalled, so vividly, the woman she had seen in the mirror, standing behind her on one leg. Her left. Goosebumps crawled over every inch of her skin. 'Poor woman,' she said. 'Poor, poor woman.'

'Terrible.'

Jenny drained her tea. Meg offered her another cup, but the woman looked at her watch anxiously. 'I have to be going,' she said. 'I have a charity fundraising committee meeting.'

'What else can you tell me about Alwyn Hughes?'

She saw Jenny glance at the portrait, as if it was making her increasingly uncomfortable. 'Well, the thing is – the thing that is so sad – is that she loved this house so much. But she had no sympathy from the mortgage company, nor their bank. Her husband hadn't got any life insurance – well, he had, but he'd stopped payments apparently some months before because things weren't going too well at work for him. She did her best to try to get a job, to earn enough to keep up with the mortgage payments, but who wants a middle-aged woman with one leg? The building society were in the process of foreclosing. She should have let them – they had some equity in the house, and she could have bought a little flat with it – but, poor thing, she couldn't see through that. So she hung herself in their bedroom.'

*

The story is best told from Francis Wells' perspective from now on.

I was approached by the Reverend Michael Carsey, a vicar of the Church of the Good Shepherd, and parish priest for the area of Hove 4 in the city of Brighton and Hove. He had been contacted by two of his parishioners, Paul and Meg Ryerson, with a story that he found convincing, but was uncertain how to deal with the situation. He suggested I should talk to them myself.

I visited their very pleasant house, and found them to be very down-to-earth people, both from Anglican backgrounds, but lapsed. The wife, Meg, was more of a believer than her husband, Paul – but that's not to say he was a sceptic; in my view he was more of an agnostic.

I listened to their story, about the apparition of the one-legged woman, and the subsequent verification of her identity from a neighbour. I studied the portrait myself and compared it to photographs I was subsequently able to obtain of the deceased, Alwyn Hughes, and there was little doubt, in my own mind, that the two were the same person.

I decided that, perhaps owing to the manner of her death – suicide – the spirit of Alwyn Hughes was earthbound, which in layman's terms means that the spirit was unaware the body was gone and was manifesting in familiar territory in an attempt to find it.

Whilst nothing of a specifically malevolent nature was occurring, the sightings of Alwyn Hughes were clearly deeply distressing to both Paul and Meg Ryerson, and affecting their quality of life. After interviewing them in depth I became further convinced that they genuinely believed what they had seen.

Neither of them had suffered any bereavement of a family

member or friend within the past two years, and they were both, in my opinion, of sound mind, intelligent and rational people.

The tragic story they told me of the past occupants of their property checked out, with the death of Mrs Alwyn Hughes registered, following the inquest and the Coroner's verdict, as suicide whilst the balance of her mind was disturbed.

I decided that the appropriate, if exceptional, action to be taken in the first instance should be a requiem mass, held in the room in the home where the sightings of the apparition had taken place.

On 3 June, I attended the Ryersons' home, accompanied by a young curate, an extremely rational young man who had begun his career as an engineer and who, I knew from many conversations with him, had a problem, as I did myself at that time, with the conventional image of the Biblical God. So, if you like, we were two sceptics turning up to help two equally sceptical, but very scared and confused people. However, I had decided on a highly conventional approach. We were to hold a full requiem mass, essentially a full, high-Anglican funeral service, in an attempt to lay the unrested spirit to rest.

We set out on a table all the requisites for a full communion, and began the service, with Paul and Meg Ryerson standing in front of us. Part of the way through, as I had broken the bread and given them both the host and was about to offer the communion wine, suddenly each of them went sheet white and I saw them staring past me at something.

I turned around, and to my utter astonishment I saw a woman standing on one leg, on crutches, right behind me. She gave me a quizzical smile, as if uncertain what to do.

Totally spontaneously, I said to her, 'You can go now.'

She smiled at me. Then, as if in a movie, she slowly dissolved, until she had vanished completely. I turned back around to face the Ryersons.

'Incredible!' Meg said.

'That is unbelievable!' her husband said.

'What did you both see?' I asked them.

Each of them, fighting to get it out first, described exactly what I had seen.

I was invited to their home, for a very boozy dinner, a year later. It looked, and felt, like a totally different house. It wasn't just the complete décor makeover it had had. It was imbued with a positive energy that had been totally lacking, or suppressed, previously.

I often think back to that night I saw the one-legged lady, Alwyn Hughes. Had she been a product of my imagination? I think not. But if not, then what, in this rational world of ours, had I seen? A ghost?

Yes, I truly think so.

TIMING IS EVERYTHING

It was finally Tuesday. Tuesdays were always a special day of the week for Larry Goodman, and this one seemed to have taken an extra-long time to arrive. He was excited, like a big kid, his tummy full of butterflies. Not long now! He shaved more closely than normal, applied an extra amount of his Bulgari cologne that the lady of his life particularly liked, dressed carefully, and ate a quick breakfast.

At 7 a.m. he kissed his wife goodbye. Elaine, who was breast-feeding their baby son, Max. She told him to have a great day at the office. He assured her he would, and left their swanky Staten Island home with a broad smile on his face. It was a beautiful, warm, cloudless morning, which made his mood even better, if that was possible. Oh yes, he would have a great day all right – well, a great morning at any rate!

Forty minutes later he alighted from the ferry onto Manhattan, took the subway up to 57th street, and walked the short distance to the midtown Holiday Inn. His secretary would cover for him, as she did every Tuesday and Friday morning at this same time, telling anyone who was looking for him that he had a breakfast meeting out with a client.

Bang on cue, his cell pinged with a text, just as he entered the foyer.

2130 xxxxxxxxxxxxxxxxxxxx

He cast a nervous eye around, but all he saw was a cluster of Japanese tourists, a group of elderly ladies, and a young couple standing at the front desk wearing huge backpacks. This was not a place where players from Wall Street hung out, nor high-powered attorneys.

He texted back:

Get naked xxxxxxxx

He rode the elevator up towards the twenty-first floor, feeling horny – and happy – as hell. Another text pinged:

I am. Hurry or I'll have to start without you xxxxxxxxxxx

He grinned. Marcie had the dirtiest mind he'd ever known. And the most stunning body. And the most beautiful face. And the silkiest long, wavy, flaxen hair. And she smelled amazing.

They always met here, in this anonymous barn of a hotel where neither of them was likely to bump into anyone they knew. Marcie didn't have to lie to her husband about where she was; he was so wrapped up in himself these days, she had told Larry, that he rarely bothered to ask her how her day had been, and even less what she had done.

But with Elaine it was different. Elaine quizzed Larry about every detail of every day, and all the more so since she was now home alone with just Max to occupy her. She called him every few hours, asking him where he was, how his meetings were going, telling him about Max – who had recently started to crawl. Luckily, Erin, his secretary, was a rock.

He was paranoid about divorce. He'd already been through one, brought about by his affair with Elaine, four years back, and it had almost wiped him out financially. He needed to be careful with Elaine, who did not suffer fools gladly and was no fool herself. She was a high-powered divorce lawyer, known affectionately by her colleagues as 'Gripper', owing to her legendary reputation for never letting go of any of her clients' husbands until their balls had been squeezed dry.

Elaine was bored witless being home alone. But not for much longer – she was going back to work as soon as possible. He relished that happening, because then the incessant calls from her would stop. That was the one problem with their relationship having started as an affair – she was permanently suspicious of him, and never more so than now she had time on her hands to think, and fret.

The elevator doors opened and he stepped out, taking a moment to orient himself with the direction arrows for the room numbers. He popped the chewing gum out of his mouth, balled it into a tissue and stuck it in his pocket as he strode down the corridor towards room 2130. Then, his heart pounding with excitement, he stopped outside the door and savoured, for an instant, this delicious moment of anticipation. He could hear music pounding on the other side. Marcie was big into music; she always brought her iPod and two powerful little portable speakers. 'Love Is All Around' by Wet, Wet, Wet was playing, the song which had become his and Marcie's song – corny but potent for them both.

He knocked.

The door opened almost instantly, and he gasped.

'You lied!' he said.

She had.

She wasn't naked at all. Not totally, anyhow. She was wearing black suspenders. And a silver necklace, which he had given her. But nothing else.

Kicking the door shut behind him, he fell to his knees, wrapped his arms around her bare midriff and buried his face into her stomach, then instantly began to explore her with his tongue.

She gasped. He breathed in her scents, the one she had sprayed on, and the natural scents of her body. 'Oh my God, Marcie!'

'Larry!'

She dug her hands so hard into his shoulders he was scared, for an instant, that her nails were going to score his skin. He didn't want to have to try to explain scratch marks to Elaine, and that was one of Marcie's dangers – she could be a bit too wild at times.

Then, as he stood, she tore at his clothes like a wild animal, her lips pressed to his, their tongues flailing, her deliciously cold hands slipping inside his boxers.

She pulled her head back a fraction, grinning, her hands moving around inside his pants. 'Someone's pleased to see me!'

'Someone sure is! Someone's been missing you like crazy all weekend.'

They stumbled across the small room, his trousers around his ankles, and fell, entwined, onto the bed.

'God, I had such a shit weekend. I've missed you so much. I've been dreaming of this, wanting you so badly,' she said.

'I've been wanting you so badly too, babe.'

'Take me from behind.'

He took her from behind. Turned her over and took her again from the front. Then he slid down the bed, down between her slender legs, and pressed his tongue deep inside her. Then she sat on top of him.

Finally, sated, they lay in the soft bed in each other's arms. 'You're amazing,' she said.

'You are too.'

Van Morrison was singing 'Days Like This', and Larry was thinking, *Yes, this is life. Days like this are truly living life!*

'You're the best lover ever,' she said.

'Funny, I was thinking the same about you!'

'You've done this before, haven't you?' Marcie teased.

'Nah – just read about it in a magazine.'

She grinned. 'So how was your weekend?'

'Great,' he said. 'Max vomited over me. Twice.'

'Sweet.' She traced a finger across his forehead. 'But you love him?'

'I do. It's an amazing feeling to be a father.'

'I'm sure you're a great father.'

'I want to be,' he murmured. He glanced at his watch. Time flew when they were together. It had been 8 a.m. only a few moments ago, it seemed. He had a board meeting scheduled for 11.30 a.m. Just a few more minutes, then he'd have to jump in the shower, dress, take the subway back downtown to the reality of his job as a hedge fund manager. And not see Marcie again until Friday.

'I don't know what's going on,' she said. 'Lot of sirens outside.'

But he barely registered what she was saying – he was thinking for a moment about a tricky client meeting he was due to have this afternoon. A major client who was threatening to move a large amount of money to a rival firm.

His meetings with Marcie were affecting his work, he knew. Ordinarily he'd be at his desk by 7.30 a.m., and would begin his day by updating himself on all the overnight changes to the market positions of his clients, then scan the morning's reports from the analysts. Recently, two days a week, he had been neglecting his work – and that was why he now had one very pissed-off client.

He listened some more to Van Morrison, savouring these last moments with Marcie and feeling too relaxed to care. He heard another siren outside. Then another.

Suddenly, his cell rang.

He rolled over and looked at the display. 'Shit', he said. It was Elaine. He pressed the *decline call* button.

Moments later, it rang again.

He declined the call again.

It rang a third time.

He put a finger to his lips. 'It's *her*,' he said. 'Third time. I'd better answer in case there's a problem.'

She rolled over and silenced the music. And now, outside, they could hear a whole cacophony of sirens.

'Hi darling,' he said into the phone. 'Everything OK?'

Elaine sounded panic-stricken. 'Larry! Oh my God, Larry, are you OK?'

'Sure! Fine! Never better – why?'

'Where are you?'

'I'm in the office – just about to go into a board meeting.'

'In the office?'

'Uh-huh.'

'You're in the office?'

'Yeah, I'm in the office, hon.'

There was a long silence. Then she said, her voice almost a shriek, 'You're in *your* office?'

'Yeah, I am. What's the problem? What's going on? Is everything OK? Is Max OK?'

'You haven't been hit on the head?'

'Hit on the head?'

'You're in your office?'

'Yes, shit, I'm in my office!'

'What can you see?'

'What can I see?'

'Tell me what you can see out of your fucking window?' she demanded.

'I see beautiful blue sky. The East River. I—'

'You goddamn liar!' The phone went dead.

Marcie, rolling over, said, 'What's with all the sirens?' She picked the television remote up from her bedside table, and pressed a button on it. The television came alive. She clicked through to a news channel. A panicky looking female news reporter, holding a microphone in her hand, was standing with her back to the building Larry recognized instantly. It was where he worked. Up on the eighty-seventh floor of the South Tower of the World Trade Center.

The newscaster had not seen, yet, the horror unfolding behind her as the skyscraper collapsed in on itself. Terrified people were running past her, some with blood on their faces, many covered in grey dust.

'Shit . . . what . . . what the—?' he said, shooting a glance at his Tag Heuer watch, on which the time and the date were clearly displayed.

It was 9.59 a.m., 11 September 2001.

ART CLASS

This is a true story. It was told to me by a friend whose father was a well-known art dealer in Mayfair, and it took place in 1962. I have changed the names, but little else.

The Denempont Gallery was located on Albermarle Street in Mayfair where, along with neighbouring Cork Street, many of London's smartest art dealers were housed. The gallery specialized in French Impressionist paintings with impeccable provenance, and it was generally acknowledged that no London dealer knew more about this particular period than its proprietor, James DeVere Denempont.

Sellers would come to him as their first port of call, because of his reputation for either paying the highest prices, or arranging the sale of important works at what were regularly record prices. Potential buyers came to him because they knew they would always get the real deal.

Denempont was a portly, balding, bon viveur of fifty-five, who had a penchant for chalk-striped, double-breasted Savile Row suits, Turnbull and Asser shirts and hand-made shoes from Lobb. He usually wore the salmon pink and cucumber green tie of the Garrick Club, and lunched there without fail every day of the working week. In fact, on this particular Thursday in June, he was just about to leave his stately office on the floor above the gallery, and take a stroll in the fine sunshine over to Garrick Street, a leisurely fifteen minutes away, just past Leicester Square, when his intercom buzzed.

It was his secretary. 'Mr Denempont, a lady's just come into the gallery who is very anxious to speak to you.'

'Could she come back later, Angela? I'm just on my way to lunch.'

'I did suggest that, but she says she has to catch a plane to Italy this afternoon.' Then, in a tone of voice that she used when something was important, she said, 'I think you should have a word with her.'

'All right,' he said, slightly irritated. He was lunching with an old friend and important client, Angus Hobart, a hereditary peer, whom he did not want to keep waiting. 'Tell her I can only spare five minutes. Shall I come down?'

'She'd like to see you in private.'

'Very well, show her up.'

He crushed out the stub of his morning Montecristo in his ashtray, buttoned up his waistcoat, stood up, pulled on his jacket and went around his desk towards the door. Moments later his secretary opened it and a tall, elegant and very classy-looking lady of about fifty entered. She was dressed in that almost impossibly stylish way that only rich Europeans knew how, and she was extremely beautiful. And despite the warmth of the day she was wearing gloves.

'Mr Denempont?' she said in an exquisite Italian accent. 'My name is Contessa Romy Di Valieria Massino.' She proferred her hand and he shook it, then offered her a seat in front of his desk.

He sat back down behind it, shooting a discreet glance at his Patek Philippe watch. 'How can I help you, Contessa?' he asked.

'I understand you have an engagement,' she said, 'so I will not keep you for more than a few minutes. Your name was given to my husband by Marcus Leigh-Hoye as someone we should talk to.'

Leigh-Hoye was a friend and fellow art dealer, who specialized in early Dutch masters, a man who was very definitely not a time-waster. Denempont's interest was immediately piqued. And it was about to become even more so. 'Ah, yes, Marcus is a good man,' he said.

'Yes,' she said. 'My husband and I have bought many pictures from him over the years.'

If she had said that she had bought just *one* painting from Marcus Leigh-Hoye, Denempont would have been impressed – and he was not a man who impressed easily. But the word *many* set all kinds of positive connections firing off in his synapses. Mostly to do with money. For, while he loved fine art, he loved money even more. If you went shopping in Marcus Leigh-Hoye's Cork Street gallery, your entry level purchase wasn't going to leave you with much change from a quarter of a million pounds.

He leaned forward. 'So how can I help you?'

'My husband and I need to raise some money – we have very expensive repairs to our palazzo in Firenze, but more importantly we are faced with some very heavy taxation which, if my husband cannot pay, could be ruinous for us. We could have many of our assets seized. One of our biggest is our collection of French

Impressionist pictures. Marcus Leigh-Hoye told my husband you are the best man to sell such a collection.'

'And what pictures do you have?' he asked. 'And by which artists?'

She opened her Hermès bag and pulled out a sheath of papers, clipped together, which she handed to him.

He pulled on his half-moon tortoiseshell glasses and began to read. She lit a cigarette and waited patiently, watching him.

Within less than a minute his eyes were almost out on stalks. This was some collection! Almost every great name among the Impressionist painters was included. Monet; Renoir; Pissarro; Manet; Cézanne; Matisse; Sisley. Included amongst them were some incredibly rare and valuable unfinished works.

When he had finished reading he looked back at her. She stubbed the lipsticky butt of her cigarette out in the ashtray alongside the stub of his cigar and crossed her legs in a sudden display of anxiety. 'What do you think, Mr Denempont?' she asked in a charming, almost innocent voice.

Millions! That's what he was thinking. Millions! This was potentially one of the most important sales in years. He was already calculating his potential commission. But there was a problem. A big, big, problem. 'May I ask where these paintings are housed?'

'In our home in Firenze,' she said.

'Excuse me one moment, please,' he said, and pressed the intercom. 'Angela, see if you can get hold of Lord Hobart and tell him I'm going to be a bit late.' Then he turned his attention to the Contessa. 'Forgive me if you already know this, but it is almost impossible to get an export licence for works of art housed in Italy. There would, of course, be a certain value for this collection sold within Italy – but nothing remotely comparable to their value here or in the United States. I've tried before for Italian clients, and even with –' he held up his right hand and rubbed his fingers together, not wanting to actually say the word *bribery* – 'it's impossible.'

'Where are they worth the most?' she asked, unperturbed. 'Here or in the United States.'

'Undoubtedly the States at present. There are a number of fabulously wealthy collectors there who will pay a premium for rare works of art, just to have them in their private collections for their eyes only. Some of them will even buy stolen works – not that I would deal with those people,' he hastened to add.

She pursed her lips. 'So you could arrange the sale of these in the United States?'

'There are plenty of potential buyers there. In New York, Los Angeles and elsewhere. I could get you the best prices for them in New York. But . . .'

He watched her tap another cigarette out of an expensive-looking holder. 'I'm being impolite,' he said. 'Can I offer you something to drink? Coffee? A glass of Champagne?'

'If you have Champagne, that would be very nice,' she said.

He pressed the intercom again and requested two glasses of Pol Roger. Winston Churchill's favourite and good enough for him as his house standard.

'I'm afraid Lord Hobart has already left to meet you,' his secretary said.

'Call the Garrick and tell them to apologize, and for him to start without me.' He looked back at the Contessa.

'And the *but* is?' she asked.

'It's rather a big *but*, I'm afraid. The *but* is that you would have to get the pictures to New York yourself. I couldn't be involved in that.'

'You mean, smuggle them?'

'That's your only option.'

He saw her eyes widen. She drew on her cigarette, holding it in her gloved fingers. She was without doubt not only a very beautiful and smart lady, but tough, too.

'So, OK, how would I do that?'

'You'd be taking a big risk. If you got caught you could end up forfeiting the lot.'

She shrugged. 'If we do nothing, we are going to lose much of what we have, Mr Denempont.' Then her eyes narrowed. 'Marcus Leigh-Hoye told my husband that you are a man he trusts completely. And that you are a man who is prepared to – how you say in your country – bend the rules? That is good enough for us. We need to bend the rules. How are we to do this?'

'You really want to know?'

'Yes.' She was emphatic.

Their Champagne arrived.

'OK, I'll tell you what I would do if these were my pictures and I wanted to get them out of Italy.'

She raised her glass and sipped. 'Yes?'

'Your biggest problem is the countries signed up to the Unidroit Convention on Stolen or Illegally Exported Cultural Objects.'

'Which are?'

'Every European nation.'

She looked unfazed. 'So what would you propose?'

'I'd take all the canvases off their stretchers, put them in the bottom of a suitcase and set off on what looks like an innocent motoring trip across Europe. The key to this being a success would be the timing of your arrival at the borders. I would suggest crossing frontiers in the middle of the night, when customs officers are tired and not so alert – at 4 a.m. no one is at their best. Get to London, where they are the least diligent about exported arts – there are no export customs at London's Heathrow Airport, for example – then fly to New York from there.'

'With the paintings at the bottom of my suitcase?'

'Precisely. Their weight will be insignificant. But you are taking a massive risk.'

'In our situation, is that a risk you would take, Mr Denempont?'

He hesitated. 'If I had no other option then yes, I think I would. But you must understand, Contessa, I cannot advise you to do this. I'm simply telling you what I would consider doing. The risk you face in any European country is serious. Confiscation of the entire collection. You could lose millions.'

'As I pointed out, we are going to lose millions if we do nothing,' she said.

'It has to be your decision.'

'So, OK, let us suppose we succeed in arriving in New York with the pictures. Will we have a problem with potential buyers because we do not have an export licence from Italy?'

'Not with the collectors I know there,' he said. 'No problem at all.'

He began once again to compute his potential commission. It would be a big sum. A very big one indeed!

She smiled and raised her glass. 'I think, possibly, we may have a plan – no?'

He raised a defensive hand. '*Your* plan, Contessa. I know nothing about it!'

She raised her glass again and drained it. 'You know – nothing! *Nada!*' She grinned, then stood up. As she reached the door she turned and said, 'I look forward to seeing you in New York. One of my favourite cities.'

'I'll be more than happy to carry your suitcases, Contessa.'

'I might hold you to that. Marcus was right, I think, when he said you were our man. I appreciate your honesty. *Arrivederci!*'

In a swirl of classy perfume, she was gone.

*

Reality was a drizzly, late November Thursday, a few minutes before midnight. While their diminutive, elderly retainer, Vincenzo, hefted the Contessa's bags into her Alfa, she stood beside her husband, nervously squeezing his hand, her stomach feeling like jelly. In the gloomy darkness, beneath the crumbling portico, with the solitary overhead lamp shining down on the wet paintwork of the car, she felt anything but confident. She had streaks of dirt on her face and her gloveless hands were grimy – all part of her cover story.

Vittorio, Conte Di Valieria Massino, a tall, elegant man, dressed in a pale blue cashmere sweater over a cream shirt, paisley cravat and crisply pressed slacks, squeezed her hand back, trying to give her reassurance, but in reality feeling very nervous, too. It should be he who was making the journey, but the London dealer, James Denempont, was experienced in helping people smuggle works of art out of Italy and was adamant that a woman travelling alone would be less likely to attract the attention of customs officers than a man.

They were taking a terrible risk. A long prison sentence for Romy and the confiscation of their works of art, which would leave them in financial ruin. The alternative was equally unthinkable, though.

This magnificent palazzo, up here in the hills close to Florence, had originally been built in 1588 as a summer home for Catherine de Medici, although she had died without ever seeing it finished. It had been in Vittorio's family for over four centuries now. He'd grown up here, and it was where, in turn, he and his wife had raised their four children. He was now its custodian. Aristocrats like himself never really viewed themselves as owning their grand houses. He regarded himself merely as a curator, trying to preserve the palazzo and hand it on to the next generation in slightly better condition than when he had inherited it.

Now he risked losing it through a convergence of unlucky factors. The first was being swindled by his trusted accountant, who had convinced him to invest vital cash, which he had been keeping in reserve for maintenance works, into a printing business. It turned out to be a scam, set up by his lawyer who had absconded to Brazil. The second was the arrival of a crippling tax bill, thanks to the same accountant, who had been siphoning off the tax Vittorio thought he'd been paying for the past decade into a Panama bank account. The third, just two months ago, was the grim news from a structural engineer that the house was riddled with dry rot, to the point where parts of the upstairs were too dangerous to inhabit and had to be sealed off. The estimate for repairs was hundreds of millions of lire.

Other than the property itself, their assets were the art treasures housed in the palazzo's grand rooms – some of which he had inherited and some which he and Romy had collected during better financial times. These Impressionist pictures, now taken off their stretchers and lying at the bottom of a suitcase in the Alfa, were the latter, so at least in disposing of them it did not feel like he was selling off the family silver. He watched Vincenzo close the boot.

They were all set.

They'd discussed for an age what car she should drive on this trip. Her convertible sports Mercedes, which she loved, might attract too much attention, they decided. As would his Jaguar. So they had bought, second-hand, an Alfa Giulietta 1600 Ti saloon. Sporty but relatively inconspicuous. And it had the advantage of a large boot.

She slipped behind the wheel. He kissed her on the cheek, wished her good luck, then slammed the door. She fired up the engine and drove off fast, as she always drove, along the driveway lined with cypress trees. After a moment he saw her brake lights come on and wondered if she had forgotten something or was having a change of heart. Then he saw a faint glow inside the car and realized she had lit a cigarette.

He went inside and had Vincenzo pour him a very large single malt. A short while later he poured himself a second one, eyeing the time. At this time of night, with the traffic light, it would be an easy two hours to the nearest crossing point, near Locarno, into Switzerland. Romy planned to stop before then and get an espresso, to kill a little more time. With luck, she would be through the border controls by a quarter past three. Then she had about a twenty-minute drive to a hotel, where she would spend the rest of the night and much of tomorrow. She had already phoned them to explain she would be hours late, giving them the same story she would give to any border official if she was challenged about why she was driving alone at this hour of the morning. Her brother-in-law had recently died; she was going to take her sister away on a short motoring holiday to Scotland.

*

The barrier at the Italian sector of the border control was up, and two officials in the booth, engaged in a conversation, didn't bother to look at her. She slowed, her stomach in knots, then drove on. There was still the more efficient Swiss border control to go through a few kilometres further on.

Sure enough the barrier was down, blocking the road. She pulled up, lowered her window and picked her passport up off the seat beside her. The official peered at her from beneath the peak of his hat and frowned, clearly studying the smears on her face. Then, as she handed over her passport, he said something in German.

'*Scusi?*' she replied.

This time speaking in fluent Italian he asked kindly, 'Have you had an accident? Is everything all right?'

'Thank you,' she said, 'I'm fine. I had a flat tyre a few miles back, but I managed to change it myself with the help of a gentleman who kindly stopped.' She raised her hands to show how grimy they were. As an additional precaution, in case anyone checked out her story, the spare wheel was lying loose with the luggage in the boot, partially deflated. Although she carried a foot pump in the car, just in case she really did get a flat.

Satisfied, he nodded, stamped her passport and handed it back. 'Be careful now you don't have a spare any more, Contessa. Are you going far?'

'No, I plan to stop at the first hotel I find and stay until the morning, then I'll find a garage to get it fixed.'

'Yes, I think that would be sensible. A lady on her own in the middle of the night is very vulnerable. Perhaps you would be safer to pull in here and wait until dawn?'

'I'll be fine,' she said. 'But thank you for your kindness.'

'I'll alert the Polizei who patrol this road to keep an eye out for you.'

The very word made her tremble, and she hoped her nervousness did not show.'

'Thank you, I appreciate that.'

'What is your registration number?'

She gave it to him and he wrote it down. 'There is a pleasant hotel about fifteen kilometres along this road. L'Auberge des Pins. I would try them, if they are open at this hour.'

'I'll look out for that,' she said. Then she gave him a cheery wave and drove on, breathing a sigh of relief. She checked in her mirror and saw a large lorry had pulled up at the checkpoint. Good, she thought, he would be distracted. She put her foot down and accelerated hard into the night.

After several minutes of driving fast along the dark road through a valley, she saw a speck of light appear in her mirror. It rapidly grew brighter and she felt a stab of anxiety. She put her foot down harder, until the speedometer needle passed 160 kph. Then 170. Still the light kept on growing brighter. In another minute she was being dazzled by it, right on her tail now.

She felt nervous, half watching the light, half concentrating on the curving road ahead. Still the light stayed on her tail. It had to be a motorbike.

Was it police? Or had one of their servants passed on information to some crooks? She pressed harder on the pedal, pushing the speed up to 180 kph, and beyond her comfort zone. Pines, road signs and occasional houses flashed past. The yellow line in the middle of the road stretched out ahead and the Alfa felt as if it were on rails, but she was too scared to feel exhilarated. She wasn't sure whether to slow and let the bike pass, or keep on to her destination. But she was scared of crashing.

God, she thought, imagine crashing, and all the millions of dollars' worth of paintings in the boot being destroyed?

Then the lights ahead picked up the name of a village, and a 50-kph speed limit sign. Could she take the risk of ignoring it? What if it was police behind her? She reduced her speed slightly and suddenly, to her relief, the motorbike roared past, carrying on at high speed, its tail light fading away into the night as she decelerated further, bringing her speed down to a much more comfortable 80 kph, until she was through the village and back out on the open road.

She was shaking, she realized, her hands trembling on the wood-rimmed steering wheel. Then, to her relief, she saw the welcoming sign for her night stop, L'Auberge des Pins, five Ks ahead. She had not told the border official that she had a reservation there and had warned them she would not be arriving until the early hours of the morning.

Drenched in perspiration, she finally pulled up outside the front entrance of the hotel. Ten minutes later, having given a massive tip to the night porter who had carried her bags up and then brought her a large brandy, she sat down on a sofa in her suite, cradling the glass, and lit a cigarette. Then she phoned her husband to say she was safe, and smiled at her two large Louis Vuitton suitcases. One contained the clothes, washbag and makeup bag she needed for the trip. The other, beneath an assortment of underwear and dresses, contained a conservative five million pounds' worth of Impressionist canvases, all lying at the bottom, removed from their stretchers.

An hour later she fell into a fitful sleep, and dreamed of being chased for a hundred miles by a whole posse of bandits on motorcycles. She awoke shortly after 7 a.m., drenched in perspiration and scared as hell. The enormity and danger of what she was doing was now really hitting her. She needed to kill a few hours in the hotel, then set off in the afternoon and head to Geneva, then up towards Jurançon to cross the French alpine border, again in the middle of the night. Then the following day on to England and a plane to New York.

She phoned her husband again and was comforted by his reassuring voice. It was easy for him to sound calm, she thought after she had hung up. She still had the Swiss and French border officials to get through. Then the English ones. No one would be interested in checking her bags when she flew into New York, he assured her. Once she was in England she would be home and dry.

*

She crossed into France at 2.30 a.m. the following morning without any problem at all. She had a bleary-eyed border official barely look at her passport before waving her through, and finally she was on the last leg. At 3.30 a.m. she checked into a lakeside chateau hotel near Annecy and fell into a deep sleep, waking at midday. She climbed out of the vast bed and, before phoning her husband, she opened the suitcase containing the paintings and their salvation for the future, lovingly, if a little sadly, thumbing through the canvases, each of them separated and protected by layers of silk dresses and underwear.

Next stop was the Calais–Dover night ferry, by her calculations an eight-hour drive, including meal stops, from here. In planning the trip with her husband and Denempont, they had discussed ways to handle a difficult customs official. They had discussed the possibility of a bribe, which was in general how it worked in Italy, and she had a large wad of lire with her, which had not been needed, as well as a large sum in French francs.

But they had ruled out any attempt to bribe either Swiss or British customs officials as too risky. If it backfired in either of these countries, she could risk arrest, and the consequences of that were unthinkable. She was going to have to rely on her charm which, with her handsome looks and aristocratic pedigree, she knew how to turn on to maximum effect, and as a fall-back, on a cunning plan that had been suggested by Denempont.

Even so, as she hit the road once more, she felt an increasing knot of anxiety with every kilometre that drew her nearer to Calais. She arrived at the port shortly after 11 p.m., an hour ahead of her estimate, and pulled into a quiet area of the ferry port car park, near some lorries. She wanted to arrive in Dover, as discussed with the art dealer, at 3 a.m., when the customs officers would be at their tiredest. With the one-hour time difference that meant catching the 2.30 a.m. boat. Three and a half hours to kill.

She could murder a coffee, but she was nervous about leaving the car unattended, so instead she sat in the car, in the darkness, listening to music on the radio, ate the baguette she had bought earlier at a filling station, sipped on a bottle of mineral water and chain-smoked until it was time to board.

She switched on the ignition and pressed the starter button. The engine turned over several times without firing and she felt a deep stab of panic. She tried again, heard the starter motor whirring and smelt a stench of petrol. No. Oh God no! She had flooded the engine. She tried again. Then again. Then again. Lorries were firing up their engines all around her and starting to roll forward.

Then the battery gave out.

She jumped out of the car and waved her arms up at a driver in his cab. He climbed down and asked her, in French, what the problem was. She explained.

A couple of minutes later he had recruited two other drivers. They told her to switch the ignition on and put the car into second gear, then they pushed. As the car gained momentum she let out the clutch and, to her intense relief, the engine fired. She sat still, soaked in perspiration, revving the engine hard, thick exhaust smoke billowing past her. She thanked them and drove forward, up to the ticket barrier.

A few minutes later she felt the reassuring judder as she drove over the ramp and down into the belly of the ferry, where she was waved forward until she was close to the rear of a Volkswagen camper van. She then climbed out and locked the car, debating whether to risk leaving the suitcase in the boot or take it with her. She realized she had not discussed this in advance. But then, she thought, it might look odd for her to be lugging the case upstairs to the passenger area. So instead, she double-checked that the boot was securely locked and made her way up the steps, her nostrils filled with the smell of spent exhaust fumes, varnish and paint, she was feeling sick with nerves.

She went to the lounge, which had a bar, and sat down nearby, waiting for it to open, badly in need of a large brandy and a double espresso. Twenty minutes later, as the ferry sailed, she sipped the espresso and drank the brandy straight down, then she went up on deck, into the salty wind and the darkness, and walked to the stern. She stayed there a long time, watching the lights of Calais disappear, and the intermittent flashes from a lighthouse, until she was shivering with cold. Then she went back below.

She bought a second double espresso and chanced another brandy. Somehow, between them, they calmed her down, yet kept her wide awake and fully alert – and confident.

Her nerves were jangling, but she thought to herself, over and over, It is going to be all right! Just remain calm. Calm.

The sea was calm and she could barely detect any motion, just the juddering of the boat's engines somewhere below her and the faint vibration of her seat.

Then she heard the tannoy announcement.

'Will all drivers please go down to A and B decks to their vehicles.'

Suddenly, she felt paralysed with fear. Please start, she thought, opening the boot of her car and checking the cases were there and undisturbed. Oh God, please start!

To her relief, the engine fired instantly, and she said a short, silent prayer of thanks. She felt the ferry yaw, then come to a juddering halt. Within moments the brake lights of the camper van in front of her came on, then it moved forward. She put the Alfa into gear and followed it – she was regretting having had that second double espresso, because her hands were shaking.

She drove up the ramp, waved forward by dock workers with batons, past a big warning sign beneath a Union Jack emblem, saying, *DRIVE ON THE LEFT.* A short distance ahead she saw the customs shed, with a lane divide. One was marked, with a green background, *NOTHING TO DECLARE.* The other with a red background, *GOODS TO DECLARE.*

She chose green, following the camper van through it. On her right was a long metal table extending the entire length of the shed and manned by a solitary, dozy-looking customs officer. He barely glanced at the van as it drove past him. She held her breath and tried to stare dead ahead, then, to her horror, she saw the official raise his arm and wave her over.

For a moment she thought she was going to throw up and began to shake uncontrollably. He was walking around to her window and signalling for her to lower it.

Taking a deep breath and trying to calm herself down, she obeyed and did her best to muster her most charming smile. 'Good evening, officer,' she said pleasantly.

But he didn't smile back. He had an intensely serious face; it was long and mournful beneath his peaked cap, rather like a horse. 'Where have you come from, Madam?'

'Italy,' she said in her broken English. 'Near Firenze – Florence.'

'And what is the purpose of your visit to England?'

'I have family here,' she said, delivering her carefully rehearsed script. 'My sister has recently lost her husband. I'm taking her on a motoring holiday up to Scotland.'

He gave her a look she could not read, but there was an element of scepticism in it. 'A motoring holiday in Scotland in November? Not the best of months to choose for the weather.'

'No!' she said, and gave a nervous laugh. 'Not the best month at all.'

He did not smile back. Instead he asked, 'May I see your passport, please.'

She handed it to him. He studied it carefully and slowly, flicking through page after page after page. 'Why did you choose to drive, Contessa? It's a long journey.'

She shrugged. 'I like driving.'

He looked at the Alfa. 'Nice car. Fast?'

'Yes, quite fast.'

He nodded and handed her passport back. She felt a tiny bit of relief. He was letting her go. Then that was shattered.

'May I see in the boot, please?'

'Yes, yes, of course, yes,' she stammered, opened the door and climbed out.

'Are you feeling all right?' he asked.

'Yes, yes, thank you.'

'You seem to be shaking.'

'I think I drank too much coffee – to keep awake.'

'Is there a reason why you have taken such a late ferry?'

She showed him her hands, which she had blackened again earlier. 'I should have taken a much earlier one, but I had a puncture, and it took me a long while to fix it. Luckily I was eventually helped by a lorry that stopped.'

Without commenting he walked around to the rear of the car and opened the boot lid. 'I'd like to look inside your cases,' he said.

She felt as though an ice-cold lead weight had dropped down inside her stomach. 'Yes,' she said. 'Yes, of course.'

He lifted the top one out and placed it on the metal table. 'Is it locked?'

'No.'

He popped the catches and raised the lid. Under her watchful eye he began working his way with his fingers down through the layers of clothes, lifting them up and peering beneath. Then he undid the securing straps and lifted the clothes out, placing them on the table, followed by her shoe bags and then her washbag. He removed each pair of shoes in turn and looked inside them, before replacing them in their bags. Satisfied all was in order he began to put them back a tad clumsily.

Finally, he nodded at her. 'OK, you may close it.'

For an instant, she hoped that was it, then her heart sank as he returned to the rear of her car and hauled out the second suitcase.

Now she was really trembling in terror. 'It's pretty much more of the same,' she said lamely.

He did not respond. Instead he placed it alongside the first case and again popped the catches.

She took a step back, her vision blurred, conscious that she was perspiring. Once more he began his almost creepy fingering through her dresses and her underwear, getting further and further down the contents. Any moment, she thought.

Oh God, any moment.

Suddenly he turned and stared hard at her. 'Oh?' he said. Then he lifted out the entire top layer of clothes that were covering the first canvas, and laid them on the table. Then he lifted up the canvas, holding it high by the two top corners.

It was an unfinished, unsigned Monet. It depicted a hazy stony bridge over a bleached-out, shimmering river. Its provenance was beyond doubt, catalogued extensively around the globe, and one of the French painter's most important works. When James Denempont had flown over to Italy to view and value their collection, he had been close to ecstatic when he had seen this particular canvas. He, too, shared the view that it was the original, and was probably the most valuable of all the canvases in their very considerable collection.

The customs official turned to her and stared hard into her eyes. His face was the very picture of cynicism. 'And what, exactly, is this, Contessa?'

'I'm having painting lessons,' she said, putting on her most charming smile. 'I'm bringing a few pieces to show my sister, who is a very talented artist, how I am progressing. I'm hoping to do some painting while I am in Scotland.'

'Painting lessons?'

His words hung in the cold air of the shed for some moments. He locked her eyes with his own. Then his inquisitor mask slipped a little and he said, 'Hmmm.'

She shrugged, and did her best to give him a disarming smile.

He did not respond but instead began to examine the canvas even more carefully, holding it close to his face. As he did so she could feel her legs threatening to buckle. He continued to inspect it for what seemed an eternity. She felt a terrible, deep sinking feeling.

Then, suddenly, to her utter amazement, he placed the canvas back into the case, and began, slowly and carefully, to replace the clothes he had removed. When he had finished he tugged the restraining straps tight, lowered the lid and pressed the catches home. When he had finished he yawned, then turned to her and said, 'OK, thank you, that's it, we're done.'

He helped her put the cases back into the boot, then she climbed back into the driving seat, her hands shaking so much she could barely turn the ignition key. As the engine fired, the officer suddenly leaned in through her window and gave her a wry smile.

'Those painting lessons you're having, lady?'

'Yes?'

'Don't take this the wrong way. But I'd have a few more, if I were you.'

DREAM WIFE

Imagine your ideal mate . . . I mean really your ideal mate . . . genetically engineered to your own specifications . . . a looker of your wildest dreams . . . who would pander to your wildest whim. Imagine someone you would be incessantly proud of . . . who would constantly adore you . . . who will never stray . . . who satisfies you intellectually . . . who is an incredible cook . . . who never ages, never gets mad at you . . . who, in short, would make your life more complete than you could ever have hoped . . .

Clive Marples sat in his den, staring at the advertisement on his computer screen, and tried to imagine it, liking what he imagined a lot. Really a lot. That could be him, he thought, having this woman. Having a whole new life. The life he had always dreamed of, with the wife he had always dreamed of.

There was just one small problem. He already had a wife.

To be fair, Shirley had once been a stunning looker. And in those early days he had been incessantly proud of her. But that had been twenty years ago, when she was fifty pounds lighter and kept herself in shape. In recent years she had become lazy, guzzling chocolates and Chardonnay and doing little else. She was like a sloth, lounging around the house and by the pool, day in, day out, when she wasn't out lounging around somewhere else with her friends.

There wasn't a labour-saving device she had not bought. A robot vacuum cleaner was one of the latest. She regularly scoured the adverts on television and at the back of her magazines for anything at all that could make her life even lazier than it already was. Clive was sure that if it was possible to buy eggs already boiled, from Waitrose or Tesco, she would do that to save the effort of boiling them herself.

They had little to talk about because she never watched the news any more. She never read a paper at all, except to see who Simon Cowell might be dating, or what the Duchess of Cambridge was wearing, or which A-list celebrity was divorcing who. He couldn't remember the last conversation they'd had about anything important that was happening in the world, beyond the pages of *Hello!* and *OK!* magazines.

Shirley had never wanted children. He'd been ambivalent about them until his friends had started having them. Watching some of his mates become fathers did not exactly fill him with a craving to do the same. Neat family homes suddenly transformed into crèches, filled with screaming and the smell of sick and poo and laundry.

When friends who were now parents came over with their sprogs, laden with rucksack baby-carriers, buggies, bags of nappies and toys and God knows what else, it was like a small army moving in for a few hours of manoeuvres.

His best mate, Charlie Carter, told him that with all his friends starting to have kids, he'd be feeling broody soon, too – and Shirley even more so. But it was the opposite with Shirley; she saw the sheer amount of effort having children took – starting with the act of giving birth itself. Any time she saw it happen in a documentary or film on TV, she would shake her head and say, 'Not for me, thanks!' Then she would quote Woody Allen's line about 'aimless reproduction' and shrug. 'And what's it all for?' she would ask. 'Become a slave to the bloody little monsters for the next twenty years? Then they either despise you and sod off, become drug addicts, or are a constant financial drain on you. And what if you got a wonky one? Subnormal or deformed? I couldn't cope with one of those. I wouldn't have the patience.'

The sister of one of her best friends had a Down's Syndrome child. Another had a boy quite seriously on the autism spectrum. Another had a daughter who would forever have a mental age of six months old. That made Shirley even more adamant never to take the risk. 'And on top of that,' she would say, 'having babies destroys your bloody sex life. If you don't have a Caesarean, your vagina gets stretched and it never fully recovers. And if you do have a Caesarean, your stomach muscles never recover from being cut through and you end up with a pot belly when you get older. It can't exactly be a turn-on for a bloke to watch a bloody, slimy baby being pulled out of your twat, can it?

'Most of my friends say they're not interested in sex after they've had all their children. One of them, Maggie, actually reads a book while her husband's shagging her. Babies? Not for me, thank you very much.'

And not for Clive, either. He was fine with that, despite the occasional bit of grief from his mother about waiting to become a gran. He was content with his life, or at least he had been, until recently. His climb up the corporate ladder of the global IT giant he worked for was going well, and he was earning a big salary and even bigger bonuses. He and Shirley had not long moved into their latest house on the property ladder, a swanky senior management home, The Cedars, with a Georgian portico, three-car garage and five-vehicle carport, in a smart, gated estate off Brighton's Dyke Road Avenue, called The Foresters. The property included a large, well-stocked garden with an infinity pool, a Zen water feature, three mature cedar trees and a view across the rooftops of Hove to the sea.

All the other houses were similar, but not completely identical. Each had its own idiosyncratic features and name, rather than a street number, to make it sound classier – The Oaks, The Firs, The Pines, The Willows, The Elms, The Maples, The Aspens – with, of course, the appropriate three trees in the garden. All their carports boasted latest, top-of-the-range Beemers, Audis, Jags, Mercs, Lexuses and Porsches, all gleaming, as if fresh out of their boxes.

All the occupants of The Foresters lived, it seemed to Clive Marples, high on the hog. In winter there were plentiful drinks and dinner parties. In summer, a constant round of barbecues and pool parties. All the residents took regular, expensive holidays. And, Clive assumed, they were all getting plenty of sex – until the kids came along, of course.

His problem was an increasing belief that everyone on the estate was actually having a better, happier and more fulfilled life than himself. As well as all the other members of his golf club, where he played a regular game on Sunday mornings.

Driving home from the station some days, he found himself starting to envy his neighbours more and more. Not their houses or their cars – his large, hybrid Lexus was up there with any of them, and so was Shirley's convertible Mercedes SL – no, it was what seemed to him to be their contentment. Couples actually happy to be with each other. In truth, he did not look forward to coming home very much.

It tended to be much the same most nights. Shirley, in some shapeless tracksuit or onesie, lying back on the sofa, stroking the cat, which had become as fat as her, watching some rubbish on the box and stuffing her face with some confection from a chocolate box lying on the sofa beside her, and swigging it down with Chardonnay.

She'd raise a hand, as if to warn him to be silent and not interrupt her programme, and say, 'Dinner's in the microwave – give it three minutes.' Then she'd pop another chocolate in her mouth, take another swig of wine and return her intent gaze to the screen.

Once a week they made love. A perfunctory, clinical function of mutual relief that rarely involved kissing, more a quick groping around each other's erogenous zones, the right movements discovered and fine-tuned over two decades, then it would be done and she would return to watching the television and he to the papers or a book.

On Saturdays in winter he went to watch his football team, The Albion, when they were playing at home, or else he watched television. On the days at the stadium when it wasn't his turn to drive, he'd enjoy a few beers with his mates, and then a few more, inevitably arriving home later than he had promised, to be greeted by an angry Shirley, all dolled up, tapping her watch, telling him they were embarrassingly late for some dinner they were going out to.

Up in the bedroom, getting changed to go out to dinner, frequently with Shirley's closest friend and her husband, neither of whom he particularly cared for, he would think to himself, dismally, is this it? Is this my life? Is this how it's always going to be?

Is this all it's ever going to be?

And increasingly, late on Saturday night when they returned home, while Shirley went to the bathroom to begin her ritual of removing her make-up, and then putting on her bedtime war paint, he would nip into his den and go online. To the DreamWife website.

And read, and dream.

DreamWife Corporation will genetically engineer the perfect wife. All you have to do is describe every detail of your perfect woman, have your brain scanned and downloaded, and DreamWife.com's computerized technology will do the rest. Using advanced, accelerated genetic development, your woman will be created at the age you specify, and come to you complete with all the memories of your actual married life implanted in her brain, but with the bad stuff edited out by cunning search-and-replace technology.

She will be everything you had hoped your wife would be, but never was. Delivery is just twelve months. Full refund if not satisfied.

*

At a mere £550,000, it was a bargain. Or would be, if he happened to have a spare £550,000 sitting around – and no wife.

Then late one Saturday night, Clive had a light-bulb moment. He realized that the two things could, actually, be elegantly combined – and how it could be done. While Shirley slept, looking like a ghost, with her face caked in anti-wrinkle mask, he lay awake, thinking, planning, scheming, hatching.

First thing on Monday morning, in the office, he phoned his IFA and told him he felt it was sensible for him to have a life-insurance policy. He did his best to make it sound innocent and altruistic. If anything happened to him, he wanted Shirley to be able to continue in the lifestyle she currently enjoyed. So the policy should be big enough to pay off the mortgage, and provide her with a continued decent income.

'Well, Clive, if you are going to do this, might I suggest you also take a policy out on Shirley. Just in case, you never know . . .'

'Well that's a thought,' Clive replied.

'You share the house. If anything should happen to her, you've no idea how you might react. You might be too grief-stricken to carry on with your work. It happens. You'd be wise to take precautions.'

Clive knew what his IFA's motivation was. Simple. The fat commission. And that suited him down to the ground. It was a small price to pay for the benefits to follow. He decided to follow the sound advice and take precautions.

A month later, after he and Shirley had completed all the forms and been visited by a doctor from the insurance company for medical examinations, the policy was in place. Both their lives were now insured for two million pounds. Now all he had to do was bide his time. Idiots got caught by not waiting long enough after taking out a policy on a loved one, before killing them. He had read about that in newspapers and in crime novels, and had seen it in crime shows on television. He had to give it plenty of time. Allow clear water between taking out the policy – and then claiming on it.

Clear water.

Another light-bulb moment!

The more he thought about clear water, the more he liked the idea. Water. The sea. Big, deep oceans. And it was their twenty-fifth wedding anniversary in a little over a year's time. What better way to celebrate than by going on a cruise? Shirley would like that. She could eat all day long. And all night long. What better place for a sloth?

A really nice, long cruise. In a nice big ship. Across a big, deep ocean.

Perfect!

Shirley was thrilled to bits when he told her it was all booked. In fact he could hardly remember a time when she had looked more pleased. Within minutes of springing the surprise on her, she was on the phone to her friends, telling them all about the fantastic cruise he was taking her on. One of the best cruise lines, all around the Caribbean. Utter pampered luxury. An hour later she was on the internet, starting to buy her cruise wardrobe. Even though it was still almost a year away.

Without telling Shirley, he remortgaged the house, giving him the extra money he needed to pay the DreamWife deposit. When he had completed the formalities, he received by courier a large, heavy wrist-watch. It contained a micro-scanner and camera, which, he had been informed, would download all the memories from Shirley's brain and implant them in his new wife. It was accompanied by detailed instructions on when to activate the camera – in the presence of any woman he met or saw, either in the flesh, on television or in a movie, whom he fancied; elements of her would then be incorporated in the manufacture of his dream woman. You just had to remember to switch it off after the download was complete or else it would continue to download going forward.

It was a very long year, in which Shirley talked about the cruise almost daily until he was heartily sick of it. They would be visiting twelve islands, including Barbados, St Barts, St Lucia and Antigua, and she regularly showed off to him, with her increasingly fat and dimpled body, the twelve different daywear outfits she had chosen and the twelve different evening dresses. With, of course, the twelve different pairs of shoes and the utterly essential matching handbags. And with each new outfit, he stared with increasing gloom at the monthly credit card bills. Within the first six months she had spent more than the entire cost of the cruise on her bloody outfits.

Way back in the early, heady days of their relationship, when he had been head over heels in lust – and in love – with Shirley, she would often show off a new dress to him when he came home from work. And back then, each time she did so, he would hold her in his arms, kissing her neck and gently reaching around behind her to unzip or unbutton the dress, until it slid down to the floor. Then he'd nuzzle her ear and tell her that the dress a man most liked to see on a woman was the one he most wanted her to take off.

That was then. Now, when he saw each new one, he desperately wanted her to keep it on. All night if possible. Even in the bath.

But Clive was sustained by his plans. The ones he carefully nurtured for life after the cruise. The plans for his new life. While Shirley continued relentlessly shopping for her cruise wardrobe, Clive wrote down another list altogether. His secret list. The requirements that he would be giving to the DreamWife Corporation.

And finally the big day arrived!

*

On their first night at sea, as the *SS Gloriana* sailed from Southampton, Clive and Shirley – who was wearing a particularly slinky first-night-at-sea gown – found themselves sharing a table with a grim couple. Plump, bald and boastful, Harry Tucker, was a self-made mail-order-cutlery tycoon, and his even ghastlier wife, Doreen, a peroxided sixty-year-old blonde who wore a frou-frou miniskirt and high-heeled leopard-skin bootees.

'Nice watch!' Harry Tucker said to him admiringly.

'Thank you,' Clive said, and dutifully admired back the large chunk of male bling attached to the fat man's wrist, realizing it was almost identical to his own.

'We've obviously got the same taste in watches,' Tucker said. 'I collect them, actually.'

'I like watches, too,' Clive said evasively.

'I've got two Breitlings. A Tag. A vintage Rolex Oyster, three Cartiers and a Patek Philippe.'

'Very nice,' Clive replied, not wanting to get drawn into a conversation about the provenance of his own watch.

Helped by the fact that Clive had secretly been lacing Shirley's drinks, in the hope that she would pass out later before making any demands on him in bed, she began flirting shamelessly with Harry – while Doreen started flirting with him. Clive became a little worried about where this might be going. The ship's photographer, who had already taken one snap of Clive and Shirley entering the dining room, now took another of the happy foursome at the table. Well, to be strictly accurate, happy threesome.

Their first night at sea was calm. For a change, it was Shirley, in an alcoholic stupor, who kept Clive awake by snoring, instead of the other way around. But he was fine with that. It gave him the excuse, not that he needed one, to dislike her even more intensely. They awoke to a gentle Atlantic swell, and when they were showered and dressed, they went down to breakfast. Shirley ate modestly for a change, just a few mouthfuls of a chocolate-coated cereal, her complexion a tad pale, while Clive happily munched his way through a full English. They whiled away the morning, checking out the geography of the ship, with Clive showing a particular interest in the stern, before having a Bridge lesson, accompanied by their new best friends, Harry and Doreen.

Clive couldn't help noticing that Harry seemed to have taken a bit of a shine to Shirley, and she to Harry, and that was fine by him. Flirt away, baby, he thought.

By lunchtime the swell had increased. Shirley, increasingly pale now, managed a few mouthfuls of chicken salad, while Clive ate a lobster, followed by fillet steak and chips and then chocolate cake. In the afternoon they sat through a dull lecture on the Caribbean islands. Clive ate a hearty tea, while Shirley managed to down a cuppa and a solitary mouthful of dry toast.

By early evening, as they headed out towards the mid-Atlantic, the weather had deteriorated to a Force 7 gale. Shirley, lying back on their bed, her face the colour of alabaster, said, 'Clive, darling, maybe you should go to dinner on your own.'

'Nonsense, my love! Get dressed and a stiff brandy will sort you out!'

Holding her pudgy hand, he helped her up to the bar, where they met Harry and Doreen, both of them already quite smashed on Martinis. 'Shirley's feeling a bit off-colour!' Clive announced.

'A stiff brandy's what you need! Brandy and ginger ale!' Harry told her, and insisted on buying her a very large one. Followed by another. And then another. All of which was perfect, Clive thought. Harry was, unwittingly, doing his work for him. A short while later, in the dining room, Harry and Shirley were engrossed in conversation, and that was fine by Clive, too, as they downed first a bottle of fine white burgundy, then a bottle of red. What was less fine was the ghastly Doreen's legs entwining themselves around his ankles, and her constant winking at him.

He played along with it, happy to see Shirley so distracted, drinking more and more as the Atlantic swell worsened. All around them, one at a time, people were getting up from their tables and staggering towards the exit. One old man fell over and had to be helped up and out by two Filipino waiters. As their puddings arrived, a huge, silver-haired woman, wearing what could best be described as a chiffon wigwam, fell over close by them and vomited on the carpet. As the stench reached their table, Shirley turned towards him and slurred, 'Clive, darling, I shink I need shome fresh air.'

Excusing himself, he helped Shirley to her feet and escorted her, holding her tightly, towards the exit and up the stairs. Then he took her out onto the blustery deck in the pitch darkness.

'Better, my darling?' he asked.

'Sh'I'm not shure.'

Slowly, steadily, he escorted her towards the rear of the ship, until they reached the stern rail. Below them was the turbulent wake, with flashes of phosphorescence dancing on it. He could feel the pitching and yawing of the great ship, its stabilizers increasingly ineffective against the rough sea. After a couple of hundred yards, the wake became invisible in the inky, moonless darkness.

'Stare at the horizon, my love,' he said, looking around at anything but. He was checking out the deck behind and above them. Checking carefully. Oh so carefully. Making sure there were no witnesses.

'I – I shhhcnan't see it,' she said.

'Maybe this will help,' he replied, lowering his arms down to her waist. Then, with one swift movement, he hefted her heavy body up in the air and pitched her over the rail. She vanished without a sound. He listened for the splash, but never heard it. He stared down at the wake, but could see no sign of her. He stood for several minutes, shivering with cold, then turned around, looking about him, then up and around him again.

Then, stealthily, avoiding his face being seen by any crew or passengers, he made his way back down to their deck and along to their cabin.

In the morning, after a mostly sleepless night in which the sea had become even rougher, he climbed out of bed, showered and shaved, picked up the daily copy of the *Gloriana News* that had been slid under their door, hung the DO NOT DISTURB notice on the door handle, then made his way along to the dining room, where he found Harry sitting on his own at their table, tucking into bacon, sausage and black pudding, despite the now quite violent motion of the ship.

'Morning, Clive!' he greeted him chirpily. 'No Shirley?'

'She's feeling a bit green this morning,' he replied.

'Doreen, too!' Harry said. 'No sea legs, these women!'

'Too right! She spent most of the night vomiting.'

'Just like Doreen!'

Clive had little appetite, but managed to down a couple of pieces of toast and a poached egg.

After breakfast the two men joined in the Bridge class once more and were paired up with a couple of doughty elderly women. After the session they went to their respective cabins to check on their spouses, then met in the bar for a couple of large gin and tonics, and lunched together.

'She's a tasty lady, your Shirley,' Harry Tucker said.

'Doreen's very beautiful,' Clive lied.

'She is. I'm a lucky man,' he replied.

'You are indeed!'

*

The following morning, Clive decided, was the time to raise the alarm. The ship's motion was still very uncomfortable as he staggered along to the purser's office on B deck and informed the officer, 'I'm worried about my wife. She's been feeling sick as hell for the past day and a half. I woke up this morning and she wasn't in the cabin. I've searched the ship high and low and can't find her. Could you please help me?'

An hour later, after the crew had searched every inch of the *Gloriana,* the captain made a decision to turn the ship around, and also to send out a Mayday signal for all ships in the area to look out for someone in the water. Although, the captain told Clive, the chances of surviving for any length of time in this cold water were not good.

'Even someone fat?' Clive asked.

'That might give them a few extra hours,' the captain told him. 'I've done my best to calculate the current, and we'll retrace our steps as close as possible to where she might be. There's also an RAF Nimrod search plane on its way.

For the rest of that day, Clive, accompanied by Harry Tucker and a large number of the ship's company, stood around the bow rail, several of them with binoculars, staring down at the ocean or towards the horizon dead ahead. For several hours the Nimrod flew low above them. But all any of them saw were occasional bits of driftwood, a half-submerged container that must have fallen overboard from a vessel and a school of dolphins. At dusk, as the light began to fail, the captain abandoned the search.

Clive Marples was inconsolable.

As his mother said to him much later, at least if they found her body, there could be some closure. Tearfully, he agreed with her.

*

Eight months on, after a good show of mourning, much sympathy from everyone he knew and copious quantities of alcohol downed with his friends and frequently on his own, attempting to obliterate what he had done, one rainy Thursday morning in early June, Clive Marples's phone rang. It was from a cheery lady at DreamWife.com telling him that Imogen was ready for collection. When would be convenient?

The following morning, Clive threw a sickie from work and spent much longer than usual in the shower. He inserted a brand-new blade in his razor and shaved extra carefully. He rolled on deodorant and sprayed himself liberally with his favourite cologne. Then, with his iPhone playing his favourite music through the car's hi-fi, he headed off from his house in Brighton, the satnav in his Lexus, programmed for the DreamWife Corporation's headquarters, near Birmingham.

He sang along to his favourite tracks all the way, feeling in a great mood, if a tad apprehensive about just how Imogen would turn out. He felt he was on the verge of a whole new adventure, the start of his new life. He could not wait!

In truth, he was a little disappointed when he reached the address. He wasn't sure quite what he had been expecting to find, but certainly swankier and more glamorous premises than the address he pulled up outside. It was a large, but very ordinary-looking unit in an industrial estate, sandwiched between an exhaust-repair outfit and a timber warehouse. But there was no mistaking he was at the right address: There, beside the door in small letters, were the words 'DreamWife Corporation'.

He went in and found himself in a small front office, with a plump lady in her mid-sixties sitting behind a tiny desk, eating a Pot Noodle. The walls were decorated with large colour photographs of smiling, beautiful young women, and there was a drinks dispenser. He gave the receptionist his name.

She looked at her computer screen, frowning. 'Mr Marples, did you say?'

'Yes.' He was irritated by her manner.

'Did you bring ID with you? Your passport and driving licence?'

He handed both to her and she looked at her screen again, frowning further. He felt his heart sinking, and started to wonder if he had been conned. Then, suddenly, she smiled. 'Ah, yes! Here we are! Imogen?'

'Imogen.'

She handed him a receipt to sign, then she picked up her phone and pressed a button. 'Mr Clive Marples to collect Imogen,' she said to someone. Then she pointed to a chair. 'Do take a seat,' she said. 'Help yourself to a tea or coffee. She'll be down in a few minutes.'

He made himself a coffee, sat on the hard plastic seat and waited. And waited. Then he needed to pee. The receptionist pointed at a door and gave him directions. A few minutes later he returned to the reception area and stopped in his tracks.

An apparition awaited him that totally took his breath away. A tall, leggy blonde in a short, clingy dress that showed off every contour of her voluptuous body and stopped several inches short of her knees. She had, quite simply, the sexiest legs he had ever seen in his life. And the most beautiful smile. And two elegant suitcases on the floor beside her.

'Clive!' she said. 'I've been dreaming about you for so long!' She threw her arms around him and gave him a long, deep, kiss that made him instantly, incredibly horny.

He carried her bags out to the car and put them in the boot. A couple of minutes later they were heading out of the industrial estate.

'Turn left here, and then in one and a half miles make a right,' she told him.

'You sound like my satnav,' he said.

'Oh yes? Well, I'll bet your satnav lady doesn't do this,' she replied, fumbling expertly with his belt and then his zip. By the time they were four miles down the M40 he'd had his first orgasm.

The rest of their journey home passed as if it was a dream. They chatted easily. She knew everything about him, as if they had been together for years, as if they were soul mates.

For the first two heady days after they arrived back at his house, they made love for most of the weekend, only interrupted by Imogen cooking him meals and rushing to the shops to get him the Saturday, then Sunday newspapers. At ten o'clock on Sunday night, falling into a blissful, sexually sated sleep, Clive Marples considered himself the luckiest man on the planet. He truly had his dream wife.

Imogen rapidly became the envy of all Clive's buddies on The Foresters estate, and at the Dyke Golf Club. A few Sundays after Imogen had come into his life, having had one too many beers at the 19th hole, Clive announced to his regular golf buddies, 'Know what they say? The perfect wife should be a chef in the kitchen, a lady in the living room and a whore in the bedroom? Well, my Imogen is all of that and more!'

Of course, they all wanted to know where he and Imogen had

met. And Clive had the perfect answer ready. 'Online,' he said. 'On a dating agency website.'

All his pals agreed he was one lucky bastard.

The following Friday night, Imogen proved to be the perfect hostess when Clive entertained his new boss and his wife to dinner. The five-course meal she prepared was, their two guests declared, some of the most delicious food they had ever put in their mouths. And after they had gone home, Imogen, just as she did every night, treated Clive to the most delicious love-making he had ever experienced. Never had he felt so alive, so fulfilled, so youthful!

His friends at the Dyke Golf Club told him he looked ten, maybe even fifteen years younger. It had to be down to the new lady in his life. What was his secret? How the hell had a middle-aged git like him pulled such a lovely woman? Several of them – all married men – surreptitiously approached him, asking for the number of the dating agency. Cheekily playing the moral ticket, he told them he could not possibly give such temptation to married friends.

And his life with Imogen carried on being sweeter than he could ever have imagined. Every evening, it seemed to him, Imogen reinvented sexual pleasure. She took him to new heights, doing new things to his body that he could never, ever have dreamed of. He just loved everything they did together, in bed and out of it. He even found himself enjoying things he had once considered chores, like accompanying her food shopping, and even clothes shopping. And all the time they talked and talked. She was a voracious reader of newspapers and books, absorbing everything, and she had intelligent views on every topic they discussed.

Then one Saturday morning, shopping in the Marks & Spencer superstore at Brighton's Holmbush Centre, his arm around Imogen as they headed towards the food hall to select items for their dinner, Clive stopped in his tracks. There, walking down the aisle towards him, was Shirley.

Clive instantly turned, sweeping Imogen around, and rapidly led her away, convinced he had seen a ghost. He dragged her out of the store and into the car, wondering, had he imagined it?

'What's the matter, my darling?' Imogen asked sweetly.

'I'd rather go to Tesco,' he said.

'Tesco's good,' she replied.

That was one of the many things he loved about her. She never questioned his decisions. But, boy, was he shaken. That couldn't have been Shirley. Impossible! It was his imagination playing tricks. His guilty conscience?

Had to be.

All the same, when he tried to make love to Imogen that night, he couldn't perform, despite everything she tried. With every caress, every touch of her lips, he saw Shirley walking down the food hall aisle towards him.

Then on Monday morning, driving up Brighton's Queen's Road to the station to catch his regular commuter train to London, Clive suddenly saw Shirley walking along the street, heading to the station herself.

Impossible!

As he turned his head he failed to notice that all the cars in front of him had stopped for a red light. Too late, he jammed on the brakes and slammed into the rear of a large, bronze Jaguar. As he climbed out, a furious-looking short, fat man clambered out of the Jaguar. To his amazement he recognized Harry Tucker, their plump, odious table companion from the cruise last year.

'My God!' he said. 'Harry! Harry Tucker! Remember me? Clive Marples from the cruise last year – the *Gloriana*? I'm so sorry!'

Not entirely surprisingly, considering the circumstances, Harry did not seem at all pleased to see him, and appeared very flustered and distracted. They exchanged few words. Harry seemed in a hurry to swap insurance details, ignoring all Clive's questions about how he was and what had brought him down to Brighton. Then he drove off after muttering vague promises about calling him and meeting up for a drink sometime.

On the train, Clive sat, deep in thought, mystified by the strange encounter. Had he imagined Shirley? Had he imagined Harry? Had he seen a ghost? Could Shirley possibly still be alive? Could Harry Tucker be having an affair with her?

But how the hell could she still be alive? It was impossible. The thought was absurd! But Clive could not stop thinking about the two extraordinary coincidences. He fretted about it all day. That evening, arriving back at the station, he hurried across the car park to his Lexus and went straight to the front of it. There indeed was a dent, and a broken headlight.

A week later, seated at a table at a restaurant in Brighton with Imogen, he saw, across the room, Harry and Shirley being shown in by the maître d' and seated at a table only a short distance away.

This time there was no mistaking. It was Harry and Shirley. Holding hands. Chinking Champagne glasses. Clearly deeply into each other.

Despite his efforts to keep his head low, he realized that Harry, who was facing his way, had recognized him. But Shirley had not.

A few minutes later, Harry got up and headed towards the toilets, giving him a nod on the way. Clive joined him at the urinal. Before he could utter a word to Harry, who seemed embarrassed as hell, Harry said, 'Clive I know this must sound pretty weird to you. But before Doreen and I went on that cruise I discovered this amazing site on the internet called DreamWife.com. You pay quite a big sum and they issue you with a watch that can scan memories and faces and create your dream woman, out of anyone you meet and fancy.'

'Really?' Clive said, feigning surprise.

'It's amazing! Well, here's the thing – sorry I was short with you the other day over that prang.'

'You had every reason to be.'

'Didn't want to get drawn into a conversation about why I was down in Brighton. Shirley had a hankering to visit. You see, I took an incredible fancy to your Shirley on that cruise.' Then he held up his watch. The one identical to the one Clive had worn on the cruise. 'A scanner, just like yours, right?'

Clive said nothing.

'I've had it a while. I used it on the cruise to download stuff from your Shirley's brain and to take pictures of her. The only thing was I forgot to switch it off when the download was complete! When I returned home, I sent it all to DreamWife and requested a replica of her. Then I dumped Doreen. I only took delivery of Shirley a couple of weeks ago. I didn't think you'd mind, too much, seeing how badly you and she were getting on. And then with her being dead and all that?' He grinned, lasciviously. 'Dunno why you weren't getting on, she's a cracker. My God, she's a goer!'

'I'm glad you're finding that, Harry,' he said.

'She's wild, mate! Know what I mean? Never known a lady like it in the sack! You don't mind?'

'Be my guest.'

Clive was feeling a terrible stab of panic. How much did Shirley remember? What the hell was she going to be telling this fat dick-head?

Then Harry Tucker put an avuncular arm around him. 'She told me everything, Clive,' Harry said. 'How she was seasick, and you took her out on the rear deck and then threw her overboard. Don't worry, matey, I know it all.'

'You do?'

'I don't mind a bit! How else would we have got together? Seems like you did us both a big favour! Our little secret, eh?'

'Our little secret.'

Harry gave him a pat on the back. Then he nodded back towards the dining room. 'That bird you're with, she's a cracker.'

'Thank you, Harry. She is.'

'Oh, I know! I know she is. You can just tell, can't you? Maybe we should go on another cruise sometime? In a year or two when you're getting bored of her. Give me a call. Just give me a call. I'd always be up for it. Know what I mean?' He winked.

Clive returned to his table. As he sat down, Imogen said, 'That man you were in the loo with – how do you know him?'

'I met him in another life.'

She smiled wistfully. 'So did I.'

A DEAD SIMPLE PLAN

Fifteen years ago I wrote a short story about a man who gets buried alive in a stag-night prank that subsequently goes horribly wrong.

It was about a guy, Michael Harrison, who is extremely unreliable, but who persuades his beloved Ashley to marry him, on the promise that he's going to change his ways. Then, on his stag night, his friends decide to pay him back, big time, for all the terrible pranks he has played on some of them on their stag nights . . . by burying him alive, in remote woodlands, for a couple of hours. They intend to return within two hours to dig him up again, but it all goes south.

I never put this story forward for publication because I always felt there was something more that I could make of it than simply ending it the way I did. That turned out to be a good decision. One of the best I've ever made in my life! Because many years later I realized that what I had, rather than being a short story with a short shocker of an ending, was actually the start of a novel. Dead Simple *became my most successful novel, and it launched the Roy Grace series.*

This is how it all began . . .

It was Wednesday night, their last date before their wedding on Saturday, and, true to form, Michael was late. Very late. Actually, Ashley thought, that was being charitable. He was incredibly sodding bloody f***ing late. Ridiculously late. Over an hour late.

As usual.

On two occasions he had failed to turn up at all, and eight months ago, totally exasperated by his unreliability, she had dumped him. They had spent five months apart, during which time Michael was miserable as hell. He bombarded her, sometimes daily, with extravagant flowers, loving emails and tearful phone calls. She'd begun dating another guy, but he just wasn't the same – neither as a companion nor as a lover. Michael was just such fun to be with, so full of energy and *joie de vivre*. It was a miserable time for her, too.

Finally she realized she could not live without Michael. They'd begun seeing each other again, and four weeks later he proposed and she accepted.

She looked at her watch and poured her third glass of wine, starting to feel a little smashed. It was now approaching 8.45 p.m. and he'd promised faithfully he would pick her up at 7.30 p.m. sharp. He was turning over a new leaf, he assured her. He would start their married life a changed man. Yeah, right.

In spite of herself, she grinned. God, she loved him, but why the hell wouldn't he wear a damned watch? Well, maybe she could change that. She'd bought him an insanely expensive Tag Heuer Aquaracer, as a wedding present, and she was going to give it to him tonight. And make him promise to wear it!

Fifteen minutes later her doorbell rang. He stood outside her flat, his contrite expression barely visible behind the vast bouquet of flowers that almost dwarfed him.

After a long, passionate kiss, she broke away and teasingly asked, 'So what happened this time? Were you kidnapped by aliens again?

Had to take a phone call from Barack Obama? Rescue a runaway horse?'

He scratched the back of his head, looking contrite. 'I'm so sorry, my darling. Mark rang. I had to go through some stuff urgently on the planning application. There's just so much to do before we go away, and I want to have our honeymoon free and not be thinking about work. I'm trying to clear my desk and my email inbox, so I can devote the next two weeks to cherishing you, making love to you and then making love to you again.'

'I like that plan!' She grinned and kissed him again. 'Want a drink, or shall we go?'

'I rang the restaurant and changed the time, but we need to be there by nine. Or . . .' he looked at her suggestively. 'We could just go to bed and phone for a takeaway?'

'I'm all dressed up, I think it would be nice to go out. We've got a ton of stuff to talk about. And I want to know all about your stag-night plans, coz I'm worried.'

'Nothing to be worried about.' He picked her wine glass up off the coffee table and took a long sip. 'We're just going on a pub crawl around Sussex – Mark's hired a minibus. I'll have the whole of Friday to recover from my hangover, Ash, and I'll be fresh as a daisy for Saturday!'

She gave him a dubious look. 'Why does that not reassure me?'

He gave her a hug and nuzzled her ear. 'Come on, we're just going to have a few drinks. No strippers, I've told the guys I don't want it getting messy. We're just going to have a few beers and then go home.'

'Ha!' she said.

*

An hour later, as their starters were being cleared away and the waiter poured more Champagne into their glasses, Ashley said, 'How can I not worry, darling? You guys have a history of carrying out crazy pranks on stag nights.'

He shrugged and raised his glass. 'Yep, well, they've promised nothing bad's going to happen.'

'I know them,' she said. 'And I don't trust them.'

'Trust me!' he said.

She stared hard at him, tossing aside her long dark hair, and blew him a kiss. 'I wish I could!'

'You can, I promise!'

'I'll trust you when I turn up to the church, go inside on my father's arm and see you standing, looking at me, with Mark by your side, on Saturday afternoon. Until then, I'm going to be worried witless.'

'You have nothing to worry about.'

She curled her fingers around her glass, as the waiter set down her sea bass and Michael's steak, followed by the vegetables. 'I just don't want to be stranded in the church, Michael, OK? I don't want to find myself standing there for an hour until you rush in, all out of breath, saying you're sorry, but you had some urgent emails to deal with!'

'That is so not going to happen!'

'It had better not,' she said. 'Because I won't wait.'

He slid his arm across the table and squeezed her hand. 'I love you, Ashley. More than anything in the world. Saturday is going to be the best day of my life. I promise you faithfully I will be there, on time and horny as hell for you. I'm a changed man.'

'Like you just showed me tonight? You are so damned unreliable, my darling. I love you to bits. But – I don't know – I just have this feeling that you aren't going to turn up to our wedding.'

'That's ridiculous!'

'Then prove me wrong!'

'I will, I absolutely will!'

So far, apart from a couple of hitches, Plan A was working out fine. Which was fortunate, since they didn't really have a Plan B.

At 8.30 p.m. on a late May evening, they'd banked on having some daylight. There had been plenty of the stuff this time yesterday, when the five of them had made the same journey, taking with them an empty coffin and five shovels. But now, as the green Transit van sped along the Sussex country road, misty rain was falling from a sky the colour of a fogged negative.

'Are we nearly there yet?' said Josh in the back, mimicking a child.

'The great Um Ga says, "Wherever I go, there I am,"' responded Robbo, who was driving, and was slightly less drunk than the rest of them. With three pubs notched up already in the past hour and a half, and four more on the itinerary, he was sticking to shandy. At least, that had been his intention; but he'd managed to slip down a couple of pints of pure Harveys bitter first – to clear his head for the task of driving, he'd said.

'So, we're there!' said Josh.

'Always have been.'

A deer warning sign flitted from the darkness then was gone, as the headlights skimmed glossy black-top macadam stretching ahead into the forested distance. Then they passed a small white cottage.

'How're we doing, pal?' said Mark in the back, with a big grin on his face, doing a passable impression of a caring best man.

Michael, lolling on a tartan rug on the floor in the back of the van, head wedged against a wheel-brace for a pillow, was feeling very pleasantly woozy. 'I sh'ink I need another a drink,' he slurred.

If he'd had his wits about him, he might have sensed, from the expressions of his friends, that something was not quite right. Never usually much of a heavy drinker, tonight he'd parked his brains in the dregs of more empty pint glasses and vodka chasers than he could remember downing, in more pubs than had been sensible to visit.

Of the group of friends, who had been muckers together since way back into their early teens, Michael Harrison had always been the natural leader. If, as they say, the secret of life is to choose your parents wisely, Michael had ticked plenty of the right boxes. He had inherited his mother's fair good looks and his father's charm and entrepreneurial spirit, but without any of the self-destruct genes that had eventually destroyed the man.

From the age of twelve, when Tom Harrison had gassed himself in his car, in the garage of the family home, leaving behind a trail of debtors, Michael had grown up fast, helping his mother make ends meet by doing a paper round then, when he was older, by taking labouring jobs in his holidays. He grew up with an appreciation of how hard it was to make money – and how easy it was to fritter it.

Now, at twenty-eight, he was smart, a decent human being and a natural leader of the pack. If he had flaws, it was that he was too trusting and, on occasions, too much of a prankster. And tonight the latter chicken was coming home to roost. Big time.

But at this moment, he had no idea about that.

He drifted back into a blissful stupor, thinking only happy thoughts, mostly about his fiancée, Ashley. Life was good. His mother was dating a nice guy; his kid brother had just got into university; his kid sister, Jodie, was back-packing in Australia on a gap year, and his business was going incredibly well. But best of all, in two days' time he was going to be marrying the woman he loved and adored. His soul mate.

Ashley.

He hadn't noticed the shovel that rattled on every bump in the road, as the wheels drummed below on the sodden tarmac and the rain pattered down above him on the roof. And he didn't clock a thing in the expressions of his two friends riding with him in the back, who were swaying and singing tunelessly to an oldie, Rod Stewart's 'I Am Sailing', on the crackly radio up front. A leaky fuel can filled the van with the stench of petrol.

'I love her,' Michael slurred. 'I s'hlove Ashley.'

'She's a great lady,' Robbo said, turning his head from the wheel, sucking up to him as he always did. That was in his nature. Awkward with women, a bit clumsy, a florid face, lank hair, beer belly straining the weave of his T-shirt, Robbo clung to the coat-tails of this bunch by always trying to make himself needed. And tonight, for a change, he actually *was*.

'She is.'

'Coming up,' warned Luke.

Robbo braked as they approached the turn-off, and winked in the darkness of the cab at Luke seated next to him. The wipers clumped steadily, smearing the rain across the windscreen.

'I mean, like I really love her. Sh'now what I mean?'

'We know what you mean,' Pete said.

Josh, leaning back against the driver's seat, one arm around Pete, swigged some beer, then passed the bottle down to Michael. Froth rose from the neck as the van braked sharply. He belched. ''Scuse me.'

'What the hell does Ashley see in you?' Josh said.

'My dick.'

'So it's not your money? Or your looks? Or your charm?'

'That too, Josh, but mostly my dick.'

The van lurched as it made the sharp right turn, rattling over a cattle grid, almost immediately followed by a second one and onto the dirt track. Robbo, peering through the misted glass and picking out the deep ruts, swung the wheel. A rabbit sprinted ahead of them, then shot into some undergrowth. The headlights veered right then left, fleetingly colouring the dense conifers that lined the track, before they vanished into darkness in the rear-view mirror. As Robbo changed down a gear, Michael's voice altered, his bravado suddenly tinged, very faintly, with anxiety.

'Where we going?'

'To another pub.'

'OK. Great.' Then a moment later, 'Promished Ashley I shwouldnt – wouldn't – drink too much.'

'See,' Pete said, 'you're not even married and she's laying down rules. You're still a free man. For just two more days.'

'One and a half,' Robbo added helpfully.

'You haven't arranged any girls?' Michael said.

'Feeling horny?' Robbo asked.

'I'm staying faithful.'

'We're making sure of that.'

'Bastards!'

The van lurched to a halt, reversed a short distance, then made another right turn. Then it stopped again and Robbo killed the engine – and Rod Stewart with it. '*Arrivé*!' he said. 'Next watering hole! The Undertakers Arms!'

'I'd prefer the Naked Thai Girl's Legs,' Michael said.

'She's here, too.'

Someone opened the rear door of the van – Michael wasn't sure who – and invisible hands took hold of his ankles. Robbo took one of his arms, and Luke the other.

'Hey!'

'You're a heavy bastard!' Luke said.

Moments later Michael thumped down, in his favourite sports jacket and best jeans – not the wisest choice for your stag night, a dim voice in his head was telling him – onto sodden earth, in pitch darkness that was pricked only by the red rear-lights of the van and the white beam of a flashlight. Hardening rain stung his eyes and matted his hair to his forehead.

'My . . . closhes . . .'

Moments later, his arms yanked almost clear of their sockets, he was hoisted in the air, then dumped down into something dry and lined with something soft that pressed in on either side of him.

'Hey!' he said again.

Five drunken, grinning, shadowy faces leered down at him. A magazine was pushed into his hands. In the beam of the flashlight he caught a blurry glimpse of a naked redhead with gargantuan breasts. A bottle of whisky, a small flashlight – switched on – and a walkie-talkie were placed on his stomach.

'What's—?'

'We've preset the channel,' Robbo informed him. 'Don't want you chatting to any strangers.'

Michael heard a scraping sound, then suddenly something blotted the faces and all the sound out. His nostrils filled with the smells of wood, new cloth and glue. For an instant he felt warm and snug. Then a flash of panic.

'Hey, guys – what—'

Robbo picked up a screwdriver as Pete shone the flashlight down on the oak coffin.

'You're not screwing it down?' Luke said.

'Absolutely!' Pete said.

'Do you think we should?'

'He'll be fine,' Robbo said. 'Mark checked it all out, didn't you, Mark?'

'Yeah, I looked it up on the internet. Even if a coffin's completely airtight, you'd have enough air for three to four hours. Unless of course you panicked and began hyperventilating. Then you could knock it down to under an hour.'

'I really don't think we should screw it down!' Luke said.

'Course we should – otherwise he'll be able to get out!' Josh admonished him. 'We just have to tell him to remain calm and he'll be fine!'

'Hey!' Michael said.

But no one could hear him now. And he could hear nothing except a faint scratching sound above him.

Robbo worked on each of the four screws in turn. It was a top-of-the-range hand-tooled oak coffin with embossed brass handles, borrowed from his uncle's funeral parlour where, after a couple of career u-turns, he was now employed as an apprentice embalmer. Good, solid brass screws. They went in easily.

Michael looked upwards, his nose almost touching the lid. In the beam of the flashlight, ivory-white satin encased him. He kicked out with his legs, but they had nowhere to travel. He tried to push his arms out, but they had nowhere to go, either.

Sobering for a few moments, he suddenly realized what he was lying in.

'Hey, hey, listen, you know – hey – I'm claustrophobic. This is not funny! Hey!' His voice came back at him, strangely muffled. He pushed up against the lid above him, but it wouldn't budge an inch.

Pete opened the door, leaned into the cab and switched on the headlights. A couple of metres in front of them was the grave they had dug yesterday, the earth piled to one side, tapes already in place. A large sheet of corrugated iron and two of the spades they had used lay close by.

They all walked to the edge and peered down. All of them were suddenly aware that nothing in life is ever quite as it seems when you are planning it. Right now, the hole looked deeper, darker, more like – well – a grave, actually.

The beam of the flashlight shimmered at the bottom.

'There's water,' Josh said.

'Just a bit of rainwater,' Robbo said.

Josh frowned. 'There's too much, that's not rainwater. We must have hit the water table.'

'Shit,' Pete said. A BMW salesman, he always looked the part, on duty or off. Spiky haircut, sharp suit, always confident. But not quite so confident now.

'It's nothing,' Robbo said. 'Just a couple of inches.'

'Did we really dig it this deep?' said Luke, a freshly qualified solicitor, recently married, not quite ready to shrug off his youth, but starting to accept life's responsibilities.

'It's a grave, isn't it?' said Robbo. 'We decided on a grave.'

Josh squinted up at the worsening rain. 'What if the water rises?'

'Shit, man,' Robbo said. 'We dug it yesterday and it's taken twenty-four hours for just a couple of inches to accumulate. Nothing to worry about.'

Josh nodded thoughtfully. 'But what if we can't get him back out?'

'Course we can get him out,' Robbo said. 'We just unscrew the lid.'

'Let's get on with it,' Mark said. 'He's going to be fine. OK?'

'He bloody deserves it,' Pete reassured his mates. 'Remember what he did on your stag night, Luke?'

Luke would never forget waking from an alcoholic stupor to find himself on a bunk on the overnight sleeper to Edinburgh. As a result he arrived forty minutes late at the altar the next morning.

Pete would never forget, either. The weekend before his wedding, he'd found himself in frilly lace underwear, a dildo strapped to his waist, manacled to the Clifton suspension bridge, before being rescued by the fire brigade. Both pranks had been Michael's idea.

They hefted the coffin off the ground, staggered forward with it to the edge of the grave, and dumped it down, hard, over the tapes. Then giggled at the muffled 'Ouch!' from within.

There was a loud thump.

Michael banged his fist against the lid. 'Hey! Enough!'

Pete, who had the walkie-talkie in his coat pocket, pulled it out and switched it on. 'Testing!' he said. 'Testing!'

Inside the coffin, Pete's voice boomed out. 'Testing! Testing!'

'Joke over!'

'Relax, Michael!' Pete said. 'Enjoy!'

'You bastards! Let me out! I need a piss!'

Pete switched the walkie-talkie off and jammed it into the pocket of his Barbour jacket. 'So how does this work, exactly?'

'We lift the tapes,' Mark said. 'One each end.'

Pete dug the walkie-talkie out and switched it on. 'We're getting this taped, Michael!' Then he switched it off again.

The five of them laughed. Then each picked up an end of tape and took up the slack.

'One . . . two . . . three!' Robbo counted.

'Fuck, this is heavy!' Luke said, taking the strain and lowering.

Slowly, jerkily, listing like a stricken ship, the coffin sank down into the deep hole. When it reached the bottom they could barely see it in the darkness.

Pete held the flashlight. In the beam they could see the lid, and they all grinned at the thought of Michael beneath it.

Robbo grabbed the walkie-talkie. 'Hey, Michael, are you enjoying the magazine? If you get a hard on you might be able to raise the lid with your dick!'

'OK, joke over. Now let me out!'

'We're off to a pole-dancing club. Too bad you can't join us!' Robbo switched off the radio before Michael could reply. Then, pocketing it, he picked up a spade and began shovelling earth over the edge of the grave, and roared with laughter as it rattled down on the roof of the coffin.

With a loud whoop Pete grabbed another shovel and joined in. For some moments both of them worked hard until only a few bald patches of coffin showed through the earth. Then these were covered. Both of them continued, the drink fuelling their work into a frenzy until there was a good couple of feet of earth piled on top of the coffin.

'Hey!' Luke said. 'Hey, stop that! The more you shovel on the more we're going to have to dig back out again in two hours' time.'

'It's a grave!' Robbo said. 'That's what you do with a grave, you cover the coffin!'

Luke grabbed the spade from him. 'Enough!' he said firmly. 'I want to spend the evening drinking, not bloody digging, OK?'

Robbo nodded, never wanting to upset anyone in the group. Pete, sweating heavily, threw his spade down. 'Don't think I'll take this up as a career,' he said.

They pulled the corrugated iron sheet over the top, then stood back in silence for some moments. Rain pinged on the metal.

'OK,' Pete said. 'We're outta here.'

Luke dug his hands into his coat pocket dubiously. 'Are we really sure about this?'

'We agreed we were going to teach him a lesson,' Robbo said.

'What if he chokes on his vomit or something?'

'He'll be fine, he's not that drunk,' Josh said. 'Let's go.'

Josh climbed into the rear of the van and Luke shut the doors. Then Pete, Luke and Robbo squeezed into the front, and Robbo started the engine. They drove back down the track for half a mile, then made a right turn onto the main road.

After a few miles, Mark switched on the walkie-talkie. 'How you doing, Michael?'

'Guys, listen, I'm really not enjoying this joke.'

'Really?' Robbo said. 'We are!'

Luke took the radio. 'This is what's known as pure vanilla revenge, Michael!'

All five of them in the van roared with laughter. Now it was Josh's turn. 'Hey, Michael, we're going to this fantastic club, they have the most beautiful women, butt naked, sliding their bodies up and down poles. You're going to be really pissed you're missing out on this!'

Michael's voice slurred back, just a tad plaintiff. 'Can we stop this now, please? I'm really not enjoying this.'

Through the windscreen Robbo could see roadworks ahead and a green light. He accelerated.

Luke shouted over Josh's shoulder, 'Hey, Michael, just relax, we'll be back in a couple of hours!'

'What do you mean, "a couple of hours"?'

The light turned red. Not enough time to stop. Robbo accelerated even harder and shot through. 'Gimme the thing,' he said, grabbing the radio and steering one-handed around a long curve. He peered down in the ambient glow of the dash and hit the talk button.

'Hey, Michael—'

'ROBBO!' Luke's voice, screaming.

Headlights above them, coming straight at them.

Blinding them.

Then the blare of a horn, deep, heavy-duty, ferocious.

'ROBBBBBBBBOOOOOOO!' screamed Luke.

Robbo stamped in panic on the brake pedal and dropped the walkie-talkie. The wheel yawed in his hands as he looked, desperately, for somewhere to go. Trees to his right, a JCB to his left, headlights burning through the windscreen, searing his eyes, coming at him out of the teeming rain like a train.

*

Michael heard a long scream. Then a huge, echoing, metallic clang, as though two cosmic-size dustbins had swung into each other. Then a clattering sound. Then silence.

In panic, he shouted, 'Hallo? Hey, guys! Guys! You OK?'

Silence.

'GUYS!'

Silence. In the beam of the flashlight he stared at the lining that was inches above his eyes, fighting panic, starting to breathe faster and faster. He needed to pee, badly, going on desperately. And he was seriously claustrophobic.

Where the hell was he? What the hell had happened to the guys? Mark, Josh, Luke, Pete, Robbo? Were those effects for his benefit? Were they standing around, giggling? Had the bastards really gone off to a club and left him?

Then his panic subsided as the alcohol kicked back in again. His thoughts became leaden, muddled. His eyes closed and he was almost suckered into sleep.

Opening his eyes, the lid of the coffin blurred into soft focus as a roller wave of nausea suddenly swelled up inside him, threw him up in the air then dropped him down. Up again. Down again. He swallowed, closed his eyes again, giddily feeling the coffin drifting, swaying from side to side, floating. The need to pee was receding. Suddenly the nausea wasn't so bad any more. It was snug in here. Floating. Like being in a big bed!

His eyes closed and he sank like a stone into sleep.

*

Michael awoke with a start in pitch darkness, his mouth parched, tried to sit up and hit his pounding head on something hard. He lay back down, confused and disoriented. Was he in bed with Ashley?

He tried rolling over and reaching out for her, but his arms went into something soft, inches away. He raised them and instantly they touched something hard and unyielding.

He tried rolling to his left. But again, instantly his hands touched something soft. His nostrils were filled with the smell of wood.

Where the hell was he?

He felt as if he was waking from a bad dream. He rolled right, then left, then raised his arms again. Slowly it was coming back. The pub crawl. They'd put him in a coffin. Surely to hell he wasn't still in it?

He raised his hands and felt the hard wood above him.

Shit. Oh shit. Panic enveloped him. 'Hey!' he cried out. 'Hey!'

His voice sounded oddly flat.

'Hey!'

He lay still for a moment, desperate for water, his head agony. 'Hey, guys, enough! OK? Get me outta here!' he shouted.

Silence greeted him. Utter silence.

He felt a sudden shiver of fear. What if something bad had happened?

'I'm claustrophobic, OK? Enough! Get me out, NOW!' He began pushing with all his strength at the lid, but it would not budge. He kicked out hard, pushed up again, banged his arms sideways. 'LET ME OUT!'

More was coming back to him. The journey in the van. The strange glances between them all. Yelling and yelling, he hammered with his fists on the roof until they hurt so much he had to rest for a moment. Then he stopped. Remembering.

Remembering a newspaper article he had read some years back about coffins. About how much air was in them. Three to four hours if it was well made and you breathed normally. But you could knock that down to less than an hour if you hyperventilated.

Instantly, he tried to calm his breathing down.

As he did, more details came back to him. The torch. The walkie-talkie.

He put his hand on his stomach and felt something hard, long and thin. He fumbled with it, twisted the end. Twisted it again. A feeble glow emerged, for a few seconds, then faded. Shit, the battery had died.

Then he found the walkie-talkie. Pressed a button on it. There was a weak, green glow. Enough for him to see the wood inches above his face and quilted white satin to his right and left. He held the instrument in front of his eyes, squinting at it, and pressed a button marked talk.

'Hello!' he said. 'Pete, Josh, Robbo, Luke, Mark? Enough, OK? Get me out of here, I'm scared.'

He heard a *bip-bip-bip* and a signal flashed on the display. 'LOW BATTERY'.

'You stupid bastards, you could have charged the bloody thing for me! Hello! Hello! Hello!'

Static came back at him.

He tried again, with the same result.

There was another sharp *bip-bip-bip*. Then the display light went out.

'God no, please no!'

He pressed the talk button again. Again. Again. Nothing. It was stone dead.

*

Then he remembered his iPhone in his pocket. Slowly, with difficulty, sliding his hand down against the white satin, he reached his pocket and teased the phone out. Then he dropped it. Fumbled. Found it again, brought it to his face and pressed the power button. The display almost dazzled him.

Three minutes past one.

Friday morning.

He was getting married tomorrow.

There was no signal.

A shiver of fear rippled through him. He tried to remember what time they had been in the van. It must have been around 9 p.m. Four hours?

They hadn't come back. Two hours they had said.

He remembered the scream. The clanging sound.

What the hell had happened?

It was hard to breathe. How much air did he have left?

He pressed the green button on the walkie-talkie again, but still heard no sound. 'Guys,' he said. 'Joke over, OK?' He was having to suck harder and harder to get air into his lungs. 'Guys!' he said desperately. 'Hey, come on!'

Silence.

He took another long, deep breath that barely filled his lungs.

Ashley darling, he thought. His eyelids were feeling heavy. He was drowsy and calm, and growing drowsier and calmer. His headache had gone. Almost delirious he murmured, 'Ashley, darling . . . if I'm not there in the church tomorrow, you are so not going to believe my excuse, are you?'

*

The police never found Michael. The boys, who had all died instantly in the crash, had kept their plans such a tight secret that no one else had an inkling what they were going to do that fateful night. It was a secret that Michael, unfortunately, took literally to the grave.

SUN OVER THE YARD ARM

Tony Trollope was a man of routine. He would arrive home from the office at almost exactly the same time every weekday evening, other than when the train from London to Brighton was delayed; kiss his wife, Juliet; ask how the children were and what was for supper. Then he would glance upwards, as if at the masthead of a yacht, and announce, 'Sun's over the yard arm!'

That was Juliet's cue to make him a drink, while he popped upstairs to change – and in earlier days, to see their children in bed.

'Sun's over the yard arm' became, to Juliet, almost like Tony's mantra. But she had no idea, any more than her husband did, just how ironic those words would be one day.

After a few minutes he would come back downstairs in an over-sized cable-stitch sweater, baggy slacks and the battered, rope-soled deck shoes he liked to slob around in at home as much as on their boat. Then he would flop down in his massive recliner armchair, feet up, TV remote beside him and the latest edition of *Yachting Monthly* magazine open on his lap. A couple of minutes later, Juliet would oblige him with his gin and tonic with ice and a slice of lemon in a highball glass, mixed just how he liked it.

Over the years, as the stress of his commute and his job at the small private bank increased, the quantity of gin got larger and of tonic smaller. And at the weekend the timing of just when exactly the sun appeared over the yard arm steadily reduced from 1 p.m. to midday and then to 11 a.m., regardless of whether they were at home or away on the boat.

'Eleven in the morning was when sailors in the British Navy traditionally took their tot of rum,' he was fond of telling Juliet, as if to justify the early hour of his first libation of the day. Frequently he would raise his glass and toast 31 July 1970. 'A sad day!' he would say. 'A very sad day indeed!'

It was the day, he informed her, that the British Navy abolished the traditional tot of rum for all sailors.

'So you've told me many times, darling,' she would reply patiently. Sometimes she wondered about his memory.

'Yes, I know I have, but traditions are important, they should never be allowed to die. Now the thing is,' he would go on to explain, 'a tot is actually quite a big measure. Half the ship's company would be totally smashed by midday. That tradition was there for two reasons. Firstly to ward off disease, and secondly, as with many military forces around the globe, to give the sailors courage in combat. Historically, many soldiers went into battle totally off their faces on alcohol or drugs. The Zulu warriors were sky high on drugs during the Zulu wars. Half the US troops in Vietnam faced the enemy stoned on marijuana or heroin. Dutch courage indeed! Didn't get its name for nothing.'

Tony had never actually been in the Royal Navy, but the sea was in his blood. From the age of ten, when his father had bought him a Cadet dinghy, which he sailed out of Shoreham Harbour near Brighton, he had been smitten with the sea. On their very first date, when he was twenty-three and Juliet was just twenty, he had sat opposite her in the little Brighton trattoria and asked her if she had ever been sailing. She replied that she hadn't, but was game to try it.

The following weekend he took her out into the Channel on his 22-foot Sonata, the entry-level yacht he had bought with a small inheritance from an uncle. She was instantly smitten – both with Tony and with being out on the open water. And Tony was smitten with her. His previous girlfriend had thrown up fifteen minutes beyond the Shoreham Harbour moles, and had spent the rest of the short voyage lying down below on a bunk, puking into a plastic bucket and wishing she was dead. Sitting in the cramped cockpit of the small boat, he fell in love with Juliet's sea legs. And with – erm . . . well – her very sexy legs.

And with everything else about her.

Juliet loved that Tony was so manly. Loved that she felt so safe with him out at sea. He knew everything there was to know, it seemed, about the craft of sailing and seamanship. He taught her how to tie a reef knot, a bowline, a round turn and two half hitches, a clove hitch, and helped her create her very own knot board. She learned from him how to navigate with the satnav and then, far more basic, with a sextant. How to read charts. How to learn from the clouds to predict squalls and rain. Tony seemed capable of fixing anything on the boat, from taking the engine apart to sewing torn sails. Gradually, in their modest little craft, they ventured further and further afield. Down the south coast to Chichester, then to the Hamble and up the Beaulieu River, and then further afield still, to Poole and then Torbay.

A promotion at work, coupled with a large year-end bonus, enabled him to splash out on a bigger yacht, with more comfortable accommodation, and a larger stateroom – or master-bonking quarters – as he liked to call it.

A year later he proposed to her on the stern of the *Juliet*, the Nicholson 27 he had named after her, in Cowes Harbour on the Isle of Wight at the end of the year's round-the-island race. She accepted without an instant of hesitation. She loved him truly, deeply, as deep as the ocean below them.

As his career advanced and he climbed higher up the corporate ladder and salary scale, their boats became bigger. Big enough to comfortably accommodate their three children as they grew older and larger, culminating in his dream Oyster 42 with hydraulic roller reefing. A substantial yacht that, thanks to all the electronic technology, the two of them could easily handle, with or without the help of their youngsters on board.

And then suddenly, without realizing how time had crept up on them, with two of their children at university and one married, they found themselves planning for Tony's retirement.

And his dream. To circumnavigate the world. Spending time in each country on the way. America. Then Australia. Then Asia. South Africa. Up through the Suez Canal. Then maybe a couple of years in the Mediterranean. 'Hey, what does it matter how long we are away?' he said to her. 'What's time to the Irish?'

'We're not Irish,' she replied.

'So?'

She shrugged. It was a strange thing he had said, she thought. And he had become a little strange, if she was honest with herself, during this past year leading up to his sixty-fifth birthday. She couldn't place a finger on what it was exactly. He seemed to have become a little distant. Distracted. Grumpier. He had always been good-natured. She used to tell her friends that they had the best marriage, that they never argued, that their sex life was still wonderful.

But there was a wrinkle. Deeper than the ones that gradually appeared over the years on their increasingly weather-beaten faces. Tony began to joke more and more about sailors having a woman in every port. And in his now senior position with the bank, he had become responsible for its overseas client development, which meant he regularly flew around the world. And with each trip, when he returned home, his interest in making love to her seemed to wane further and further.

She tried to put it down to a natural decline in libido as he aged, knowing from discussions with her girlfriends, and from looking it up on the internet, that a man's testosterone levels diminished as he grew older. Nevertheless, she began to have nagging doubts about what he got up to on the trips, which were becoming even more frequent and often prolonged – very prolonged at times, with some two-day trips turning into a week or even longer. He also became a little furtive, guarding his mobile phone carefully, getting an increasing number of texts at all hours of the day and night, and frequently disappearing to his den to make or take calls.

At dinner one night, with friends, he told a jokey story, but one she did not find particularly funny. 'Did you know,' he said, 'that in naval-base towns like Portsmouth and Southampton, wives of seamen whose husbands were away at sea for long periods of time used to put a pack of OMO washing powder in their front windows to signal to their lovers, *Old Man Overseas!*'

Everyone laughed, except Juliet. She just stared quizzically at her husband, wondering. Wondering.

For Juliet, the day of his sixty-fifth birthday, and the big retirement party the bank held for him in the City of London, could not come soon enough. Because they had planned their round-the-world sailing trip to start soon after, and they were going to spend the next five glorious years away. They would be together for all that time, and Tony seemed really happy and had spent months planning every last detail and provisioning the yacht.

He told her, repeatedly, how happy he was at the thought of the trip and spending all that time together. She began to think that maybe she had misjudged him, and had been jumping to the wrong conclusions. All those long trips overseas in the past few years had, perhaps, been totally innocent after all. He had just been working as hard as hell to justify his worth to the bank. He was a good man, and she loved him, truly, deeply, as much as ever. More, perhaps. She realized that of all the choices that life had presented to her, nailing her colours to his mast had been the right decision. She began to prepare for the voyage with a sense of excitement and adventure she had not felt since she was a child.

And Tony told her, after a bottle of Champagne celebrating their fortieth wedding anniversary, and using one of the nautical phrases that were part of his language, that being spliced to her was the best thing that had ever happened in his life.

She and Tony pored over charts, looking at routes that famous round-the-world sailors had taken. Through the Bay of Biscay, around Spain and Portugal, then through the Med and down through the Suez Canal was one option. Another was to carry on after Spain down the coast of Africa. But the one they preferred was to cross the Atlantic first, cruise the East Coast of America, then head through the Panama Canal, down the coast of Ecuador, across to the Galapagos, then Fiji, then circumnavigate Australia, before heading up to Indonesia, then across to South Africa, around the Cape of Good Hope, over to the East coast of South America, to Brazil, then across to the Canary Islands, Morocco, then home to England.

*

Finally the big day came. Their children, with their own young families now; a large group of friends, who had sponsored them on Just Giving to raise money for the Martlets Hospice in Brighton; a photographer from the local paper, *The Argus;* a television crew from BBC South, and a chaplain friend, Ish, from Chichester Cathedral, who had renewed their wedding vows on the stern of *Juliet 3,* were all there to wave them off and wish them luck.

The next two years were, for the most part, a blissfully happy time. They had plenty of scary moments, particularly when they lost their self-steering gear during one severe Atlantic storm, and another when they lost their mainsail off the coast of Florida. But, one by one, they made their destination ports and got things fixed or replaced.

Most importantly for Juliet, Tony and she were getting on better than ever. By the time they berthed in Perth, nearly three years into their voyage, she had never, ever, in all their years, felt so close to this man she loved so much. Enjoying the luxury of a hot shower in a deluxe hotel room, then making love to Tony afterwards and falling asleep in his arms in soft, clean hotel bedding, she decided she never wanted this voyage to end – although she did miss her children and grandchildren. He told her that he didn't want it to end, either. And why should it? They were in the happy situation of being able to afford this life at sea – why not continue it for as long as they were both able-bodied?

They only had one real argument. That was when they were in Darwin, three years and six months on, and two more of their grandchildren had been born. Juliet realized that if they did not get back to the UK, at least for a short while, their grandchildren would be total strangers when they finally returned.

It didn't seem to bother Tony, but it was an increasing concern to her. 'Why don't we take a straight route back home, spend a year there, bonding with the kids, then set off again?' she asked.

'I really want to go to Singapore first,' he had replied. 'We've never been and I've always wanted to sail there.'

'But you've been there on business,' she said. 'Several times. And you always said it wasn't that special. I asked you one time if I could join you on one of your trips and you said it was too hot and humid, and I wouldn't like it.'

'I did?'

'Yes.'

He had shrugged. 'It's so totally different when you arrive by boat, darling,' he said. 'Can you imagine what it must have been like for Sir Stamford Raffles when he first arrived there? I'd love to experience that sensation with you.'

For the first time in the voyage, Juliet had bad vibes, which she couldn't – or wouldn't – explain. 'I want to get back to England,' she insisted. Then she pointed at the chart. 'We could take that route, couldn't we? Sri Lanka, then across to Oman, then up the Suez Canal?'

Momentarily he had a far-away look in his eyes. 'Sri Lanka? I think you'd like it there.'

'Didn't you have a client there? You used to go there a lot.'

He nodded. 'Yes. Yes indeed.' And suddenly his whole countenance lit up. 'Sri Lanka's a good plan!'

'So let's do it!'

'Sri Lanka it is!'

Then he pointed at the chart again. 'If we're going to sail that route, it's about three thousand, seven hundred miles. At our average speed of six knots that's about thirty days sailing across open ocean, and there's a risk of Somali pirates all the way. We'd have several days out of radio contact with anyone – we would be totally on our own – at the mercy of whatever happened.'

'I feel safe with you. And besides, what interest would pirates have with us? They're after big commercial ships – like in that film *Captain Phillips*.'

'Not always. They take Western hostages, too. We'd be sitting ducks.'

'I want to get home, Tony, OK? I'm prepared to take that risk.'

'Right, fine, we'll have to establish a watch routine all the way – like we had to do during some other crossings on this trip.'

'Yes, no problem.'

For some reason he seemed particularly keen to get this idea of the watches across to her. 'It will mean long, lonely vigils on deck,' he said.

'I'm used to that.'

'Of course you are.'

There were a couple of occasions over the next two days, while they provisioned the boat, when Juliet's old suspicions about Tony returned. He seemed to need the toilet on the harbour rather a lot, and always took his satellite phone with him. And he had become particularly irritable with her.

Once, she ribbed him, only partially in jest, saying, 'You're going to have a crap, darling. Does your phone help you or something? Do you have a crap app on it?'

He just gave her a strange look as he jumped ashore and strode up the quay.

God, she loved him. But there was something, always something, thinking back throughout their time together, that she felt he kept from her. And she hated that. She had never kept anything from him, not from the very first moment they had met. Her biggest wish was that she could trust him just as much as she loved him.

She stared at the chart over his shoulder and could see it really did look a long way. An awfully long way. They would be leaving Borneo, and then Singapore, hundreds of miles to starboard. There was just a vast, blue, fathomless expanse of Indian Ocean. Of course, they could just berth the boat here and fly home. They'd be back in England in twenty-four hours, instead of three months, minimum. But she thought about the huge send-off they'd had, and all the donations, some per nautical mile covered, that were still clocking up, and she knew they had to arrive home, just as they had departed, by boat.

Three days later they set off. Tony, with his tanned face and beard flecked with white, was at the helm, motoring them out of the harbour while Juliet stowed the fenders into the hatches. It was a calm day, with a gentle force three breeze. Once they were clear of the moles, Juliet, still spritely, energetic and agile, unfurled the roller jib. When it was set, with the breeze on their port beam, she pressed the button to raise the mainsail.

Then Tony cut the engine and they sailed, with smiles on their faces, in the blissful, sudden silence. Just the crunch sound of their prow through the water, the clatter of the rigging, and the occasional caw from the handful of seagulls that accompanied them, hopeful of a snack of any scraps that they might jettison overboard.

After their long stay in port, Juliet moved around the deck, tidying away or coiling loose ropes, and checking for any loose tools Tony had left lying around. Then when her chores were finished, she went aft, leaned on the stern rail and watched the coastline of mainland Australia slowly, but steadily, fading into the heat haze.

Suddenly she felt a prick of apprehension. As if she had a presentiment, which she could not define, of the horror that lay ahead. They faced a long, long, voyage ahead of them. It would be one of the longest times they had spent at sea, unbroken by any landfall. In many ways she had been looking forward to it. On a long sea voyage, routine took over your lives, and she liked that routine. Taking turns on deck at the helm, on watch for other craft, especially at night in bad weather, when you were in the shipping lanes and there was the constant danger that a container ship or supertanker with a lazy crew on the bridge might not spot you, and could run you down without ever even noticing the impact.

Then preparing meals. Sleeping. And plenty of time for her passion: reading. They had a good supply of books, and she had her Kindle loaded with all the books she hadn't yet got around to reading, including *War and Peace* and the complete works of Charles Dickens.

The first two weeks passed without incident, and they had a steady, benign wind on the beam, giving them slightly faster progress than they had expected. If this continued, they could be home several days ahead of schedule. She was looking forward to seeing her family more and more with every passing day – and becoming increasingly excited. About two weeks to landfall in Sri Lanka, then up towards Europe.

The first inkling of what was to come happened while she was asleep in the stateroom with two hours to go until her turn on watch, when suddenly the yacht pitched violently, almost throwing her out of bed. She could hear the rigging clattering more than usual, and the yacht pitched again. It felt like the sea was getting up.

She slid out of bed, made her way across the saloon and climbed the steps up to the cockpit into the pitch darkness of the night, with Tony's face looking grim and paler than normal in the glow from the instrument binnacle. For the first time since they had set sail on this leg of the voyage, she could see no stars above them. 'Everything OK, darling?'

'Wind's getting up,' he said.

The forecast earlier had said a mild depression was heading their way, but Tony had not been worried. Now he looked a tad concerned. 'Take the helm, will you, I want to go below and get a forecast update.'

She could feel a strong, warm wind on her face, and the boat's motion was now so violent she had to hold onto a grab rail as she stumbled over to the wheel. The bitumen-black sea was flecked with phosphorescence from white horses. 'Are you OK, darling?'

'I'm OK – well – I don't feel that great, to be honest.'

'In what way?'

'I sort of feel a bit clammy. But I'm OK.'

'Clammy?'

'That curry we had – I think I may have eaten a duff prawn.'

'You poor darling. Go below and I'll take over for a while.'

'I want to get an update on the forecast. But I'll be fine.'

'You don't sound fine,' she said, alarmed now. 'You sound short of breath.'

'I'm OK, really. All shipshape and Bristol fashion! We may have to reef in a bit if the wind gets up any more.' He told her the course to stay on, advised her to clip on to the safety wire, gave her a peck on the cheek and disappeared down the companionway steps.

The wind was very definitely strengthening. The boat was heeling over, and pitching and rolling increasingly violently. They had far too much sail up. Reducing the mainsail was a matter of pressing a button and the reefing mechanism would wind it in. If necessary they could lower the main completely, as they had done on several occasions previously, and just sail on under a reduced jib – they could do that from the safety of the cockpit by winding in one of the sheets. In configuring the boat for this voyage, Tony had sensibly ensured that anything they needed to do at night to reduce the amount of sail could be done without leaving the cockpit.

Above her head, the rigging was clacking and pinging alarmingly. Suddenly, in a violent gust, the boat almost went flat on its side. She only just averted disaster by violently swinging the wheel, bringing the prow around into the wind. Below, she heard Tony bellow in anger – or shock or pain; she couldn't tell which. Immediately she obeyed his earlier instruction and clipped herself on.

Moments later he reappeared, his face looking like thunder through the hatch, and blood pouring from a gash in his forehead. 'What the hell are you bloody doing, woman?'

'I'm sorry, darling, we've got too much sail up. Let me put some antiseptic on your head and a bandage.'

'Bugger that,' he said. 'Get that ruddy main down, fast! We're heading straight into the eye of a force ten!'

'That's not what the forecast said earlier!'

She didn't like the panic in his voice. Tony never panicked, ever. But he was looking extremely worried now.

'OK!' She leaned over and pressed the button to begin the hydraulic roller reefing. The boom would rotate, furling the mainsail around it. With a force ten imminent, they needed to lower the main completely and take in the jib. The strength of the wind would power them forward just on their bare rigging. And they could do what they had done on two previous occasions, which was to go below, batten the hatches and ride it out. Fortunately they were well past all the major shipping lanes, and they could drift for days, if necessary, without any danger of striking land or rock. They had plenty of what sailors called sea room.

There was an alarming clanking sound from the boom, a loud whirr and nothing happened. The boat keeled over, and again, only her fast reactions on the helm prevented them from being knocked flat by the wind. Then it began pelting with rain, hard needles on her face.

'Get that sodding main down!' he yelled, clinging onto the companionway rail, unable to move with the angle of the boat.

'It's not working!' she shouted back.

'Turn into the wind!'

'I am, I'm trying to hold us there!'

Tony ducked down, out of sight, then reappeared holding a large rubber torch. He shone the beam up the mast, to the top. And they could both immediately see the problem. The very top of the mainsail had torn free, and was tangled in the rigging; the Australian courtesy flag, which they had run up weeks earlier and forgotten to take down after leaving the country, was fluttering hard.

Also clipping himself onto the jackstay safety wire, Tony stumbled across the wildly pitching deck and stabbed at the buttons on the reefing controls. The sail jerked up a few inches, then down. Then up again. They both smelled the acrid fumes of a burning electrical motor.

'Struth!' he said. 'Struth!'

He stabbed at the control buttons, but now nothing happened at all.

'What's happened?' Juliet asked

'Sodding motor – it's either burnt out or fused.'

'Put another fuse in!'

'It's not going to help, you bloody stupid woman! It's all a bloody mess of knitting up there! I'll have to go up in the bosun's chair and sort it! You'll have to winch me.'

'You can't, darling, it's too rough, I can't let go of the helm!'

They'd had the self-steering replaced last year in Perth harbour with a completely new system, but this, too, had failed in today's storm.

'We don't have a choice. We're going to go over unless we get that damned main down – keep her into the wind while I pull in the jib.'

A few minutes later, puffing and wheezing, and looking exhausted from the effort, Tony managed to get the jib completely furled. But with the wind rising, by the second it seemed to Juliet, it was making minimal difference, and she was fighting, with all her strength, to stop the boat being knocked flat. Rain continued pelting, and the troughs into which the prow was plunging were deepening. Each time it felt more and more like they were shooting down a big dipper. Spray roared over them, stinging her face.

'I've got to go up!' Tony shouted.

He pulled on gloves, climbed up over the cockpit onto the deck, holding on to the grab rails for dear life, and wormed his way forwards towards the mast on his stomach. He reached the webbing harness, which was like a trapeze attached to a pulley system, and managed, with difficulty, to haul himself into it and secure himself with two straps, forming a seat, and one rising up between his legs. Then he clipped everything securely in place and shouted out, 'OK, darling! I'm going up!'

He released the safety wire attaching him to the boat, then slowly, inch by inch, hauled himself up the nylon rope by the handle. As Juliet did her best to hold the boat head-on into the wind, the mainsail thrashed at him with enormous force – so hard in one gust he thought it had broken his arm. The boat was pitching and rolling ever more crazily, and there were several moments on the way up when he was convinced he was going to get a ducking.

The boat could ride this out, he was confident of that. Even if they did get knocked over, provided the hatches were all shut, it would right itself. What he was most scared about was losing this mainsail. They didn't have enough fuel to motor the 15,000 miles they still had to go to Sri Lanka. And if they had to rely on the jib alone, it would add weeks to their sailing time.

He hauled himself ever higher into the night sky, getting increasingly breathless. Almost at the top now! He was going to sort out this bastard! Then suddenly he felt a stabbing pain shoot up his right arm and his head swam. The darkness turned into a fairground ride. And suddenly it seemed as if a steel tourniquet was being tightened around his chest.

'Darling! Darling? How are you doing?' Juliet yelled. 'Are you OK?'

He shone his torch at the tangle of wire and rope. As he did so the boat keeled over violently and the wind ripped at his face and hair. Below him, he heard Juliet scream. The bosun's chair was swinging wildly, and suddenly, despite his efforts, it stopped. Tangled up in the mess, too.

'Bugger!' he shouted out in frustration.

'What is it, Tony?'

There were times when you had to make fast decisions at sea. This was one of them. The companionway hatch, which he had climbed up through, was open. If they did get knocked flat, the sea would pour in and down into the saloon. If that happened, they were doomed. Juliet and he would stand no sodding chance of survival 15,000 miles out into the Indian Ocean in the little inflatable life raft with its emergency provisions of a small quantity of water and a couple of bars of chocolate. It was designed to keep them alive for a few hours, or a couple of days at the outside, before they were rescued. There was only one option.

He began to cut the mainsail, stabbing it, ripping it, then moving his knife as far as he could reach. Within seconds, the wind made the tear wider. Then wider still.

'Tony!' Juliet called. 'What's happening?'

He tried to shout back, but he couldn't find the energy. Instead he spoke softly into the brutal wind. 'It's OK, we're safe!'

'Tony?'

The band was tightening around his chest.

'Tony?'

He saw faces appearing out of the darkness. The faces of beautiful women. All of them were calling out, 'Tony! Tony! Tony!'

Somewhere in the distance he heard Juliet's voice, anxiously calling, 'Tony? Tony! TONY!'

The yacht was easier to steer now, with the torn mainsail flapping around like laundry on a line above her. But the wind was so intense that whenever she tried to let go of the wheel, the yacht keeled over so sharply she was scared it would go flat, even on its bare rigging. She fought the wheel, trying as desperately hard as she could to keep the prow head-on into the strengthening and constantly veering wind, which seemed as if it was playing a weird game of catch-me-if-you-can, and constantly having to close her eyes against the stinging spray and rain. Again and again, she called out, 'Tony! Tony! Tony!'

Finally, without the storm letting up, dawn began breaking, slowly, after the longest night of her life. She kept on shouting her husband's name. As the sky steadily lightened, she could see Tony's silhouette at the top of the mast appear intermittently, as a strip of torn mainsail alternately wrapped itself partially around him, then flapped away. Steadily he became more detailed. He sat up there, silent, strapped into the bosun's chair, his head slumped forward, swinging to port and then starboard with each roll of the boat.

Her voice was hoarse from shouting. The rain and spray had long since stopped and now her eyes were raw from crying. This wasn't happening, please God, this was not happening.

'Tony!' she called again. 'Wake up, Tony, please wake up!'

He rolled around like a rag doll in his yellow T-shirt, blue denim shorts and plimsolls, the gloves making him look like some kind of mechanic.

'Tony!' she called again and again, with increasing desperation. The storm was beginning to ease. The swell was still very heavy, though, with the boat riding waves and almost pitchpoling. Over the course of the next two hours, the wind dropped steadily, and as it did, the sea slowly calmed down.

Finally, she felt able to leave the helm. She locked the wheel, clambered up onto the deck, still clipped to her safety wire, and stumbled on all fours to the mast. She stared up at her husband and called out again, repeatedly, her throat raw and her voice croaking, 'Tony, Tony, TONY!'

She tried to climb the mast, but each time, swaying wildly, she only got a few feet above the deck before sliding down and burning her hands, painfully, on the raw wires. 'Tony! Tony! Tony!'

There was no response. And now in full daylight, as the torn strip of sail flapped away from him again, she could see why not. His eyes were wide open, but he wasn't blinking. They just stared, sightlessly.

Sobbing, she pulled at the wires, trying to free the bosun's chair high above her from the tangle, but all that happened was the burns on her hands became worse. Finally, she gave up, crawled back to the cockpit and went below.

She switched on the radio and tuned it to Channel 16, the international maritime channel. But all she got was a buzz of static. She tried other channels, but the same buzz greeted her. All the same she returned to Channel 16 and sent out a Mayday distress signal. The satnav wasn't working, and she could only figure out their approximate position from Tony's last plot of the chart on the chart table. She gave their approximate position and asked for urgent medical help.

The only response she got was more of the same static buzz.

She went back on deck and looked up with a shudder, past her husband's swinging body by the spreaders, close to the very top of the mast, where the radio aerial, transponder and satellite navigation receptors were – and where the yard arm would have been on an older boat. And she saw, to her dismay, that they had gone. Presumably torn away by the tangle of rigging in last night's storm.

She wept uncontrollably. 'Tony, please don't do this to me. Don't leave me. Not here. Don't, please no!'

She stared up at the dark grey sky. And then at the expanse of dark green ocean all around them, which stretched out to the horizon in every direction. According to the chart, Christmas Island was a couple of hundred nautical miles behind them. Sri Lanka was still well over a thousand miles ahead of them. Indonesia was several hundred miles to starboard. It would be days of sailing to reach them, days taking her away from the most direct route home.

Tony was dead. She had to accept that, she knew. It wasn't going to make any difference whether it was a few days now, or two weeks. Her best option, she decided, was to keep to their course, and hope that her Mayday had been heard. If she saw a commercial ship or another yacht on the horizon, or if a plane flew overhead, she would fire off one of the flares they had on board. Her best hope was that her distress signal had been picked up, but she wasn't confident about that.

Maybe a helicopter would appear? But she was pretty sure they were out of range for one. Then, cursing herself for forgetting it, she swore aloud as she suddenly remembered Tony's satellite phone.

'Of course! How could I be so stupid?' It didn't need a mast! Tony had bought it for emergencies, justifying the expense by telling her that even if they lost all their electrics, they could still use it to call for help.

She clambered back down into the saloon, and found it safely stowed in the cupboard to the right of the chart table. She unclipped it, studied it for some moments, then pressed the power button. After a few moments, the display came on. Several symbols appeared, one showing that there was 80 per cent of the battery life left. Then, to her dismay, there was a request for the code.

And she had no sodding idea what that was.

'For God's sake, Tony,' she cursed under her breath. 'Why the hell did you need a pass code?'

Then she remembered a piece of wisdom Tony had once given her a long time ago, and that was to never panic. Panic was what killed people, he had said. Survivors of disasters were those who were able to keep calm and clear-headed, no matter how bad the situation they faced.

And bad situations did not get much worse than the one she was currently in.

'Good advice, Tony!' she said aloud. Doing her best to keep calm and clear-headed, she thought about the pass codes they had always used. The one for their burglar alarm at home was the first one that came to mind. Her year of birth: 1954. Whenever they had stayed in a hotel anywhere and there was a code required for the safe in the room, they had used the same one: 1954.

She tapped the numbers in expectantly. But all she got was an angry buzz and the display shook.

Sod it! Why the hell hadn't he used that one? Just to make sure she hadn't made a mistake she entered it again. And got the same response.

She stared at the phone, thinking. She knew there were settings on some phones that only permitted you a limited number of tries at a pass code before locking you out. How many did this allow?

What the hell might he have used? On such an important phone, it must be a sequence of numbers that he would remember easily. What about his date of birth?

She entered 1948, and instantly got the same angry buzz and short, sharp shake of the display.

'Stupid bastard!' she said, out aloud this time. What else? She tried the numbers backwards. Same result. She tried her own date of birth backwards. Same result again. Then she shouted at the phone. 'Come on, you are my sodding lifeline! Give me your bloody code!'

It required four numbers. How many sodding combinations of four numbers could there be? She started trying, at random, different sequences. His birth date, day and month: 1607. Day and year: 1648. Then her own. Then 0000. Each time she got the same response.

'Please!' she said. 'Oh God, please let me in.'

She took the phone up on deck and saw, to her alarm, that they had veered way off course whilst she had been below. She brought the boat back round onto the correct heading, but the wind had dropped so much that she was barely making any progress at all. She needed to get some sail up, or else start the engine and motor, but she was worried about the amount of fuel they were carrying. She had always left that to Tony, but remembered that he had always been careful not to run the engine for longer than necessary. He always told her that they needed to conserve their fuel for charging up the boat's batteries and for entering and leaving ports. *Juliet 3* was a sailing yacht, not a power boat. They did not have long-range fuel tanks. How far would their fuel take her, she wondered?

The mainsail was useless, way beyond repair, one large strip of it listlessly flapping around Tony's body, like a shroud, before slipping away and fluttering around. She would have to sail under the jib, because when she did reach Columbo harbour at Sri Lanka, she would sure as hell need to motor in – she didn't have the skills to go in under sail.

She freed the jib sheet from the cleat, then pulled hard to unfurl it. After a few minutes of exertion, the massive sail was fully extended and filled with the wind that was coming from the stern. She could feel the boat accelerating forwards, and watched the needle on the dial steadily climb from one knot to three. The mainsail, now a huge, tattered rag, flapped uselessly.

Three knots, she thought. How long would it take to get to their destination, sailing with only the jib, making seventy-two nautical miles a day? Somewhere between two to three weeks. She stared, warily, up at her husband's motionless body. Then, in a sudden fit of anger, she shouted up at him, 'You want medical help, Tony? Give me your sodding phone code!'

Then she wept again. She had not prayed for years, not since she was a child. But suddenly, she found herself pressing her hands against her face and praying.

'Oh God, please help us. Please help us.'

As if in answer, she suddenly heard a horrible, ugly cry above her. '*Aaarrrggghh! Aaarrrrggghh!*' She looked up and saw a gull-like bird with a sinister hooded face, as if it was wearing a mask. Spooking her, it circled the boat several times, unfazed by the sail that continued to wrap around Tony's body then flap away, free, again. After a few minutes, slowly, unhurriedly, it soared away.

Did the bird mean she was closer to land than she realized, she wondered?

She watched it warily, until it became a tiny speck, remembering, suddenly, the albatross in the 'Rhyme of the Ancient Mariner'. Was it bad luck to see a gull, too? There was a country superstition in England that it was bad luck to see just one magpie, you needed to see another quickly. Did the same apply to gulls?

Shakily, she went below again to try the satnav and radio once more, but the satellite navigation screen was just a mass of squiggly lines and the radio continued to produce nothing but a buzz of static. She gave up on them and instead tried to study the chart, to see how far they were from the nearest port. But for several minutes, sitting at the chart table, all she could do was cry, her grief pouring out. She felt so alone, so scared and almost as if nothing mattered any more. She had lost the man she loved. Lost their life. The easiest thing would be to climb back up the steps, go to the rear of the cockpit, haul herself over the stern rail and let go.

But then she thought about her children and her grandchildren, and dabbed her eyes, blotted up the tears that had fallen onto the chart and did her best to pull herself together. It was having no one to talk to – no one at all – that was the worst thing at this moment. No one to share her grief or fear with. And the prospect of two weeks like this. Two weeks of sailing, with Tony stuck up there by the spreaders, in the full glare of the sun when it came out. There had to be a way to get him down.

Had to. Please God.

She studied the chart carefully and took measurements. Indonesia was definitely a lot closer than Sri Lanka. Five or six days' sailing instead of about fourteen. But she wasn't confident enough about her navigation skills to risk changing course. She could have programmed the satnav if that had been working, but although Tony had taught her how to plot a course, calculating currents and, where relevant, tides, she didn't trust herself enough to do it alone. And for a start, she didn't even know her exact position.

If the sky had been clear, with the sun or stars out, she might have been able to figure out her exact position from the sextant. But there was only thick, unbroken cloud. Tony had drawn, in pencil, a circle around their last position, which he had plotted yesterday evening. There was no land showing, although she knew that if she just steered a course east she would be almost bound to reach somewhere on the Indonesian coast – the country virtually formed a barrier in that direction.

But that would be taking her off the planned course, and she could not be sure of landfall remotely near anywhere that had an airport. At least if she kept going towards Sri Lanka she would be heading closer to home. And when she reached there she could find an undertaker and fly home with her husband.

Although, she suddenly remembered in her misery, Tony had always told her that he wanted to be buried at sea, and she had promised him that if he pre-deceased her, she would arrange that. How ironic, she thought now, that he had died at sea, doing what he loved, and she wasn't able to get him down and do at least that.

Perhaps, if the authorities permitted it in Sri Lanka, she could arrange it there?

Maybe, she wondered, they were closer to land than she thought. How far could gulls fly from land? Thousands of miles? Perhaps. Some birds flew great distances when they migrated, didn't they? Where had that one, with its sinister hooded face, come from?

She went back up on deck, swung the wheel to bring them back on course, then looked at the broken self-steering mechanism, wondering if there was any way she could fix it. But she could see that a whole central cog had ripped away. Nothing short of welding was going to fix it.

She resigned herself to having to man the helm for as long as she could, and sleeping for as little as possible.

The sun was high in the sky now and, despite the light breeze, it was sweltering on deck. She tried to look up, but the sight of the lifeless body of the man she had loved so much swinging around in the bosun's chair, and the creepy sail that kept furling around him like a shroud, was too much for her to bear. Instead she stared, steely-eyed, ahead, her gaze fixed on the far horizon beyond the prow of the vessel.

After half an hour, she suddenly saw two tiny specks, high in the sky, heading towards her. For an instant her hopes rose. Helicopters? But then, a few minutes later, her spirits sank again; she could see from their motion that they were birds.

And as they got closer still she could see their masked faces. Was it the one she had seen before returning with a friend? Keeping one eye on the compass binnacle, she watched the birds circling, soaring around in a wide loop, then a tighter loop. Then a tighter one still.

She felt a sudden prick of anxiety as they began to circle her husband's body. Tighter and tighter, showing increasing interest.

'Sod off, birds!' she called out.

Then one darted at his face, made a pecking motion and flew away. Then the other flew in and pecked.

'Sod off! Go away! Don't touch him!'

Suddenly she saw more dark specks on the horizon. She counted five, six, seven, eight, ten?

Within minutes there were a dozen gulls swarming around her husband, all pecking at his face.

'NOOOOO!' she screamed. She swung the helm wildly left and right, heeling the boat over to port then to starboard. But it made no difference to the birds. They were crying out, a hideous *caw-caw-caw* shriek, batting each other with their wings, darting in, pecking at Tony's eyes, lips, nose, ears.

'NOOOOOOOOOO!'

She locked the wheel and hurried down below, opened the locker where they kept the six emergency flares, unclipped them and clambered up on deck with them. There were even more gulls now, hideous creatures with demon faces, all fighting each other for a morsel of his face.

She held up one flare, trying to read the instructions, but her hands were shaking so much the tiny print was just a blur. Finally she succeeded, aimed the flared directly at them and pulled the small plastic ring. There was a sharp whoosh, and it fired, sending something like a firework rocket shooting up, well wide of the gulls, high into the sky before exploding in a sheet of red light. They took no notice at all.

'GO AWAY YOU BASTARDS!' she screamed and seized another flare.

She aimed again, pulled the loop, and this time scored a bullseye, sending it right into their midst. It hit one gull in the belly, then arced down into the sea, exploding as it struck the water off her port beam. The gull spiralled downwards, helicoptering, unconscious or dead, and landed motionless on the water. As if in wild panic, all the other gulls, cawing in anger and confusion, scattered and flew off towards the horizon.

She was shaking uncontrollably. The motionless gull passed by the port side and soon was way behind her. 'Bloody serves you right, you ghoul,' she muttered.

Ten minutes later the gulls returned, some singly, others in groups. Now there seemed even more than before. She fired off another flare, but she was shaking so much she missed altogether. Ignoring it totally, the gulls were now on a feeding frenzy.

Tears were running down her face, blinding her as she fired off another flare, then another, with no effect. She realized now she had only one left. She couldn't fire it, she needed to preserve it in case she saw a ship on the horizon. It would be her last hope, she knew. The nightmare of Tony dying, which she could not have imagined getting any worse, now had. She had to stop these vulture birds, but how?

She clambered forwards, gripped the mast and desperately, using all her strength, tried to climb the narrow aluminium pole. She felt a splat of bird shit on her forehead. Then another. The din of their cries above her was almost deafening.

She screamed at them, again and again and again. Gripping the mast with her arms and her legs she made it up a few feet, but then, obstructed by the rigging and parts of the ripped sail flapping in her face, she could get no higher.

She slid back down, weeping uncontrollably, and returned to the cockpit. They were heading wildly off course. She turned the wheel and watched the compass needle slowly swing back round. She shouted at the birds until she was hoarse, but it made no difference.

The gulls stayed until there was nothing left of his face to peck, and then, as dusk began to fall, they gradually, some singly, some in pairs, flapped away into the falling darkness.

High up above her, swinging in the bosun's chair, was her husband's skull, with a rictus grin and patches of hair on the scalp.

Her stomach was burning, but the rest of her felt numb. Totally numb. She prayed. Prayed that she would wake up and find this had all been just a nightmare.

The gulls returned soon after dawn. Now they were pecking through his clothes, bits of fabric from his orange Henri Lloyd yachting jacket fluttered in the air as they greedily found the flesh beneath it.

By the end of the third day, Tony resembled a scarecrow.

*

It was twelve more days and nights before, in the early afternoon, she finally saw the lighthouse, the long, welcoming concrete harbour arms of the port of Colombo, Sri Lanka, and a speed limit sign. She was utterly exhausted, almost out of her mind from lack of sleep, and during the past two days she had started speaking out aloud to Tony, holding imaginary conversations with him. The gulls had long departed, having, she presumed, picked his carcass clean. Some bits of his clothes still clung, raggedly, to his skeleton.

There was no wind on this searing hot afternoon, and fortunately, the strip of sail had once more furled around Tony, almost completely covering him. She was motoring, the fuel gauge on empty, praying there was enough left to get her to a berth in the yacht basin that she had found identified on the harbour chart and marked in red by Tony. She was thankful, at least, for his meticulous planning.

Through bloodshot eyes, behind sunglasses that were long fogged with salt, she watched the bunkering stations pass by, cranes, a huge lumber warehouse and an endless line of berthed container ships and tankers. Then finally, to her relief, she saw a whole forest of yacht masts through a gap to starboard and headed towards them.

Fifteen minutes later, passing a refuelling station, she saw a sign for visitors' berths and, slowing her speed to a crawl, scrambled forward and removed a bow line from its locker, then pulled out several fenders and hung them over the side. She wasn't sure how she was going to manage the actual berthing, though.

Then, to her relief, an elderly man in a battered peaked cap, with the appearance of a port official, suddenly appeared, signalling to her with his arms. She threw him the bow line, which he caught expertly and secured around a bollard. Moments later he caught the stern line and secured that, and steadily, as if he had done it a thousand times before, reeled her in alongside the pontoon.

Sobbing with relief, she did not think she had ever been so happy to see another human being in her life.

She jumped ashore and then, pointing towards the top of the mast at Tony's remains, tried to explain what had happened. But he spoke no English and failed to take any notice of her gesticulations, nor did he look up. All he kept saying, repeatedly and insistently through a sparse set of yellow teeth, one gold and several missing, was 'You Passeport? Passeport? You papers? Papers, documentation?'

She went below, found the boat's papers and her passport and handed them to him. Signalling he would be back, he hurried off. She stood on the deck, watching him head towards a cluster of buildings, shaking with relief that she was no longer at sea. As she had sailed in, she had passed several yachts flying British flags. If she walked along, with luck she would find someone who could tell her where to find the British consul, or at least let her use their phone.

But before that, she badly needed a drink. She went below and pulled one of the bottles of rum that Tony had been fond of drinking at sea out of the booze cabinet. Just as she was pouring herself a glass, she heard a female voice above her, calling in broken English, 'Hello? Tony? Hello?'

Frowning, Juliet looked up and saw a very attractive-looking Indian woman, in her early thirties, peering in.

'Can I help you?' she asked.

'This is the *Juliet*?' the woman asked. 'The yacht *Juliet*?'

'Yes, it is.'

'I'm meeting Tony.'

Now Juliet frowned again, more severely. 'Tony Trollope.'

'Yes!' Then she hesitated. 'You are the cleaner?'

Bloody hell, Juliet wondered. Did she look that bad after all this time at sea? Without commenting she replied, 'Might I ask who you are?'

'Yes, I am Tony's fiancée.'

'Fiancée?' Juliet could barely control herself.

'Yes, Tony was sailing here to meet me, to get married here.'

'Who was he sailing with?'

'He said he was sailing alone, solo.'

A sudden chill rippled through Juliet. Was that why Tony had chosen this route? Three weeks at sea, away from land. Three weeks out of radio contact. Three weeks where anything could have happened to either of them, and no police would have had any evidence that a crime had been committed?

Had that been his plan? To push her overboard and then sail on to a new life with this beautiful young woman.

The bastard.

'What is your name?' Juliet asked.

'Lipika.'

'That's a very pretty name!'

'Thank you. Is Tony on board?'

'Yes, he's just a little tied up at the moment. You know what, I think we should have a drink, Lipika, to celebrate your engagement!' She pulled a second glass out of the cupboard.

'No, thank you,' Lipika said, and smiled sweetly. 'I don't drink.'

Ignoring her, Juliet filled the second glass. 'You're going to need one, dear, a very large one!'

She carried both glasses up into the cockpit and stared at the woman in daylight. She really was very beautiful indeed. Beautiful enough to kill for?

But what did that matter any more? It was over now. The past. She raised her glass and clinked the young woman's. 'Cheers!'

Lipika hesitantly clinked back.

Then Juliet said, 'Sun's over the yard arm!' and raised her glass high. 'Here's to the happy couple. Tony and Lipika! He's all yours!'

The woman raised hers high and followed Juliet's gaze. And at that moment, a light gust of breeze unfurled the strip of sail that had wrapped around Tony's body, and it flapped free, exposing his ragged skeleton, his skull picked clean apart from a few sinews and a small patch of hair.

Lipika's glass fell to the deck and smashed.

Her scream shattered the calm of the afternoon.

YOU'LL NEVER FORGET MY FACE

It was almost dark when Laura drove away from the supermarket. Sleet was falling and strains of 'Good King Wenceslas' echoed from the Salvation Army band outside Safeway. She wound down her window and pushed her ticket into the slot. As the barrier swung up, a movement in the rear-view mirror caught her eye and she froze.

Black eyes watched her from the darkness of the car's interior. She wanted to get out of the car and scream for help – instead, her right foot pressed down hard on the accelerator and the rusting Toyota shot forward.

She swerved past a van, zigzagged between a startled mother and her children, who were walking on a zebra crossing, and raced across a junction.

The eyes watched her, expressionless, in the mirror.

Faster.

The windscreen was frosting over with sleet, but she couldn't find the wipers. She swung out too wide on a bend and the car skidded, heading on to the wrong side of the road. She screamed as the Toyota careered towards the blinding headlights of a lorry.

The lorry's bumper exploded through the windscreen. It slammed into her face, ripping her head from her neck, hurling it on to the back seat. The car erupted into an inferno. Flames seared her body . . .

Then she woke up.

The room was silent. She lay bathed in a cold sweat and gasping for breath. Suddenly, she remembered the old gypsy woman who'd tried to force a sprig of heather on her outside the supermarket.

The gypsy had blocked her way and had been so insistent that Laura had finally lost her temper, shoved past the woman and snapped, 'Sod off, you hideous old hag!'

The gypsy woman had followed her to the car, rapped on the

window, pressed her wizened face with its piercing black eyes against the glass and croaked, 'Look at my face. You'll never forget my face. You'll see it for the rest of your life. The day you stop seeing my face will be the day you die!'

Laura turned for comfort towards her sleeping husband. Bill stirred fleetingly. She smelled the raw animal smell of his body, of his hair. He was the rock to which her whole life was anchored.

Christmas Eve tomorrow. It was going to be just the two of them together this time and she had been really looking forward to it. She snuggled closer, wiggled her toes – hoping faintly that he might wake and they could make love – pressed her face against his iron-hard chest and began to feel safe again.

In the middle of the next night, Laura woke again, startled by a sharp rapping. The room was flooded with an eerie sheen of moonlight. Odd, she thought, that she hadn't drawn the curtains.

Then she heard the rapping again and her scalp constricted in terror. The face of the old gypsy woman, a ghastly chalky white, was pressed against the bedroom windowpane.

'Look at my face!' she hissed. 'Look at my face. You'll never forget my face. You'll see it for the rest of your life. The day you stop seeing my face will be the day you die!'

Laura turned to Bill with a whine of terror, but he was still sound asleep. 'Bill,' she whimpered. 'Bill!'

'Urrr . . . wozzit?' he grunted, stirring.

'Someone's at the window,' she said, her voice so tight it was barely audible.

She heard the sound of his hand scrabbling on his bedside table. Then a sharp click and the room flooded with light. She stared fearfully back at the window and a wave of relief washed over her. The curtains were shut!

'Wozzermarrer?' Bill grunted, still half asleep.

'I had a bad dream.' She turned towards him, feeling a little foolish, and kissed him on the cheek. 'I'm sorry.'

In the morning, Bill brought them both breakfast in bed. Then he gave her a huge card and three gift-wrapped packages. 'Happy Christmas,' he said, and blushed – he was never very good at sentiment.

Laura gave him his presents – an expensive bottle of aftershave and the cordless screwdriver he'd hinted at wanting – then she opened hers.

The first package was a sweater with daft-looking sheep appliquéd on the front. It made her laugh and she kissed him. The next was a bottle of her favourite bath oil. Then she saw his eyes light up in anticipation as she gripped the final package. It was small, square and heavy.

'I . . . er . . . hope you like it,' he mumbled.

With mounting excitement she unwrapped a cardboard box. It was filled with sprigs of heather. Buried in their midst was a small porcelain figurine.

Laura froze.

Bill could sense something was wrong. 'I . . . I got it yesterday,' he said. 'For your collection of Capo di Monte peasants. I thought it had . . .' his voice began to falter, '. . . you know – a real presence about it.'

'Where did you get it?'

'A junk shop. Something made me stop there – I just knew I was going to find the perfect present for you inside.'

Quite numb, Laura stared at the black, piercing eyes of the hag that leered up at her with lips peeled back to reveal sharp, rat-like incisors.

'It's lovely,' she said flatly, seeing how hurt he looked. 'Really lovely.'

Laura kept the figurine on her dressing table over that week, to please Bill, but the thing's presence terrified her.

The following Sunday, he left to drive his container lorry to Italy. She didn't start back at her office until the day after next, so she busied herself with housework. As the afternoon drew on, she felt increasingly uncomfortable.

Finally, she made a snap decision, went to the bedroom, put the figurine in its box, took it outside and dropped it in the dustbin.

Feeling better, she ate supper on a tray and watched a weepy movie on television, wishing Bill was home.

Shortly after eleven, she went upstairs. As she switched the bedroom light on, her eyes fell on the dressing table, and a slick of fear travelled down her spine. The figurine was back, sitting in exactly the same position it had been that morning. Laura's eyes shot to the undrawn curtains, then returned to the dressing table. The floor seemed to sway. She backed unsteadily out of the room, clutching the door frame to stop herself falling, then slammed the door shut.

She stumbled downstairs, pulled the sitting-room curtains tight, switched all the bars of the fire on, curled up on the sofa and listened, petrified, for a sound upstairs. She lay there all night, finally dozing for a brief spell around dawn.

In the morning, she put the figurine in the boot of her car, drove to the tip three miles away and threw it on to the heap. She watched it fall between the discarded fridges, busted sofas and tangle of rubble and old tyres, until it finally disappeared beneath a fire-blackened cushion.

When Laura finally got home, she realized that it was the first time she'd felt at ease since opening that damned present. At two in the morning, she was woken by a sharp rap. The room felt as cold as a deep freezer. As she switched on the bedside light, she let out a curdling yelp of terror. The figurine was back on her dressing table.

Laura sat up the rest of the night, too frightened to sleep. Next morning, she carried the dreaded figurine out on to the patio and smashed it to smithereens with a hammer. She carried the fragments in a rubbish bag to her office, and during her lunch break dropped them in the incinerator. All afternoon she felt elated, as if she'd finally freed herself. When she finished work, she drove to the outskirts of town and went to Safeway to do her weekly shop.

As she pushed her trolley down the aisles, she found she was smiling to herself. Smiling at her little triumph and smiling, too, at her own stupidity. Probably the figurine hadn't looked anything like the old gypsy, it was just her wild imagination, the same way she must have imagined throwing it in the bin and on to the tip but hadn't.

'Got spooked by the old hag and now I'm cracking up.' She grinned to herself. 'Silly fool.'

It was nearly dark as she left the store. There was no sign of the gypsy woman, but even so, Laura looked carefully at the back seat of the car before climbing in and quickly locking the doors. She reached the exit, pushed her ticket into the slot and the barrier rose up. As it did, a sudden movement in her rear-view mirror caught her eye. The temperature plunged. Goose pimples as hard as rivets spiked her skin. In the mirror, she could clearly see the piercing black eyes watching her out of the darkness. The dream flooded back. She remembered how she'd accelerated helplessly and she found her right foot pressing down now. The car surged forward as if it had a will of its own. Laura let out a tiny whimper of fear, and saw the rat-like teeth grinning at her in the mirror.

'Got to stop this somehow. Got to change the dream. Got to break the spell.'

Gripping the wheel with both hands, her heart thrashing, she turned to face her tormentor. There was no one there, just the empty rear seat.

I imagined her, she thought, with immense relief. I imagined her!

The blare of a horn filled her ears. As she spun her head back to the road, she saw, far too late, the blazing headlights of the oncoming truck. In that last split second before the little Toyota exploded in a fireball, Laura remembered the gypsy's words. 'Look at my face. You'll never forget my face. You'll see it for the rest of your life. The day you stop seeing my face will be the day you die!'

SANTA DROPS IN

Roy Grace had that nightmare again last night. The one in which he woke up on Christmas morning and realized he'd forgotten to buy his beloved wife, Cleo, a card or any presents. It was the same dream he used to have regularly a week or so before Christmas, all those years back before his first wife, Sandy, had disappeared.

But the Sussex Detective Superintendent was in better shape than usual this year. At least he'd made a start, and had bought Cleo a card and a few silly bits for her stocking. But he wanted to buy her a nice piece of jewellery, and he had in mind a silver bracelet, which he'd seen in the window of the jeweller Stanley Rosen, in Brighton's Lanes. He still had time, it was Friday today and Christmas Day was not until next Tuesday.

The current murder enquiry into a woman found dead on the beach, which his team had been working on for the past two months, was winding down after a successful conclusion, with the suspect charged and on remand in Lewes Prison. Friday afternoon, and an air of frivolity had settled on the normally sombre major incident room where his team was housed. Glenn Branson, Emma-Jane Boutwood, Guy Batchelor, Norman Potting and all the rest of them were unwrapping their Secret Santa gifts. This was their last day all together before the Christmas holidays, although some of them would remain on call over the holiday period.

Norman Potting eagerly unwrapped his gift, then chortled, as he held up a knitted willy warmer. Roy Grace grinned at his, an ancient copy of a Ladybird Easy Reading Book entitled, *People at Work – The Policeman,* wondering which of his colleagues had bought that for him. He felt in a relaxed mood. For the first time in many weeks he had a free weekend ahead – and tomorrow he planned to nip down to the Lanes and buy the bracelet. Although he was well aware that as the on-call Senior Investigating Officer, there was always a risk of a major crime occurring. In particular, levels of domestic abuse rose around Christmas time. Tensions could run high. Last year there wasn't even a let-up in the number of 999 calls made during the fifteen-minute duration of the Queen's Speech. Fights, accidents, vehicle thefts and even robberies.

There was one shadow on his mind as he drove home, taking a detour past the swanky homes of Dyke Road Avenue to enjoy the Christmas light displays outside some of the houses. Some miscreant the press had nicknamed Scrooge had committed several attacks on displays in the main shopping precinct. Hopefully he would be caught soon by Brighton CID, who had deployed undercover officers in an attempt to apprehend him before he hurt someone, or by the city's network of CCTV cameras.

Then, as he drove down towards the clock tower in his unmarked Ford Focus estate, he saw a long tailback ahead. As he pulled up, a patrol car screamed past him on blues and twos. He frowned, wondering what was happening. Clearly a major incident. He turned up the volume on his police radio and called the duty Ops 1 controller, Inspector Andy Kille, to ask what was happening.

'The Christmas tree in Churchill Square has fallen over, sir,' he replied. 'Reports of two casualties.'

'I'm close by,' Grace said. 'I'll attend and take a look.'

The spectacular tree, one hundred feet high, was the biggest the city had ever erected. Visit Brighton, the city's tourist board, had decided to give its retailers a recession-buster of a Christmas this year, and they had really gone to town on the street decorations. Tomorrow afternoon the city was having its biggest ever Yuletide event. A concert on the Hove Lawns, headlined by local superstar celebrity Norman Cook, aka Fatboy Slim. And the highlight of the day was going to be Santa Claus arriving by parachute. A crowd of twenty thousand was expected, and he was planning on taking Cleo and their baby, Noah, to see what promised to be a spectacular occasion.

The Detective Superintendent switched on his blue lights and siren, pulled out and raced down to the clock tower, then made a right turn into Western Road. Ahead was a blaze of strobing blue lights. He could see several police cars, two fire engines and an ambulance. Two uniformed officers were taping off the road ahead of him.

He climbed out and saw the mayhem in the square. The massive tree was lying on its side, some of its lights still twinkling, and part of the tip lying through the shattered shop window of WHSmith, surrounded by demolished festive displays of books. Several of the crowd of onlookers were taking pictures with their phones. He ducked under the tape and walked up to the figure of Bill Warner, the duty Inspector.

'What happened?' Grace asked.

'Evening, sir. I have reports from two witnesses who saw a man rush up with a chainsaw, cut through the base of the tree and run off. Hopefully we'll get something from CCTV. We have two injured – a mother and her small boy, neither serious – and several in shock. One of the undercover CID officers gave chase, but lost him. It appears Scrooge is stepping up his attacks.'

'I was just heading home. Anything I can do?'

'I think we have it under control, thank you, sir.'

The Inspector took him over to see the severed tree stump. 'What a miserable bastard,' Grace said, staring at the clean cut, and the raw, fresh wood that was exposed.

'My thoughts exactly. I think John Street CID can handle this. I'd go home if I were you.'

'OK, but keep me posted.'

Bill Warner promised him he would.

*

Half an hour later, changed into jeans and a sweatshirt in Cleo's town house, he was helping her put the finishing touches to the tree. There were bowls of festively scented pot pourri around, and several beautifully wrapped presents around the base of the tree, which reminded him of his shopping task tomorrow. Cleo was making sure that Noah's first Christmas was going to be special indeed, even if he was too young to appreciate it.

Noah, in a striped onesie, was lying on his play mat, blinking up at his Christmas mobile under the watchful eye of Humphrey, their black rescue Labrador-Collie cross. Marlon the goldfish was circumnavigating his bowl, as ever. Must be a bit dull for a fish, he thought.

At least a dog could get excited by wrapping paper and appreciate a few extra Christmas treats. Maybe Marlon could at least enjoy the Christmas lights, he wondered. He stared lovingly at Cleo, her long blonde hair clipped up and looking gorgeous, and suddenly felt an overwhelming feeling of happiness. Their first Christmas together and their baby son, Noah's, first ever.

Then his mobile phone rang.

'Roy Grace,' he answered, his heart sinking. He hoped desperately this wasn't going to be a fresh murder inquiry, which would put pay to all his plans. To his relief, he recognized the friendly but serious voice of Chief Constable Tom Martinson. Although it was unusual for the Chief to be calling him personally, it would not be about a murder.

'Sorry to bother you on a Friday evening, Roy,' he said, 'but we have a potential problem. Brighton Council and the Police and Crime Commissioner are extremely worried about crowd safety tomorrow, in light of all the recent attacks, and especially today's. I should also mention that a minibus bringing kids from the Chestnut Tree House hospice is coming along. As you know, it's a charity Sussex Police have raised a lot of money for; they're our special guests tomorrow and we don't want them disappointed.'

'Yes, sir, I do.'

'Although the Public Order Team have had all leave cancelled for tomorrow,' the Chief Constable continued, 'and we have drafted in officers from all over the county, I've had a discussion with the Assistant Chief Constables, and we've decided we should have the Major Crime Team as additional observers in the crowd tomorrow. How many of your officers could you muster?'

Inwardly, Roy Grace groaned. He would be spending the next two hours solidly on the phone. 'About twenty, sir.'

'I want them all deployed. Liaise with Nev Kemp who's Gold Commander for tomorrow.' Chief Superintendent Nev Kemp was the Divisional Commander for the city, and heading the police operation for the event tomorrow.

'Yes, sir, I'll get onto it right away.'

'Good man.'

The phone went silent. Along with Roy Grace's festive joy – for tonight, anyway.

*

Snow was forecast for the week ahead, but at 10 a.m., beneath a cloudless cobalt sky, Roy Grace was snugly wrapped up inside a fleece-lined parka, rubbing his gloved hands together as he stood on the promenade, above the sparkling, frosty grass of Hove Lagoon, which surrounded Norman Cook's Big Beach Café. Half a mile to their left was the bandstand that had been erected overnight. Earlier, he'd briefed the eighteen members of his team that he had been able to muster in the warmth of the Conference Room of the Sussex CID HQ, and now they stood in a ragged circle around him as he deployed each of them in turn to their points.

A large white circle had been taped on the promenade – the drop zone, where Santa would make his landing, wind permitting. Fortunately there was only the faintest breeze – the weather could not be more benign for a parachute jump.

He yawned. Bill Warner had phoned him after midnight, to tell him he was emailing him CCTV footage of the suspect who had chain-sawed the Christmas tree. There had been several sightings of him across the city caught on camera.

A few joggers and dog-walkers passed them by. The tide was out, and a wide expanse of mudflat, riddled with worm casts, lay beyond the pebble beach. Over to the east was the skeletal ruin of West Pier, and glitzy Brighton Pier half a mile beyond that, beneath the ball of ochre that was the low winter sun. The Detective Superintendent watched, warily, an elderly man in gumboots working his way along the beach with a metal detector, and another man with a bucket, digging for lugworms in the mud for bait. To his trained, suspicious eye, everyone at this moment was a potential suspect.

Parked all along the road behind was an endless line of police vans. The entire area, as far as the eye could see, was ring-fenced with blue and white police tape and a massive presence of uniformed officers, most of them huddled in groups, nursing beakers and Styrofoam cups of tea and coffee. It was going to be a long morning.

Members of the public were starting to arrive. The first of two warm-up bands, both local groups, was due on at 11 a.m., and they would play until midday. The second band would play until 1 p.m., when Norman Cook was due to come on. He would end his act by announcing the arrival of Santa Claus overhead. With luck, the whole event would start winding down after Santa landed on schedule at 2 p.m., and he would have time to rush over to the Lanes and buy that bracelet for Cleo from Stanley Rosen.

Over the course of the next hour the crowd swelled, parents with their excited children bagging the best spots, closest to the circle. By the time the band was halfway through its set, there were several thousand people amassed. Grace left his station on the promenade to enter the Police Mobile-Command-Centre vehicle, equipped with cameras covering a large part of the surrounding area. So far, everything was fine. The band was great and the crowd seemed happy. Queues were lengthening outside the mobile burger and hot-dog stalls and portable loos, which had been placed on site. Street vendors were out in force, flogging Santa hats, festive balloons and other seasonal tat. Excitement was growing.

By midday the crowd was estimated at over fifteen thousand. So far there were no incidents, other than a couple of arrests of people drinking alcohol in public and one pickpocket caught on camera. By the time Fatboy Slim came on, to a tumultuous cheer from the crowd, there were well over twenty thousand people. On one of the cameras, Grace saw a group of children, mostly in wheelchairs, leaving a Chestnut Tree House minibus. He felt a pang of sadness, thinking about his own baby son. These were all children suffering progressive life-shortening or life-threatening illnesses. This was his son's first Christmas, but for many of these kids, it would be their last. Despite himself, looking at their happy faces, he dabbed tears from his eyes.

It was easy to forget, amid all the excitement and happiness of Christmas, that for so many people it was the very opposite. For the lonely, and particularly the elderly on their own, it was a time when their loneliness felt more acute. For parents of sick kids, it was a time of emotional turmoil. But at least at this moment, as he carefully scanned the crowd through the monitors, everyone here was having a good time. Occasionally he picked up a local villain he'd encountered in the past. But all those he saw seemed to be with their families, looking happy.

He spoke to key members of his team at their stations. Glenn Branson; Norman Potting; Guy Batchelor; Nick Nicholl and Emma-Jane Boutwood. All of them reported nothing suspicious, so far. A great time was being had by all. Somewhere in the melee were Cleo and Noah, though Grace had no idea where. He glanced at his watch – 2 p.m. was fast approaching.

He stepped out of the command centre and walked down to the promenade, eager to watch the spectacle for himself. Just as Norman Cook's music was reaching a crescendo, a breakbeat remix of Paul McCartney's 'Wonderful Christmas Time', he heard the sound of an aircraft overhead and looked up. A small plane was banking and beginning a wide arc overhead. He watched the crowd. At first, only a few people seemed to notice and start looking up. Then Fatboy Slim raised his hands in the air. 'Happy Christmas everyone!' he shouted into the mic. 'Here's Santa!'

Grace saw the awesome sight of thousands of faces all turned to the sky. A banner trailing from the plane, now low in front of them, bore the words '***MERRY XMAS!***'

In the silence following the music, Roy could hear the gasps and cheers of the crowd. The excitement was palpable when, moments later, a second plane appeared, higher up, flying directly overhead. Suddenly an object fell from it. It grew larger as it dropped, until Grace could see it was red. He heard the excitement building in the crowd. More cheering. He watched the sea of upturned faces, then Santa again. Steadily, over the course of the next fifteen seconds, the falling figure grew bigger still. And bigger. And the red became brighter and brighter.

And brighter.

He was leaving it late to open his parachute, Grace thought. All part of the thrill!

The figure became brighter red. And brighter. At any moment the parachute would deploy.

But still it didn't.

This guy was good, Grace thought!

He kept on falling. Getting closer, bigger, brighter.

Santa was heading towards the ground now at a speed Grace could almost measure. Surely he was going to pull the ripcord now?

Surely?

He kept on falling.

So close now that Grace could even see what he was wearing. A Santa outfit, the coat flailing upwards, red leggings, black boots, beard being blown ragged, and something trailing upwards above him like a sack.

Open your chute man, open your chute!

The figure grew bigger. Bigger. Bigger.

He was heading towards the beach.

The crowd fell silent.

And Grace, holding his breath, realized that his parachute wasn't opening.

Santa Claus continued to plummet towards the promenade, only his sack trailing above him, no sign of a parachute deploying. He missed the carefully marked-out white circle on the promenade by about one hundred yards, and instead hurtled down onto the pebble beach, a good twenty feet below the promenade railings. Mercifully, Roy Grace thought, he was out of sight of the twenty-thousand-strong crowd gathered on the Hove Lawns.

The Detective Superintendent was as stunned as everyone else as he heard the impact. A sickening crunch, as if a giant sack of potatoes had fallen from the sky. Except it was a human being.

For several seconds you could have heard a pin drop.

Then, his training kicking in, Roy Grace sprinted forward. He yelled instructions to the line of uniformed Constables on crowd duty, keeping the area of promenade around the drop zone clear. 'Make sure everyone stays back!' He ran over to a Public Order Sergeant he knew. 'Get crime scene tape and seal the area! Don't let anyone near the beach!' He sprinted up to the promenade railings and looked down.

And wished he hadn't.

Surrounding the horrific sight of a clearly dead Santa Claus, gift packages, their pretty wrapping torn and their contents broken, lay scattered on the pebbles. These were the presents that Santa had been destined to hand out to the children from Chestnut Tree House, who had been given a front row view of his arrival.

Grace's brain was racing, wondering, speculating. Was this a terrible accident, or was there something more sinister behind it? The handiwork of the creep who had chainsawed the tree in Churchill Square?

He thought quickly through what he needed to do. His immediate priority was to secure the beach and surrounding area to protect the scene. Subsequently, it would be to find out everything about the unfortunate skydiver who was acting the role of Santa Claus, to interview the pilot of the plane that had dropped the skydiver, to impound the plane and to find out, urgently, who had packed the skydiver's main and reserve parachutes.

He could hear the cacophony of sirens above the wailing of children, and the quiet hubbub of shock and disbelief from the subdued crowd, and then the sound of his phone ringing. He knew who the caller was before he answered, and exactly what he would be saying. He was right on both counts.

It was Chief Constable Tom Martinson, asking for an update on what was happening at the scene. This was a tragedy for everyone, not to mention a disappointment for all the children in the crowd who had just seen Santa Claus die in front of their eyes.

'I'm cancelling all leave for my team until we establish whether this is just a tragic accident or if there's something more sinister behind it, sir. I haven't worked out how yet, but I'm going to make sure that at least some of the kids will see Santa in one piece,' he added grimly.

*

At the briefing later that day, Detective Sergeant Norman Potting, well known for his politically incorrect comments, said, 'Maybe we could get a better flat-pack Santa from IKEA than the one on the beach.'

There were a few stifled grins, but no one laughed, other than Potting chortling at his own joke.

'Thank you, Norman,' Grace chided. 'I think we can do without gallows humour right now.'

'I was just thinking about elf and safety, Chief,' Potting continued blithely.

That did produce a titter of laughter, and even Grace found himself grinning, for a brief, guilty moment. 'Thank you, Norman. Enough, OK?' he said sternly.

The fifty-five-year-old, with his bad comb-over and ill-fitting suit, looked suitably chastened and mumbled an apology.

Roy Grace, his Policy Book open in front of him, glanced down at his hastily prepared notes, then up at Potting, who despite his appearance and appalling sense of humour was one of his most trusted detectives. He nodded at DS Guy Batchelor. 'Can you and Norman report on your visit to Shoreham Airport?'

'Yes, boss,' DS Batchelor said. 'The aircraft that carried Richard Walker, the skydiver dressed as Santa, has been impounded. We interviewed the pilot, Rob Kempson, who told us that Walker is – was – an extremely experienced skydiver. He'd represented England in many international stunt-jumping events and was qualified to pack and check his own main parachute and his reserve. Apparently his wife, Zoe, was equally experienced but hadn't jumped for several years after a bad landing, following which she suffered back problems. He tended to rely on her to pack his parachutes, as she had done on this occasion. The procedure today was the same as always and nobody noticed anything untoward.'

'Did the pilot have any comment on the relationship between Walker and his wife?' Grace quizzed.

'We did ask him that, Chief,' Norman Potting said. 'So far as Kempson knew they had been a happy couple, but lately they were in severe financial difficulties, and Walker had got mixed up with some loan sharks, who were making threats to recover their money. We are following this up – whoever he owed money to must at this stage be considered a suspect, Chief.'

'There's a specialist team from the British Parachute Association coming tomorrow,' DS Batchelor said. 'Hopefully we'll find out more from them.'

Grace nodded, mindful that he needed to hold a press conference at some point during the next morning, which he was dreading. 'What time will this team be here?'

'Nine a.m., boss,' Batchelor said.

'There is another thing of possible significance,' Norman Potting said. 'According to the pilot, Walker had joked that he had a big life insurance policy and that if he ever died, his financial woes would be sorted and his wife, Zoe, would be well taken care of.'

Grace noted this down. 'Nice work,' he said.

Detective Constable Emma-Jane Boutwood raised her hand. 'Sir, an officer spotted someone who fitted Scrooge's description shedding his Santa hat ten minutes after the Christmas tree was felled in Churchill square last night, and replacing it with a baseball cap. He's been identified as Sidney Carp.'

'Sid Carp?' said Potting. 'He was always a fishy blighter.'

The entire team groaned in unison. But they all knew the name. Sid Carp was a frequent flyer with Brighton Police. An old lag and a true recidivist – or revolving door prisoner as they were known – a nasty petty thief and small-time drug dealer. 'Sid Carp?' Grace said. 'He must be older than God.'

'Got to be nudging seventy,' Potting said.

'Old enough to play Santa, anyway, sir,' DC Boutwood continued. 'He'd been the resident Father Christmas in the Churchill Square shopping mall until a week ago, when he turned up drunk and was fired. Apparently he went round telling several of the staff that if he couldn't be Santa, no one would be, and the store and Brighton were going to regret it. So it sounds like this could all be about his revenge.'

'How on earth did he get past the security vetting?' Grace asked, shaking his head. Then he turned to Potting. 'Norman,' Grace said. 'I want you to come with me to see Walker's wife – we need to find out if, in his financial predicament, she thinks he might have been unstable.'

*

An hour later, Roy Grace and Norman Potting climbed out of Grace's car in front of a smart, mock-Tudor house on Woodland Drive – a street nicknamed by locals as Millionaire's Row. It was freezing cold, the stars glittering like heavenly bling above them. There would be a frost in the morning for sure, the Detective Superintendent thought, as they strode past two cars on the driveway, a convertible Audi and a BMW coupé. He rang the doorbell, waited, then rang again. Then he rapped hard on the door.

After a good couple of minutes it was opened by an attractive blonde, with dishevelled hair and streaked make-up. She was wearing a slinky dressing gown with her boobs half falling out.

Grace showed her his warrant card. 'Mrs Zoe Walker?'

'Yes?'

'Detective Superintendent Grace and Detective Sergeant Potting from Surrey and Sussex Major Crime Team. I understand you have been informed of the very sad news about your husband?' he said.

'I have, yes.' Tears rolled down her cheeks. 'Would you like to come in?'

'Just for a moment, thank you.'

The two detectives entered the hallway and she shut the door behind them.

'Can I offer you gentlemen a drink? Tea or coffee, or something stronger?'

'We're fine, thank you,' Grace replied. They briefly talked through what had happened that afternoon, and gave her an outline of the police investigation to date. 'We don't want to keep you tonight,' Grace said. 'But I understand your husband may have had financial worries. I believe he owed a lot of money and had recently been threatened.'

'That's right,' she said. 'I'm afraid he was a bit of a gambler. He told me he was sorting it all out. I . . .' She hesitated for a moment and he saw her shoot a sudden glance upstairs. He studied her eye movements carefully.

'What do you think has happened?' she asked.

'It's really too soon to say – we need more information. We have to establish whether this was a terrible accident, murder or possibly suicide.'

'Well now you mention it, Richard did mention suicide occasionally, but only in the way many people do when things are bad – you know. I never thought he – you know – he would actually do it. He's not the type.'

'What do you think might have happened to your husband?' Grace pressed.

'I don't have an explanation,' she said and began sobbing. The detectives waited for her to regain her composure. 'He was highly experienced, and even if his main chute didn't open, his reserve should have done, for sure.'

'Accidents do occur,' Grace said, 'from what I've read up today.'

She shook her head vehemently. 'No, I packed his parachutes immaculately. I know I did.'

Grace nodded. 'OK, well, we have the British Parachute Association team coming down tomorrow, so hopefully we will be able to establish exactly what happened. I won't trouble you any more until we have all the facts.'

As she closed the front door on them, Potting gave him curious look. 'That was a bit short, Chief.'

Grace patted the bonnet of the Audi, which was icy cold. 'Nice cars, these,' he said. Then he touched the bonnet of the BMW and could feel the heat from it. 'I like Beemers. Always have.' He made a mental note of the registration number.

'Know what BMW stands for, Chief?' Potting said as they climbed back into the car.

Grace stared at him, knowing it was going to be something rude. 'Don't go there,' he warned. He started the engine, drove a short distance from the house, then pulled over and radioed for a PNC check on the BMW, reading out its index number to the controller.

*

Roy Grace delayed the Sunday morning briefing to the afternoon, to give the parachute investigation team a chance to carry out their work. Meanwhile his own officers were still trying, urgently, to trace Sidney Carp. At 10 a.m. Roy held a press conference at which he gave public reassurance about the numbers of officers on the case, leave being cancelled, and his enquiry team working through the holiday period to establish what had happened and make the city safe.

In the early afternoon, just as his briefing was about to commence, Norman Potting came hurrying in. 'We've netted our suspect, Sidney Carp!'

'Brilliant work, Norman!' Grace said.

Then Potting looked gloomy and shook his head. 'Not good news, I'm afraid, chief, he's going to be the fish that got away.'

There was another loud groan from the team.

Potting continued. 'He was arrested at Victoria Station in the early hours of Sunday morning, in a drunken state, with a holdall containing a chainsaw, and is still in custody, having refused to give any details or explain why he was carrying a chainsaw.'

'That doesn't necessarily eliminate him,' Grace said, 'but he's no longer our best suspect. I think I have a better one.'

*

An hour later, Grace was armed with the preliminary, but fairly conclusive, information about why both parachutes had failed. The two detectives returned to Woodland Drive. As they climbed out into the sub-zero air and walked to the front door, Grace noted that both the Audi convertible and the BMW were coated in frost.

This time, slightly to Potting's surprise, Roy Grace enthusiastically accepted Zoe Walker's invitation for coffee. She sat them on the large sofa in the sitting room, and proudly pointed out the two cabinets filled with Richard Walker's sky-diving trophies.

'There is something I've remembered, Detective Superintendent. When I was at Shoreham Airport yesterday, I'm sure I saw a man sitting in a car on the perimeter road who I recognized – he was one of the men who had been threatening my husband.' She stood up. 'I'll just go and get the coffee.'

The moment she had left the room Grace said, 'Norman, I want you to go outside, slam the front door loudly behind you, get in the car and drive off.'

The DS frowned at his boss. 'You do?'

'Come back when I call you,' Grace said. 'Go!' He could see all kinds of doubts in Potting's face. 'Go!' he said again.

Potting shambled off, and a moment later, Grace heard the door slam, even louder than he had intended. Then he heard the sound of his car starting.

A few moments later, just as Zoe Walker came back in, holding a laden tray, a gruff male voice called down from upstairs, 'Was that those coppers again, darling? What did they want this time?'

She turned sheet white and froze in the doorway. The tray slipped from her hands and crashed to the floor. Roy Grace leapt to his feet, ignoring the mess. 'You always packed your husband's parachutes, is that correct?'

'Yes. Well, almost always.'

'Well the reason his parachutes failed is fairly clear. The lines on both the main and reserve chutes had been cut clean through. You've got your husband's former business partner, Jim Brenner, upstairs in your bed. And your husband had a two-million-pound life-insurance policy. More than enough to cover his debts and for you to start a new life.'

She said nothing. He could see her eyes darting around nervously.

'Not smart to let your lover leave his car on your driveway with a warm engine when your husband's body's not even cold, Mrs Walker.'

'It's not like you think it is,' she said.

'Oh it is, trust me. It's all too often exactly how I think it is, sad to say.'

He pulled a pair of handcuffs from his pocket. 'Zoe Walker, I'm arresting you on suspicion of the murder of your husband Richard.' Then he read her out the formal caution.

'What . . . what . . . do you mean?'

He snapped the cuffs on her wrists. 'I'm also arresting your bedfellow on suspicion of conspiracy to murder. The one bit of good news I can give you, as it's Christmas, is that in prison you get an excellent turkey dinner, with all the trimmings. Some local villains have themselves banged up deliberately every December so they can enjoy it. There'll be plum pud and crackers. You'll have a lovely time. A much nicer Christmas than your husband will in the mortuary.'

*

It was almost midnight by the time Roy Grace left the custody centre and drove home. Although Zoe Walker had broken down and confessed, he would have to appear in court tomorrow in front of a magistrate, to get an extension to keep her and her lover in custody whilst enquiries continued. In addition to this, he would have a morass of paperwork to wade through.

She thought she could blame the people her husband owed money to, but there was one flaw in her plan – she didn't know he had already paid off his debts a week earlier, after a huge win at the casino. He'd been planning to tell her the good news as a Christmas present.

Then, as Grace stepped out of the shower, his phone rang.

Dreading news of another homicide, he picked it up with trepidation. But it was the Chief Constable again.

'Well done on your fast work, Roy,' he said. 'I understand you have two in custody.'

'Yes, sir.'

'There's one problem the arrests haven't solved though: all the kids who now think Santa Claus is dead. I'm particularly concerned about the children at Chestnut Tree House hospice – for some of them, sadly, it might be their last Christmas. You're a resourceful man, Roy, and a father yourself. Any thoughts?'

'Leave it with me, sir,' he said. 'I'll come up with something.'

*

A life-size wooden reindeer stood in the gazebo-style porch of the sprawling mansion, Chestnut Tree House, along with a huge inflatable snowman. Fairy lights twinkled all around in the late afternoon darkness. Snow was falling and there was a sense of the magic of Christmas in the air. A crowd of fifty adults and youngsters, all wearing Santa hats, were outside, singing a carol. In the front row were children in pushchairs or wheelchairs, and one small boy on a wooden chair playing a trombone larger than himself.

Out of the darkness came a loud, 'Ho-ho-ho! Hello boys and girls!' Santa Claus, in his full costume and thick beard, staggered towards them under the weight of a huge, laden sack. For twenty minutes he chatted animatedly to each child in turn, before handing them a beautifully wrapped gift with their name on the tag.

When he had finished, the director of the hospice called out, 'Let's all say, 'Bye, Bye, Santa!'

All the kids shouted out in unison, 'BYE BYE, SANTA!'

Roy Grace fought back tears as he trudged back down the driveway to his car, safely out of sight of the house. He wiped snow off the windows and mirrors and climbed in, desperate to remove the beard and moustache, which were itching like hell. It was 6 p.m., he realized with a heavy heart. It had taken him all afternoon, since leaving court, to get the kit sorted out and buy the presents, ticking each off the list he had been given by the hospice, paying for them himself, then wrapping and labelling them. He had been determined to show all the kids that Santa was alive and well.

But the shops would all be shut now, and it was too late to get to The Lanes to buy that bracelet. Cleo was going to be disappointed in the morning at not getting a proper present, and he felt lousy about that.

A shadow fell and there was a sudden rap on the window, momentarily startling him. He saw a man he recognized in a smart overcoat – one of the parents he'd seen in the crowd – standing by his door. Grace wound down the window.

'I just wanted to say, Detective Superintendent, how grateful all of us parents are for what you did. If there's ever a way any of us can repay your kindness, please let me know. I hope you get all you wish for this Christmas.'

'That's very nice of you,' Grace said. He grinned. 'I have only one wish. If you could get Stanley Rosen, the jeweller, to open up his shop in Brighton tonight for just five minutes that would really make my Christmas!'

The man smiled. 'I think that could be arranged.'

'You do?' Grace said, surprised.

'I am Stanley Rosen.'

An hour and a half later, Roy Grace drove out of the underground car park and turned left onto the seafront, towards the pier. Heading home to Cleo. It was 8.30 p.m., and Christmas, for him, was really beginning. He'd phoned her to say he was on his way, and she'd told him Champagne was in the fridge, waiting.

On the seat beside him was the blue velvet box with the name 'Stanley Rosen' monogrammed in gold on the lid. He couldn't believe his luck! They truly were going to have a great Christmas after all. His and Cleo's first Christmas together, and Noah's first Christmas ever. He felt a surge of deep happiness.

Then his phone rang.

CROSSED LINES

At five o'clock, Henry Henry got up from his typewriter and walked quietly to his window. It wouldn't have mattered if he'd jumped there in hobnail boots, there was no one to hear him, but this was his ritual and he stuck to it. Rituals marked his day like punctuation on a printed page.

He peered nervously at the row of terraced houses the other side of the street. It was impossible to tell the quality of the residences inside. Some were elegant flats, some were bedsits, like his own.

He found the window straight away, out of habit. Damn. She was not there. He muttered to himself, as if he had been deprived of something that was rightfully his. And then he saw a flicker of movement – or had he imagined it?

Suddenly she came into view, clutching a drink and a paperback. She was completely naked, as usual; only now it was summer and her body was brown, with slim white bands around her breasts and bum. She kicked off her high-heeled shoes, placed her buttocks on the pink chaise longue, leaned back and swung her long legs onto it. She took a sip of her drink, put down the glass and opened her book.

What was the drink, he wondered? What was the book? Why did she keep a bikini on whilst sunbathing when she clearly liked to be nude? So many questions, he thought. So much he would like to know about her. All last autumn, he had seen her tan fading; now the bands were back, appearing whiter every week. There were surely things she would like to know, too? Not, perhaps, the fact that he watched her every night, no. But would she be pleased that she was the heroine of the book he was currently writing? Would she care for that type of book – the romantic novel? Perhaps not, he thought wistfully. It seemed to him that the people who cared for his romances were a dying breed. Old hat, people called them. Old hat – and he was only thirty-two!

A wave of panic squeezed his stomach like a tourniquet. What had he forgotten? Something important? Damn. He stared at the long brown legs longingly. He remembered, and tore his eyes away reluctantly, like sticking plaster from an old wound. He looked up the telephone number and dialled with short, timid stabs of his index finger, as though he were testing the warmth of a soup.

He was surprised to hear a squawk, instead of the ringing tone, followed by a woman's voice, then a series of clicks.

'Hallo,' he ventured timidly.

'Hallo,' came the reply.

Silence.

'I believe we have a crossed line,' he said.

'Yes,' came the reply. 'I believe we do.'

His eyes were transfixed across the road once more. She was on the phone too!

'I was just dialling,' she said, there was humour in her voice. It was a nice voice, someone who had learned to cope with the world and was still young enough to be full of hope. Across the road she had stopped speaking and was listening. She looked puzzled. Was it really possible this was her?

'I was here first,' he said, and then winced. He was doing it again. His wife had always told him he could never argue without attacking; now he was attacking the nice voice.

'OK,' she said, her tone unaltered, the lips of the girl across the road moving once more. 'I'll hang up.'

The lips stopped moving.

'No – no, don't do that. I'll hang up. It wasn't an important call. I was trying to get the weather you see.'

Her lips moved again. 'You must be an optimist, to spend money on a weather report.' The lips stopped again.

The coincidence was too great now. It had to be her! Then a cloud moved in front of the sun. Optimist, he thought. No. She did not know him at all. Optimism was something that eluded him like a butterfly in a summer field.

In a moment, she would be gone. He could not bear that, not now, not having got so close.

'Meet me!' he blurted out. 'For a drink? You know – a coffee, perhaps. Or lunch?' He looked across at her. She was smiling; her eyes lit up! 'Are you free for lunch one day?' She was thumbing through something, turning pages. A diary? Where had his courage come from, he wondered? She was searching, searching with her long naked arm. Say yes, please say yes.

'How about Thursday?'

He gobbled her words down greedily, like a starving man eating a stew.

'Yes, Thursday is good for me. It's the only day I have clear this week,' he lied, and immediately was annoyed with himself for lying. But he knew she would not have been impressed with the truth: that all his days were free, stretching out ahead like the blank white sheets in the box of A4 paper he had to fill with words – of love, bravery, heroism, desire and, ultimately, success.

'You do live in London?'

'Yes,' he said, conscious that his voice was blurting; it was as though his mouth had become a brass horn and his voice a rubber bulb; he kept squeezing it at the wrong pressure.

'Where do you work?' he said. 'I mean, which part of London? I'm not trying to be nosey, it's just important to choose somewhere – er – convenient.'

The good humour stayed with her voice, without effort. 'I don't mind coming over to where you work.'

'No,' he said, and realized that he had nearly shouted.

'What I mean is that I couldn't inconvenience you. I work in Oxford Circus.'

'That's perfect. I have a meeting in Bond Street on Thursday morning,' he said, selecting Bond Street because he felt it sounded smart. His mind raced. Where could he suggest? Bond Street? What names. Claridge's? Classy, but he had never been in; he wouldn't know where the bar was, where the restaurant was. He could do a recce; it was only Monday today. But no, Claridge's seemed too formal. Somewhere romantic – Italian? Yes, the hero and heroine of *Sweetness and Light*, his new book, fell in love with each other in an Italian restaurant, while a mandolin player serenaded them.

'Do you like Italian food?' he blurted again, wondering what the hell had happened to his voice.

'Oh yes, I adore it,' she replied.

'Me too. Have you a favourite restaurant? I'll leave the choice up to you.' He began to flounder. 'I . . .' he said, 'I . . .' He searched for words, like a man rummaging through a key ring.

'It's been a while since I was around that area.'

'What about Fifty-Five?' she said.

'Fifty-Five?' He paused. 'Fifty-five which street?' he said, feeling slightly foolish.

She laughed. 'No, that's the name of the restaurant. On the corner of Bond Street and Maddox Street.' He found a laugh, too, from somewhere within him, easier than he had thought he would. 'Oh yes, I know it,' he said. 'Very nice. Yes, I'll book – what time?'

'Will your meeting be over by one?' He delayed replying, trusting this implied that he was pondering the agenda. 'Yes,' he said finally. 'It should be. And if not,' he added, with bravado, 'it will just have to go on without me.'

'Right,' she said. 'I'll see you there at one. How will we recognize each other?'

She was practical, he thought.

'Just ask for my table.' He paused, like a dry bather at the edge of a pool.

'I don't know your name.'

'Henry,' he said.

'Henry what?' she said.

He stuck a toe in the water and watched the ripple. 'Henry Henry – surname and Christian name.' Don't laugh, he said to himself, please don't laugh. He remembered his wife laughing the first time they met. The name had annoyed and embarrassed her throughout the eight years they were married.

She did not laugh. 'I'll see you at one o'clock on Thursday, then.' She paused and added sweetly, 'Henry.'

'What – what's your name?' he blurted.

'Poppy,' she said, and left it at that, without revealing her surname.

His heart sank, very slightly, at this tiny element of mistrust. He hung up the phone and watched across the road. She was replacing the phone and smiling – yes, smiling! She lay back. 'Poppy,' he said to himself. Yes, he liked that name. Suddenly he realized he was humming 'Waltzing Matilda'; it was something he always did on the rare occasions when he was happy.

*

The tune deserted him at ten to one on Thursday, when he arrived at the restaurant. It was pleasant enough, yes, but not romantic. The tables were small and too close together, with hard wooden seats; it was too crowded and cramped. There was no mandolin player, either, although one of the waiters did occasionally sing a few bars of 'O Sole Mio' as he weaved his way to and from the chef's hatch.

He informed a harassed man in an open-neck shirt of his reservation.

'Ah, Signor Hairy,' he said, finding the name amid a page of ballpoint scribblings. He guided him to a table at the back of the room. Henry sat, and began to rehearse his opening line.

'Drink, Signor?' Henry coughed with surprise, nearly swallowing his breath-freshener spray. What drink would impress her?

'Vodka martini on the rocks, with a twist,' he said, emulating his heroes, who always emulated James Bond.

'A tweest, Signor?' He looked anxiously past the waiter; she could appear at any moment.

'Of lemon,' he said.

'Limonada?' The man was infuriating him.

'No, no, lemon; forget the lemon.'

'One vodka martini, no lemon? Correct. Martini Rosso or Bianco?'

Struth, he thought. When Bond ordered that drink, the waiters always knew exactly what he wanted. 'Dry white vermouth,' he said patiently.

A short, dumpy girl was talking to the waiter in the open shirt. Henry looked beyond her at the street. A group of businessmen crowded in the door.

'Onna the rocks?' said the voice.

He nodded. 'Yes, on the rocks.' Then he changed his mind. 'No, er, not on the rocks. Shaken – shaken, not stirred.'

The dumpy girl stood behind the waiter, patiently, smiling. The waiter moved and she stretched out a hand; it smelt of expensive perfume.

'Henry?'

Henry stared at her. Who the hell was this, he thought? And would she please go away, he had an important date. Was she a fan? He did not want Poppy to come in here and see him talking to her. He wanted her to see him alone at the table, calm and suave, sipping his vodka martini.

'I'm Poppy!' The words did not immediately register; he was still willing her to go away, watching the door and not wishing to be discourteous to a fan, of whom he had far too few, all at the same time.

'I'm Poppy.' The words registered like a kick in the shin.

Mechanically, he stood up, shook her hand, found a smile from somewhere inside him, put it on his face and bade her to sit down. A joke, was his immediate reaction: Poppy must have chickened out and despatched a friend instead. But when she spoke, he knew that no, this was indeed the girl he had been talking to. Disappointment seeped into his body like rainwater into a leaky shoe. She was all wrong. He stared across at her, wondering whether to cut and run now and save himself the price of lunch. But no, he knew he was committed to it.

Perhaps she would offer to split the bill at the end? He chided himself for being so petty. It wasn't her fault he had made such a ridiculous mistake.

'Would you like a drink?'

'Why not,' she said. 'I think I'll have a spritzer.'

Henry looked for the waiter with one eye and studied Poppy with the other. Black blazer; open-neck white blouse; twinset and pearls; hair straight and short. Too short for her face. She had made a lot of effort over her appearance; she reminded him of a gift-wrapped box of chocolates. He caught the waiter's attention and ordered the spritzer. The waiter knew what it was, which was more than Henry did. Poppy folded her hands and laid them in her lap. She smiled across. Too much weight, he thought; she would look much better if she was slimmer

'Well,' she said. 'Hello, Mystery Man.'

Henry smiled. Might as well be cheerful, try and make the best of it. The menus arrived. They chose their food and he ordered a bottle of Barolo; he knew little about wine, but he knew Barolos were sturdy. He felt like getting drunk – drunk enough to forget the hopes he had cherished throughout this long week.

She raised her glass. 'Cheers,' she said. 'Henry Henry.' Then she bit her lip, realizing from his expression that it was something about which he was sensitive.

'It's a nice name,' she said, very quickly. 'It's elegant.'

They chinked glasses.

Henry knew his name would need explaining; it always did.

'A christening joke,' he said dully. 'My father was a stand-up comic. He found life outside the stage so sad, he tried to carry on his routine the whole time; tried to make the whole of his life a joke. Now he's dead and I have to continue the joke.' He raised his glass and nearly drained it.

'That's sad,' she said. 'But you mustn't think of it as a joke; it's a very classy name; it's unusual and it suits you.'

She smiled again.

Henry realized she was prettier than he had at first thought; he felt guilty about his hasty judgment of her. 'What do you do?'

She was a kitchen planner, she told him. He wasn't exactly sure what a kitchen planner did, but he suspected it was important in kitchen planning to appear slightly plump, to give the impression of a healthy appetite and the enjoyment of a good kitchen. 'What do you do?' she salvoed back.

Rather nervously, he told her. What would anyone think, he wondered, of a man in his thirties who wrote unknown romantic novels?

'How wonderful! An author!' She said the word slowly, relishing it, as though it were a piece of fine steak. She leaned forward a little, her eyes shining. 'I've never met an author before.'

'I'm afraid I'm not very well known.'

'Henry Henry?' she said thoughtfully.

'No, I write under a nom-de-plume: Sebastian de Champlain.'

She allowed herself a slight giggle. 'Sebastian de Champlain – how frightfully grand. But that does ring a bell. I love romantic novels, you see. I read them all the time.'

'You do?' He became aware that hope had crept inside him, quietly, when he was not looking.

'Yes; tell me some of the titles of your books?'

'*Desire of the Heart*?' he replied. '*Summer Wind*? *The Scent of the Orchid*?'

'Goodness!' she squealed. 'I'm reading *The Scent of the Orchid* at the moment! It is so – real – you must have spent a long time in Singapore researching it.'

Henry smiled and nodded. It was not appropriate, now, he thought, to tell her that he had not been to Singapore, but had gleaned the information from a film and a couple of books he had borrowed from the library.

'Gosh!' she said.

Halfway through their main course, Henry Henry ordered a second bottle of wine. He had never met a fan before, never been so flattered and complimented before.

He had forgotten all about the girl in the window opposite. Poppy and he had already made a date to go and see a film that evening, and a concert tomorrow. On Saturday, she would cook a very special meal for him at her flat.

'Who'd have thought this could happen from a crossed line?' She giggled.

He smiled back, almost too happy to talk.

'Where was it you said you lived?' she said.

'Pembroke Terrace.'

'It's an extraordinary coincidence,' she said, taking another long sip of her wine. 'I have a friend who lives in Pembroke Terrace. I was just dialling her number on Monday night when I got you instead. Incredible, isn't it!'

'Yes,' he replied. 'Incredible.'

'She's quite a character, you know – I'll introduce you one day. Some time ago, nine or ten months I think, she got absolutely drenched in a rain storm. She took off all her clothes and was trying to dry herself in front of the fire when she looked out of the window and saw some pervert leering at her from the other side of the street.'

'Really?' said Henry. 'Good lord. I suppose there are some pretty peculiar people who live in that street.'

She giggled. 'She's wicked, you know. Do you know what she does now? Every evening, she takes all her clothes off and lies in front of that same window; and every evening, bang on cue, this fellow appears and gawps at her. You really must meet her some time, she's a hoot.'

'Yes, I'd enjoy that,' said Henry.

'Cheers!'

'Cheers!' he replied, raising his glass.

'To our crossed line,' she said.

'Yes, to our crossed line.'